Praise for *Pretty*

"From the moment I started readin completely immersed in the gripping, twisty, diffuser-filled world of a posh spa wedding, where four college friends reunite, each with old baggage and new. Sparkling with insight, wine, humor, and a drop of blood, the women in this book leapt off the page and straight into my heart. *Pretty Guilty Women* is a must-read!"

—Susan Crawford, bestselling author of
The Pocket Wife and *The Other Widow*

"Love the strong female characters and the dark underlying themes—a perfect summer read."

—Harriet Tyce, author of *Blood Orange*

"I loved *Pretty Guilty Women*—totally gripping with a fabulous cast of characters. A wonderful summer read."

—Vanessa Savage, author of *The Woman in the Dark*

"LaManna deftly unpacks her characters' baggage in this twisty tale."

—*PEOPLE* magazine

pretty

guilty

women

pretty

guilty

women

A NOVEL

GINA LAMANNA

Published by Sourcebooks Landmark, an imprint of Sourcebooks
P.O. Box 4410, Naperville, Illinois 60567-4410
(630) 961-3900
sourcebooks.com

Library of Congress Cataloging-in-Publication Data

Names: LaManna, Gina, author.
Title: Pretty guilty women / Gina LaManna.
Description: Naperville, Illinois : Sourcebooks Landmark, [2019]
Identifiers: LCCN 2019001141 | (hardcover : alk. paper)
Subjects: | GSAFD: Suspense fiction.
Classification: LCC PS3612.A55347 P74 2019 | DDC 813/.6--dc23
LC record available at https://lccn.loc.gov/2019001141

Printed and bound in the United States of America.
VP 10 9 8 7 6 5 4 3 2 1

For Alex, my husband and my very best friend.

And for my parents and sisters:
Mom, Dad, Kristi, and Megan.

prologue

H ush, little baby, don't say a word…"
Quiet footsteps filled the nursery. A woman padded
over the thick, plush carpet, carefully selected to greet
the newborn. Moonlit lines lay etched on the floor, carved into
bars by the halfway-closed blinds. Thin strips of light gave the
impression of an ethereal jail cell, a prison holding the baby—*her*
baby—captive.

"Mama's gonna buy you a mockingbird…" Happily grinning
cartoon giraffes had been lovingly pressed against the wall, their
necks arched toward the ceiling in a quiet watchfulness. "And if
that mockingbird won't sing…"

The singing ground to a halt as she listened for the groan of
the garage door—the sound of it inching up, a gaping, ugly black
mouth ready to swallow him into the belly of the beast. To bring
him here.

While she waited, her pulse racing, she listened for the creak
of the front door, the depression of his heavy sole striking the
hardwood staircase. If it was him, she would recognize the fifth step
squeak as he ascended, and then the seventh step sigh.

But she suspected he knew about the squeak. He'd skip over the
fifth step, but not the seventh.

That *sigh* would save her life.

When neither the fifth nor the seventh steps wailed their
trusty alarms, she eased to the side of the crib and smiled down at

the sleeping baby. In a few more minutes, they'd be free. Alone and safe.

"Mama's gonna buy you a diamond ring…"

She lifted the baby to her chest, cradling the newborn bottom against her arm, savoring the feel of the tender little head against her chest. Sweet-scented bubble bath clung to the baby's skin like an exquisite perfume.

"And if that diamond ring turns brass…"

"Papa's gonna buy you a looking glass." The low, throaty voice came from the doorway, where a man, flanked in shadows and charmingly handsome, rested against the wooden trim. He watched her through glittering black eyes.

He gave a slow, dangerous smile as she spun toward him. Her pulse skittered as she realized with horror that he'd discovered the seventh step sigh.

"And if that looking glass gets broke…" She hoarsely continued singing as if nothing strange had occurred. She belonged here with the baby, after all. Nothing—no one—could take that away from her.

"That's where you're wrong, sweetheart." He gave an ugly smile, fingered the gun at his waist, and shook his head. "You're already broke."

one

Detective Ramone: Please state your name for the records.

Lulu Franc: My name is Lulu Franc, and I am sixty-eight years old. My last name is spelled *F-R-A-N-C*. Please make sure that gets spelled correctly, as it's a nightmare to correct on legal documents.

Detective Ramone: Ms. Franc, we're recording this interview. Your name will be transcribed accurately. Please state the date you arrived at Serenity Spa & Resort and your purpose for being here.

Lulu Franc: I arrived August 16 with my husband, Pierce Banks. We have a suite booked for a week as we're attending the DeBleu/Banks wedding. I'm the groom's aunt by marriage. Not that my nephew would notice if I wasn't in attendance, but he'd most certainly notice if we didn't leave him a check as a wedding gift.

Detective Ramone: I assume you know the reason you're here. We discovered a body tonight, Ms. Franc.

Lulu Franc: Yes, a dead one.

Detective Ramone: That's implied.

Lulu Franc: Good. Because that's the way I saw him last.

Detective Ramone: Are you confessing to murder, Ms. Franc? Let me remind you this conversation is being recorded and whatever you say can and will be used against you in a court of law.

Lulu Franc: Must I repeat myself? For the last time, let me state for the record: I, Lulu Franc, am guilty of killing this man. When you write that down, remember, Franc is spelled *F-R-A-N-C*. If you add a *K* at the end, I will be very upset.

L ulu Franc was desperately annoyed.

She was supposed to be at the salon, relaxing while Delilah curled her hair and touched up her manicure, but *no*. Instead, she was stuck at home, rattling across her gorgeous wooden floorboards as she poked her head into the freezer and ducked under tables. Lulu's joints creaked as she bent low, and despite her attempts to ignore all signs of aging, she couldn't help but notice the glaring evidence to the contrary. However, her darling husband's elusive (and very fat) wallet was not nearly as obvious. It simply insisted on remaining lost.

She straightened, flicking dust off her new cashmere cardigan as she heaved a sigh of frustration. Her sweater was lined with real raccoon fur and had cost her husband a fortune. No matter, as Pierce Banks was both loaded and happy to indulge his wife's taste in fashion. Not that Lulu didn't work for it. Being married to Pierce Banks was a full-time job on the South Carolina social circuit.

"Relax, sweetheart. It'll turn up," Pierce called as Lulu blazed passed him. "Don't be late for your appointment."

"Have you forgotten that you need identification to fly?" Lulu asked. "Please call Marsha and have her come by. Maybe she saw your wallet when she was cleaning yesterday."

"I'm not calling Marsha on her day off," Pierce said. "It will turn up; it always does."

Lulu gave up her search in the kitchen, where Pierce Banks lounged against the counter in a luxurious, black robe, watching her with a gleam in his eye as he waited for the coffee maker to warm. Lulu returned the flirtatious look with one of her own, forgetting her annoyance almost at once as she surveyed her husband, a man who by any measure appeared quite perfect.

"What is that look?" Lulu asked with a coquettish tilt of her head. "I'm annoyed, Pierce Banks. Don't think you can distract me with those beautiful baby blues."

"I don't think I can make the one and only Lulu Franc do anything she doesn't want to do." Pierce grinned back at her. "Otherwise, your name would be Lulu Banks."

"You knew my rules when you married me." Lulu added a lighthearted snip to her tone. "It's a lucky thing you're charming enough to make me forget why I was frustrated with you in the first place this morning."

Pierce crossed the room, pulled Lulu in for a quick kiss on the cheek. "I am the luckiest man alive."

Lulu inhaled the fresh scent of Pierce after his shower, his expensive gels and shampoos both familiar and comforting. She didn't think there'd ever come a day when she wouldn't be madly, brutally in love with her husband.

"Pierce," she protested against his chest. "I'm going to be late!"

Pierce let her back away to arm's length, but he held her there, his eyes fixed on hers with a lingering gaze that at once melted Lulu's heart, and then set her at unease. There was a hint of love in his eyes and, more curiously, a longing. Something Lulu hadn't seen from Pierce in quite some time.

"Is everything all right?" Lulu asked. "What's wrong?"

"Nothing." Pierce looked startled. "Nothing at all. Just taking in the moment."

"Yes, well, next time you take in the moment, do you mind taking in your wallet as well? We really do need to find it." Lulu gave a smile that was meant as an olive branch. In the background, the coffeepot gurgled to life and the delightful scent of freshly ground beans reached Lulu's nose. She inhaled deeply. "I've got to finish getting ready. Will you pour me a cup for the road?"

As Lulu pecked her husband on the cheek, she allowed herself one additional moment to wonder about Pierce's strange look. He was kind and loving, almost too generous for his own good, but he wasn't overly affectionate. At least not anymore. That look in his eyes set Lulu on edge, and it wasn't the first time he'd acted somewhat strangely as of late.

She waited in the hallway until she heard Pierce puttering around, pouring a cup of coffee for himself and then another for her, before easing into his favorite kitchen chair where he flicked a newspaper to attention during his typical morning routine.

Lulu took his silence as an opportunity, easing farther down the hall before she paused outside Pierce's study. It was the one place she hadn't gone to look for his wallet. The one place she normally avoided, with the drawer she normally ignored. But she couldn't shake that look in his eye. Something wasn't quite right.

And despite her husband seeming quite perfect, Lulu knew she was missing something. Nobody was perfect—Lulu included. Her four (failed) marriages proved that. Ironically, Lulu had thought this would be her last marriage. She'd toyed with the idea of changing her last name when she married Pierce, especially after he'd emotionally pleaded his case and explained how much it would have meant to him to share a surname, but it hadn't been enough.

In the end, Lulu had made the decision with her head, not her heart. She'd kept her maiden name—Lulu Franc (without the *K*)—because that was the way she'd held onto her independence, her identity, after nearly seven decades of life. Four men, five marriages, and through it all, she'd maintained a certain sense of freedom. Clung to it with greedy little fingers, even though it had disappointed Pierce to hear her decision. He'd said he understood, but Lulu wasn't sure if he ever truly could.

After all, Pierce hadn't been married before. He claimed to have no secrets. No ex-wives or tangled relationships following him around. At least, none that Lulu had heard about. But somehow, she suspected that all might change if only she could open the damn drawer.

Lulu slipped into her husband's study. She knew with confidence that she had at least ten minutes until Pierce would finish his coffee, crinkle up his paper, and pour himself a second cup before heading to his study to check his emails.

She didn't ever mean to pry, but Lulu was nothing if not curious. Her fingers curled around the handle on the drawer and gave a light tug, but it didn't so much as budge. She knew it wouldn't, just like she knew Pierce wouldn't be fooled if he found her in here, yanking against a handle and claiming to be looking for his wallet. The truth was, the drawer had been locked for more than a year now.

Do all couples have secret drawers? Lulu wondered, casting a guilty glance over her shoulder. She paused to listen again, her heart pounding against her chest with such intensity that she checked her left arm for signs of a heart attack. Unfortunately, her arm was fine, and her erratic pulse was due solely to the fact that her perfect husband was keeping a secret, and Lulu was positively dying to find out why.

two

Detective Ramone: Please state your name for the record.

Ginger Adler: Ginger Holly Adler.

Detective Ramone: What is the nature of your trip to Serenity Spa & Resort?

Ginger Adler: We're attending a college friend's wedding. It's pretty obvious, I thought. Aren't you supposed to be the detective? I mean, there are signs for the ceremony everywhere. Did you see the letter board out front?

Detective Ramone: I haven't.

Ginger Adler: It's got a week's worth of activities on it. In my day, weddings were a one-day event. And the money they're putting into this! There's a flower arrangement the size of the Taj Mahal outside the resort, spelling their initials in a heart. They even gave me a bottle of custom wine as part of a welcome basket in our room. Not the cheap kind either, with a label just stuck on the outside. It's an actual bottle of some special blend made exclusively for them. Don't you think it's all a bit much?

Detective Ramone: Let's stick with me asking the questions. Mrs. Adler, when did you arrive at the resort?

Ginger Adler: We were supposed to arrive on August 16 at 3:00 p.m. We didn't arrive until 8:00 p.m.

Detective Ramone: 8:00 p.m. on August 16? What was the reason for your delay?

Ginger Adler: A missed flight. I almost killed my husband because of it.

Detective Ramone: I assume you were able to get on a different flight.

Ginger Adler: Yes, luckily. My husband lives to see another day.

Detective Ramone: Mrs. Adler, I assume you understand why I've called you in here this evening.

Ginger Adler: Of course. Let's cut to the chase and save us some time—I am responsible for a man's death tonight. Is that what you needed to hear?

E lsie, get your shoes!" Ginger tugged a hand through her strawberry-blond hair, now showing a smattering of gray. (She'd meant to get that highlighted before the wedding, but there was no time now.) "Poppy, did you pack a bathing suit? You should bring two, honey. Tom. *Tom!* Put down your dinosaur and go potty. We have a long flight ahead of us, and we are not stopping on the drive to the airport."

"Mom," he moaned. "I'm seven. I use the bathroom."

"Potty, potty," Poppy singsonged in her sweet little voice. "Tom has to go to the potty."

"Shut up," Tom said. "I do not."

"Mommy!" Poppy's sweet voice turned into a wicked scream. "Tom told me the s-word."

"Kids, now," Ginger roared. "Anyone not in the car in ten minutes is going to be left home alone. Move it, troops."

Ginger's children grumbled and groaned and moaned in camaraderie. It seemed the only time they called a truce and worked together was when they were ganging up on their mother. All three kids seemed to agree on how horribly awful she was to have picked up double shifts for the past six months at the hotel where she worked as a receptionist, just so they could afford the trip. Anything less, and the Adlers wouldn't have been able to foot the bill for the ungodly sum of money it was costing her to fly a family of five across the country.

Who did Whitney DeBleu think she was, anyway? It was ridiculous that she needed to get married in some exclusive resort on the coast of California. And even more ridiculous that the wedding festivities lasted an entire week! What happened to nice, heartwarming Midwestern weddings in a barn with sloppy buffet food and a raucous dance party? That'd done the trick for Ginger and Frank, and they were still married sixteen years later with three gorgeous (albeit not very cooperative) children.

In reality, Ginger would rather not have received an invitation to

Whitney's wedding at all. She and Frank really couldn't afford to be going, but the wedding would only happen once, and Ginger and Whitney really had been good friends in college. Of course, Emily and Ginger had been best friends, but that relationship had fizzled once Emily had gone and turned into a complete and utter bitch.

"If I don't see your butt on the toilet in two seconds, Tom, I am going to put you there myself," Ginger called. "Frank, where are you? Can you find Poppy's other shoe? The pink one. She needs it for the ceremony. Elsie, you've packed a library in this backpack. Do you need ninety-four books for a week? And they're all so torn up and mutilated. Can't you choose a regular-looking book to read by the pool so people think we're a normal family?"

Ginger limply picked up a battered, dog-eared, somewhat stained paperback that her daughter had likely acquired from the neighbor's Little Free Library. Elsie had a thing for random books and preferred to choose an odd freebie from next door rather than buy her own, which fit very well with Ginger's budget, but not so much with the image of a neat little family vacationing at a luxury resort.

However, Elsie was almost sixteen and almost impossible to be around. Arguing with her only made things worse. She'd developed some sort of new attitude that revolved around obnoxious technology, an inability to string a full sentence together, and a general moodiness that affected the entire house. Even vacationing in California had barely tipped the edges of her lips into a smile.

"Frank!" Ginger looked toward her feet where there were four full-size suitcases, three halfway-zipped duffels, and Poppy's little backpack—along with an entire zoo of stuffed animals. "A little help here?"

"Sorry, honey, I didn't hear you." Frank Adler careened in through the front door of the suburban three-bedroom house—just a touch too small for the five of them—with a goofy grin on his face. "I was watering the tomatoes."

"You were…" Ginger felt her lips parting in shock. "You were watering the tomatoes?"

"Yeah, well, Leslie won't be here to care for the plants until Wednesday, and we're really in for a heat wave. Would hate to see those babies die. I figure a good soak will keep them healthy for a few days." Frank paused, running a hand through his already ruffled hair. "Hey, I forgot all about my potted lemon tree. And the raised garden bed. Honey, I'll be right back—"

"No you won't." Ginger felt her voice turn ugly. "Frank, what about your *real* children? Tomatoes are not living things."

"Well, actually—"

"Forget the damn tomatoes," she said as her phone burst into a jingle. "I've got to answer this. Can you help get the children ready for the trip that *you* wanted to take?"

Ginger's shoulders stiffened with resistance at the horribleness in her voice. This wasn't like her. Ginger was fun and patient and exuberant. She wasn't a nag, and more importantly, she loved Frank. She loved his silly hobbies and stupid projects. His very zest for life was one of the reasons she'd fallen head over heels for him in the first place.

But then life had happened, and kids, and finances, and insurance, and lost pink shoes. And somewhere in the mess of suburbia and second jobs and the monotony of daily life, love just seemed so hard sometimes.

"Sorry," Frank mumbled. "I—Er, what did you need me to do?"

"Forget it," she said, pulling her phone out from beneath the mounds of other things she had in her arms. "Water your garden. Be in the car in ten minutes, and I'll take care of the kids and the house and the suitcases and the snacks and the paperwork and the money."

"Really?" Frank's face turned into a childish expression of jubilee. "You're a doll, honey. Kids, listen to your mother. We're going on vacation!"

"Hello?" Ginger was already on the phone. She'd barely glanced at the number as she pushed the phone against her ear and juggled the socks and the suitcases and one of Elsie's books that had plopped on the floor, looking sad and dead. "Sorry, I can't hear you. Who is this?"

"It's me, Whitney" came a tinkling, manicured voice. "Is everything okay? It sounds like you're in a war-torn country, sweetie."

"Well, that's the Adler household for you," Ginger said. "How's everything going with the wedding? Is something wrong? I swear, Whitney, if Arthur is having cold feet, I'll stick those frigid toes up his—"

"No, no, it's nothing like that," Whitney said quickly. "Arthur is wonderful. I've just stepped out to the spa to get my nails done, and I thought I'd give you a call while I had a second to myself. I'm positively booked every minute from now until the ceremony."

Of course Arthur is perfect. Whitney deserved all sorts of wonderful, so why was the image of Whitney—wildly in love, chatting easily while a masseuse rubbed her shoulders and a nail technician pampered her feet and yet another professional waxed her lady business—so dang frustrating? As if Whitney's blissful naivete was some sort of sin.

Just you wait… Ginger thought. *Wait for the third kid, the tightening budget, the sleepless nights.* Then Ginger would call Whitney back and daintily inquire about her delightful marriage and beautiful children, picturing her baggy-eyed with roots showing and a child on her breast while Arthur watered his fucking tomatoes.

"I'm thrilled we'll be seeing you so soon," Ginger said instead. "We're trotting out of the house now."

"Excellent," Whitney said. "But that's sort of what I was calling about."

"Go on," Ginger said, gritting her teeth as a shoe came flying over the upstairs bannister and nearly took her eye out. "What's bothering you, sweetie?"

"Emily called," Whitney said in a rush. "She wanted to know if it would be super rude to last minute change her RSVP and attend."

"It's a little late, don't you think?"

"Yes, but, well…" Whitney had always been uncomfortable with confrontation. Everything from her angelic blond hair to her precious pale skin shrunk at the first sign of an argument. "I was thinking of telling her she could come. It's…she thought she'd be traveling, and now she's not, and—anyway. I thought you should know she's going to be there."

"That's great," Ginger said in a high-pitched falsetto. "Thanks for calling, but I'll be fine. We're all adults. Now, you just focus on getting married and looking marvelous. We're running late for our plane, so I'm going to let you go get pampered. See you soon!"

Ginger sighed and collapsed on the couch, the phone cradled in her limp hand as she stared at the muddy shoe on her white floor. She should have never RSVP'd to this wedding. She'd have to face Emily while towing tomato-loving Frank on one arm and three children headed straight to the juvenile detention center behind her.

three

Detective Ramone: Please state the time and date you arrived at Serenity Spa & Resort, as well as your name, for the record.

Emily Brown: Emily Brown. I arrived the sixteenth of August at 4:00 p.m.

Detective Ramone: Did you go straight to your room?

Emily Brown: No, but I suspect you already know that.

Detective Ramone: I have an eye witness who claims you joined a man in his room.

Emily Brown: Yes, Henry. I met him on the plane.

Detective Ramone: The flight you took on August 16?

Emily Brown: Yes.

Detective Ramone: Please describe the nature of your relationship with Henry, for the record.

Emily Brown: What does that have to do with anything?

Detective Ramone: I'm sure you're aware this is an investigation into how a man died, Ms. Brown.

Emily Brown: I could get a lawyer.

Detective Ramone: You could.

Emily Brown: But there's no need. I fired that gun, Detective. I killed a man tonight.

W hy don't you hand me both of those, please and thank you." Emily Brown gestured at the flight attendant carrying two glasses of champagne and forced a smile at him. "I really hate flying."

"Of course," he said, setting both glasses on Emily's tray table before respectfully bowing his head and returning to the front to retrieve more drinks for the first-class passengers.

That's a laugh, Emily thought. She wasn't a first-class passenger by a long shot, nor was she scared of flying. However, when the airline bumped her up at the last second, what was she supposed to do—decline free drinks?

Emily settled deeper into her seat, closing her eyes in an attempt to relax. She came up short when a passenger clunked her head with a hefty backpack in passing. Emily's eyes flashed open as a stressed-looking woman with two small children in tow leaned over and apologized. An apology that was lost when one of her sons elbowed Emily in the thigh during a heated argument with his brother.

"Gosh, I'm so sorry," the woman said again. "We're terrorizing you. Boys, what did I say about behaving? You get none of the cookies we packed if you don't say sorry this instant."

"Sorry," they chirped in unison.

"It's really okay," Emily said. "I understand. I used to be a teacher."

The woman gave her a grateful smile as the line moved along, and she barked at her children to keep up.

Emily had been a preschool teacher for long enough to understand exactly how difficult it was to get small children to do much of anything in an orderly way, let alone behave on a cross-country flight. But her patience for that sort of work had expired long ago.

Her career as an educator had been short-lived after college, and over the past ten years, she'd transitioned instead to corporate America. She had eventually settled into a comfortable position as a project manager at a marketing company. It was much safer there.

Wincing at the memories, Emily took her first sip of champagne and glanced at the empty seat next to her. With a small laugh, she shook her head and then closed her eyes again. The only reason they'd bumped her to first class was probably because she was still single, no children. At thirty-eight, her biological clock was winding down.

Emily finished her second glass of champagne and stacked the two cups on top of each other when a shadow appeared over her shoulder. She glanced up at the hulking presence, noting that her new seatmate was one fine specimen of man.

But when Emily truly laid eyes on him, her first impression was that he was tired. The same sort of bone-tired she herself often felt. She continued her assessment of him, ticking off observations on some arbitrary mental checklist: handsome, worn, rugged. A hint of reckless. This man had lived a lot of life—but Emily didn't care. She only wanted to be left alone with her champagne.

This man had ruined everything. She'd almost had the row to

herself until he showed up. A surge of illogical frustration bubbled in her chest as she sat pointedly back in her seat and ignored him. It wasn't as if the man had actually said something; he just waited, expectantly, as if she were supposed to read his mind.

He cleared his throat and edged closer.

Emily still gave him nothing. She had no idea why she was being so rude except she was tired too. A lifetime ago, she would've apologized and made a huge effort to move out of his way, offering polite niceties and appropriate small talk. That was before the incident. Now, Emily was a bitter shell of herself, and the more she noticed it, the more she sank into the role like a comfortable, old sweatshirt.

"Ma'am, I think that's my seat." The man's voice was deep and rocky, like a desert gravel road crunching against tires.

"Ah." Emily moved her legs ever so slightly closer toward the seat. "Can you get by?"

He threw a small backpack in the bin above and then climbed roughly over her. Apparently both of them were in a mood, but it was nothing Emily couldn't handle. If he knew half of what Emily had gone through, he might think twice about getting on her bad side.

As he adjusted and buckled his belt, Emily couldn't help but glance over. He brought no personal items with him to stash under his seat, a choice that always mystified Emily. What was he planning to do all flight? Stare out the window? Pick at his fingernails? Sleep? Heaven forbid his plan was to talk to her.

"Sir, can I get you a beverage?" The flight attendant appeared again, politely ignoring Emily's two empty glasses. "We have sparkling water, champagne, sodas, liquor, wine…"

The man's eyes flicked toward Emily's empty cups, then to her hands clenching around the seat arms, then back to the flight attendant. "Whiskey for me, two champagnes for the lady."

The flight attendant stared blankly at him. He clearly didn't believe in serving Emily four glasses of champagne before the wheels lifted for takeoff, but there was a certain weight to the way this guy carried himself, as if it would be unwise to mess with him, so the attendant nodded. "Very well, sir."

The more Emily studied the man next to her, the more intrigued she became, albeit reluctantly. Her champagne savior looked something like a cowboy with worn jeans and a simple, buttery-soft black sweater. The alcohol already twirled lazily through Emily's brain, and she wondered what it would be like to rest her cheek on his shoulder and close her eyes. To have his hand come up and dance lightly over her skin as she drifted into the safety of a nap.

Emily gratefully reached for a glass when it arrived and held it up, clinking the cheap plastic lightly with his. "Cheers. What's your name?"

"Henry," he said. "And yours?"

"Emily."

"Emily no last name?"

"Henry no last name?"

Henry raised the glass of whiskey to his lips and downed it in one gulp.

Emily watched him with interest. "So, are you from Chicago, Henry Anonymous?"

He glanced out the rain-streaked windows and watched men and women dressed in neon-orange vests shuffle around below, carting bags and directing traffic beneath the gray clouds hovering over O'Hare. "No. I'm only passing through."

"I moved here a few years ago from Minnesota after college," Emily offered. "That's the reason I'm headed to California—I've got nothing better to do, and an old roommate of mine is getting married. I fucking hate weddings."

Henry sucked his teeth. "Is that why you're still single?"

Emily saw Henry glance at her bare ring finger. She raised her hand, wiggling her fingers to make it easier for him.

He arched an eyebrow and looked out the window again, and

Emily found herself peeking for a glimpse of a ring on Henry's hand, but it was equally as naked as hers.

"One more question," she said as she reached down to her own bag stashed beneath the seat and pulled out headphones, a marker, and a small photo album. "What are you planning to do for a whole flight?"

Henry's eyes flicked toward Emily's supplies. "Not an art project."

"I never understand why people don't bring a book or a tablet with them on the plane," she said. "Won't you be bored staring out the window?"

"I inevitably sit next to women who want to talk the entire flight."

"If you'd brought headphones," Emily pointed out, "you could've plugged them in and pretended you couldn't hear those annoying women."

Henry gave a half smile for the first time all flight, reached into his pocket, and withdrew two earbuds. Without another word, he popped them into his ears and rested his head against the seat, staring out the window. The other end of the cord dangled uselessly between his knees.

"Nice." Emily shook her head and looked away. "Subtle."

He gave a soft laugh, and it changed something in Emily. It warmed her blackening heart, softened the bitter taste in her mouth, like tea that'd steeped too long, and added a hint of honey to make it palatable. She—Emily Brown—had made this surly, fine-looking gentleman laugh. A stranger.

As Emily polished off her champagne, she studied the man next to her more overtly, counting the grooves on his face like battle scars, noting the laugh lines that seemed to have softened over the years, as if Henry hadn't had a reason to smile in quite some time. She could relate. And if the weekend went as awfully as she expected, she wouldn't be smiling again anytime soon.

So why had she called Whitney and RSVP'd at the last moment? Emily still didn't have an answer. Part of it had been curiosity. In college, some fifteen years ago, Emily, Whitney, Kate, and Ginger had been the best of friends. Then Emily had made one choice that had sent the four spiraling down wildly different paths through life.

The thought sent a chill along Emily's spine. She hoped Henry didn't noticed her reluctant shiver. Turning toward the album on her lap, she thumbed through pages of happier times. She racked her brain for captions to add beneath the photos while the flight attendants prepared everyone for takeoff. However, her time was mostly spent chewing on her pen and daydreaming instead of jotting down lovely, heartfelt phrases—even after the pilot had gotten the four-hour trip well underway.

Sometime later, Emily found her head bobbing forward. Her hand slid over the book, and she closed it, sensing Henry's curious glance at her lap. She resolutely turned her head the other way, let her eyes collapse shut, and before she knew it, she found they were halfway to California.

Shaking herself awake, Emily dropped the tray table before her and placed the photo album on top, still disoriented from her unexpected doze. She wiped at her eyes and blinked a few times until the alertness settled back in her brain, hampered only by the slight lingering effects of her champagne.

Hunching over the weathered album, Emily resumed her scan of the images. The book featured those smallish square photos from disposable cameras, the stills taken long before phones or digital versions had made perfection so much easier.

Emily smiled at one particular image where the four girls had smooshed together, crammed with limbs entangled underneath one teensy tiny Christmas tree they'd decorated with whatever junk they could scrounge up in their college apartment.

Emily recalled Ginger's playful cackle as she'd made paper snowflakes out of old exams she'd bombed from a certain history

professor she'd sworn had a vendetta against her. They'd sipped
spiked eggnog and belted Christmas carols at the top of their lungs
until their resident advisor had pounded on their door with a noise
violation in hand. Ginger had made a paper snowflake out of the
violation too.

Emily's thoughts were interrupted as Henry glanced over her
shoulder and spoke. "How old were you there?"

She considered. "Oh, I don't know. Twenty? This must have
been junior year of college."

Emily knew for a fact it had been junior year because she recognized the present under the tree she'd wrapped to give to Ginger.
It was a silly thing, a set of matching Christmas pajamas for her and
Ginger to split. After all, they'd shared everything. An apartment,
a friendship, a life...until Emily shared one thing too many and
ruined everything.

"Do you keep in touch with all of them?" Henry asked. "Seems
like a lot of work."

"No, actually," she said. "I mean, the occasional Christmas
card, maybe. But Kate—this one, here—she lives in New York.
Whitney's in California. Ginger's in Minnesota, and I'm in
Chicago, and we don't make a habit of meeting up."

"Why are you going, then? You hate weddings, you don't talk
to these people—seems like it makes sense to skip the damn thing."

"Maybe I should have." Emily shrugged. "But I have a week of
vacation to burn, and it's supposed to be a very nice spa and resort.
I will probably barely see them at all."

Or maybe that was a lie. Maybe Emily longed to be a voyeur
more than anything else. To peek into the life of her ex-best friend
and marvel over Ginger's flourishing, secure marriage. To watch
her chirpily dote upon three flawless, cherub-faced children. To
examine in person the gifts Ginger had been given, and to make
certain—absolutely certain—that Ginger appreciated what she had
in front of her. (Emily had Facebook, and even though she and

Ginger weren't friends, Emily could see her profile picture of a bubbling, joyful family.)

God only knew how Emily had suffered. And God only knew how much Emily admired, envied, desired what Ginger had. If it weren't for one terrible decision in college, maybe things would have been different. Maybe Emily would be sitting in economy class with three children climbing on her lap, shooting knowing, lovely little glances at an adorable, loving husband. Instead, she was groveling over photos from years past, longing for simpler times.

"Well, that doesn't make any sense to me, but maybe it's different for a man and a woman." Henry sat back in his seat, closed his eyes. "You're an adult. You clearly don't like these women anymore, so why torture yourself?"

Emily's fingers shook, and she capped the marker she'd been holding so no stray flecks of ink marred the irreplaceable photos. There were no backup copies. "What makes you think I don't like them?"

Henry opened his eyes to glance at his watch. "It doesn't seem like the captions are coming easily to you. If they were still your friends, it wouldn't be so hard to write your little love notes."

"It's a wedding gift," Emily clarified. "I'm trying to make it nice for the bride."

However, as Emily peered down at the book again, she was surprised to find Henry Anonymous was right. She'd only written a handful of captions on a thirty-page photo album in the span of a few hours.

"I'll finish at the resort," she said. "I'm not in a rush."

However, the truth was that Emily had been so lost and twisted in her thoughts of yesterday that the sound of Henry's voice was disorienting as it dragged her back to reality. She pinched at her forehead as she felt the beginnings of a champagne headache take hold and wondered about the logistics of getting another glass to keep her buzz going strong.

She leaned over the arm of her chair, glancing up the aisle in search of the attendant. When she caught Henry watching her, she gave a wry smile. "Who do I have to sleep with around here to get a glass of champagne?"

"He's not going to serve you again," Henry said, returning the smile. "I think the flight attendant is a bit frightened of you."

"That's ironic," she said. "Seeing as I'm not frightening at all. I only wish he'd top up my glass, or this headache is going to get worse."

"Why don't I buy you a drink when we land?"

"I really should get to the resort and get checked in."

"What are the chances you're staying at Serenity Spa & Resort?"

Emily choked back a noise of surprise. "Did you see the reservation on my phone?"

"You wrote the date and location of the wedding on the front of your album." Henry's gaze flicked downward. "It wasn't hard to guess you've been suckered into attending the DeBleu/Banks wedding too. That's where I'm headed, and I figure there are only so many weeklong extravaganzas in California at one time."

"That would be correct," Emily said, somewhat mystified and quite unsure how she felt about sharing a hotel with this gorgeous and mysterious stranger. "I'm obviously friends with the bride as you saw from the photos. You?"

"Cousin of the groom." Henry gave a polite shrug. "We're not close, but it's family."

"I suppose you could buy me a drink at the resort, then," she blurted, feeling a bit shy. "If the offer still stands."

"I'd hate to be interrupted by a bunch of family I haven't seen in years," he said, giving her a somewhat lopsided smile. "They say my room has a great view and a complimentary bottle of champagne waiting for my arrival. You're welcome to join me."

"Oh."

"Like you, I don't have a desire for small talk and mingling. I've got a work project due next week, so I'll be holed up in my room most of the weekend fighting a deadline—which is fine by me."

"Ah," Emily said, feeling a thrill cascade through her body at the thought of his implication. "I see. What do you do?"

"I've got a big case," he said. "But if you'd like to join me for a drink this evening, I could use a break."

"We'll see," Emily said, knowing full well that was exactly what she wanted to do. "I should probably check in with the bride first. See what's on her agenda."

"Is this Whitney? I haven't met her yet."

Henry leaned over, his breath hot against Emily's neck as his finger extended in a point toward the photo open in her book. It was one of Emily and Ginger, their faces squished together with smiles of glee painted across their lips. They were sitting in a bundle of blankets in the back of Frank's beat-up truck at the drive-in movie theater on a hot summer's evening. If she closed her eyes, Emily could feel the warm Midwestern breeze, smell the buttery flavor of popcorn, feel the stickiness on her fingers.

When she opened her eyes, she realized Henry was watching her curiously.

"Sorry," she said quickly. "No. It's not. It's a different friend… or was."

Henry passed over his glass of whiskey. Emily hadn't remembered him ordering another, but she took a grateful sip regardless.

"It's been a long time since I've seen these friends," she admitted. "I'm a little on edge."

"Will this help?" Henry leaned forward, his fingers tilting Emily's chin upward. He waited there, paused, his eyes telling her she needed to meet him halfway.

Emily tipped forward, lost in the pull of him. The comfort of a man's arms, the allure of a stranger who knew nothing about her but could make her forget it all for one tiny minute. Their lips met in a soft test of wills.

Henry pulled back first, and, if Emily wasn't mistaken, he looked quite pleased with their kiss. She blatantly studied him, noticing the thick, sturdy head of hair. She wondered how a man as handsome as Henry wasn't married. She wondered if he had children. She wondered if she asked, would he lie? The dark hair cascading over his eye gave him a mysterious, standoffish sort of charm. Emily itched to brush it away, as if that were the key to opening his secrets.

What happened next was a blur. It was a mix of the alcohol simmering in her blood, the thought of showing up alone—fat, ugly, old—for the sole purpose of lording her misery over Ginger. As if Emily had been some self-sacrificing guardian angel in college.

Maybe that was why Emily reached over and brushed the lock of hair from Henry's forehead. Their gazes cemented a concrete bond between them. A knowing, reckless dare. The pulling of two broken souls toward each other in a poisonous, futile swirl of lust.

Henry leaned forward, grabbed her chin roughly with his hand, and pressed his mouth to hers. They tangled together, hot, heavy, until he nodded toward the back of the airplane. Emily felt her heart race, her stomach twist. She returned his nod.

They screwed in the airplane bathroom, Emily's foot wedged on the sink as Henry pounded into her, his eyes—jungle green, flecked with gray—studied her with surprising intention as she moaned his name against his neck. His grip was hard, their pace fast as they fucked like teenagers, tasting whiskey and champagne, smelling a fresh, spicy cologne mixed with cheap airplane bathroom sanitizer. She grasped his delicious, buttery sweater between her fingers as they finished.

The two shared a cab to the resort. They checked in at the same time at different desks.

They met at the elevator.

"I'm in 509," he said.

"411," she said.

"Your room or mine?"

four

Detective Ramone: Please state your name for the record, the time and date you arrived at Serenity Spa & Resort, and your purpose for being here.

Kate Cross: Kate Cross; August 16 at approximately 3:36 p.m.; attendance at the DeBleu/Banks wedding.

Detective Ramone: Thank you, Ms. Cross. Now, please tell me, do you recognize this man?

Katie Cross: Yes.

Detective Ramone: Please state your relationship with him.

Kate Cross: There isn't one, considering he's dead.

Detective Ramone: Please state the nature of your relationship with him while he was alive.

Kate Cross: Let's be efficient here. You want to know who killed him? I did.

Detective Ramone: Ms. Cross, were you acting as part of a group?

Kate Cross: No. We were alone when it happened—end of story.

Detective Ramone: Ms. Cross—

Kate Cross: I'm a lawyer, Detective. I know my rights, I know you're recording, and I know you can use this in a court of law. I hit a man over the head with a wine bottle tonight, and he never woke up. I acted alone. Now, can we move along?

W here are you? I've got lunch!"

"In here!" Kate called. She glanced through the window of her newly purchased condo—not quite the penthouse in her building, but close enough. This was New York. Real estate was expensive, and the fact that she had secured a two-bedroom, two-bath space with a view of Central Park said enough about her financial situation.

The sound of Max tooling around the kitchen filtered into the bedroom. Her long-time boyfriend (she really was too old to be calling him *boyfriend*, but Max was skittish about getting married) had been debating moving in with her. He spent more nights sleeping over than not, but still refused to give up his own apartment.

Part of the reason she'd bought this new space at such an exorbitant price was so they'd have room to grow here together, and hopefully ease his fears on marriage. He was forty-five, for God's sake, and she was thirty-eight. They weren't getting any younger, and they had both agreed to have one child. Ticktock and all that.

"Leave the food in the kitchen," Kate called, twirling the satin ribbon of her robe between two fingers. "I've got a surprise for you."

The sounds in the kitchen quieted, but they didn't stop. She couldn't be sure if she heard Max sigh or if she'd imagined it, but finally, the unwrapping of takeout food calmed, and he made his way to the bedroom.

Kate's smile faltered as he stopped in the doorway with a stony expression. But she recovered quickly; after all, she was a professional at keeping her emotions chilled. She'd made partner a year ago at William & Brooks, and she couldn't have done so without the ability to keep her personal feelings on ice.

"There you are, babe," Kate said, letting the exquisite robe that'd been delivered to her work that morning drape open to reveal a flat stomach. Underneath, she wore La Perla lingerie that cost more than most Americans paid monthly in rent.

"Kate, I'm hungry." Max's eyes skimmed briefly over her. "Can't we eat lunch like a normal couple?"

Kate felt the sting like the crack of a whip, but she forced herself not to let it show. "Come on, one little quickie."

"Kate—"

"Don't you like my outfit?" Kate preened under the lavish fabrics. She ran her hand seductively down her neck, fluttered her eyelashes, then continued her caress between her breasts and over her distinct abs (thanks to Marvin, the marvelous, bank-draining personal trainer who came five mornings per week), down between her legs. "I've been waiting for you."

Max rolled his eyes and stalked away from the door. "Forget it. I'm going back to work. There's food on the table if you want— I'm not hungry."

"Max!" She fought back the panic rising in her chest. "Don't you dare walk out of here!"

Slipping her feet into gorgeous cream slippers, Kate tread into the living room, her long, bare legs failing to draw the attention of Max like they used to. Once upon a time, he would've come running to the bedroom and pounced on her. They would've torn the sheets apart in a hot and sweaty lunch date, then followed it up with a giggling rinse in the double-headed shower she'd installed exactly for such occasions.

"Stop right there, dammit," she said, her voice taking on that possessive, growly sound that was unlike her. "Don't walk out on me, Maximillian Banks."

"I'm not walking out on you! I only said I wanted to have a normal lunch." Max stopped in the kitchen to face her, shooting her an expression eerily close to disgust. "If you can't give me that, I'm leaving."

"I'm ovulating."

"Congratulations." Max narrowed his gaze at Kate. "How do you know that little detail, anyway? We're supposed to be on a break."

"Max, please," Kate said, her heart pinging with the sense of impending loss. "You can't give up hope."

"Hope?" Max started to run a hand through his hair, then stopped so as not to disrupt his meticulous style. Instead, he massaged his forehead. "We agreed after the last failed round of IVF that we'd take a few months off. No temperature charting. No medicines. No pregnancy tests. It's too much, Kate—it's driving us both out of our minds. It has taken over our lives."

"I haven't been charting anything! I haven't taken a pregnancy test in weeks, nor have I taken my temperature. I was only attempting to be romantic. We agreed to try to bring back a little spontaneity to our sex lives."

"And the way to do that is by discussing your ovulation cycle?" Max's gaze was tinged with disdain as his eyes raked over Kate's body. "I'm sorry, but I think we both need to come to terms with the fact that we are not meant to have a baby. It's just not going to happen."

"You don't know that!"

"We've been through five rounds of failed IVF," Max said. "I know that much, and so does my bank account."

"But the statistics say there's a chance it could still happen naturally—"

"I don't care what the statistics say," Max said. "It doesn't matter. And even if it did, we fucked last night. So you should be good either way."

"Is that what it was?" She raised her voice in anger to avoid sounding hurt. It was the way Max phrased things that infuriated her. They'd made love! They were in a loving, adult relationship. Kate had tried to raise the romance factor last night too—wine, candles, a massage. "Who knows? Maybe today is our lucky day. Please—we've got to at least try."

"Do you not understand what a fucking break is? We need time to de-stress and regroup. The way you're acting now—I don't call this a break. Why is it so hard for you to accept it's not going to happen for us?"

"Well, it's certainly not going to happen naturally with an attitude like that!" Kate cried, dangerously close to losing her cool. She was either going to snap or cry, and neither would be acceptable. "I thought you wanted this."

"I do...I *did*. But with all we've been through, I feel like I'm your dog—like you're using me for breeding purposes."

"I want to marry you! Stop being ridiculous."

"Forget it," Max said. "I'm going back to the office. I suggest you put some clothes on and do the same. While you're at it, have a serious think about whether you'd like to focus on me or your uterus. It's one or the other, Kate."

"Is that an ultimatum?"

Max stepped close, took Kate's hand in his. "I'm here, and I'm real. Tangible. This obsession you have with a baby—well, there is no baby. There's never been one. Is it worth ruining our relationship over something that may never happen?"

"Max, you're not making any sense. Can we sit down and discuss this?"

"There's nothing more to say." Max leaned in, kissed her forehead. "I'll see you tomorrow."

"Tomorrow?"

"We're flying to my cousin's wedding, remember? This is what I'm talking about. You're so obsessed with your cycles and ovaries and eggs that you don't have room to consider anyone else."

"No, I know about the wedding, but..." Kate felt flustered, a totally foreign feeling. "Aren't you staying over tonight?"

"I don't think that's a good idea. I'll meet you at the airport."

"Max!" Kate's voice felt scratchy, her heart thumping with what could only be described as panic. "Can we at least talk?"

"No, I don't think so," he said quietly.

Then he turned, his feet carrying the rest of his impeccably clad body down the hallway. He punched the elevator button and, without looking back, stepped through the doors and disappeared.

Kate closed the door and leaned against it, struggling to breathe. After a moment, a burst of rage at Max's words coursed through her, and without thinking, she spun to kick the door childishly with her gorgeous cream slippers and tried to ignore the prickling in her eyes.

She shook, her fingers running through a three-hundred-dollar blowout she'd gotten yesterday after work that had been for one purpose only: to seduce her boyfriend of over two years. She unceremoniously pushed her dark hair back from her face, impatiently fighting the full-body trembles that rocked her shoulders as she slumped against the door. She played back every one of her interactions with Max, trying to determine where things had gone wrong.

Of course everything would come crashing down the day before their trip. Whitney's stupid wedding was at some posh resort in California, and Kate vaguely remembered asking her assistant to book her and Max tickets a few months back. Kate had attended college with Whitney, roomed with her at the University of Minnesota, where they'd both completed their undergrad degrees.

Bossy, organized Kate and painfully shy, waifish Whitney had been the perfect match in some bizarre universe. While Kate lived to argue, Whitney avoided confrontation at all costs, and the two had managed to create an odd sort of friendship through bookish nights and boozy weekends.

Kate had always suspected, even now, that on some level their friendship had only worked because Whitney had wanted to *be* Kate, and Kate had liked the attention. An only child born to two wealthy lawyers, Kate's family had money in excess while Whitney—the youngest of four kids raised by a single mother—had never had enough to go around. Whitney had always been a bit in awe of her friend, and Kate had appreciated the admiration.

Ironically, Kate's first thought when she'd received the beautifully embossed invitation to Whitney's wedding was that Whitney had met her goals. She was marrying rich and could now afford the wedding of Kate's dreams. And it was clear Whitney wasn't hesitating to show off her newfound social status.

Still, Kate had to wonder—what about the wedding of Whitney's dreams? A rich, posh wedding would fit the style of Kate and Max. It was who they *were*. For Whitney, Kate had always pictured a more intimate family gathering, complete with a slew of close friends, loud music, and a dance party that carried on into the wee morning hours.

Strangely enough, it had been at one of the drunken college parties Kate and Whitney had attended together where Kate first met Max when he was in town visiting his cousin Arthur Banks—a study buddy of Whitney's. Although Kate and Max hadn't reconnected until years later in New York, Whitney had received credit for the initial introduction. It wasn't lost on Kate that while Whitney and Arthur had recently reconnected and found blissful love, Kate and Max were struggling to get through the lunch hour without a nasty argument.

Now, Kate was due to face Whitney in a reunion…with nothing aside from a career to show for her fifteen years of post-college life. The only ring on her finger was the two-carat diamond she'd bought herself for her last promotion. She had no children. She couldn't even get Max to officially move in with her. There was no life to speak of outside of her glaringly successful career.

Kate heaved herself to her feet, idly wondering what Whitney's reaction would be when they saw each other in person. They kept in touch in vague, distant ways, but they hadn't met face-to-face for nearly five years. Living on opposite coasts, aging out of weekend girls' trips, and demanding careers had a deteriorating effect on friendships. Would Whitney gloat? Kate didn't think so. Whitney wasn't the type to gloat.

She would be polite and demure, offering quiet sympathies like the time in college when Kate had scored lower than Whitney on an exam. It'd been only once—a stupid history test, no less—and Whitney had pulled out an A while Kate had been enraged to find an angry red B+ scrawled on her paper. Kate hated turning in work that was anything less than perfect—she always had, and she always would.

Whitney had peeked over, and despite her mumbled apologies and her declarations that their teacher was absolutely nuts for the deplorable comments he'd left on Kate's page, Kate had seen the gleam in her friend's eye. The hint of pride, the sweet joy of victory. No matter how Kate sliced it, her relationship with Whitney had always had an element of competition to it. And in the world of weddings, Whitney had won.

Kate let the sensation of emptiness wash over her. It wasn't the wedding that upset her. Kate was under no illusion that she was anything less than fabulous without a rock on her finger put there by a man. It was the utter sense of hopelessness that had begun simmering in her gut lately, the feeling that she was on the cusp of losing everything. The man she'd been meant to grow old with. The children she'd dreamed of having. The warmth that came with a full house instead of an empty, expensive cage.

Easing her way back into the kitchen, she wondered when Max had begun to look at her with disgust in his eyes. They'd been trying for over a year and a half to bring a child into this world together. Unfortunately, there was simply nothing happening in Kate's uterus.

They'd been to doctors, specialists—the best money could buy—and none of the expensive professionals had any sort of diagnosis for her. They claimed both Kate and Max were completely healthy. Sure, Kate was creeping toward forty, but that didn't explain the last year and a half. She'd had her blood drawn, swallowed pills, peed on more sticks than she could count, and gone through the rigorous IVF process not once but on five different occasions, and still, nothing had worked.

Kate was barely clinging to the last dredges of hope. Max had already given up, if this afternoon's display of frustration was anything to go by. Then again, he had been the one encouraging them to listen to the doctor's advice and take a break while Kate had wanted to do anything but. She'd been dying to dive into the sixth round of IVF, but Max had claimed he needed time to heal, or to recover, or some other bullshit that Kate knew wasn't true.

Max took pride in never displaying emotion, aside from the occasional burst of anger. He hadn't needed to heal. Max wasn't tired and worn from the physical, mental, or emotional process of it all—he was sick of Kate. Kate was broken, and Max didn't like to play with broken dolls.

So, for the past several months, instead of trying for the baby she so desperately desired, Kate had been forced to watch precious eggs cycle through her body. She never cried when it happened, but the crushing sense of emptiness was worse, if anything. Lately, her periods had been so light from the stress and anxiety of *not* trying that she feared it would be more impossible than ever to conceive naturally. The very hope that had been sustaining Kate was gradually fading away into oblivion.

Kate felt a bit wobbly and leaned against the kitchen table, a whiff of wasabi and soy sauce making her stomach roil. She found a sushi platter from her favorite restaurant sitting on the spotless counter, the plastic lid already wrestled off and placed neatly next to the sashimi. Kate felt like puking at the sight of it. The spicy wasabi, the tangy ginger, the crunch of sesame seeds.

She tipped it into the trash. If she were pregnant, she wouldn't be able to eat it anyway. Storming to the bedroom, she shed her outer layer and slipped into a fine skirt and jacket combination fit for the office. She added pearl earrings, a matching necklace, and a bracelet that Max had given her for Christmas last year. Maybe after work, she'd stop at Max's place and apologize.

Kate clipped her hair into a neat bun, loose enough to give her face the feminine curves people admired, severe enough to give off the impression she meant business in the workplace. As she grabbed a handbag that matched perfectly, she fingered the dress sitting out on the hanger that Max had demanded she wear to Whitney's wedding.

He'd picked it out, ordered it straight from a French designer's website, and had given it to her as a gift for Valentine's Day. The gown was a floor-length stunner, made from a silky red material meant to skim Kate's trim hips. It had been tastefully decorated with a delicate lace pattern across the chest and two exquisitely thin straps that would hang sweetly from Kate's shoulders. The slightest of trains would swish behind her as she walked, ensuring that all eyes would be on her—or rather, on Max and his date.

The whole thing was excessive and over the top for some stupid wedding, but Max didn't seem to care. Kate sometimes had the feeling he saw her like a Christmas ornament—a beautiful piece of art to display when convenient, and then tuck away in precious papers when she was no longer needed.

As Kate held the dress in front of her body, examined her lithe figure in the mirror, and pictured her hair and makeup tucked in *just so*, she smiled. Max needed the night to cool down. Tomorrow, they'd be on the plane together to a lush spa, and there was a chance she'd still be fertile. Between her agreement with Max to stop charting her temperatures and her irregular periods, she couldn't be sure of her exact ovulation date. A week spent away together, under the influence of a romantic wedding and candlelit dinners and relaxing massages, was just the ticket.

Kate would come back pregnant from that damn spa if it killed her.

five

Detective Ramone: Thank you for joining me here today, Ms. Anderson. Please state your name and occupation for the record.

Cindy Anderson: I'm Cindy Anderson, and I'm one of the bartenders at the lobby bar.

Detective Ramone: Ms. Anderson, what was your first impression of Lulu Franc?

Cindy Anderson: She is… It's hard to describe. She's the sort of woman everyone wants to be when they get older.

Detective Ramone: What does that mean? Please include specifics.

Cindy Anderson: Well, she's quite glamorous. She showed up in this big fur coat. I mean, the woman must be pushing seventy, but she carries herself in a certain way that's quite intimidating. She doesn't seem old, though, if that makes sense. There's this classiness to her that I really love. Then again, I suppose you're not asking

about looks. Are you wanting to know if I think
she could have killed someone?

Detective Ramone: Do you have any reason to
believe Lulu Franc was involved in a man's death
this evening?

Cindy Anderson: Well, she was pissed that first
day she arrived at the resort. She was convinced
her husband was seeing another woman. I remember the conversation well because I was staring
at that fur coat of hers and listening very
intently. For a minute, I wanted to be like Lulu,
but of course, I work eighteen-hour days to keep
my six-month-old in diapers, and that's not very
glamorous, is it?

Detective Ramone: Lulu's husband, Mr. Pierce
Banks, was seeing another woman? Are you certain
that's what you heard?

Cindy Anderson: I don't know for sure if he was
or wasn't. Neither did Lulu, for that matter.
Nothing was confirmed as far as I know. But do
I think Lulu is capable of murder? Absolutely.

Detective Ramone: What makes you say that? It's
a bold statement, Ms. Anderson, and not one I
take lightly.

Cindy Anderson: Of course not. But she really
loved her husband, you know? It was easy to see.

Clear as day. And yet, there was this other side to her that was…I don't know, cold? Calculating? Her eyes were very intelligent. The thing is, I don't think she knew how to handle rejection. Love drives people to do strange things.

Detective Ramone: Remind me how you know Lulu Franc, please.

Cindy Anderson: Oh, well, I don't, really. But being a bartender means I double as a therapist. You wouldn't believe the things people tell me, especially during weddings. Weddings seem to bring out the worst in people—or at least, that's the side of them I see.

Detective Ramone: So you don't actually know Lulu?

Cindy Anderson: No, but I've been bartending for ten years—I know a thing or two. By the way, have they released the victim's name yet? I heard his head got so smashed up that his face was completely destroyed.

Detective Ramone: Thank you for your time, Ms. Anderson. That'll be all.

I'll take a mimosa," Lulu said to the startlingly young bartender. She thought the woman looked barely old enough to drink alcohol herself. "Light on the orange juice."

"A mimosa?" Pierce asked. "For a nightcap?"

"I told Mavis and Edna I'd have a drink for them," Lulu explained, resting a hand on her husband's as she thought fondly of her closest friends back in South Carolina. The two sisters were both unmarried old women who lived together and rarely left the comfort of their front porch, choosing instead to get their fill of adventure through Lulu's stories. "I might as well get it out of the way early on. Mavis will be calling me any minute, wondering what we've been up to so far—the woman is a gossip."

Pierce nodded along with his wife, looking supremely distant, as he had all evening. The pair had landed in California a few hours back, and after a quick nap, a shower, and refreshments, Lulu had convinced her husband to meander down to the bar for a drink before bed.

"It's good people watching," she'd said while she toweled her hair after her shower. "All the wedding guests will be arriving. Aren't you curious to see who was invited?"

"Not really." He had shrugged and looked longingly at the bed. "It's family. How interesting can it be? I'd rather stay here and watch a movie."

Pierce Banks was used to doing what Lulu wanted. He adored her, or at least he had when they'd first gotten married. These days, however, she caught him staring into space more than usual. Distant, uninterested.

It seemed the harder she fought to sustain their (previously vigorous) sex life, the less interested he was in maintaining it with her. Lulu had heard this happened with older adults, only she'd never considered herself one of them. Then again, she was barely on the right side of seventy—could she blame her husband for losing interest when there were women half Lulu's age who'd give their right foot to be with him?

They watched a lot more movies these days, and Pierce always drifted off during the most climactic scenes. He was seventy-four (a handsome seventy-four), so Lulu tried to forgive him for an early bedtime, but that didn't help her anxiety over the feeling that her husband was gradually floating away. Like a beach ball when, after a bit too much fun in the sand, it landed in the water and lazily bobbed out to sea—lost forever.

Honestly, it'd been like pulling teeth to get Pierce out of the room. He'd claimed to be exhausted from travel, not in the mood for an in-room massage or a bubble bath drawn by one of the innumerable resort staff specifically tasked to keep the guests pleased. Well, Lulu wasn't pleased.

She sighed. It would have pleased Lulu to see more of the man she had married instead of his distant shell. She wanted the eye-twinkling laughter, his soft kisses and silly jokes. But she hadn't seen much of the man she'd fallen in love with over the last few months. And while she hated to admit it, Lulu recognized the signs of a deteriorating relationship.

Unfortunately, those niggling signs were hardly subtle any longer, and it was only Lulu's desperate desire to remain married to her husband that kept her firmly in a state of denial. She'd noticed the little white lies that didn't quite make sense. She just didn't want to believe them.

So Lulu ignored Pierce's references to late-night meetings when he claimed to be at the office and wasn't. (Lulu was an excellent gossip, and she'd made great friends with Pierce's receptionist.) She deliberately looked past the appointments he would schedule that couldn't be moved for any reason, but whose purposes remained a mystery to Lulu. And above all, she pretended not to notice the tiny black *S* notation in his planner that appeared two or three times a month with no location attached, no time specified, and no further explanation as to what—or rather, who—this *S* character could be.

Lulu was staring down the deadline of her five-year anniversary with Pierce, which would make for a record. Out of her five marriages, she'd never had one last longer than five years (although her two unions with Anderson had collectively totaled seven years), and she was determined to make it to the mark this time around.

She had sincerely hoped this weeklong getaway at a renowned resort on the coast of California would rekindle their romance. But the truth—the sort of truth Lulu only admitted to herself while tears ran down her cheeks in the privacy of her own shower—was that she suspected her husband was getting ready to leave her. And that was impossible.

Men didn't leave Lulu Franc; she left them.

Lulu squeezed her husband's hand tighter, then released it when he didn't reciprocate. Pierce didn't seem inclined to speak, so Lulu took her time soaking in the relaxation bubbling around them. The entire venue had been set up to ease away stress, to enhance romance, to promote wellness.

Cucumber and watermelon ice water sat in elegant pitchers on every spare surface, flanked by silver coffee and tea warmers with dainty little teacups. The spa and minibars, of course, stocked only low-calorie, plant-based sweeteners and raw, natural sugars, and none of the cheap yellow packets of Splenda found in every other resort.

Lulu's keen gaze caught sight of a woman dressed in an all-pink pantsuit as she ushered in an ice sculpture the shape of a dove. Leaning toward Pierce, Lulu gently patted his hand and pointed out *the* Miranda Rosales.

"Mavis is going to die when she hears about this," Lulu said. "That wedding planner costs two grand to get on the phone. Can you imagine spending that much on a single day? Well, I suppose a week, this time around. Did you see that letter board with the itinerary out front? It's a bit military how much the bride has sched-uled. I felt like I was reporting for boot camp when we arrived."

Pierce looked at his water glass without acknowledging Lulu's attempt to make him smile, which had her feeling ridiculously self-conscious. The original Pierce Banks would have humored her at least, smiling in amusement and chuckling good-naturedly. He wouldn't have ignored her entirely.

Lulu watched her husband more carefully, wondering if he was thinking that in Lulu's case, it would have been five separate occasions she'd have needed to hire Miranda Rosales. Five weddings to four different men. Four failed marriages and a fifth on the way. Lulu leaned back, disconcerted as she watched Pierce study the countertop.

A resort manager propped open the front door, drawing Lulu's attention as the cool night breeze of a California desert flitted through the lobby, pushing the scents of fat, pink peonies and delicate, white baby's breath to the far corners of every room. Lulu loved the romance; she thirsted for it. Prayed even a droplet would rub off on her husband.

"Here's your mimosa," the bartender said, sending the drink across the countertop to Lulu and startling her from her reverie. "And you, sir?"

"Er, whiskey," Pierce said. "Rocks. Top-shelf."

Lulu glanced at her mimosa, the drink a design worthy of a photo. The colors were expertly intertwined and adorned with a beautiful sprig of berries and greenery. Even the beverages were exquisite and, as Pierce commented, so were the prices.

"What would you like to do while we're here?" Lulu rested her hand on Pierce's thigh. "What about a nice massage tomorrow?"

"Hmm?" Pierce raised his eyebrows in question and glanced over at his wife. "What was that?"

"Maybe we can sign up for a Jacuzzi treatment and ditch the god-awful itinerary. I think they draw the bath for you right in the room, but then they leave. It's been a while since we relaxed in the tub together and played hooky from all our responsibilities. Doesn't that sound nice?"

"Sure. Whatever you'd like."

When she'd fallen in love with Pierce, they'd been equal partners. They'd argued, they'd laughed, they'd joked, they'd made passionate, desperate love, they'd fought and made up. There'd been none of this demure "sure, dear" and "whatever you like." Lulu was a fighter, *dammit*! She wanted to be married to one too.

"What's wrong with you?" she snapped finally, hoping to draw him out of this miserable funk and into some sort of conversation. She'd take a feisty argument over this lackadaisical attitude; in fact, she was hankering for an argument. "I feel like you don't listen to a thing I say anymore. Do you even want to be here with me?"

Pierce looked at her, his brows lifting once again, this time in shock. He had inherited that unfair George Clooney gene that God seemed to only bestow on men—the one that made them look better as they aged.

Still, Pierce was unique. His nose was a touch crooked, and his left eye squinted smaller than his right when he smiled. It was his smile, however, that melted her heart—and the heart of practically every woman he encountered. There was a cheeky happiness to it that matched the twinkle in his eye, and when coupled with his broad shoulders and a spattering of salt-and-pepper gray hair, the combination was mesmerizing. Pierce's imperfections made him perfect.

"I-I'm sorry. I'll be right back." Pierce stood, pushed his untouched whiskey across the bar, and threw a fifty underneath it. With a single glance back at Lulu, he pressed the button for the elevator and stepped into it.

Lulu gaped after him, holding her husband's gaze until the door severed their bond. Something had changed. *Something big*, she thought, and he wasn't going to tell her what it was. He was simply going to slip away, and there was nothing she could do about it.

Her heart felt as if it were cracking, slowly crumbling like an old terra-cotta pot. Where it had once held such beauty, a blooming tree of love and desire, only five years later, it'd become worn and grooved. Salt deposits stained the outside; the flowers blooming inside had disintegrated to dust. Soon enough, it would shatter, the shards tossed unceremoniously into the garbage.

She gripped the bar for stability as a *whoosh* of breath left her body. When she inhaled again, she tasted fear and bile. Lulu didn't tread carefully on eggshells through her relationships. She loved fully, completely, and when love had run its course, she left it behind without a backward glance.

There was only one problem: her love for Pierce had not run its course. She'd even pondered if Pierce would be her last husband. She'd never particularly believed in soul mates, though Pierce had just about converted her. But what good was it having a soul mate if he didn't love her back?

six

A baby's cry pierced Lulu's blue, melancholy musings as she wondered who had brought a baby to a bar. Sure, it was the lobby bar, and the cry was coming from the lounge area. *But this is a five-star relaxation resort*, Lulu thought as she glanced behind her for the source of screeching. Surely there was five-star (soundproof) child care somewhere around here.

"What a lovely child," Lulu said as the bartender topped up her mimosa with a bit of champagne. The young woman smiled fondly across the lobby but was whisked away by her colleague before she could comment.

Lulu spun on her delightfully comfortable barstool and scanned the room for the source of the noise. Spotting a young mother with a baby clasped to her chest, Lulu studied her and waited to feel a twinge of remorse. Lulu had never heard the *ticktocking* biological pull that so many of her female friends had felt in their late twenties, early thirties, and onward. It had simply never hit her.

"Such an adorable little one," Lulu murmured to nobody in particular as she tested another phrase on for size, waiting to see if the words unearthed any latent feelings of longing from somewhere deep within. When nothing stirred, she tried again. "So sweet."

"Excuse me?" A woman two seats down was giving Lulu an odd look. "Are you talking to me?"

Lulu turned to face the woman. A woman nearly half Lulu's age was watching her carefully. "Oh, I'm sorry. I'm mumbling to myself. My name is Lulu."

"Emily."

For a moment, Lulu was lost in her own thoughts as she sized up Emily. Lulu wasn't particularly envious of youth, but what she saw in Emily disappointed her. Lulu placed Emily in her late thirties, and when Lulu had been that age, she'd been thriving. Young and beautiful, desired and pursued. Men had eaten from the palm of her hand, and Lulu had liked the feeling of being in control.

But Emily, somehow, didn't appear to be at the peak of anything. She might have been pretty once upon a time, but now, her lips were turned into a contemplative pout and her gaze didn't hold contact for long. Her clothes didn't do a thing for her figure, and while her accessories weren't exactly cheap, they were just… plain. Everything about Emily seemed a bit drab, as if she'd lost the will to try for the sparkle that belonged in a woman. A shame, if you asked Lulu.

"I'm sorry about that," Lulu said quickly. "I was mumbling to myself. My husband ran upstairs to freshen up." She glanced over at Pierce's recently emptied seat. "But if you're bored, you can slide over and join me for a drink until he returns."

"Sure," she said. "I hate drinking alone."

"Like I said, I'm Lulu." She stuck out her hand for a shake. The woman had a cool grip and still didn't meet Lulu's eye. "What are you having?"

"Is that a mimosa?" Emily glanced at Lulu's glass. "I started with champagne on the plane, so I should probably stick with it. I'm not eighteen anymore, and you know what they say about mixing alcohols."

"I don't know what you're talking about," Lulu deadpanned. "I've only just turned twenty-one."

Emily stared at Lulu for a long moment, that critical second in time where one stranger is supposed to determine whether the other stranger is joking or a little bit psychotic. Finally, she cracked a small smile and then burst out laughing. "I like your style, Lulu."

The bartender appeared with a smile. "What can I get you ladies?"

"I'm fine, but she will take a mimosa," Lulu said, patting the seat next to her and flicking a glance at Emily. "Go on, scoot over into Pierce's seat for now so I'm not shouting across the bar."

"Hold the orange juice, will you?" Emily muttered to the bartender. "Thanks."

Lulu smiled. "What brings you here, Emily?"

"To this monstrosity of a resort?" Emily gestured around her, looping in the white, gauzy fabrics dripping from the rafters, the signs sitting on every spare corner that had been adorned with the bride and groom's initials outlined in hearts made of pearls. "I'm here for the wedding. Seems to have taken over the place, don't you think?"

To Lulu, the resort was an extravagant oasis located in the California desert—a location chosen, according to Pierce, because of its exclusivity and reputation as the ultimate luxury spa. Whitney DeBleu and Arthur Banks wouldn't—absolutely couldn't—get married in a normal fashion like everyone else. They needed opulence.

And if their goal was over-the-top luxury, they'd certainly achieved it. With tiny portions of food that tasted like money and drinks more expensive than liquid gold, one couldn't walk into the space without going into debt. The very chandelier dripped bits of warm light onto the deep, heavy wooden bar top, meeting the flickering of Himalayan salt candles and the hiss of diffusers pushing out humid bits of scented mist. Even the palm trees outside swayed in time with the soft, relaxing pump of music through the speakers as if they, too, were part of the very core of the ambiance so carefully crafted.

While Emily didn't seem to approve of the resort choice, Lulu didn't mind it. Lulu's life had always been about luxury. Marrying into money, divorcing with money. Of course, money wasn't everything; marriage was about love and passion. If Lulu didn't believe in romance, she wouldn't have gotten married five times.

"I don't think it's so horrible," Lulu said. "I read on the website that the resort staff leaves beautiful petit fours every night on the bedside table. How lovely! And these drinks? They could be featured on the cover of a magazine."

"Can I be honest?"

"If you'd like."

"I hate weddings." Emily heaved a sigh. "Seeing all these old friends who aren't really friends anymore, figuring out the perfect gift, making small talk with strangers I'll never see again."

Lulu gave a perfunctory smile. "Do you consider this small talk? If so, we can sit here quietly. I won't be offended."

"Not you." Emily's cheeks flushed a rosy pink. "I'm sorry, I'm not thinking straight. I had a long travel day, and I met a man on the plane. Somehow, things are already complicated."

"Ah, men." Lulu shifted to get more comfortable in her seat and settled in for the long haul. "Well, I'm always up for a good story. And I've been married five times, so if it's advice on men, maybe I can help. Advice on relationship longevity, not so much."

Emily smiled, looking gratefully over at Lulu. "I'm impressed."

"Don't be," Lulu said, though she enjoyed the compliment nonetheless. "Getting married is the easy part. Staying married is the difficult portion."

"Tell me about it." Emily stared deeply into her drink, studying the champagne bubbles as if they held the answers to her deepest questions. Then she added quickly, almost as an afterthought, "But I'm not married, of course."

Lulu sensed Emily was on the verge of spilling some of her secrets, the details closely secured against Emily's chest, but at the last second, she appeared to pull herself back from the ledge. Emily shook her head, obviously distracted, and plucked something from the purse she'd slung over Pierce's chair.

"I need an honest opinion." Emily ran her hands over a slim photo album in a gorgeous shade of rose. "Is this a stupid idea as a wedding gift?"

"Is it a photo album? I do love that shade of pink." Lulu leaned farther over and gently stroked her finger along the velvety exterior. "Oh, you must be friends with the bride. College days?"

Emily gave a hesitant nod. "We lived together for a while. There were four of us who were close—though when I think back, I wonder how we ever got together. We were all so different."

"May I?" Lulu waited for Emily's nod.

When it came, she pulled the album closer to her and flipped it to the first page. Four young, pretty faces smiled gleefully back at her, all of them shoved under a Charlie Brown–style Christmas tree that looked as if it'd been pulled out of a dumpster and decorated with bits of leftover trash. It was charming in a funny sort of way.

"Well, it's obvious how the four of you got along," Lulu said, unable to keep the smile from her own face. "Look at the fun you all are having. It's a different sort of fun before you have money, isn't it? You know, I married my first husband when he was a poor schmuck. My best memories of him are from before he went and got rich."

Emily watched as Lulu flipped a few pages further into the album. Clearly, Emily had been struggling to come up with captions to the photos. The first three contained silly little quips written in a shaky hand, but they quickly trailed off to blank lines where loving words belonged.

"Don't think about your notes so hard," Lulu encouraged. "This is a great idea for a gift. I'm sure Whitney will love it, and it will be a great way to reconnect with your old friends. Maybe the other two can help come up with some of the captions."

"I doubt that," Emily said. "I'm not on the best terms with either of them."

"College was a long time ago." Lulu didn't make eye contact with Emily as she flipped to an image of two girls—Emily one of them, an unfamiliar woman beside her—and laughed out loud. "What is happening here?"

Emily grinned wryly. "Halloween our sophomore year. We

went as a bra—it was Ginger's idea. It was a dare, I think, or maybe that was during the phase when she was protesting something for women's rights—I can't remember. Either way, I went along with her because that's what we did back then. Our other friends—Kate and Whitney—were too embarrassed to be seen with us until they'd finished the better part of a wine bottle. Then, they came out dressed as a devil and an angel."

The next page revealed another photo of Emily and Ginger, this time wearing swimsuits. The photo was so dark, they were mere blobs of pasty-white skin against a star-spattered night sky as they stood on the edge of a dock.

"Oh, this one!" Emily exclaimed with the first hint of excitement she'd shown all evening. "This was when we got Whitney to go skinny-dipping for the first time. She was so nervous, poor thing. She only did it because Kate went with her—those two were attached at the hip."

"But Whitney's not in the photo," Lulu said gently. "In fact, most of these are you and Ginger, and a few are of the four of you."

"Er, right," Emily said. "Kate and Whitney were inseparable, and so were me and Ginger. Sophomore year, we all shared a four-bedroom apartment on campus, and that's when we all started hanging out. We spent so much time together over the next three years, I guess we didn't have a choice but to become friends."

"This one is sweet." Lulu stopped on a photo clearly taken in the library. Poor Whitney was facedown with her head on one of the books in such a deep slumber that her mouth was cracked open. "All-night study session?"

Emily snorted. "Sweet, yeah right. That was the week of finals. Our school had one of those late-night pancake breakfasts to help us fuel up for exams. Whitney ate too much and passed out. Not a good idea when you have Kate and Ginger around."

Lulu frowned in confusion. "Why ever not?"

In explanation, Emily flipped the page and found an inappropriate piece of artwork drawn on Whitney's forehead. Even Lulu found it hard to hold back a smile at their naive immaturity, the girls' eyes squinted with suppressed giggles. "I see what you mean. Emily, promise me—if I happen to fall dead asleep after this next mimosa, do me a favor and shuffle me off to my room before your friends get here, will you?"

Emily laughed. "You have my word. Though, I think we're all a little past that now."

"There's no outgrowing some things," Lulu said. "Take it from me. A little youthfulness is always good."

"Maybe." Emily snapped her book closed, shuffled it back to her purse. "I guess I'll finish that later. I should probably just write Whitney a check, though—it does seem a little odd giving her a book where she's not even in half the photos. Anyway, all those memories have me thinking I could use another drink."

Lulu stifled her urge to raise an eyebrow and instead beckoned the bartender over and gestured for Emily's glass to be refilled.

"I normally don't drink like this," Emily explained. "It's the college photos bringing me back, I guess. It's been a complicated sort of day."

"So you said. This man, what is it about him that's making everything so difficult?"

"Um…" Emily tapped her hand nervously against the bar counter. She glanced toward Lulu, then took a fortifying sip of her drink. "The sex."

"Oh." Lulu licked her bottom lip in thought. "Yes, that does tend to complicate things. Is he married?"

"God, I hope not. He told me he wasn't. He didn't have a ring on, but men have been known to lie before."

"Well, don't expect judgment from me," Lulu said. "As long as you're two consenting adults, I don't see anything wrong with having a little fun on vacation."

"We all have our secrets, I suppose." Emily lifted her glass to her lips and raised an eyebrow, offering Lulu a half smile. "I've told you mine."

Lulu mused for a moment, unsure how to feel about offering up her greatest fears on a platter. It felt a little like standing naked in front of a room full of staring strangers. Then again, there was something tempting about it, something freeing.

For so long, Lulu had held her cards close to her chest. When she'd married her first husband, she'd been so young, and so in love. Joe hadn't been rich, but that hadn't stopped Lulu from understanding a woman's place—and power—in society. After her relationship with Joe ended, she'd set her sights toward upward mobility and secured Anderson, a true catch in all senses of the word.

From then on, Lulu had access to money, and that allowed her to slip easily behind a charade of furs and gowns, sparkling accessories, and high-end makeup products. She'd learned to smile a certain way, to tilt her head at a certain angle when listening to men. She'd accumulated invitations to the most prestigious of events and learned how to survive among the elite.

There was a specific walk Lulu now used when entering a room, and a particular laugh she knew captivated men and women around her. Lulu's friends claimed she was polished, but Lulu saw it more as a form of camouflage. Her mother had always said Lulu wouldn't amount to much, but Lulu had known differently. She'd been convinced of it. And look at her now.

The thought startled Lulu. *Look at me now.* Was she really as happy as she claimed to be? She had the furs and the home, the husband...but did she really have him? Lulu cast a glance at Emily, who ran an unpolished finger around the lip of her champagne flute. Maybe it would feel good to bare everything. Or at least *something.*

"I really don't think—"

"A minute ago, I told you I had sex with a stranger on an

airplane," Emily interrupted. "If you think what you've got to say is bad, trust me—I've got worse."

Lulu struggled to put this woman's dark confidence in context with the bubbly college student she'd seen in photos. And Lulu made a decision to trust her, at least for the night.

"I think my husband might be planning to leave me."

"Well, shit," Emily said. "That's not good."

"No," Lulu said, feeling the tremble of frustration burn to a boil in her chest. It might have stemmed from hurt, but it had spilled over into a helpless, desperate anger. "No, it's not good at all."

Detective Ramone: Ms. Franc, are you aware that a man was killed this evening at Serenity Spa & Resort?

Lulu Franc: We've already gone over this, Detective. I'm well aware a man is dead, seeing as I killed him. I swung a wine bottle at his head and cracked it wide open. There was a lot of blood.

Detective Ramone: Was it an accident?

Lulu Franc: Does it sound like that was an accident?

Detective Ramone: Was anyone else involved?

Lulu Franc: No. It was only me out on the patio.

Detective Ramone: Were there other people with you at the time of the incident? Even if not directly involved?

Lulu Franc: I've already told you this, so if you didn't hear me the first time, listen back to the recording. But since we don't have time for that, I'll tell you again that the answer is no. It was just the two of us. And then I killed him.

Detective Ramone: Ms. DeBleu, thank you for taking time out of your wedding weekend to speak with me. I assume you know what this is about?

Whitney DeBleu: The man who died, I imagine. But I don't understand what I have to do with it. I mean, I was in the middle of my rehearsal dinner when it happened—ask anyone.

Detective Ramone: You're not under any suspicion, Ms. DeBleu. But I would like to talk to you about several of your wedding guests, specifically Lulu Franc, Ginger Adler, Emily Brown, and Kate Cross. You invited these women, yes?

Whitney DeBleu: Well, Lulu was a family invite. I've met her once or twice in passing. She's married to my fiancé's uncle, but I can't tell you much more than that about her. The others, yes—I invited them. I lived with Ginger, Emily, and Kate during college.

Detective Ramone: Can you please describe the nature of the relationship between the four of you?

Whitney DeBleu: I don't understand the question. I already told you, we were friends in college. We don't keep in contact much anymore, but I thought it would be fun to get together after all this time.

Detective Ramone: How often do you keep in touch with these women?

Whitney DeBleu: Kate and I exchange a few texts a year, maybe. But gosh—I haven't seen her in person in probably five years. As for Ginger, we do the Christmas card thing now and again. I did end up calling her before she left for the trip to let her know Emily would be attending the ceremony also. I don't keep in touch much with Emily, but it would have been rude not to invite her if I invited the other two. We were a foursome back in our day.

Detective Ramone: Why would Ginger care if Emily was in attendance at the wedding?

Whitney DeBleu: There was a little tiff between those two back in college, and I wanted to make sure they were over it.

Detective Ramone: And was Ginger over this little tiff?

Whitney DeBleu: I don't know, Detective. Would you be over it if you caught your best friend wrapped around the person you loved?

Lulu watched the bartender as she dropped off a glass of water in front of Emily and gave both women a fleeting, polite smile before she was called over by another customer. Lulu studied the young woman as she flitted between patrons, wondering if she herself might have accepted a job as a bartender had she not married a series of rich husbands. After all, it wasn't as if Lulu had many marketable skills in the workforce.

But Lulu wasn't sure her feet could've handled the long shifts standing behind the counter, nor would she have stood for the disenchanting hourly rate that came with the demands of such labor. Though she probably could have scored great tips thirty years ago, Lulu just hadn't been all that interested in working.

"Cheers." Emily raised her champagne glass, looking eager to have a sip. "To new friends."

Lulu tapped her glass to Emily's, wondering when the last time was that she'd made a friend. A real friend. Mavis and Edna went back fifty years in their friendships with Lulu, but the rest of Lulu's acquaintances were exactly that. Acquaintances.

"Will you look at that?" Lulu gave a faux-appalled shake of her head as she nodded toward the front doors to the resort. "That's the third ice sculpture that's been wheeled in here this evening. Rumor is that Whitney hired Miranda Rosales to plan the ceremony. I've heard it costs two grand to get her on the phone."

"I suppose that's fitting for Whitney."

"How do you mean?" Lulu asked. At Emily's curious expression, she continued. "I'm recently married into the family—I've only met the bride once or twice. My husband, Pierce Banks, is an uncle to the groom."

"Ah, well, Whitney's always been interested in…" Emily studied the mahogany bar in thought. "I'm trying to figure out how to say this nicely."

"I think we've passed the point of being polite," Lulu coaxed easily. "I won't tell a soul."

"The only thing I'll say is that Whitney has always been interested in things she qualifies as better than her," Emily said in a rush. "I'm not saying it's true, but Kate and Whitney—you saw them in the photos—had a strange sort of friendship throughout college. Almost parasitic, if you know what I mean. Kate came from wealthy parents and always had money for things that Whitney didn't. Plus, have you met Kate yet?"

Lulu shook her head.

"Well, you'll know her when you see her." Emily paused, looking lost in thought. "She's got a certain presence about her. Polished, classy, always gets her way. You'll know what I mean soon enough. Anyway, it always seemed to me there was a bit of competition between the two girls—one that Whitney could never quite win."

"I suppose we all need each other in some way," Lulu said, thinking of her own friends back in South Carolina. "Friendships are strange; they come in all shapes and sizes."

The more Lulu considered it, Edna and Mavis—Lulu's closest female companions—had latched onto Lulu because she was their eyes and ears into the social circuit. She brought spice to their lives, breaking up the monotony of the last few decades in which the sisters had spent their time raising a porch full of dead plants and one blind cat.

In turn, Lulu adored regaling them with her (often exaggerated) tales of parties and vacations and gossip from the hair salon. They gasped and applauded in all the right places, and because they were both nearing their eighties, Lulu still felt like the spring chicken among her friends. It was a win-win for all.

"That's true," Emily agreed. "All I meant is that this wedding... Well, it feels a bit like Whitney is trying to... Oh, I don't know. Forget I mentioned it."

"You feel like all of *this*"—Lulu spoke softly, pausing to gesture at the dimly lit sanctuary—"is Whitney's way of showing Kate and the rest of us that she's made it in the world."

"More or less," Emily admitted. "I mean, I'm happy for her—really, I am. And I think she and Kate genuinely care about each other, or at least they did."

"Well, there's no better way to marry into money than to snag a Banks." Lulu gave a tinkling laugh. "I should know."

"How long have you been married?"

"Oh, now you've opened a can of worms," Lulu said, glancing over her shoulder to make sure Pierce was nowhere to be seen. "It'll be five years this weekend with Pierce. Though as I mentioned, I've been married several times before."

Lulu didn't like to talk about her past relationships in front of Pierce. It felt so classless compared to his impeccable history: a thrilling career as a trial lawyer, a gorgeous house and fat retirement account, no annoying failed marriages following him around. His only baggage was the fact that he'd lasted the better part of seventy years as a single man.

When Edna and Mavis had heard the news of Lulu's engagement, however, they'd warned her about him. *A man single for that long is too good to be true*, they'd said. *There's no such thing as the perfect husband.*

Lulu wondered if they were right.

"Did you ever have a wedding like this one?"

"No, see, I don't particularly love the fanfare," Lulu said. "I love *love*. Romance and passion and desire. Weddings are an entirely different matter. Have you been married before?"

"It's complicated," Emily said. "Are things complicated with your ex-husbands?"

"Not with two of them. They're dead. And I've tried things twice with Anderson. Third time would not be a charm, I'm afraid."

"I'm sorry," Emily said, not appearing sorry in the slightest. "How'd they die?"

"Ah—"

"Sorry," Emily said. "You can tell me to fuck off whenever you like."

"It's complicated," Lulu finally said. "Shall we have another drink?"

"Let's."

After requesting a bottle of champagne from the bartender, along with a side order of chili cheese fries—was it really girl talk without a generous helping of junk food?—Lulu and Emily gave another toast to new friends, then launched into a professional form of people watching that only two women of a certain age could manage with success.

"Look at them. Sickening, isn't it?" Emily pointed out a young, twentysomething couple as they strode toward the front desk in itsy-bitsy swimsuits, wrapped around each other as they giggled to the front desk clerk. "They're so in love now, but just wait. It never lasts."

Lulu fell silent at Emily's observation.

Emily recoiled. "Oh, shit. I'm so sorry—I didn't think. Is your husband…"

"I don't know if he's truly leaving me," Lulu said. "But I think he might be interested in another woman."

"Do you have proof?"

"Not exactly, but we'll call it women's intuition." Lulu reached for her glass, surprised she'd opened up once again to this stranger. Not that what she'd told Emily was entirely true; Lulu did have some proof, but it wasn't enough. The appointments, the meetings, the mysterious *S.* After a fortifying sip of champagne, she sighed. "I do hope that if he's planning to leave me, he does it quickly. It's embarrassing to be hanging on by a thread."

Lulu was normally the one encouraging others to share, sympathizing with breakups and heartaches and losses with a bit of savory relish on the side, as if Lulu herself would never be affected by such tragedies. Why this Emily character had drawn out her only real fear, she had no clue.

"Why don't you go ask him?" Emily asked, and then winced as a child's cry pierced the thrum of soft lounge music pulsing through the bar area. "What is that awful sound?"

"The baby?" Lulu turned her attention to the wails, which had resumed after a brief respite. Still intent to try on her soothing words for size, Lulu smiled at Emily. "Precious, don't you think?"

"Not really," Emily snapped in a way that had Lulu sighing in relief. "It's cracking my skull in half. I can't breathe. Can someone *shut that baby up*?"

Lulu's breath came out in a startled, giggly gulp. Even she didn't feel that strongly about children one way or another. Emily, on the other hand... "You don't have any children?" Lulu asked.

There was a stony silence that followed, and Lulu wondered if she'd misread the situation. But the woman had already confided in Lulu about having sex with a stranger. Lulu couldn't understand how a simple question about children could be the imaginary line in the sand.

"No," Emily said finally. "I don't."

"Me neither." Lulu gave a hearty nod. "I never wanted them. Always thought something was wrong with me. What about you?"

Emily cleared her throat and downed her glass of champagne. "I don't want them anymore."

Lulu realized she was dancing too close to the veil Emily kept pulled tightly across her features. She made a mental note, then treaded lightly away from the subject of children and resumed watching as guests entered the lobby and checked in at the front desk. There was now a red carpet being rolled out through the entryway, and piles upon piles of white roses being carried in and placed in bundles on either side of the hall to create a living, breathing, flowery canopy.

Emily only pinched her head in response. "I'm sorry to cut things short, but I think it's time I retire to my room. I have a splitting headache."

Lulu glanced over her shoulder. "That crying baby probably isn't helping."

Emily gave a wan smile. "It's not the most relaxing sound I've ever heard."

"Well, get some rest. I should head out too," Lulu said, albeit reluctantly. She wanted to find Pierce and curl against him in bed. She wanted to read a trashy magazine while he pondered World War II or some other infinitely impossible-to-grasp subject, and she wanted to drift off to sleep together.

"Actually, do you mind waiting here for a minute?" Lulu asked. "I'd like to check on my husband, but if he comes back before I return, I don't want him to think I've left. My phone's upstairs, so…"

"No problem." Emily waved her off halfway through. "I don't mind at all."

"Can I get you another drink for the trouble?" Lulu eyed the almost-empty champagne bottle. Lulu hadn't had more than two sips of her glass. "I'll have my husband catch the tab when he comes down. That's the benefit of marrying an old wealthy man who has manners that date back to the Great Depression."

"No, I think I'm good for the night," Emily said in that slightly dreary tone. "You go on, and I'll wait here."

Lulu made her way to the elevator and hit the button for her floor. As the doors closed, she watched while Emily gestured to the bartender for another round.

Secrets, secrets, Lulu thought. *Secrets are no fun…*

Speaking of secrets, Lulu wondered where her husband had gotten to while she befriended the curious Emily. Had he come up to make a phone call to the ever-mysterious *S*? Lulu hated having such paranoid thoughts about her husband—it weighed on her, made her feel guilty for harboring suspicions of Pierce when she hadn't scrounged up the confidence to broach the subject head-on with him.

Sure, she'd dropped hints that she knew he hadn't been at the office when he'd claimed to have been, and she'd tiptoed around the fact that she wished Pierce would confide in her about those appointments he couldn't miss. But he hadn't offered additional information, and she hadn't pressed further.

Until Lulu demanded the answers from Pierce's mouth, she preferred to hold out hope that maybe there was a logical explanation for everything. Including the money that had been transferred out of their account in large sums over the past few months. Lulu wasn't stupid. And she was nothing if not honest. That was exactly why she'd been divorced four times; she refused to pretend things were *just fine, thank you very much*, when they were not. And things were not fine.

As she reached her floor, she sidestepped out of the elevator and made her way down the hall, practicing what she'd say if she found Pierce in some sort of compromising position in her room. Would she beg him to stay? Demand a divorce and storm out? Emily would be downstairs ready to have a drink with her and wallow, if need be. If nothing else, that was a small comfort to Lulu.

Halfway down the hall, her husband stepped out of the resort room and looked furtively around. (*Furtive!* Such a covert word. Lulu was too old to be sneaking around and dealing with furtive glances from her seventy-four-year-old husband.) He glanced curiously down the hallway toward Lulu, but he didn't appear to see her. Quite possibly because Lulu had ducked behind a plant, her heart pounding. She hadn't felt this way since she'd played kick the can as a knobby-kneed girl, and she was so nervous, she felt the sudden urge to use the restroom.

After a few moments of glancing around, Pierce turned the opposite way from Lulu and headed toward the elevator at the other end of the hallway. Lulu breathed a sigh of relief and waited until the bell dinged, the doors closed, and her husband began the descent to the lobby.

Letting herself into the room, Lulu flipped on the lights to reveal a carefully prepared suite that spared no luxury. She scanned the area, her gaze flicking past the large whirlpool tub outfitted with the best bath salts money could buy and over the chamomile pillows she'd ordered earlier in the evening.

A king-sized bed with a fat, perfectly proportioned mattress and fresh-scented, hypoallergenic pillows waited for a lovestruck couple to slide between the sheets. To make gentle, passionate love before drifting off to sleep beneath the lavender-scented diffuser.

Someone, likely Pierce or one of the staff, must have snuck in while Lulu had been at the bar and started the diffuser, clicked on the television, and changed it to the *relaxing* advertisement channel flicking on repeat through the resort amenities.

The staff had also deposited the promised tray of sweets Lulu had been looking forward to sampling with Pierce by her side, along with a complimentary welcome basket from the bride and groom. In it, Lulu spotted a bottle of wine adorned with a custom label stating its contents had been created by a vintner in Napa specifically for the upcoming nuptials.

Lulu pushed the chocolates away, her stomach churning with frustration and champagne.

The service here was impeccable. *It's my husband who's flawed*, Lulu thought, on second thought, grabbing one of the expensive petit fours from the tray beside the bed and shoving it unceremoniously between her lips. On any other occasion, she might have fawned over the gold-dusted surface and the way the delicate chocolate melted between her lips, but not this evening.

Swallowing the sour-tasting treat, she began piecing together Pierce's footsteps, dragging her gaze over the surface of their combined belongings. That was the thing about marriages: they accumulated a lot of stuff. Always a headache to split said stuff up, which was why Lulu had begun tossing everything after a divorce and starting fresh. Problem solved.

Pierce kept his things very neat and orderly, unfortunately for him. It made snooping very easy for Lulu, and she quickly spotted the paperback book on the bed. She crept across the room and noted the title—something about war, of course—resting on the bed with its spine cracked open. It hadn't been there when they'd left.

Lulu picked up the book, giving a sniff at the title. *War.* That was what Pierce would get if he planned on leaving her. Or maybe she'd leave him first, and...*oh, God.*

There it was. Her worst nightmare.

The note fluttered to the bed. A crumpled piece of loose-leaf paper with writing that was undoubtedly Pierce's. Even worse? The man was an oaf. He'd dated the piece of paper. There was absolutely no mistaking the fact that Pierce had come upstairs specifically to write this sordid little letter.

Lulu's hands trembled as she began to read the sweet words surely written to *her.*

seven

Detective Ramone: Mrs. Adler, before your bathroom break, you confessed to killing a man.

Ginger Adler: Yes.

Detective Ramone: Walk me through how it happened— and please don't leave out any details.

Ginger Adler: I was at the rehearsal dinner in the ballroom when I decided I needed a break. So, I went outside for a breath of fresh air and wandered over to peek at the wedding setup for tomorrow, but I wasn't the only one who had that idea. There was a man there. It was the two of us outside—everyone else was still eating. I had no clue what this man was doing, but it was clear he was no good right from the start.

Detective Ramone: How could you be certain if you hadn't met this man before tonight?

Ginger Adler: Probably because he came after me before I had time to think. I barely know what happened next. I remember trying to run, but I wasn't fast enough. Instead, I fought. There was

a bottle of wine sitting on a rack outside, and
I just picked it up and swung. I hadn't meant to
kill him, but I knew right away when he went down
that he wasn't getting back up.

Detective Ramone: Mrs. Adler, if that's the full
truth, then *why* does the victim have a bullet in
his body?

S ee, honey? I told you we'd make it," Frank said good-
naturedly. "Everything always works itself out."

Ginger bit her lip. She wouldn't call missing a flight
"making it," but that was her husband, all right. Everything always
"worked out" no matter the bumps and bruises and twists along
the way. The airline had been accommodating enough to get their
family of five on the next flight out, even though it meant they
wouldn't all be seated next to one another.

As Ginger led the way down the aisle of the plane with three
little ducklings (Elsie, Tom, and Poppy), and one big duckling
(Frank), waddling behind her with the biggest bag, she wondered if
she was being too harsh on her husband. She'd been furious when
they'd arrived late to the airport and missed the flight. Absolutely
furious.

Ginger had always thought Frank should have been born a rich
man. Based solely on his attitude and the way he walked around
without a care in the world, touting inspirational quotes like
"everything will work out" and "relax, sweetie, you work too
hard." It wasn't fair that Frank had the attitude of a rich man with
the wallet of a poor schmuck, and it didn't help Ginger's mood.

She flinched as she remembered the way she'd blown up at

Frank in the car. It was a given that she shouldn't have exploded in front of the children, and Ginger owed her husband an apology. But it was more than that. Lately, Ginger had been feeling like the worst wife, and an even worse mother. She worried constantly. She worried about flights and Elsie's withdrawn new attitude. She worried about the cost of Tom's new soccer cleats and Poppy's medicines.

On some level, Ginger even worried about her relationship with Frank—he probably wasn't a fan of this new, snappy, short-tempered version of Ginger. It seemed the only thing Ginger was successful at these days was the ability to wear the same yoga pants for an alarming number of consecutive days.

Ginger had pondered why she might be spiraling out of control, watching it happen like a hamster getting trapped on its rotating wheel, as life spun faster and faster around her. Sure, Elsie's mood was driving her nuts, and her job at the hotel was keeping her up until all hours of the night working double or triple shifts when they let her. Frank was constantly getting on Ginger's nerves with his stupid little hobbies that weren't bringing in any money whatsoever, and honestly, if Ginger didn't get ahold of her temper soon, she just might kill someone.

Ginger rolled her shoulders, massaged the permanent knot that had appeared on her left side. Frank noticed the movement, the probable look of exhaustion, and thank the Lord, he snapped to attention.

"Okay, troops," Frank chirped. "Bags in the overhead bins! It looks like we're a bit split up now. Elsie, what if you sit with Tom? I'll sit with Poppy over here, and we'll get your mother her own seat for a bit of relaxation. Wouldn't you like that, honey?"

Ginger wouldn't exactly call sitting trapped in a tin sardine can with no legroom and screaming children (thank goodness her children had passed the baby phase) a relaxing time, but she'd take what she could get.

"But I want to sit with Dad," Tom moaned. "He said we could play a game together."

Ginger opened her mouth to approve the plan when Poppy gave a huge stomp. "But I want to sit by Daddy!"

"No!" Tom shouted. "I'm the boy. You sit with the girls."

"But Daddy said he'll let me have chocolates," Poppy said. "Mom won't let me have chocolates."

"Frank, I thought we talked about bribing them," Ginger said halfheartedly, knowing she'd done the same thing that morning. Only she hadn't been caught. "No chocolates anywhere unless you listen."

"I don't want to sit next to the baby," Elsie moaned. "Let me sit next to Dad."

"What about me?" Ginger asked. "Nobody wants to sit next to me?"

The plane suddenly fell silent.

"Great," Ginger said. "I suppose I'll take my seat then and leave you all to fight over the rest."

"Er, honey," Frank said, beginning to panic. "But the children."

"Rock, paper, scissors," Ginger said, heaving her pack above her seat. "I'm done. Hurry along, though; you're blocking the aisle. Here—Elsie, give me your pack so I can throw it up there."

"No, Mom—I want it."

"You can only keep one bag with you. Purse or backpack?" Ginger asked. "The attendant will take it away if you don't store it, and by then, the overhead bins will have filled up. Hurry, Elsie. People are waiting."

Grudgingly, Elsie shoved her backpack toward her mother and plopped on the end seat, making Poppy crawl over her to sit in the middle. Ginger grunted, promising she'd deal with Elsie's manners later, after she got this ragged backpack shoved into bins that were meant to hold a pair of socks, not luggage. Who was the idiot without children that had made planes so cramped?

"Excuse me," an older gentleman said from behind Ginger. "Can we keep things moving?"

"Sorry," Ginger muttered. "Trying to help my kids get situated. We'll be out of your way in a second."

"It's been a second," he said, and inwardly, Ginger rolled her eyes. This old man, who seemed to not understand the stress of traveling with children, was ironically acting quite like one himself.

"Sorry," she said again. "This bag isn't quite fitting—"

"Maybe if it wasn't so loaded with stuff," he said, "it would fit. It's oversized. That should have been checked."

Does he think he's a flight attendant? Ginger gritted her teeth so hard, she suspected her dentist would suggest a mouth guard (again) at her next visit. Ginger would jokingly laugh it off (husband, kids, ha-ha-ha, I'm so busy I must grind my teeth with stress!) when the real stress of it all was the ridiculous cost of a mouth guard. She couldn't afford it. She was ready to stick Tom's old hockey mouth guard in at night to save a few bucks so they could afford to send Poppy to the gymnastics camp she'd been dying to attend.

"Just—about—there," Ginger said, giving the backpack a final shove punctuated by a loud *riiipppp*. Before Ginger could process the sound, an avalanche of her daughter's things began spilling out in every direction. The books she'd stacked on top were the first to go, sending Ginger into a scramble to catch the free fall of dented, mutilated books her daughter liked to collect from local donation bins and library shelves. "Shit."

"Mommy!" Poppy said. "You can't say that in public! Only when you stub your toe in private!"

"No, you shouldn't say that ever," Ginger said, her face flooding with embarrassment. Why was it that Poppy could remember every curse word she'd ever muttered under her breath, but she couldn't remember the rhyme to tie her shoes?

"Great, then," the man said behind her. "Shall the rest of us take our seats?"

Ginger barely heard the gentleman's request because she was too busy staring at the ripped pocket on Elsie's backpack. Ginger could see the zipper had come completely undone, and her daughter's stuff—so much stuff!—had gone everywhere. Eyeshadows spluttered blue and pink powder everywhere (hadn't that gone out in the '80s?), lipsticks broke and smeared, a compact mirror hovered on the verge of a nasty death-by-shattering, and one last book plopped past Ginger's arms to the floor. That was the least of her problems.

"Excuse me," the man pressed again. "I'd like this plane to take off someday."

Ginger was too busy staring in horror at the long, thin sleeve of foil packets dangling down from her daughter's bag (her fifteen-year-old daughter) to respond. Her eyes locked on those little foil squares that meant her baby girl was no longer as innocent as Ginger thought.

Condoms. *Condoms?* Since when did fifteen-year-old girls begin carrying condoms around? A whole *rope* of them? Ginger's ears burned, and her heart pounded. The sounds around her melted into a mushy slush of broken phrases.

Excuse me!

Mom, my shoe!

Mom, where's my tablet?

Ginger! What's happened, honey?

My shoe, Mom! Where did it fall? Can you find it?

Mom, I thought you packed my tablet.

Mom didn't pack your tablet. You had it in the van, buddy. Where'd it go?

Excuse me, ma'am!

That's my wife, sir. She seems to be…er, Ginger? What are you doing?

Ginger slowly unfroze, shards of icy horror flaking away as she reached up, pointed a finger, and turned her gaze on Elsie. Her eyes narrowed, and two sides warred in her—the angry mother (rule maker!) and the friend (why won't my daughter talk to me?)—and she gave a deathly hiss. "Elsie?"

Her daughter, the fearless teenager, suddenly looked terrified. The unshakable, invincible Elsie Adler, trembling in her seat—all from a word. "Mom, it's not—"

"Condoms?" Ginger breathed, and then she snatched them from the overhead bin.

With the force of an Olympic shot-putter, she slammed her arm upward until the compartment crunched shut. The breaking glass signified the end of the poor compact's life, and a snap of plastic told Ginger at least one lipstick had bitten the dust. Elsie looked mortified.

Good, Ginger thought in a moment of weakness. And good on the compartment for busting up makeup and mirrors—good riddance. Her daughter should barely be wearing lipstick, let alone keeping condoms in her makeup kit.

"Where did I go wrong?" she asked, more to herself than anyone else. "I loved you, I hugged you, didn't I? I breastfed you, even though it nearly killed me."

Unfortunately, the man behind Ginger saw fit to answer: "You went wrong when you stopped in the middle of the aisle. Can you move out of the way, lady? This is ridiculous."

"I drove you every day to volleyball practice," Ginger said, trembling as she looked at Elsie. "I fed you veggies and painted your nails and read books to you with good morals in them. I censored movies and books that were too old for you. Sure, I haven't been around as much the last few months because I have been working, but that's because I love you too."

"Mom, you're making a scene." Elsie found her scowl and snarled. "Get out of the way. It's no big deal."

"Ginger, honey, I think the flight attendants are coming back to warn us, and we can't miss another flight," Frank said. "Why don't we discuss this later?"

"Frank, your daughter packed condoms on a family vacation," Ginger blurted. "She's fifteen."

"At least she's being safe!" Frank spluttered right back, his ears turning red. "Now, can we talk about it later?"

Fuming, Ginger stepped into her seat to let the impatient man pass. If she wasn't mistaken, his eyes quickly flicked over Elsie. (Admittedly, maybe it was Ginger's imagination. Suddenly, every male looked like a potential walking hormone with the hots for her daughter. Horrifying.)

Luckily for him, the man passed right by Elsie and found his seat a few rows back, settled in, and grumpily closed his eyes. He was one of those passengers who didn't feel the need to bring entertainment like the rest of the world to occupy his attention during the painstakingly long, uncomfortable flights. If Ginger weren't so furious at her daughter, she'd be furious at him. *Fury, fury, fury.* Ginger's new state of mind.

Frank had been right about the attendant. She was bustling down the aisle, her gaze fixed not-quite-impolitely on Ginger as she worked her way back. "Everything okay here?"

No! Ginger wanted to scream. Instead, she gave a thin smile. "Just a bit of stress."

"Traveling with children will do that to you," the flight attendant said, resting an understanding arm on Ginger's shoulder. "However, we really do need to get you and your lovely family situated so we can take off."

Lovely? Ginger wasn't certain that was the best word to use to describe her family at the moment. Nothing seemed inherently lovely anymore. In fact, as she glanced forward and saw the champagne glasses being handed out in first class along with hand towels she suspected were blissfully warm, she had the flitting thought of trading it all in.

Giving her kids and Frank away (for a few days—nothing permanent of course) so she could get pampered in first class and go away to a resort where Serenity Spa & Resort actually meant serenity and relaxation and massages and not: *Mom, can we go to the pool? Mom, I lost my shoe. Mom, I'm having sex with some random boy you don't know!*

She closed her eyes. She knew she could never trade it in. But she did wonder how everything had gotten so far out of control. Back when she was first married, everything had seemed more manageable. Everything was new and exciting and fresh.

The first trip to the zoo with Elsie, the first smile, the first fart (giggle!). Now, passing gas was a nightly dinner table discussion, and they'd practically been banned from the zoo because Poppy continually tried to feed the flamingos and Tommy banged against the glass at the gorillas while Ginger had turned her head (for two seconds) to find Elsie making eyes at the Boy Scouts.

Ignoring the shuffling sounds of curious onlookers, Ginger slid out of her chair and tapped Frank discreetly on the shoulder. She marched determinedly toward the back of the airplane, and her husband, good man that he was, heaved himself out of his seat. He gave Tom a fond little ruffle of the hair before following his wife down the aisle.

Good old, fun-loving Frank, Ginger thought, annoyed that even the sweet things her husband did were turning bitter in her mind. Frank loved her. He loved his kids. He wasn't the problem.

"What is it?" he asked when he reached her side, using a purposefully soft voice, as if Ginger needed to be handled with kid gloves. "Is this about the, er... Well, you saw..."

"Condoms, Frank," Ginger said firmly. "A whole strip of them. Half the plane is probably ready to proposition our daughter. She's fifteen."

"Er, right. I'll, ah, have a chat with her at the resort? Unless you want to do it? Girl talk and all that."

"She hasn't spoken two words to me lately, unless you count *Mo-om* as two words. The way she drags it out, those can't be called syllables anymore. I'd love to talk to her, but apparently, she thinks she can't confide in me. Where did I go wrong?"

"Honey, I think you're overreacting."

"She can't drive. She can't vote. She's not eighteen," Ginger said. "She's not legally an adult. She can't make decisions like that."

"You're forgetting about us," Frank said, leaning closer. His hand came to rest on her hip as he lowered his voice in a nostalgic sort of way. "We started fooling around at that age."

"Yes, but we loved each other. My mom knew your mom. Our friends were friends," Ginger said, her hands coming to rest on her husband's waist in a surprisingly intimate gesture in an otherwise tense moment. "We were officially together. I don't have the first clue who Elsie might be sleeping with! Oh, God, I can't even say it. I have cotton mouth. Frank, I need a glass of water. I can't breathe."

"Ginger Adler," Frank said in the calm, firmly patient voice he adopted whenever Ginger began to lose her mind. "I love you. You love me. We have three beautiful children. Elsie is a teenager, and she's going through some things—it's normal. Maybe this is a good thing. We have a week together; maybe we can get her to open up while we're relaxing."

"Fine," Ginger said. "But if I find anyone on that trip laying a finger on Elsie, I'll kill them, Frank. I'm not kidding."

Detective Ramone: Please state your name for the record.

Frank Adler: Frank Jonathan Adler.

Detective Ramone: Tell me a bit about your wife, Mr. Adler.

Frank Adler: Ginger? Well, you already talked to her. Frankly, she's a saint. She holds our house together. We have three kids, and Elsie is a real handful at the moment. Teenagers. Do you have kids, Detective?

Detective Ramone: No, sir.

Frank Adler: Oh, you wait, pal. Teenage girls— every event is the apocalypse. We were having a life-altering discussion in the car on the way to the airport about bangs. *Bangs!* Frankly, I didn't even notice Elsie got her hair cut.

Detective Ramone: Mr. Adler—

Frank Adler: Sorry, I'm getting distracted. What do you want to know about Ginger? She's beautiful, she's smart, and she's the hardest worker I know. She picked up a ton of extra shifts at the hotel over the last few months because my work hasn't been paying all that well lately. She should be managing that place by now, but she took time off when we had the children, and so she's stuck behind the reception desk. The woman is a godsend. Honestly, I'm not sure why she stays with me. She's not my better half, she's my better 90 percent. If I didn't have her in my life, I'd… well, I'd probably die. I'd starve or something.

Detective Ramone: Frank, I need you to be honest with me: Has your wife ever threatened you?

Frank Adler: Well, she was about ready to kill me when I made us late for our flight, but that was my own fault. Hold on—are you serious? Of course not. Ginger wouldn't hurt a fly. What are you getting at, Detective?

Detective Ramone: Mr. Adler, your wife has confessed to killing a man tonight.

Frank Adler: That's impossible.

Detective Ramone: What makes you say that? Can you give her an alibi for this evening?

Frank Adler: It doesn't matter—my wife is squeamish at the sight of blood! She's gotten a little better, what with the kids banging their knees or elbows every other day, but…you can't be serious, Detective.

Detective Ramone: Were you with your wife during the rehearsal dinner tonight?

Frank Adler: No.

eight

She *knows.*

Emily stared after Lulu until the elevator doors cinched shut to carry the peculiar woman upstairs. Emily saw the look in her eye, the sharp turn of Lulu's head when Emily ordered another drink. The older woman had seen right through her; she'd figured Emily out. Lulu had peeked into the dark spiral that one drink, two drinks, three drinks quickly became. The thirst that didn't quit.

Lulu had been too polite to stare and, instead, had averted her eyes to avoid looking at Emily with the same biting, familiar disappointment she'd seen in her family and friends over the years. A disappointment that had prompted Emily to excel at holding herself at exactly the right level of happily buzzing when around others. It was a place where, in public, nobody suspected a thing because Emily always appeared to be in control. *Control, control, control.*

Emily could stop drinking when she wanted to, and that was why she wasn't an alcoholic. In fact, she'd turned down a drink! Alcoholics didn't do any such thing. They couldn't. (Never mind the fact that Emily had ordered another right after—she'd chosen to do that. It had been a coherent, logical choice, not a compulsion.) She just hadn't wanted Lulu to pay for it.

Even now, Emily wasn't drunk. Sure, she'd felt the spirals of fuzziness tugging at the edges of her consciousness on the plane after a few glasses of champagne, and that was probably why she'd been inclined to climb Henry like a tree in the airplane bathroom. The alternative reasons weren't appealing.

Then again, it wasn't as if Emily had a great track record with men even when sober. It had been nearly a decade since she'd been involved with a man in any serious sort of way, and she intended to keep things that way. It was much easier.

A decade was also the exact same length of time Emily had been in mourning. Granted, she'd told her therapist she'd really been mourning for three years because the other seven were blurred out and fuzzy. (Emily's therapist didn't think she was very funny.)

Get back out there, Sharleen had said.

Then had come the tried and true: *It's not your fault. There's nothing you could have done.* Sharleen had a knack for the cliché.

Bullshit, Emily thought, glancing around the bar, looking for Lulu. She was nowhere in sight, and neither was her husband. So Emily pulled out her phone and dialed Sharleen. Emily wasn't sure if she wanted to shock her therapist or genuinely hear her advice. Maybe a bit of both.

"Hello?" the therapist answered, sounding surprised to be receiving a call on her work cell well after polite calling hours. "Emily, are you okay?"

"Dr. Sharleen, I wanted to give you an update," she said. "I met a man."

"Are you drinking, Emily?"

"A little, but I'm not drunk, I promise you. A few celebratory glasses of champagne."

"Emily, where are you? I'm concerned," Sharleen said. "You didn't drive anywhere, did you?"

"No, I'm fine, really. I'm at a hotel—excuse me, *resort*—for a friend's wedding," Emily said. "I met a very nice man on the airplane, and we sort of had a date. He's very handsome."

"That's…wonderful," Sharleen said carefully. "And you liked him? He treated you nicely?"

"In a manner of speaking," Emily said, adding an extra, sly giggle. "I thought you might be proud."

"Of course, but, Emily, I would really encourage you to hold off on the alcohol. We've discussed this before, and I thought we were making progress—"

"Sharleen, you said it yourself. You can't help me until I'm ready to help myself."

"Yes, but I care about you, and I care about your well-being. You've been doing so wonderfully. But one step backward doesn't have to ruin all the forward momentum we have going for us. Why don't you have a glass of water and head up to your room? This will blow over in the morning, and we'll start again. Remember, wine won't make your problems disappear."

"What about champagne?"

"Emily."

"Look, Sharleen," Emily snapped. "You don't know what it's like. I'm here alone. I'm facing my ex-best friend who hates me. And there's a baby that won't *fucking stop* screaming!"

"Oh, honey." Dr. Sharleen let her professionalism slip as emotion eased into her voice. "But you have tools to deal with this. Remember, it's been over ten years."

The slight judgment that'd followed Emily's outburst diminished into pity. Or sympathy. Emily could never tell which. "And time is supposed to make everything go away?" Emily said harshly. "I'm sorry I called you. Sorry I disrupted your night, Sharleen."

"Emily."

"I have to go," Emily said. "I can't handle that crying anymore."

After Emily hung up on her therapist, she ordered a water from the bartender, who looked relieved. It was hard to tell whether it was something Sharleen had said or whether it was the screaming baby that had flipped a switch in Emily's brain, but something had changed. A sort of curiosity that'd crept into her veins, poisoned her blood, sucked her toward the unhappy infant.

Before she could stand, however, Lulu's order of chili cheese fries arrived at the same time as a lost-looking older gentleman. *Pierce*, she thought, knowing with certainty it was him when he looked quizzically at the seat Lulu had recently abandoned.

Emily gave a jerky little wave toward him. "Are you looking for your wife?"

"Lulu," he said carefully, easing toward Emily. "Have you seen her?"

Pierce Banks had a head full of thick hair, meticulously styled in a perfect part and combed to either side, while a few tufts poked out in a lovably charming, disheveled way. He was dressed in a fine suit, looking quite adorable with a pair of suspenders added underneath, caught between the distinguished-older-gentleman and lovely-grandfather-type phases of life. He was quite handsome for his age, and Emily was willing to bet he'd been a knockout in his prime.

"Yes, we were chatting a bit," Emily said, gesturing to Lulu's abandoned seat. "She asked me to wait here for you so I could let you know she'd be right back. She had to run off somewhere for a second, and she was worried you'd think she'd forgotten about you."

Pierce gave a laugh that brightened his features, and Emily was surprised to feel a surge of fierce hope for the couple. The hope that they'd last forever because, despite Lulu's flippant dismissals of her past marriages, it was clear as day to Emily that the woman had found true love in Pierce and would be devastated if he left.

"Where exactly did you say my wife went looking for me?" Pierce asked abruptly, and Emily flinched, as if Pierce had wandered into her mind and knew she'd been told more than she was letting on. "I think I should go find her."

"No, that's exactly what she didn't want," Emily said quickly. She wasn't sure what her new friend had planned, but Emily sensed Lulu wanted to be left alone. "Stay put. She'll be back in a jiffy.

Have a fry. They're Lulu's. I'm going to go see if that woman there needs help."

Emily pushed the fries toward Pierce and tottered in the direction of the baby, pleased to find she was more sober than she thought. *Control.* Her wobbling was kept to a minimum, and when she glanced in her compact, her eyes were clear.

It also helped that Emily looked the part of a rich social drinker. She wore her most expensive jeans and heels, topped with a slim black blouse rimmed with lace. She'd added a few of her favorite accessories—a slim wristwatch she'd had for ages, a pair of small diamond studs in her ears, and an inexpensive but sentimental silver necklace she'd received as a gift from Whitney during college. It wasn't a luxurious outfit by any stretch of the imagination, but she'd made an effort to look put together. It was all part of the charade.

As Emily moved closer to the crying baby, her almost ethereal vision of a blissful mother with her child faded before her eyes. Stress crinkled on the young woman's forehead, and dark bruises lived under her eyes, detailing a chronic lack of sleep. The woman appeared barely old enough to have a child of her own, looking more like she should be hoofing it across campus with a backpack strapped to her shoulders than attending a baby at her breast.

The young woman's hair had been pulled back into a messy bun, and Emily could see it'd once been long and beautiful but was now strapped helplessly on top of her head. She wore faded jeans and an unbuttoned flannel shirt with the sleeves rolled to her elbows. Underneath, a tiny black crop top peeked through, exposing a brush of pale skin at her waist.

Emily stood there for a long moment, transfixed by the little child more so than the curious young mother. Emily couldn't seem to make herself speak. She hadn't been this close to one in so long, not since…

"Can I help you?" the woman asked. "Oh, I'm so sorry. I must be bothering you. I know I probably shouldn't be sitting here in

the lobby with a crying baby, but I had to get out of my room."
She shuddered. "It felt like the walls were closing in on me, and it
was so dark, and Lydia wouldn't stop crying, and…"

"She doesn't bother me," Emily lied. "I'm Emily."

"Hi, Emily. I'm Sydney," the mother said, and she went stiff as if
she'd said the wrong thing. Her face quickly recovered, the shadow
passing as she shifted, attempting to hold out her hand.

Emily waved her off. "You've got your arms full."

"Sorry," Sydney apologized, biting down on a lip rimmed in
what looked like cherry lip gloss. "I should be a pro at this by
now—she's four months old already—but it doesn't always come
naturally to me."

Emily found herself sinking into a chair next to the woman, the
fluffy, fake sort of armchair that resort lobbies use to say: *Sit here,
relax, rich one; we'll take care of you.* As Emily sat, she noted the seat
felt like cardboard.

"I'm sure that's natural," Emily said, feeling a swirl of emotion as
she shifted on the hard chair, in the lobby filled with all the obvious
(and very expensive) signs of love and commitment, watching the
baby fuss against her mother's chest. A baby, the ultimate sign of
love. *Or is it?*

A howl of anger worked its way through Emily. Instead of trying
to fight it, she let the feeling envelope her, let pricks of black and
red and stars burst behind her eyes as she studied the baby, drawn
to it with the same sort of interest as a moth to an open flame.

"Do you have kids?" Sydney asked, and it was as if a knife had
gone straight into Emily's gut, scooped her out, and then left her
to bleed.

Emily shook her head, her eyes fixed on the baby. "No, I don't
have any children."

"You're probably thinking you're lucky," Sydney said with a
wry smile. Then, she must have caught a look of something on
Emily's face, because she automatically retracted her sentiment

with a guilty flick of her eyes toward Lydia. "I didn't mean that. I'd never trade Lydia for the world, it's just…I'm so exhausted. So tired. All the time."

"I can't imagine."

"My husband—er, well, I suppose he's not my husband anymore," Sydney said, her eyes downcast. "We're separating, so I'm doing this on my own. I know plenty of single moms who do it, but frankly, I can't figure out how."

"I'm sorry to hear that."

"You're probably thinking what a horrible mother I am for not making my marriage work when we have a little girl together," Sydney said as if she thought the very same thing herself. "I really think it's for the best, though. It has to be this way."

Emily didn't know what to say, so she merely inclined her head to show she was listening. Emily knew about toxic men. One might say she was the *queen* of them: falling for them, stealing them, marrying them.

"And here I am babbling to you, a stranger, when you probably came over here to ask me to take the baby from the bar." Sydney's eyes landed on Emily's with a neediness that tore Emily's soul into ribbons. "I'm sorry. I'll take her away."

"No, please—" Emily reached a hand out in reflex and rested it on Sydney's wrist. "Don't go."

Sydney's crystalline blue eyes looked a bit grayed by her exhaustion, but that didn't hide her beauty. Pre-exhaustion, Sydney must have been a head-turning stunner with her Shirley Temple innocence and wide, trusting smile. Except now, those huge, curious eyes were filling with tears.

"Really?" she asked. "That's—that's so nice of you. I've been getting dirty looks all evening. I walked Lydia around the pool, I put her in the car seat in the bedroom, and I even… Oh God. You're going to think I'm horrible. I went to the laundry room and put her carrier on top of the dryer, because that lulls her to sleep at home. Nothing worked. I…I can't be alone right now, and sitting here around all these glamorous people having a good time helps me feel less alone."

"Believe me," Emily said. "I understand. Loneliness is a—"

"Sydney!" A voice interrupted Emily at an ironically fitting moment, turning Emily into an unwanted third party as the newcomer stalled in front of Sydney. "That baby can't be yours. I thought I just sent you a high school graduation card. I hadn't heard you'd gotten married?"

"Oh, well, it's been a long time since we've gotten together." Sydney shot Emily an apologetic smile before turning back to the woman. "Aunt Janice, this is Emily. She's—"

"Is the baby yours?" Aunt Janice leaned closer, squinted her eyes, and ran a finger down the baby's soft-looking cheek. "She's a sweetie. She must have your husband's eyes, though. How long have you been married? I assume you *are* married?"

Emily felt uncomfortable watching the somewhat invasive line of questioning that could only come from an out-of-touch family member. She busied herself by leaning back in the chair and averting her gaze toward the bar. With a sigh of relief, Emily saw that Lulu had returned from her journey upstairs and was easing into the seat next to her husband, who was speaking to her with a frown on his lips.

Turning her attention back to the conversation at hand, Emily noted Aunt Janice to be somewhere in her late fifties. She dressed with the flair of a much younger woman, rings glinting from more fingers than not, her bright makeup accented by a light pink cardigan and topped with a floral scarf tied neatly around her neck.

On her feet were flip-flops adorned with golden straps that looked somewhat gladiator in nature, and tying the ensemble together was a gauzy black dress that swung around her knees and matched the designer bag slung over her arm.

"I would have sent a wedding gift." Aunt Janice tsked with

embarrassment at herself. "And a baby gift. I know how hard those early days can be. I remember when I had my little Jackie. She's the most wonderful daughter now, but as a baby, part of me wanted to hand her off to the nanny for good!" Janice paused for a cackle. "Anyway, I'm sure Whitney and Arthur will be pleased you brought the little one with you for the ceremony. Is your husband with you? What are you doing these days for work?"

"I actually gave up working when we had Lydia," Sydney said, her cheeks blushing. "My, er, husband was insistent on it, actually. Wanted my full attention on our daughter."

Aunt Janice nodded approvingly. "And who is this mystery man?"

Sydney glanced at Emily, bit her lip in a gesture that to Emily seemed to be pleading in nature. Emily looked at her feet and found a scuff mark on her heel that suddenly needed tending to. She reached down, rubbed her thumb against the white skid mark, and pretended she couldn't hear the conversation happening before her.

"We met in college. Well, not *at* school, but when I was in college," she said. "It really was a whirlwind. We got engaged a few months after we met and began dating, and the wedding followed shortly after. It was a small, private ceremony."

"Well, I must say, I'm impressed." Aunt Janice frowned, offsetting her compliment. "When did you graduate college? I don't remember sending a card. If I missed that too—"

"Didn't you say you were headed to put Lydia to bed?" Emily asked. "If you want me to take her for you, I wouldn't mind. That way you can keep chatting with your aunt. It seems like it's been a while since the two of you saw each other."

"Oh, no, I couldn't ask you to do that." Sydney gave Emily a fleeting look of relief as she made a show of shuffling Lydia to one arm. With the other, she reached for the diaper bag and hiked it onto her shoulder. "Aunt Janice, maybe we could grab coffee tomorrow and continue our chat?"

"That sounds lovely." Aunt Janice shot Emily a somewhat annoyed glance, but it passed quickly as she turned back to the baby. "Sweet dreams, precious angel."

Emily watched Sydney hold her breath until Aunt Janice disappeared into the elevator and the doors slid firmly shut behind her. Finally, she turned back to Emily and gave a sigh that turned into a self-conscious giggle.

"I'm so sorry about that," she gushed. "I haven't seen my aunt in years. And the nerve of her, confronting me like that. Especially after the way she treated my parents."

"What do you mean?"

"My last name might be Banks, but I'm not one of *them*. My parents were estranged from the family and had almost no contact with them when I was young. We weren't rich. We were a normal, working-class family…until they died." Sydney shook her head. "Did you hear the way Janice talked to me? No wonder my parents stayed away from them. I'm still amazed I got an invite to the wedding at all, but Arthur's mom really was a godsend after my parents died, helping out financially with funeral arrangements, that sort of thing. Probably out of guilt."

"I'm sorry."

Sydney shook her head, blew out another breath of frustration. "Janice has one daughter named Jackie—she's a little older than me—and she works at the local grocery store. It's not like her offspring have gone on to do great and wonderful things, yet she feels the need to critique me?"

"I really do understand," Emily said. "It's family. They can be—"

"I'm so embarrassed." Sydney rocked Lydia without seeming to realize she was doing it, the bounces becoming more energetic by the second. "I'm sorry she interrupted us. Where were we?"

"Oh, we were just talking about the baby." It was like a path had opened before Emily, a red carpet laid bare, and she had no choice but to follow it. A red carpet that led hungrily, greedily straight to the baby. What would it be like to touch her? To hold her? To sing to her? To imagine that baby might belong to *Emily*? "How difficult it is to be a single mother, to have to navigate this entire parenthood thing on your own."

"Oh, right. Well, you're an angel for sticking around and listening to me and my babbling family," Sydney said. "It feels as if it's been weeks since I talked to another adult. I hope you know how much I appreciate you coming over here. I would love to say I'm not desperate, but…" She gave a smile that said she'd be lying if she did.

Emily inhaled a sharp breath and felt a sudden burst of guilt. She hadn't come over here to coddle Sydney; she'd been intrigued by the baby. Selfishly, she'd wanted to see what sort of feelings bubbled up inside when she laid eyes on the squirming little bundle in the blanket. She hadn't been this close to a baby in quite some time, and she had needed to see if she could do it. If she could see it, smell it, hold it, touch it…without the walls closing in on her.

"Tell me more about yourself," Emily said, striving for something, anything, to keep the conversation moving. She wanted Sydney distracted. Wanted time to ignore Sydney and watch the pink bundle and analyze her own emotions in peace. "Are you close with your family?"

"Not exactly, in case Aunt Janice didn't already give that away." Sydney gave a dry, self-deprecating laugh. "I probably shouldn't be here, actually. I can't exactly afford it. I mean, I can, but I'm stretching the budget," Sydney said quickly, as if striving to prove to Emily that she was a capable, responsible mother. "But it's my cousin's wedding. I know he doesn't care all that much that I'm here, but his mother does, and she offered to help cover some travel fees. I tried to refuse, but…" She waved a hand as if to say *Here we are.*

"You're cousins with Arthur Banks?" Emily wrinkled her nose. "I think they can afford to pay your room bill."

"You might be right, but I really hate owing people favors."

"Most people do," Emily said. "But don't look at it like charity. They're family, and they want you to be here."

"I suppose. I mean, I'm not great pals with Arthur or anything, but I've always adored his mother. When my parents passed away, she was sort of a second mom. We, er, grew apart after, as I got older, but we keep in touch now and again."

"I'm sorry about your parents," Emily said, thinking Sydney really needed to *shut up* and let her stare unabashedly at the baby. "That's awful."

"It's fine," Sydney said, waving her hand. "It was a long time ago."

"Well, your mother would sure love Lydia. Your daughter is gorgeous. May I?" Emily reached out a hand and offered it to the baby, pausing to wait for Sydney's nod of approval.

"Gosh, yes," Sydney said. "Please go on. I'd let you hold her, but I'm afraid she'd break your eardrums."

"You—you'd let me hold her?" Emily felt herself stuttering, felt the heat rising unnaturally in her cheeks. Her neck would be turning splotchy red by this point, her chest a mottled mess from the wave of emotions forming a vortex inside her. "No, I don't think that's a good idea. I've had a few glasses of champagne."

"Don't be ridiculous," Sydney said. "It's not as if you're drunk or something. Would you like to? Here, have a moment with her."

"I, er—" Fingers of fear gripped at every nerve ending, drawing Emily's vision into a spiral of stars. Oxygen turned into an elusive resource, something Emily couldn't get enough of no matter how deeply she breathed. "I'm sure Lydia doesn't want me to hold her."

"Oh, I'm so sorry," Sydney said. "You probably have someplace to get to, and I'm here holding you up. Get going back to your party, why don't you! You've already been so nice to come over and say hello."

As Emily felt the first fingers of a faint clawing at the edges of her consciousness, something miraculous happened. Something beautiful and wonderful and impossibly horrible. Lydia reached out, her tiny, chubby little hand clenching around Emily's frozen pointer finger. The baby latched on, holding onto Emily as if she were her lifeboat. And miraculously, Lydia stopped crying.

"Oh, look at that," Sydney whispered fondly, her shoulders curved with relief. "She likes you."

Emily's heart burst. It exploded into teensy little crumbs of fireworks, sparks shattering through her like bits of fiery, vicious love. For one moment, Emily forgot that Lydia didn't belong to her. She forgot that Lydia was a symbol of the ghosts in her past. A mere remnant, dragging out feelings that were unfair and hurtful, even vengeful. She felt a burst of fury at this innocent little bundle and wondered why she'd survived while others hadn't.

Nothing you could do… The doctor's voice repeated over and over again in her head. *There's nothing you could have done differently, Emily. You couldn't have saved her.*

"I want to hold her," Emily demanded. Her voice came out harsh, sharp, and she realized it a second too late. "Please. If I may."

"Sure," Sydney said. "You are so good with her. Did you see how she stopped crying when she looked at you?"

The little girl is probably terrified of me, Emily thought. She thirsted to hold the baby, to drink in that newborn smell, the bubble bath clinging to her, the baby powder drifting lazily over smooth skin. Emily wondered if babies could smell fear, like dogs. Emily reeked of fear and greed and anger. And somewhere beyond the anger, there was a wound so deep, it could never possibly heal.

"Put your arm out on that pillow there," Sydney instructed. "It'll cushion her head, and you've got nothing to worry about. Babies aren't as breakable as you think."

Yes, they are! Emily shouted internally to Sydney. A hint of disdain tipped her poisoned thoughts, and Emily found herself glaring upward, frustrated by the way Sydney treated her as if she were a first-time baby holder, a clueless bystander. A non-mother.

Fortunately, Sydney was already setting Lydia in Emily's arms, and the warmth of Lydia's small body was somehow soothing. Before she knew it, Emily was holding a baby.

A baby. What would Sharleen think? Emily had the urge to call Sharleen back and fill her in on the development. Tonight was a night of many milestones. She waited for the feelings to fill her chest.

They came, slowly. Like an IV dripped through her veins, filling her with a clash, a tug-of-war that threatened to rip her body in half. She basked in the familiarity that came with all babies: the universal sweet scent and comforting weight of their bottoms against her belly. Followed by the rash unfairness of it all, the very *life* this baby had that Emily's own had lost.

The doctors had said it was SIDS. A nifty little acronym for a long string of words that meant Emily's child had died in her sleep. But Emily knew better. It had been her fault. Her penance for not leaving him sooner—and one hell of a penance she'd had to pay. She'd rather have paid with her life, if it meant her baby could have lived.

The black thoughts plagued Emily. *If only...* If only she had left him the first time it happened. If only she had trusted the cops. If only Emily hadn't been unconscious when it happened, when her child slipped away, alone. If only Emily had been awake, able to stop it—to call 911—to do something, anything to save her child's life. But she hadn't.

No, Emily thought, stroking Lydia's cheek. *I did nothing.*

It had been Emily's fault her own daughter had died.

At that moment, a family of five burst through the doors of the resort lobby, interrupting that tornado of poison threatening to suck Emily back. The gangling group poured toward the front desk, a perfectly formed family.

There was a mother, a father, and three children—a teenage girl currently struggling to understand eyeshadow, a boy with his face glued to a tablet, and the most adorable little girl with no less than nine ponytails protruding from her head like spokes on a wheel. She wore tall rain boots, despite this being the middle of the desert, and she had a perpetual smile on her face as she studied the lobby like it might be some wonderful, fascinating museum.

"Look at that gorgeous family," Sydney said softly. "You know, I thought I'd have that myself someday, but…"

Emily couldn't speak.

"It's not going to happen for me." Sydney sighed. "But it's okay. Lydia is enough."

"Why have you and your husband decided to part ways?"

"Irreconcilable differences," Sydney said, shutting the subject down as a cement wall descended over her face. "Anyway, I should actually get Lydia to bed. You've been a doll to hold her for as long as you have. Oh, *shit*—er, shoot. There, I've done it and woken Lydia after you lulled her to sleep."

Emily glanced down, startled to find the baby's eyes open. Instead of screaming, however, Lydia's lips turned into the sweetest of smiles. Her bright eyes stared directly into Emily's as her dimpled cheeks squished with unbridled joy. And then she giggled, and Emily's heart shriveled with the sheer amount of life in the child.

"Oh, look at that tiny baby!" The mother from the family of five glanced over from the front desk, whispering loudly, as if the sound wouldn't travel. Then, to Emily's surprise, the woman began wandering over while her husband completed check-in.

It wasn't until she got nearer that Emily recognized her. She'd been so obsessed, so taken with Lydia, that she'd been single-mindedly focused on the baby. But as she glanced up and met her old best friend's gaze, she felt her heart flutter in a surprising twist of anger.

"Emily," Ginger said in a flat voice. "Is that your baby?"

Emily ignored her ex-roommate. She focused on the child, on her shaking hands, on controlling the rage that had burst inside her at the arrival of Ginger. Emily had expected to feel many things at the sight of her old friend—shame, remorse, loss. But not this fiery disdain that had settled in her gut. As if this were all Ginger's fault. In a way, though, Emily wondered, wasn't it partially Ginger's fault?

"Er," Sydney said awkwardly, "do the two of you know each other? I'm Sydney."

"Ginger," Emily's old friend said, extending her hand toward Sydney. "Yes, we both went to school with the bride."

"Oh, lovely," Sydney said, but it was in an awkward, limp sort of voice.

"It was," Ginger said, emphasizing the past tense of her statement. "We lost touch a bit after school."

"That's unfortunate," Sydney said. "Though it happens all too often. Life gets busy, kids, husbands…I understand."

Ginger looked as if she wanted to disagree, but before she could, she was interrupted by a voice from the reception area.

"Oy, Ginger," the man at the counter—it must be Frank—called exuberantly across the lobby, oblivious, as he always had been, even in college. Emily couldn't bring herself to look up at him without her neck reddening in shame. "Ginger, honey, do you have my wallet? Can't seem to find that bad boy. Hope it's not on the plane!"

"Well," Ginger said with a faded smile. "It's been a pleasure to meet you, Sydney. Emily, I suppose—well, we'll see you around."

Detective Ramone: Ms. Brown, when did you meet Sydney Banks?

Emily Brown: The first night at the resort. We chatted for a bit, and I held Lydia. Her baby.

Detective Ramone: You hadn't known either of them before that night?

Emily Brown: Never seen her before that. At least, I don't think so.

Detective Ramone: And now, what would you say your relationship is with her?

Emily Brown: None of your business.

Detective Ramone: Well, then, would it surprise you to know there's no Sydney Banks registered at the resort? Who did you talk to, Emily?

nine

Kate wasn't stupid.

She knew exactly what was happening.

"Are you breaking up with me?" she asked Max once they'd been carefully seated in first class. Kate had declined her customary glass of champagne because she didn't feel the slightest bit like celebrating. Max, however, had readily accepted his.

"No. What makes you think that?"

"You stormed out of my house last night, and you've barely spoken a word to me since we reached the airport."

"I said no," Max repeated. "You're reading too much into everything."

I should have seen it coming, Kate thought. The second Max had accepted the champagne on the flight, she should have known. He was celebrating, she was wallowing.

Kate climbed out of the SUV and waited for the driver to unload her bags at the resort. She'd arranged for private transport from the airport to the spa, but one look at the impressive front doors of the sprawling resort, and Kate was ready to have him turn around and head back. A brilliant red carpet trumpeted the main entrance and propelled guests into a weeklong buffet of wedding festivities, the very last place Kate wanted to be when it felt her relationship was crumbling from the inside out.

This was supposed to be *her* wedding. After years of clomping behind Kate in hand-me-down shoes that were slightly too big for her feet, Whitney had finally surged past her. The most ironic part of all was that until Kate had turned her attention to Max a few years back, Whitney hadn't looked twice at Arthur.

Arthur Banks had always been a family friend to Whitney, a younger brother of sorts, a staple in her life. Then suddenly, when Kate reconnected with Max, Whitney had latched on to Arthur in a whole new way. Kate doubted Whitney had even realized what happened, but Kate knew. She certainly hadn't imagined the curiosity in Whitney's voice when they'd first discussed Kate's new boyfriend Max.

Shortly thereafter, Arthur had arrived on the scene in a prominent way. It was with a wry smile that Kate wondered what Whitney soon-to-be Banks would do if she found out that Kate Cross's perfect life wasn't so perfect after all. That Max was probably going to dump her the second they arrived back in New York. That Kate couldn't bear children. That Kate's life was empty, save for her wallet. Then what? What would Whitney have left to strive for?

Kate trailed behind Max out of the car and toward the entrance. The resort and spa seeped into the desert atmosphere, sitting snugly against the landscape while managing to gift its visitors with a wave of natural relaxation and the feeling of being utterly pampered from the moment they stepped foot on the front drive. Men in sharp suits waited with fresh coconut milk and sparkling crystal flutes of champagne, and the soft floral scent that pumped from the front doors came from real bouquets and not some manufactured perfume.

As it was, Kate didn't feel very Zen. She was angry, furious. She could see the closure in Max's eyes. He was keeping her around for this weekend as a pretty little trophy on his arm, and as soon as they were back to New York, he'd dump her on the doorstep. Would he bother carrying her bags in, or would he leave them outside too?

Kate stepped one stiletto in front of the other, following behind

Max into the lobby. She'd put extra effort into her clothing choices today—skintight black jeans, a V-neck that exposed significant cleavage, a glittering necklace and bracelet set Max had given her for Christmas.

She wore huge sunglasses and had her hair down in curls the way Max liked. In their early dating days, he'd called it her pre-sex hair because he *couldn't resist* when she wore it that way. Kate's lips curled as she wryly noticed he was resisting her hair just fine at the moment.

As they stepped to the front desk of the resort, Kate barely noticed the easy thump of a relaxing soundtrack or the quiet, efficient bustle of staff hurrying to appease every last whim and wish of its visitors. Instead, Kate was captivated by the sight of two women sitting in the corner, both of them focused on the baby nestled against the older woman's chest.

It took Kate a second to place the woman holding the baby, but as Kate's chest pinged at the sight of the small child, she recognized Emily, her former roommate. Kate hadn't heard that Emily had gotten married, let alone had a child. *What a pretty little life*, she thought.

It wasn't that Kate was jealous of either woman specifically, but she envied what they had. At least one of them had a baby, and they both had their friendship. They probably had loving husbands waiting for them in their rooms, sending them off with some charming quip like, "Have a sparkling girls' night!"

The young woman across from Emily was staring at Kate as if she'd seen a movie star. It wasn't an uncommon occurrence for Kate and Max to be recognized—their wedding would certainly have appeared in the social section of the paper, and every now and again, the couple had their photo picked up in some magazine. They weren't famous, but they were both rich and beautiful. They made for a handsome couple.

Funny, Kate thought wryly. *If only they knew…*

The younger woman snapped her gaze away as if she knew she'd been caught staring. Her cheeks blushed a vibrant red as she turned toward her friend and spoke in a lowered voice. The woman cupped her hands in a shield over her forehead with what looked like embarrassment, which was quite unnecessary, considering Kate had been staring back just as much.

Kate looked away to see Max at the reception counter already, and she stomped across the room to join him. Max flashed the front desk clerk a winning smile. The front desk employee, name tag Allison, gave Max an equally brilliant smile back.

"Here are the keys to your room," Allison said. "Would you like me to get some massages booked for the two of you?"

"No, thanks." Kate stepped forward, swiping the key from the woman's hand before Max could take it. She leaned on the counter, gave a knowing side-eye glance toward Max. "We'll be plenty busy on our own."

Max ran a hand through his hair. "For Christ's sake, Kate. Will you leave it alone?"

Allison blinked and glanced down at the sharpness in Max's tone.

"What did I say?" Kate asked, feeling a flutter of uncertainty. Max's furious eyes were out and in full force. Normally, he was more of an indifferent sort of fighter, but this time, she could tell he meant business. "I meant—"

"Fuck! Everyone knows what you meant," Max said. "It's all you talk about, even after we agreed to take a break. What if I want to get a massage?"

"Get a massage," Kate said. "What's the big deal?"

Max rolled his eyes. "Kate, this isn't working."

Kate tapped the room key against the counter. "What the hell do you mean, Max?"

Suddenly, Max went still. He closed his eyes, his hands folded peacefully in front of his body. "I can't do this."

"Get the damn massage if you want!" Kate tried to sound angry, but her voice cracked. "I was trying to be romantic."

Max's eyes flashed open. "There's nothing romantic between us anymore. It's business and sex, and business and sex. Everything has turned into a calculated regimen. Look, Kate, I'm sorry. I was going to wait until after the wedding for your sake, for Whitney and Arthur's sake."

"Wait to do what?"

"End things. It's over, Kate," Max said. "I didn't want to make a scene. Didn't want to ruin the wedding for our friends and family, but I can't wait. It's over."

"Max, we need to discuss this."

"Allison—" Max brushed passed Kate and leaned against the counter. "I'm going to need another room. Do you have anything available?"

Allison's long, lacquered nails click-clacked in an annoyingly efficient way. "Yes, sir. We have only one room left—"

"I'll take it," Max said. "Whatever it is."

"Please, Max! Let's talk this through."

"It's done. It's over," Max said. "It has been for a while. I was trying to wait, but…"

"Well, maybe if we actually tried harder and talked about things, we could sort everything out." Kate felt mysteriously calm as she gave a shake of her head and flicked her sunglasses to the top of her expertly curled pre-sex hair. "Yesterday was a little disagreement. We get into them all the time."

"We want different things."

"We're trying to have a baby together!" Kate's voice broke, raising the slightest amount. "We've been dating for over two years. We've discussed marriage. I'm ready to marry you tomorrow."

"I told you, I'm not interested in getting married."

"You're almost fifty, for God's sakes! Grow up, Max. You want a family, don't you?"

His eyes flickered with the smallest amount of pain in them. "Yes, I do. That's why things won't work between us. I'm sorry. I'll cover your room and instruct all your bills for the duration of your stay to be put on my credit card. Spend as much as you like, relax, heal. You'll be over me by the time you leave."

Allison continued typing through the painfully awkward silence. Eventually, the front desk clerk produced a second key card, which she handed to Max. Without even a glance at Kate, Max snatched the key and stomped toward the elevators.

That was when she knew for sure. They were over. Done. *Finito.*

Allison stood there, gaping at Kate. "I'm so sorry."

Kate couldn't find the words to speak. She'd been dumped at a wedding she didn't even want to be at. She could have cut Whitney a fat check and sent along a fake apology instead of sitting in an over-the-top gorgeous spa trying to heal. Kate didn't need to fucking heal. She needed to get pregnant.

"I'm sorry," the front desk clerk said again. "Can I send a bottle of champagne to your room?"

It was such an obviously inappropriate, rehearsed response that Kate could do nothing but stare at the woman. When Allison realized what she'd said, she began to stutter, flustered, apologizing over and over. Eventually, Kate put her out of her misery by grabbing the suitcase Max had conspicuously left behind and marching toward the elevator.

There was no way Kate was sitting around the spa for the duration of her trip. How could she possibly relax at the same lush resort where her boyfriend—ex-boyfriend—was celebrating with family and friends, probably looking for the new version of her? This time around, he'd want someone who wasn't broken, someone who could give him children.

Kate felt her eyes sting as she reached the elevator. She'd pop into her room for a second, to clear her head and reassess. Kate was a strong woman, she knew that much. She was smart and successful—and broken.

Yes, I want a family, Max said in her head. *That's why things won't work between us.*

The nerve of him! Kate jammed her room card into the door and waited for the green light to flicker on before giving the solid wooden panel a huge shove. She left her bag in the entrance, stepped over it, and strode across the thickly carpeted floor to the window.

She took no satisfaction in the fact that the room Max had booked for them to share was gorgeous. It offered a view of the desert around them, the blackened mountaintops in the distance offset by glittering pools underfoot. A full-blown Jacuzzi was the centerpiece of the living area, quite a laughable development to Kate, considering the circumstances. Hot tubs were for romance. Kate certainly wasn't going to use it alone.

Neither was she going to use the custom bottle of wine that sat in a small welcome basket near the television. Kate strolled over and retrieved it, recognizing the name of the Napa Valley vineyard printed on the label. The design was a custom one created for Whitney and Arthur, along with the blend inside. Kate read the sappy quote about love wrapped around the outside and set the bottle down with a snort of disgust. Enough was enough. She couldn't even escape the reaches of love on her alcohol bottles.

She stepped onto the balcony and stared out at the peculiarly beautiful landscape, the silent, sharp edges of the cacti and palm trees, and found it fitting. Eerily poignant, beautiful and solitary, intimidating and vulnerable.

Next to it all, interwoven, were the big, bold, beautiful touches. Carefully manicured trails wound between sapphire pools and tropical little huts offering all sorts of refreshments (for a fee). Everything glowed beneath the ethereal wash of twilight, while the hotel staff scurried underfoot like ants dressed in fine white linens, smiles pasted on their faces as they buzzed, buzzed, buzzed between customers. They delivered towels, beverages, toothbrushes—whatever pampered their high-paying guests into a sense of false security.

Security—what a laugh, Kate thought. She'd believed her relationship with Max was secure, but how wrong she'd been. She watched as a small army of workers bustled about on the beach to set up for the wedding. There was an arch someone was decorating by hand with flowers, blooms that would surely be dead before the actual ceremony. A practice run, maybe?

There was the spacious, open-aired platform made from tarnished, knotty wood and brushed with sand that would be transformed into Cinderella's ballroom. Already, white, gauzy fabrics were being hung from the rafters as twinkling little fairy lights danced beneath the stars. The wedding wasn't for another two days, but like most of the guests, Kate had arrived early due to the suggested stay dates listed on the wedding invitations.

According to the schedule in the lobby, the guests would be keeping busy with rehearsal dinners, groom's dinners, pampering parties for the ladies, and whiskey tastings for the men. Post-wedding, there would be present-opening ceremonies (plural), massage sessions to unwind for the women, and cigar-rolling extravaganzas for the men. Kate hadn't had such a full social calendar since college.

As Kate turned her attention back to the landscape, back to the natural scenery, to the trees gusting in the warm night breeze and the sand whispering across the ground, she felt a sense of calmness wash over her shoulders, followed quickly by the chill of sadness.

The sadness, however, bubbled into anger as she shivered and wrapped her arms around herself. Anger because Max had wasted two precious years of her life. Two precious years she'd never get back, two precious years that could have been put toward building something—a future, a family, a home—with the right man. Instead, Kate had nothing to show for her relationship with Max. He didn't even have a sock drawer at her house, because he preferred to keep everything at his place "just in case."

Obviously, "just in case" had arrived, and Kate realized they didn't have so much as a shared utility bill. There was no discussion needed once they got back to New York. Two days before, she'd been trying to procreate with this man. Today, he felt like a stranger.

Kate wanted to cry, but she knew she couldn't. She knew she wouldn't.

With a hit of resolve, Kate left her things where they'd fallen and stormed right back to the elevator. She descended to the main lobby. She strode through, noting the deep, manicured wood on every surface—the bar, the stools, the chairs and couches. Even the accents on the walls, the shelving, had a cabin-like sort of feel, a lush setting the resort had designed to lure its guests into a calming mindset.

Yet Kate's shoulders had never been stiffer, her mind never more ruffled.

Stalking up to the bar, she leaned over and attracted the attention of the bartender. "Glass of champagne," she said lightly. "Actually, fuck it. I'll take the bottle. Put it on the tab of Max Banks."

"Are you here for the wedding?" A well-preserved, older woman sat next to her handsome husband and smiled up at Kate, not waiting for an answer. "We're here for the DeBleu/Banks wedding. You're welcome to join us for a drink if you'd like."

"Well, I've gone and ordered a bottle of champagne, so I could use some help with it," Kate offered. "I've been freshly dumped, and my ex-boyfriend is picking up the tab this weekend."

"Oh my." The older woman's shoulders stiffened, and a frown tilted down her rose-tinted lips. "But you're so young...and gorgeous."

"Apparently, we wanted different things," Kate said.

"Well, I suppose it's something that he's footing your bill," the woman said with a cautious smile. "My name's Lulu Franc, and this is my husband, Pierce Banks. I do love a good story if you feel like talking."

"This is where I say good night," Pierce said, standing and giving Lulu a kiss on the forehead. "I really am exhausted, sweetheart. I'm going to retire to bed. I'll be waiting up, but don't rush."

"Oh, don't leave on my account," Kate said. "I'm just a sad, brokenhearted woman."

"Stay a bit longer, Pierce," Lulu insisted. "We've barely spent any time together since we arrived."

"I wouldn't want to interfere." Pierce flashed a disarming smile, rested his hand on his wife's shoulder. "I'll be upstairs in bed. Don't hurry back."

While a flutter of confusion crossed her face, Lulu kissed her husband on the cheek, then turned her attention to Kate. She regained her composure quickly and offered a fresh smile. "Looks like I've got a few minutes."

"Hi there, Lulu," Kate said, then gestured to the bartender. "Add another bottle of your finest champagne. I'll be here a while."

Detective Ramone: Ms. Feeney, tell me a bit about your job at Serenity Spa & Resort.

Allison Feeney: Well, I'm the front desk clerk, and I was working alongside my coworker, Ashley Pinkett, on the day most of the Banks/DeBleu wedding party was checking in. I assume that's what this is about?

Detective Ramone: The computer records show you

were the one to check in a woman named Kate Cross and her boyfriend, Maximillian Banks.

Allison Feeney: Ex.

Detective Ramone: Excuse me?

Allison Feeney: *Ex*-boyfriend. I mean, everything blew up right in front of me. I actually offered the poor girl a bottle of champagne, like an idiot. I was just so shocked, you know? Then again, Ms. Cross doesn't strike me as poor at all. Or a girl. She's definitely a woman with some money, if you know what I mean. I think I've seen her picture in the paper.

Detective Ramone: What was said during the breakup?

Allison Feeney: Oh, I don't know if I should share. It's very personal.

Detective Ramone: Well, this is a murder investigation. Please tell me everything you remember.

Allison Feeney: Did she kill him? Did Kate murder Max? Oh, God. Good thing I didn't ask him out! I thought about seeing if he wanted to get a drink. He was cute, you know, but... Oh, right. Is he dead?

Detective Ramone: Please describe the nature of their argument.

Allison Feeney: Well, I was so stunned, I didn't catch all that much. I can say for certain that he mentioned some things about her being broken. About how he had wanted to wait until after the wedding to break things off for the sake of their family and friends, and then she wouldn't let him get a massage, and he sort of exploded then and there. He ordered a second room, and that's when I asked her about the champagne. Stupid, I know.

Detective Ramone: In your opinion, how angry was Kate Cross?

Allison Feeney: I mean, does the scale go up to one hundred? Because she was a million. She was really upset, but then again, who wouldn't be? Her ex said the worst things you can say to a woman. I think they were trying for children or something, and it must not have worked for them.

Detective Ramone: Thank you for your time, Ms. Feeney.

Allison Feeney: Oh, it's not a problem. And I should warn you, my friend Ashley is hoping you'll interview her next. She's super single and happens to love a man in a uniform. Would you be interested in grabbing a drink with her once this is all over?

ten

"D id you see that perfect little baby in the lobby?" Ginger murmured to Frank, loud enough for the children to hear. "So sweet, so innocent, so well-behaved. Thank God it wasn't Emily's. It couldn't have been Emily's, right?"

Frank sighed. "Why are you so concerned with Emily? I thought you two had let the past go."

Ginger's shoulders went rigid, but she didn't actually want to discuss this with Frank, seeing as he'd been at the center of Ginger and Emily's feud in college. To Frank, all had worked out hunky-dory. He and Ginger had gotten married, they'd had three children, and Emily had gone trotting along with her life far, far away in Chicago. Why worry about the past when their lives had all turned out just peachy?

The elevator doors dinged open, and Frank, looking worn and harried, finally seemed to be feeling human tiredness. A day of traveling cross-country with three kids in tow would do that to a man. Or maybe the debacle with Elsie on the plane had pushed him over the edge. Ginger supposed the fact that they'd had to struggle for an hour to find a taxi that could fit their family of five at the airport hadn't helped matters either. Ginger had given Frank one job: book transport to and from the resort. But Frank had figured the family would "play it by ear" when it came to taxis and shuttles.

The wait for a taxi hadn't gone well. Poppy had been starving, the battery on Tom's tablet had died (the equivalent of the apocalypse), and Elsie had played the sullen teenager role to the max. It'd been a disaster.

The car ride to the resort had been just as chaotic as the wait. Ginger had "accidentally" loosed one of Poppy's ponytails, and the ensuing tears had been impressive. Poppy absolutely, positively couldn't live with eight ponies instead of nine on her head. Tom had pinched her to stop crying, and Elsie had elbowed Tom. It got bad enough that Ginger had asked the cabbie to pull over on the side of the road to allow her a speech. *Everyone get along or we're skipping vacation.* Even the cabbie had shut up for the rest of the ride.

You will have fun if it kills you!

Well, it was just about killing them.

They made it to the room and opened the door with a gasp of relief. It was as if they'd returned from war and were getting a full meal, some rest, and a shower for the first time in years. Decades. It sure felt like they'd been deployed a long time.

"Mom, I'm dying!" Poppy screeched. "My stomach is eating itself. Look!" Poppy pulled her shirt up to her neck and squeezed her baby fat together to show a perfectly pudgy little stomach. "It's disappearing!" Then she collapsed on a bed and dissolved into tears.

Tom scowled across the room at her. "I don't want to share a bed with the girls. Where am I sleeping?"

"There's a pullout couch, bud," Frank said. "We'll get you set up there like a man."

"Why do I have to share the bed with a baby?" Elsie moaned. "Poppy kicks in her sleep."

"I do not! I kick you when I'm awake." As if to prove her (morally ambiguous) point, Poppy lined up a punt in Elsie's direction and, despite Ginger's warning, sent a wayward toe toward her sister.

It wouldn't have disturbed a fly, but Elsie bent in half as if she were dying. "God, Mom! Do something about her."

"Watch your language," Frank said desperately, as if he knew he needed to contribute but couldn't figure out exactly what to say.

He glanced over at Tom, who had stripped down to his undies and flopped onto the second bed, trying to claim it for himself. "Tom, buddy, keep your pants on. The ladies are present."

While Tom yanked up his pants and Elsie sobbed from an imaginary bruise and Poppy disappeared from starvation (she'd had a bag of chips on the car ride to the resort, mind you), Ginger gave a deep sigh and surveyed her family.

Nobody had told Ginger Adler that having children would be her own personal war. While there were glorious victories thrown in the mix (Poppy's first smile, Tom's little giggles, Elsie's sweet toddler hugs), there were many, many failures.

This evening, Ginger felt like one gigantic failure. Why was it the days meant to be so important, so noteworthy and fun and relaxing, were always the most stressful? Birthdays, holidays, vacations—she couldn't escape the drama. It was as if the holiday gods had conspired to make all children antsy on special occasions, throwing an added wrench into the already complicated labyrinth of parenthood.

Ginger turned to Frank, her voice soft enough that the kids couldn't hear. "I can't do this."

The look in her eyes must have triggered her other half into acting. One of the long-lasting reasons Ginger loved Frank—despite, or because of, his flaws—was because he truly was her other half.

He might screw up, lose his head in the clouds, and hate to discipline the kids, but he always knew the moment Ginger snapped. The moment her life force drained out of her, and she was ready to give up. When the exhaustion reached new levels of an all-consuming high that had her ready to break, to flutter off into the wind like a dried-up, crusty stalk of corn. Despite her frustrations with her husband, she never went a day thinking she could do this without him.

"Kids," Frank said with his rare use of authority. "We're going to grab something to eat. Your mother is going to rest and shower and crack open the bottle of wine in that basket, and then she's going to find a cozy space in the lobby and read a magazine. Alone. You're not to talk to your mother, ask your mother anything, or otherwise dissolve into tears around her for the rest of the night."

"But what if I miss Mommy?" Poppy asked, her lip quivering. "Where's she going?"

"You can say nice things to her," Frank said. "You can hug her and kiss her, and you may tell her what a good mommy she is, but from here on out, any complaints go to Dad."

"So tomorrow morning," Tom puzzled out, "I can complain to Mom again?"

"We'll discuss that downstairs, buddy," Frank said. "Come on, grab your things. There's a restaurant I want to try that looks yum."

"Mommy," Poppy said, adopting her sweet, innocent little voice as she scurried over to Ginger's knees. "I'm sorry."

"Oh, honey, it's fine. It's nothing you did, Mommy's just really tired," Ginger said, feeling a twinge of remorse already as she remembered her fleeting thoughts about handing her family off to someone else, even if only for a day. "I'm going to shower, and then I'll be right as rain, okay, sweetie? Have fun wandering around with Daddy."

"Can we look at the water?" Tom asked. "Mom said there are seven pools. Are you sure you don't want to come with us?"

"She doesn't," Frank said. "Move it, gang. Five-second countdown."

"I wouldn't mind walking around the pools," Ginger said with a look at her kids, feeling the infamous mom guilt manifesting itself as a red flush around her neck. "Maybe I can rinse off quickly and join—"

"You're not lifting a finger for the rest of the night," Frank said. "I insist."

Ginger's gaze landed on her eldest daughter, who had inched over toward the television and was examining the contents of a welcome basket left by the resort staff, no doubt courtesy of Whitney and Arthur. Elsie had retrieved the bottle of wine from it, her eyes fixed on the label. Ginger's knee-jerk reaction was anger. *First, condoms—now underage drinking?*

However, beneath the scowl on Elsie's face was a look that Ginger couldn't quite place. Confusion maybe, or frustration. And Ginger knew that despite the emotional overload she herself was feeling, it was probably worse for her daughter. Teenage hormones, peer pressure from boys and girls alike, coupled with the rest of the complicated package that came with being a brand-new young woman—it all added up to a lot to handle. And Elsie didn't have a partner to share in the load.

"I'd like to talk to Elsie for a minute," Ginger said, making a snap decision. "I'll walk her down afterward."

"Honey, it might be better if you take a rest first," Frank said. "Have a shower, a glass of wine. We're on vacation."

Yes, Ginger wanted to say, *a vacation where I must size up every eligible man on the premises the second he looks at my daughter because she carries condoms and she's only fifteen.* Fifteen-year-olds were still children. Ginger was stupid at fifteen. So stupid. Reckless and dangerous and a half-formed individual.

It's lucky I found Frank when I did, she thought fondly, glancing at her high school sweetheart. Otherwise, she might have gotten in trouble. But men like Frank didn't come around often, and the more likely scenario was that Elsie would fall in love with the wrong boy and end up hurt. And Ginger couldn't bear to watch that happen to her daughter. Not if she could help it.

"I'm not talking to you," Elsie said, her mouth curling into a frown. "You're so embarrassing."

"Yes, you are," Ginger said. If she took a deep breath, remained calm, she could help Elsie. She was her mother, above all. "Go on, Frank. I'll bring her down in a bit."

Poppy and Tom must have sensed something wrong in the air,

because Tom moved out of the resort room as if his bottom was on fire, and Poppy tiptoed, quite literally, into the hallway. Frank shot his wife an apologetic grin, and it softened Ginger's harried heart. She pecked him on the cheek before she shut the door behind him and faced her eldest daughter.

Elsie smartly put the bottle of wine back before turning to glare at her mother with fury and trepidation, as if Ginger was the crooked lawyer that'd put her on death row. Why couldn't Elsie see that Ginger only wanted the best for her daughter? Why was that so difficult for teenagers to understand? As Ginger watched, Elsie kicked back on the bed and stared at the ceiling.

Ginger crossed the room and sat on the bed next to her daughter. Elsie scooted away.

"Once upon a time, you used to sit in my lap," Ginger said with a laugh. "Bet you don't remember that."

Elsie had no comment on whether she remembered or not. Ginger had said the wrong thing already. *Note to self: Reminiscing on fond memories is a no-go.*

"Honey, I just want to talk," Ginger began, folding her hands together as she eased farther onto the bed. Elsie didn't move away, but she rolled over so her back faced her mother. "I'm not judging you. I'm not even mad."

"Yes, you are," Elsie said.

"I was surprised. That's different from being mad."

"You sure seemed mad. Everyone on the plane thought you were mad."

"Okay, I admit that was not the place or time to discuss things," Ginger said. "I'm sorry if I embarrassed you, but the thing is that I care about you so much."

Elsie grunted in neither approval nor dismay.

"I didn't stop to think about the fact that it was an inappropriate time for me to react like I did." Ginger pointed across the room as if envisioning an audience sitting on the opposite bed. "I would do whatever it took to keep you safe, and I didn't care who was watching or listening."

"Screaming at me about carrying…" Elsie shuddered. "Screaming at me doesn't keep me safe."

"I didn't scream."

"You're raising your voice right now."

"I'm trying to get a point across, Elsie." Ginger rested a hand across her forehead as if she were feeling faint. "You know what? Forget it."

She took a much-needed deep breath and surveyed the room and its fixings to stall. Ginger had thought she'd calmed herself down enough to have this conversation, but she was already having her doubts. Her nerves were frayed, her daughter was tipping over the edge of hating her, and the stupid walls of their room seemed to be closing in on her. The space might be nice enough for a romantic weekend away, but to fit five people in here was a challenge in and of itself.

Sure, it was luxurious and all. There was a Jacuzzi in one corner and fancy salts sitting on one side. Ginger made a mental note to grab those bath salts—she'd need a good soak at home once this godforsaken trip was all over. The minibar was stocked with the finest treats and beverages, and someone had left fancy little cakes— petit fours, maybe?—on the bed.

But luxury didn't help a family of five. There were only *two* treats, which would mean they had to be cut in halves. The Jacuzzi took up precious space that wouldn't be used for anything romantic. Either Tommy would end up sleeping in the tub, or Poppy would want to play hide-and-seek in there. At best, Poppy would use it as a Barbie fort.

And the minibar—don't get Ginger started on the minibar. She was ready to pull out the duct tape and wrap that sucker shut for good so none of her children could sneakily cram forty-five-dollar Skittles in their sticky little mouths.

Once the pullout couch had been pulled, there'd be no extra space. Add in their exploding suitcases, and they'd barely have enough oxygen to breathe. (Ginger wasn't quite sure how, but whenever the kids packed anything, it multiplied inside the suitcase and bred until their stuff took over the room.)

"I have tried to be your friend, and I have tried to be understanding, and I have tried to speak sternly," Ginger said, reaching for the tray of petit fours. "And you aren't receptive to any of it. I don't know what to do."

"Leave me alone."

"No. I'm your mother before I'm your friend. Sorry." Ginger never thought she'd see the day she was pulling the mom card on her almost-adult daughter, but that was what she'd saved it for all these years. "Why do you have condoms in your bag?"

Ginger watched the reflection in the window and found Elsie's face crinkling in dismay. She used the silence to figure out a solution to the little sharing issue with the petit fours. If Ginger merely ate them both, the kids couldn't complain. She popped one in her mouth.

"Mom, stop talking!"

"Look, if you want to carry around protection, then sit up and be an adult and talk to me about it. Are you having sex?"

"Mom!" Her eyes turned furious as she flew up in bed. "I don't want to talk to you about this stuff!"

"There is nothing embarrassing about discussing safety," Ginger said, though internally, she cringed. She hadn't grown up talking about sex with her parents—this was new territory for her too. "If you can't have an adult conversation about sex, then you shouldn't be having intercourse. Do I know the boy you're interested in?"

Elsie closed her eyes.

"It's very important to be safe," Ginger said, trying to separate her emotional reaction from the logical one. It was normal for teenagers to be interested in the opposite sex, and Frank had a point—at least Elsie was taking precautions. "I'm not upset about the fact that you have protection. In fact, I'm proud that you'd think about it. Maybe they did teach you something in health class. Sex can be very healthy when you're in a loving, committed relationship. Your father and I—"

"Mom. Shut. Up!" Elsie flew to her feet. "I don't want to talk about it."

"I'm trying to be understanding—"

"It's not like I'm even using them. God." Elsie shot a hand over her eyes. "Leave me alone! I'm not stupid."

"I don't think you're stupid, honey." Ginger hesitated, her mind clicking through Elsie's last words. "So, you're still a virgin?"

"I'm going to find Dad. If you try to talk about sex with me again this trip, I will shoot someone!"

Elsie stormed out of the room and slammed the door behind her. Ginger got up to chase after her, but she stopped. What was she going to do? Hold her teenage daughter's hand and walk her down to Daddy? Elsie would be driving in less than a year. *Driving.* Working. Living her own life like a little, miniature adult. She'd have full-fledged adult status in a few years. How horrifying.

Ginger popped the second petit four in her mouth. She was so stressed, she didn't taste the ridiculously expensive "complimentary" chocolate. She chewed, swallowed, and hunted through the minibar, closing the door with remorse at the thought of how many hours she'd have to work at her much-less-extravagant hotel to pay for a Snickers bar. Not that the hotel where Ginger worked stocked minibars with cute treats, nor did they hand-deliver fancy chocolates pillowside at night. It was probably a good thing they also didn't offer the nicest of bath salts and lotions, or else Ginger would have been fired for pilfering work supplies into her purse.

As Ginger scoped out the rest of the room, her mind wandered to dangerous places. Ginger had always thought she'd be excited to see her little birdies grow up and leave the nest, but now the thought of Elsie setting out on her own gave her heart palpitations. Elsie was a smart girl, and usually responsible, but still. She was her innocent baby, or she had been, once upon a time.

Maybe Ginger did need that glass of wine. She eyed the bottle in the basket but quickly realized she didn't have a wine opener. So she texted Frank instead, and he confirmed they'd found Elsie and were grabbing a bite to eat. He told Ginger to grab a drink at the bar, relax, pamper herself—he and the kids would occupy themselves for the rest of the night.

As Ginger stepped into the shower and cranked the water onto the hottest setting, she vaguely wondered how she could ever hope to relax. Maybe when she was sixty-five and retired, and her children were grown and married. Even then, all it would take was a phone call from one of them with some problem or another, and *wabam.* Her back would turn into a knotted mess all over again.

After her shower, Ginger took some much-needed time to set up the room, organize clothes and suitcases and sleeping arrangements, pull out necessary nighttime gear and teddy bears and books and special pillows and pajamas. The process of getting everything in order calmed Ginger's nerves and gave her a breath of fresh air she desperately needed.

When she finished, she sat on the bed and looked around. The room was all set for bedtime…minus the children. In a strange way, Ginger already missed the noisy ruckus that was the Adler household. What would she ever do when she had an empty nest? She could barely last five minutes alone without twiddling her thumbs.

When Ginger's phone pinged, it was with relief she picked it up to find a message from Frank. Surely there was some catastrophe (Poppy's seventh ponytail had come out, for example) that Ginger needed to attend to at once. In a way, Ginger felt like a bit of an addict: *Give me something to do! I need something to keep me occupied. Busy, busy, busy, dammit!*

Frank: You're forbidden from worrying about us for the rest of the night.
         Have a glass of wine. Read a book. Soak in the Jacuzzi. We
         love you.

The one time Ginger actually wanted to be needed, and her
family was a happy little gaggle of good. It hardly seemed fair.

Ginger: Maybe I'll come down and check Poppy's temperature. She
          looked a little peaked on the plane, and she was complaining
          about her stomach...

Frank: She's fine. They're all fine. We're fine for a few hours. RELAX!!!!

Ginger had to snort with laughter at his last instruction. It
sounded like something she'd say, like something she had said.

Shrugging on jeans and a sweater, Ginger decided to make the
most of her first night "off" in years. One glass of wine couldn't
hurt. Her family seemed fine without her, and her husband had all
but threatened her to relax. She picked up a book, a light beach
read someone had left behind at the hotel where she worked, and
she glanced at the title. Something about love.

Good enough, she thought and slipped from the room with the
second key in her pocket.

The elevator carried her back down to the first floor, and Ginger
stood for a moment taking in the luxury of it all. The hotel where
she worked the front desk wasn't seedy by a long shot, but it wasn't
anything fancy. It was no *resort*. It was a get-in, get-out sort of
place meant for business travel. The place was efficient, clean, and
fluff-free—exactly how Ginger liked.

Serenity Spa & Resort, however, was quite the opposite. All
plush furniture and calming decorations, the lounge was lit by fake
torchlight and subtly scented by diffuser reeds protruding from tall,
elegant vases tucked in corners. Combined with bushels of fresh

flowers that had been carted in for the wedding festivities, the room had a wash of floral ambiance.

All in all, simply stepping foot into the lobby should be relaxing, but as Ginger stood there, clueless, she realized she wasn't sure how to relax. Did one order a glass of wine alone? Was it a normal thing to bring a book to the bar?

Ginger heard the titter of laughter coming from one end of the lobby bar and saw a group of four women. The fourth woman stood a bit to the side, slightly turned away, yet distinctly part of the group. That young mother, Ginger realized—Sydney.

Ginger deliberately ignored Emily, who was standing somewhat near Sydney, and made her way over to the bar and quietly ordered a glass of red wine. She wasn't much of a drinker, save for a glass of wine with dinner or at holiday functions. Aside from her former friends, she didn't—and wouldn't—recognize anyone here, she figured as she glanced around the lobby at the influx of finely dressed couples. Whitney was busy, and Kate was…*Kate*, and Emily was a bitch.

"Hi, thanks," Ginger said as the bartender delivered her drink. With a jolt of horror, she realized she'd left her purse upstairs. "Can you charge this to my room? I forgot my cash upstairs. Otherwise, I can run and get it."

"Sure, ma'am," she said. "What's your room number?"

"Charge it to the room of Max Banks," a woman called from across the bar. She was part of the small group gathered in the corner. "She's on our tab. Don't pretend you don't know us, Ginger."

"Um, you really don't have to do that." Ginger felt her face flush as she recognized the voice as belonging to Kate.

Glamorous, perfect Kate Cross. The very perfect Kate who'd bossed Whitney around in their odd little friendship and wore makeup to 8:00 a.m. classes. Kate who never looked hungover. Kate who dated glamorous men, paid entire bar tabs for parties, and wore designer clothes. Kate who…was everything Ginger wasn't.

"It's not like I don't have the money," Ginger spluttered. "I forgot my wallet, and—"

"Oh, we all have money," Kate said with a tight smile. "We're old now. We're trying to rack up my ex-boyfriend's bar tab. Come closer so we don't have to shout."

"I should probably just pay," Ginger said, but she inched her butt slightly closer to Kate, as if following instructions. Kate was still very bossy. "It's only ten dollars."

"He's worth four million," Kate said with a fuzziness that indicated she'd gotten into the bottle of champagne sitting on the counter. "I don't think he'll miss ten bucks."

"I would rather pay for myself."

"You never could follow my instructions, could you?" Kate snapped. "I'm *really* brokenhearted tonight, so can you please help me run up my ex's goddamn bar tab? Is that really so much to ask from an old college pal?"

Ginger stared at her, gaping at this full-grown, adult, superstar lawyer until a snort of disbelief came out of her nostrils. It was unladylike and unconscious, and Ginger coughed to cover it up. "Well, I think I could do that. How have you been?"

Kate cracked a smile. "It's good to see you, Ginger. Obviously, I wish the circumstances were different, but...what can you do?"

Ginger watched as Kate waved a glittery hand, pretending she didn't feel a slight smugness at the other woman's glaring lack of a wedding band. Kate might have sparkling rings and beautiful hair and real diamond earrings, but Ginger had something she didn't. A husband. And children, though Ginger doubted Kate wanted kids. Kids were messy. Kate Cross was classy, elegant... and bossy.

"It's good to see you too," Ginger said, realizing the small group of women had gone silent. "It's been a long time. You look marvelous as usual."

"I know," Kate said. Then added, a beat too late, "Thank you."

In the silence following the compliment, the woman next to Kate shifted on her barstool and smiled politely at Ginger. She was an older lady, her hair flecked with gray, her face quite beautiful. She was clearly a woman who cared for herself with weekly spa dates and appointments that kept her looking more put together and exquisite than Ginger, who was probably close to half her age and deteriorating at a much more rapid pace.

"Hello there. My name's Lulu," the woman said, her smile crinkling the slender laugh lines around her eyes. "Why don't you take this seat? Unless you're busy, of course. What are you reading?"

"Oh, this? I don't actually know." Ginger stared at the book in her hand, mystified, as if a ghost had put it there. "I grabbed it off a shelf. I don't have much free time, and my husband is trying to give me the night to relax, so I figured…" Ginger gave an odd little shrug. Why the hell could she not seem to carry on a conversation like a normal person? Had it been that long since she'd interacted with other women?

"Well, why don't you join us?" Lulu pressed, nodding at the empty bar stool. "You already know Kate, obviously."

"She knows Emily too," Kate said. A moment of dead silence passed in which Emily, staring a bit drunkenly at Sydney's baby, swiveled her unfocused eyes on Ginger. Kate added, "Oh, don't you two be difficult. It was a disagreement. Ten years ago. Over a stupid man."

"Frank," Ginger said. "It was over Frank."

"I'm sorry," Kate said, not sounding sorry at all. "I didn't mean Frank was stupid. I meant that it was an accident. Things happen."

"Ah, I see," Lulu interrupted in that soothing, knowing voice of hers. "Well, it sure looked like all of you were great friends back in the day. I happened to see a few photos of the four of you. Emily and I had a nice chat earlier this evening."

Emily cleared her throat, not making eye contact with the other women. "I was putting together a photo album for Whitney as a wedding gift and trying to come up with some captions for our college pictures."

"Ah." Ginger took a swig of wine, vaguely curious about the reason Emily had chosen to include her in the project. If it had been Ginger making the album, she would have expertly cut Emily's face out of most of the pictures. "Things were different back then."

"They always are. Change is never easy," Lulu said softly. "By the way, has anyone seen Whitney? I've been wanting to congratulate her in person, but she seems to have been MIA since we arrived."

"I texted Whitney when I landed," Kate said. "Her schedule is booked full. I let her know we'd be down at the bar tonight, but I don't expect she'll show. If I had to guess, we won't see her until the rehearsal dinner. And even then, it might just be a sighting from afar, the way things are going."

"Well, that sounds"—Lulu hesitated—"vigorous. What a shame she won't have time to catch up with her friends."

Ginger wondered if Lulu's particular way of speaking had developed with age, or if Lulu had been born with it. Brisk and businesslike, but gentle, somehow filled with experience. Maybe if Ginger had that sort of tone, Elsie wouldn't freak out every time Ginger tried to talk to her.

"Yeah, well, that's Whitney for you," Kate said easily. "What about you, Ginger? Are you going to come over here and tell us what's bothering you or not?"

"Oh, I don't know." Ginger's nerves told her it would be easier to go sit in the corner, sip her wine, pretend to read her book, and count down the minutes until she was needed in her mommy role again. Her feet, however, were traitors. And before Ginger could say no, she found herself standing next to her old college friends. "I have a boring life. I'm a mom to three, and I work all the time at a hotel that isn't even in the same stratosphere as this one. I don't have much that's exciting to say."

The woman with the baby smiled. "Not boring at all. I think we met before. I'm Sydney, and my daughter's name is Lydia."

"She is the cutest thing," Ginger said with genuine fondness as she studied the young woman who looked to be closer in age to Elsie than Ginger. The mere thought of Elsie with a newborn frightened Ginger to the core. "I remember you. Are you here for the DeBleu/Banks wedding?"

"Most of us are," Kate interrupted. "But if I'm being honest with you ladies, I'm debating staying. My boyfriend—ex-boyfriend— ordered two different rooms when we arrived and dumped me in this very lobby. I mean, Whitney is a doll and all, but I might fly home tomorrow."

"Hence the credit card bill," Ginger said. She surveyed Kate with a new, sympathetic eye. Where Ginger was a bit dowdy in her mom clothes, Kate was all slick Angelina Jolie in *Tomb Raider* and big sex kitten hair. Ginger's mind wandered back to that moment of wondering what it would be like—shipping off her husband and kids for a few days, and trading lives with the esteemed Kate Cross. "Sorry, but what sort of idiot would dump you? You're gorgeous. And I assume wildly successful. I mean, we always knew you'd be the one to make the big bucks."

"Yes," Kate said without modesty. Somehow, it didn't come off as cocky. "But I can't have children, and my boyfriend didn't approve of my...flaws."

Ginger shifted uncomfortably. She now felt incredibly guilty over the wave of smugness that had hit when she'd realized she had a husband and Kate didn't. Despite all Ginger's troubles, she'd never actually wish her children away. She couldn't imagine life without them.

"I'm so sorry," Ginger said. "You deserve better. That was awful of him, and I can't imagine all you've been through. Or what kind of person would say those sorts of things to you."

"Yes, well," Kate said briskly. "We've all got problems. Sydney over here is a single mom. I don't know how she does it."

Sydney shifted uncomfortably under the attention. "We're managing. I mean, it's a bit tight financially because it's hard to find a job at the moment, but we'll be okay. That's small potatoes in the scheme of things."

Ginger's heart clutched. She suddenly felt so dangerously lucky, she wanted to ditch these intriguing women and rush to be with her husband and babies. To soak them all in while she could. If the successful and stunning Kate couldn't manage to be lucky in love, what hope did Ginger have?

"I slept with a stranger this afternoon," Emily said in a monotone sort of way that told Ginger it wasn't the first time she'd said it tonight, nor was she proud of it. "I met him on the plane, and now I call him Henry Anonymous because I don't know his last name."

Ginger took another sip of wine. "And that's a *problem*?"

An awkward silence settled over the group as Ginger stared at Emily, locked in some sort of bizarre standoff. Ginger was well aware of the wine making her more forthcoming and bitchier than normal, but these other two women had laid severe, life-altering struggles on the line. Emily's vacation fling didn't exactly compete in the race full of awful problems. Then again, Ginger wasn't all that sure Emily was aware of what she was saying. Her eyes were a bit bleary, and her champagne glass seemed to have a hole in the bottom for how fast it drained.

"Well, we all have issues of different shapes and sizes," Lulu said, smoothing the situation over as Kate and Sydney gratefully nodded. "Not that it compares to what Kate's been through, or the challenge Sydney has of raising a child on her own, but I myself am wondering if my husband is preparing to leave me for another woman."

"That most certainly counts as a problem," Ginger said. "I'm sorry to hear that."

Lulu waved a hand dismissively. "It's your turn. What's on your mind? We've all told you our worries."

"Oh, I don't know," Ginger hedged. "Nothing that compares to what you ladies have shared."

"Ginger," Kate instructed. "It's your turn to share."

Ginger swallowed a fortifying sip of wine. Part of her wanted to clam up and listen to these other women discuss their lives and loves and problems, but the other half of her was ready to contribute. To join in on the first adult, female-centric conversation she'd had in months, maybe years.

Turning from Kate's expectant gaze, Ginger focused on Lulu's patient expression. "Well, if you insist... I found condoms in my daughter's backpack," she finally confessed, feeling like a breath of fresh air as she came clean. "She's fifteen. And she hates me. I feel like a horrible mother."

"There," Kate said. "Was that so hard? Now you've gone and joined the *itty-bitty pity committee*! Welcome to the club. Another round for everyone."

"I don't know what to say," Ginger said. "I haven't done this in so long. It feels..." Ginger couldn't quite bring herself to finish her thought.

Lulu's eyes twinkled. "Friends are wonderful, aren't they? Men come and go, but women, you can count on the good ones."

Ginger nodded. It was all sorts of wonderful.

Hesitantly, she raised her glass as Kate muttered a nonsensical toast. When she finished, Ginger clinked her flute against the other glasses, beginning with Lulu's, then Kate's, then Sydney's water glass, hesitating only when Emily's arm remained extended toward her.

Ginger bit her lip as she felt the pull of old anger swirling in her stomach. She should have let the emotions fade away. Everyone knew forgiveness was healthiest for the forgiver, but she hadn't. She couldn't seem to let the grudge go, preferring to hoard it close to her chest for all these years. And where had it gotten Ginger? Married to a wonderful man with three beautiful children.

Where had it gotten Emily?

Drunk and alone at a bar with old college pals. Ginger met Emily's gaze and saw a world of hurt in her expression. She could see it in the limp spiral of her former friend's hair, in the nervous blink of Emily's eyes, in the tremble of fingers as she held her glass hopefully, pitifully, toward Ginger as if this olive branch meant the world to her.

And Ginger wondered if maybe it was time to let go. Maybe karma had run down Emily in the years since college, or maybe there was something more to her story. Ginger wasn't entirely sure she cared. So with a guttural sigh, she extended her arm, pasted on a smile for Emily, and clinked glasses with an old friend.

Detective Ramone: Ms. Pinkett, please state your occupation for the records.

Ashley Pinkett: I'm so glad Allison told me you were interviewing people. I would be happy to help however I can. I work the front desk for Serenity Spa & Resort, and I've been here for, oh, five years. I love my job.

Detective Ramone: Were you working on August 16?

Ashley Pinkett: Yes, I worked a full day because Dylan called in sick, so it was me and Allison behind the counter. I started at noon and didn't finish until after bar close…around 3:00 a.m. after cleaning up. As I said, I enjoy my job, Detective.

Detective Ramone: Can you please describe the

nature of Ms. Emily Brown's check-in? Here's a photo of her to jog your memory.

Ashley Pinkett: Oh, I don't need a photo. I remember her. Brunette chick, right? She checked in with that yummy-looking man. I mean, they weren't together, but they were *together*, if you know what I mean. I don't think I've ever felt so much electricity between a couple in my life. It was like they electrocuted the lobby.

Detective Ramone: Did she have any special check-in requests?

Ashley Pinkett: Yes, as a matter of fact. A bottle of champagne sent up straightaway, even after I mentioned they would receive a complimentary bottle of wine in their welcome baskets from the bride and groom. Not that they cared. In fact, I'm pretty sure Ms. Brown was three sheets to the wind at the time of check-in. Someone had a little too much fun on the plane. I wonder if she and her man friend joined the mile-high club? I wouldn't put it past them, the way they were staring at each other.

Detective Ramone: Thank you for your time, Ms. Pinkett.

Ashley Pinkett: Happy to help. And while we're at it, what's the verdict, Detective? Are you single? And did my friend Allison mention that I think you're cute?

eleven

I t's your turn again," Lulu said, turning her sights on Ginger
after an hour or two had passed. The women had become
almost giddy, sharing the odd bits of information that seemed
so magical at the start of new friendships and rekindled old ones.
"I'm not sure you have to worry so much about your daughter.
How old were you when you lost your virginity?"

They'd been drinking for a while now, and Lulu was a happy sort
of buzzed. She'd had more to drink than she'd had in quite some
time, but it was working, distracting her enough to push thoughts of
Pierce to the back of her mind and focus on other problems.

Problems that weren't hers; problems she could make go away.
Unlike the note she'd found upstairs when she'd gone looking for
Pierce. A note that had been written to *S,* signed by Pierce, and
referenced a meeting at a local hotel. The Ritz—a place she and
Pierce had stayed a few times for their anniversary or other special
occasions. This time, however, the meeting Pierce had apparently
shared with his mysterious friend had occurred the day before he
and Lulu left for the wedding—and Lulu hadn't been invited.

"Me?" Ginger hesitated, took a small sip from her second glass
of wine. "You know, young. But things were different then. It was
a different time, and it was with my husband, and—"

"Hold on a second!" A very sober Sydney extended a finger,
her eyes sparkling with the revelation. "Are you saying you've only
ever been with one man?"

"Ginger and Frank broke up for a bit in college," Kate said, ever the stickler for accuracy. "But we all knew that was a facade. They've only ever been with each other."

"We've only slept with each other," Ginger corrected. "I'd gone on a few dates with other men, but we never got past the make-out stage. And we all know Frank has been with other women."

Emily glanced down at her feet as Ginger shot her a pointed stare.

"Don't start this again!" Kate rolled her eyes. "Ginger, get over it. Frank came to our apartment for *you*. He was drunk, Emily was drunk—it was one kiss!"

"It looked like a little more than that," Ginger said, the slight flush to her cheeks a sure sign that the effects of alcohol were working on her. "One doesn't need to remove their shirt to kiss a man, as far as I know. Otherwise, I've been doing it wrong this whole time."

"I'm not saying it was right what happened," Kate said. "But you walked in before things went too far."

"If I hadn't walked in, then what?" Ginger pressed. "Frank and I had recently broken up. Don't you think I had the right to feel a bit betrayed when I found my best friend and ex-boyfriend exchanging saliva?"

Emily winced. "Ginger—"

"You ended up with Frank, didn't you?" Kate persisted. "Both of them apologized. Emily felt awful, didn't you?"

Emily nodded, but her gaze was fixed on the bar. "Of course. It didn't mean anything. I told you, Ginger—I barely remember it happening. We were both way, way too drunk to be making good decisions. Frank was moaning to me about missing you, and I was moaning to him about getting dumped by Daniel, and it just sort of happened."

"That doesn't answer my question," Ginger said. "What if I hadn't walked in when I did?"

"Ginger, don't forget—you and Frank were completely broken up when it happened," Kate said. "Sure, I understand you being pissed because your friend kissed your ex, but they both apologized. It was a stupid, drunken error."

"I know," Ginger said. "But—"

"And if I remember correctly, you were out on a date with another man the night it happened," Kate said sternly. "I think we need to focus on the fact that everything worked out as it should have. Maybe you should thank Emily. If she hadn't kissed Frank, maybe you'd never have realized how much you loved him."

Ginger looked quite shocked at the insinuation that she should be thanking her ex-best friend, but she noticeably worked to compose herself before speaking. With a cough and another sip of wine, she expelled a breath and gave a half-hearted shrug.

"Anyway, everything ended as it should have ended. Emily got back with Daniel the week after that debacle. You and Frank reconnected. Seems to me you're still in love nearly two decades later, right?" Kate didn't wait for an answer before she continued. "I think it's time you let it go already."

Ginger watched Kate, her lips cracked open in surprise.

Kate, undeterred, swiveled toward Emily. "Speaking of, whatever did happen with Daniel? Weren't the two of you still together at graduation?"

"We were." Emily's face had gone ashen. "But it didn't work out. I don't know what he's up to these days."

Lulu suspected there was more to Emily's story than she'd let on, but she didn't push. She was too content to watch the group of women with a tidy little smile on her own face. Kate was by far the tipsiest of the group, but the poor woman had a good excuse. She'd been dumped at a wedding. How was the woman supposed to relax when Cupid was everywhere, and her heart had been battered like a piñata?

"Gosh, that is quite a story." Sydney's wide, cherubic expression was focused on Ginger. She swayed gently back and forth with Lydia clasped tightly in her arms, the baby finally sleeping with a peaceful little smirk on her chubby cheeks. When Ginger cast her a curious look, Sydney blushed and quickly corrected herself. "I mean the bit about you and Frank being destined to be together. High school sweethearts and all, and now you have three gorgeous children. Plus, you're still in love. You *are* still in love, aren't you?"

Ginger gave a shrug, obviously trying for modesty and failing to achieve it. "We drive each other up a wall sometimes, but yes. I couldn't survive without him. I was doing the math and realized I've had him as a staple in my life for over half of it. Half my life! That is wild to think about. Though the kids, they're…far from angels."

"What about you?" Kate asked Sydney. "What age did it happen for you?"

"When did I first sleep with a man?" Sydney blushed, hugged her thin, gangly arms tighter around her child. "Twenty. It's not all that interesting of a story; the guy was nice enough, and we dated for a few weeks, but things didn't last."

"Well, I, for one, was a virgin when I married my first husband," Lulu said. "I was eighteen. Married for love. Joe was a heartthrob, but his bank account was dismal."

"What about the two husbands of yours who passed away?" Kate asked with a crooked eyebrow. "Was he one of them?"

Ginger was giving Lulu a funny look, so Lulu flashed a wan smile and gave her the quick rundown. "I've been married five times to four different men, dear. Two husbands have passed away. Anderson, the fool I married twice, is still kicking."

"Ah," Ginger said. "How did they die?"

Lulu felt her own guard come up as she thought about the lone detective who'd come poking around after her third husband, Louie, passed away. "Both Joe and Louie died within a year of our divorces and left me considerable sums of money. In fact, the police thought it was suspicious."

"I thought Joe was poor," Ginger said with a frown. "I married my husband when he was poor too. We both were. We both still are."

"Oh, the silly man went and got rich around the time we separated," Lulu said with a light laugh. "He inherited some money from his father. Apparently, Joe hadn't updated his will, so a chunk of that money went to me. Similar thing with Louie. He left me a good chunk of money despite our divorce. His new girlfriend was very upset about it and made this big stink about wanting his money. I think she's the one who called the detective."

"So, did the detective…" Ginger cleared her throat. "What did he say?"

"I didn't kill anyone, dear," Lulu said. "Luck of the draw. Joe had a heart attack—he always did like his fried food—and Louie had a sudden aneurysm. They didn't do autopsies because Joe drank like a fish, and Louie had always had health issues. They were getting old. I always married older men, see. But Louie's new girlfriend kept saying I offed them to get their money."

"But you didn't," Ginger clarified.

"Of course not. I already had my sights set on Anderson, again, and he's as rich as they come," Lulu said. "He was my second and fourth husband. We didn't manage to stay married, but we're still quite close and talk often. He's a good man."

"Has someone written a book about you?" Ginger asked, her voice tinged with surprise. She gestured to the romance novel on the table. "Your life story is incredible."

"Oh, I don't know," Lulu said, but she secretly didn't mind the flattery. Lately, she'd been doubting herself, her choices, her failed marriages. After all, she was the largest common denominator in all four of her failed marriages. That thought hit her like a lightning bolt.

"Oh, dear," Lulu murmured, a sudden panic arcing through her heart. Could that be true? Was she the problem? It wasn't until she felt the stare of four sets of eyes on her that she realized she'd spoken aloud.

"I'm positive you are not the problem," Ginger said. "Marriage is hard. It takes two people to make it work."

"Exactly," Lulu said. "Which means that if I'm the problem, none of my marriages had any hope of sticking."

"That's ridiculous," Kate said. "But if you're worried, why don't you ask?"

"Ask who?"

"You said you're close with your ex-husband," Kate pointed out. "Call him and ask why you broke up. Maybe it'll give you some peace of mind."

Lulu paused in thought. "I'm not sure that's a good idea."

"Do you want to know?" Kate pressed. "Or not?"

"Excuse me for a second, ladies." Lulu stood. "I need to make a phone call."

Lulu pushed back from the bar and dodged the group of chattering women with ease. She grabbed her cell phone—an expensive thing that Lulu only pretended to know how to work—and carried it across the lobby to a private corner of the space. Flipping to the appropriate phone number, she hit dial.

"Lulu," a deep voice answered on the other end of the line. "Is everything all right?"

"I'm fine, Anderson," Lulu said briskly. "This isn't a social call. I have a question for you."

"Fine."

"What broke our marriage apart?"

Anderson gave a wry laugh. "The first time or the second?"

"Um, either one," Lulu said, feeling uncharacteristically nervous. "I'm sorry to be calling you and asking. I realize it's late, but…I need to know."

"You're serious."

"Dead serious."

"This isn't some sort of joke, is it?" Anderson asked, his voice clipped. "Have you left Pierce? My heart can't take a third time with you, Lulu, as much as I enjoyed our first two attempts."

Her breath caught in her throat. "No, I haven't. It's our five-year anniversary this weekend."

"Big moment. Momentous, actually."

"I hope so too." As she spoke, her voice shook. Lulu almost didn't recognize herself. She didn't get nervous as a general rule. "Anderson, I think Pierce is going to leave me."

The line on the other end went silent. "I'm sorry, Lulu. I truly mean that."

"Is it me?" she asked in a painfully small voice. "Did I push you away?"

"No, I don't think so. Well, in a way, I suppose it was you," Anderson amended. "But only because you broke up with me—both times, remember?"

"Yes, but maybe it was inevitable. Maybe I'm the problem, the broken one." Lulu distinctly remembered Kate saying something similar on repeat all night. "Maybe I can't handle being married."

Another long beat of silence passed. "He's the real deal, isn't he?"

"Yes," Lulu insisted. "He is. I'm surer of it than anything before, and I can't stand to lose him. What do I do?"

"I don't know that I have the right answer for you, seeing as I couldn't convince you to stay with me," Anderson said, pausing as if weighing what to say next. "But I can guarantee you one thing, Lulu. If you're feeling these emotions for Pierce, he's worth fighting for."

"I think you might be right," Lulu whispered. "Maybe it's not too late. Maybe…"

"Talk to him," he encouraged. "Don't make any rash decisions."

"You're right." She exhaled a shaky breath. "Five-year anniversary. Damn. Love is hard."

"For what it's worth, I didn't think love was hard when I was with you," Anderson said lightly. "Until you dumped me."

Lulu grinned, then she glanced at the group of women behind her and bid her ex-husband goodbye. As she hung up, she realized that somehow, over the course of the evening, her shoulders had tensed with the anticipation of holding a discussion with Pierce she wasn't ready to have. Lulu loved to talk, but for some reason, the only conversation she needed to have was one that felt just out of reach.

She knew Anderson was right. If she could find the courage to confront Pierce with her questions, it could solve everything. Maybe there had been some misunderstanding. Lulu had jumped to conclusions before. Pierce loved her, and she loved him. She hadn't seriously doubted that, had she?

Maybe it was the weight of this five-year anniversary milestone making her see things that weren't there. Like Anderson had said, everything would be fine. She'd finish up here with the girls and then head upstairs to find her husband and clarify a stupid miscommunication. Then, she'd happily call it a night and snuggle in next to him.

Lulu returned to the conversation as Kate leaned toward the group and giggled. "I was twenty-three," she was saying. "Can you believe it? I thought I was saving myself for marriage. Good thing I didn't, because I'm still not married!"

"Really? You—twenty-three?" Ginger leaned inward, her forehead crinkled in concentration as if the math didn't make sense. "I could have sworn, in college…"

"That's older than me," Sydney said. "I mean, my current age."

"Oh, my," Kate said and touched her face. "I'm almost double your age."

Sydney looked mortified. "I swear, I'm much older in spirit. I'm like a grandma—not that I think you're a grandma! Oh, Lordy, please—"

Lulu caught and met Sydney's gaze and threw the poor girl a life vest.

"Oh, quiet you," Lulu said. "I'm the only one of grandmotherly age here. Thankfully, Pierce and I don't have children, so I don't ever have to worry about carrying that title formally. I'm more than happy to be Aunt Lulu, and so on and so forth. Right, Emily? You know what I mean."

Emily looked up with a startled expression. "Um, sure. Of course."

Lulu wondered if she'd overstepped her bounds, but it wasn't as if she'd been assuming. Emily had told her flat out she didn't want children earlier at the bar. Lulu shook it off and declared to the group, "I'm absolutely wiped, ladies. I'm going to turn in for the night. What do you all say we meet for a massage tomorrow?"

"Oh, I couldn't," Ginger said. "I'll have the kids with me."

"Same," Sydney said quickly, looking relieved to have an excuse. "Sorry. Maybe I'll meet up with you all after?"

Kate waved a hand. "If you change your mind, massages are on Max at one o'clock tomorrow afternoon. I hope to see you all there. I'm sure the resort has child care."

"My oldest daughter is also a babysitter," Ginger said to Sydney. "I'm sure she'd love to look after Lydia for an hour if you'd like a massage. She is very good with children, and she'd do it for free. It'd do me a favor too, keeping her out of trouble. I'd be there too, of course, as a supervisor."

"That's sweet of you to offer," Sydney said. "But I wouldn't want to impose on her vacation."

"Well, good night, girls!" Lulu blew kisses to her newfound friends and gave a wave as she eased from the bar. "I hope to see you all tomorrow."

It was with a pleasant sort of buzz that Lulu ascended in the elevator to her floor, then walked, humming, to her room as she replayed her conversation with Anderson. A quick few words with

Pierce and both parties would be right as rain. Lulu would be able to heave this heavy weight off her chest and get on with all the festivities.

Pierce, however, had other plans. As Lulu pushed the door open, she found him sleeping on the bed with a book across his chest—a different book from the one Lulu had peeped through earlier. The offending book was nowhere to be seen.

As gently as possible, Lulu reached for the novel and removed it from her sleeping husband's chest. She felt tenderly loving toward him, almost more of a fondness than a love, and she realized her spark for Pierce had faded into something else, something new. A level of comfort she hadn't obtained with any of her past relationships.

It was with tears in her eyes that Lulu realized Anderson right: she was deeply, madly, truly in love with Pierce Banks.

twelve

Detective Ramone: Ms. Brown, please tell me about Lulu Franc. You met her the night of August 16? That would be your first night at the resort.

Emily Brown: I know which date I arrived at the resort.

Detective Ramone: I understand you met Lulu at the lobby bar?

Emily Brown: Yes, I did.

Detective Ramone: I understand the two of you grew close over your stay at the spa.

Emily Brown: I suppose you could say that. As close as two strangers can get over the course of a couple of days.

Detective Ramone: What did you discuss?

Emily Brown: The well-known fact that men are assholes.

Detective Ramone: I see. Did Lulu mention anything about her husband?

Emily Brown: She said she loved him.

Detective Ramone: What else do you remember from that night?

Emily Brown: Not a whole lot, seeing as I was at least a bottle of champagne in when I got to the bar, and I didn't stop there. Can you get to the point?

Detective Ramone: Ms. Brown, Lulu admitted responsibility for a man's death this evening. Here's a photograph. Do you recognize him?

Emily Brown: Well, she can't have killed this man.

Detective Ramone: Why not?

Emily Brown: Because that's the man *I* shot.

Detective Ramone: You're admitting to shooting and killing this man? Did you have help from Lulu?

Emily Brown: No, I was alone with him under the pergola when it happened.

Detective Ramone: Then why would Lulu confess to killing this man?

Emily Brown: I don't know, Detective. All I know is that it's impossible for a man to die twice.

E mily waited a respectful amount of time for Lulu to disappear into the elevator before she sidled over to Sydney. "Your arms must be killing you. I've been around children quite a bit; I was a preschool teacher for some time before I got a job in marketing," she said. "You've been standing for hours. Would you like me to take Lydia again?"

"Are you sure you don't mind?" Sydney blinked in surprise. "I don't mean to be foisting my baby onto you all evening. This is supposed to be your vacation."

Emily couldn't think of anything she wanted more than to hold Lydia to her chest and imagine that, for a moment, Lydia belonged to her. But if she said any such thing aloud, if she even thought about it too obviously, she'd sound like a psychopath, and any good mother would never let Emily near her child again.

So instead, Emily said, "Oh, I don't mind a bit. Have a bite to eat. You are so thin."

Sydney wrinkled her nose. "Well, it's not as if I can compete with Kate's body. When she walked into the resort, I was convinced she was a celebrity."

"Get used to it," Emily said, single-mindedly focused on the baby. Now that she was this close to Lydia, it had become more than a fascination. A sort of addiction, like a vampire's thirst for blood. "Kate has been perfect since I met her in college. Some things never change."

Kate was ordering another bottle of champagne from the bar—for whom, Emily had no clue. Emily had switched from booze to water an hour ago when she realized Ginger was giving her an odd, pitiful sort of look. Emily knew how to manage, how to abstain, how to blend in, and she'd decided that holding this baby and feeling something again was far more important than blacking out her past.

Emily surveyed Kate too. She had the lean, muscular look of someone who paid big bucks for trainers and gyms and equipment. Then, she looked over to Sydney who had the scrappy, thin look of someone who'd lost weight to stress and lack of proper nutrients. Emily had never been thin, nor had she particularly had a problem with her body size or weight, but she knew it was a rare thing for a woman to be comfortable in her own skin. The thing was, Emily had much bigger problems than a number on a scale.

"I don't know that you need to look like anyone else," Emily said to Sydney. "I think you look great. Plus, you need to be kinder to yourself—you just had a baby, and you're going the road alone. I think that makes you pretty damn strong. Here, let me get Lydia for you."

"Wow, that's really nice of you to say." Sydney stretched, maneuvered her arms so that Lydia blinked sleepy eyes and settled, then passed her to Emily. "I can't tell you how much it means to me."

For some reason, the gratefulness in Sydney's voice combined with the weight of the baby sent pings of feeling to Emily's heart. It'd been so long since she'd dared step foot in the same room as a baby without babbling some excuse and backing away. She wasn't sure what had come over her tonight, but something had changed. Everything had changed. Nothing had changed. She wasn't entirely sure which.

Yet with a fierce longing for Lydia, and a blackened hate for her own destroyed life, she suddenly blamed *him*.

The fury was overwhelming, and Emily trembled as she tightly curled the small child to her chest. A wave of annoyance washed over her as she heard Ginger complaining about something her children had done on the flight to California.

At least you have children you can complain about! Emily wanted to scream. But it was Emily's fault for not coming clean with the truth. When Lulu had mentioned Emily not wanting children, it had stung.

You have it all wrong, Emily wanted to tell her. How could she ever want another child after what had happened to Julia? It would be disrespectful to her memory. Emily hadn't been strong enough to save her first daughter—she didn't deserve to have a second chance.

However, she'd kept her mouth shut and nodded, and now the women thought she was purposefully child-free. She'd felt too guilty to contradict Lulu, as if her desires were a dirty little secret. As if she'd be betraying Lulu by voicing her true feelings.

Emily protectively curled Lydia closer to her chest, wishing she could slip away with the baby for a private, cozy little feeding. With a start, Emily realized her baby would be almost the same age as Ginger's oldest. Julia wouldn't need feedings anymore; she'd make herself a sandwich or go out to eat like other teenagers.

The thought jolted Emily with surprise. She'd never thought of her daughter as someone who might've grown up; Julia was forever a baby imprinted in Emily's mind, but that wouldn't have been true. Emily should be worrying about her teenage daughter counting calories and talking to boys and demanding social media when Emily thought she was much too young for that nonsense, but no. Ginger had all that and still couldn't manage to be grateful, while Emily, once again, was empty.

"Hey, maybe I can get a little snuggle?" Kate took a few tipsy steps toward the baby. "She is the sweetest thing, Syd. My God, she's an angel."

No! Emily shrieked in her head. *Get away!* Trying to control the irrational curl of anger that'd snapped in her stomach, Emily sidestepped the question and said instead, "But I just got her, and she really does smell divine. I can't get enough of the baby scent."

"I shouldn't hold her actually. I've dined on a bit too much champagne, but maybe I can have a sniff." Kate leaned a little closer, took an exaggerated inhalation, and grinned. "Seriously delicious. I could gobble her right up. Maybe a snuggle tomorrow?"

"Of course," Sydney said, looking up at Kate in awe. "Speaking of tomorrow, I hate to cut the party short, but I really need to get this little miss to bed. Thank you all for your help."

Emily felt the life drain out of her as Sydney finished her goodbyes and turned expectantly toward her. Emily lingered a touch longer than necessary with the baby, knowing Ginger's eyes were fixed on the exchange, yet unable to muster the energy to care. When Sydney held her arms out, Emily reluctantly handed Lydia back.

"Well, I think I'm a bit too tipsy to find my room," Kate said with a laugh. "I'm going to stroll outside, grab a coffee—stretch my legs for a bit." She glanced down at her watch. "Damn, it's after midnight. Does anyone remember when the juice bar closes? I really could use some fresh coconut water or the bags under my eyes will be horrendous tomorrow."

"There's a market open all night to the left of the doors," Sydney said. "I don't think they'll have fresh juice, but they'll have water and other things. I'll walk you there if you like—it'll only take a minute."

"Perfect," Kate said. "Shall we?"

"I should go check on my family and turn in for the night," Ginger said, her eyes quickly flicking toward Emily. "It's been great talking to you all."

Emily realized everyone was looking at her. She'd been so dead focused on the child that she'd already pushed the women to the back of her mind. "Right! I'm headed to bed too. Long day."

Sydney waggled her eyebrows. "I'll say."

Kate snorted with laughter. Even her snort was somehow ladylike and adorable. *Not fair,* Emily thought. If Emily snorted, she'd sound like an asthmatic horse.

She gave them each a good-natured smile, but anyone watching closely would have seen it wasn't genuine. The ache persisted in her gut. The wave of tears that'd built up in her chest pressed to come out, to wash over her like Niagara Falls.

Why couldn't Emily have picked a perfectly acceptable time to cry and defuse this mess? Last night when she'd been alone in the shower. This morning when she'd been too hungover to get out of bed. In the bathroom on the airplane after Henry had left her alone. This, here, was a horribly awful time to feel the urge to cry.

"I'm exhausted," Emily assured the group. "Thanks for the drinks, Kate."

"Thank Max," Kate shouted happily over her shoulder. "See you for the massage tomorrow?"

"Yep." Emily agreed before she could talk herself out of it. Whatever it took to get out of there. She suddenly couldn't bear the thought of one more look at Lydia tucked snugly against her mother's chest or Ginger's eyes watching her with a brutal intensity, filled with judgment for things she knew nothing about.

Emily ascended in the elevator, well aware the time was much past polite calling hours. However, nothing about her relationship with Henry Anonymous had been polite. So, she marched right up to his door and knocked.

The door opened to reveal Henry Anonymous standing there in his jeans, almost as if he'd been expecting her. He had no shirt on and his stomach was a tanned, glorious six-pack. (Eight-pack? Was that possible?) His physique was incredible, but it was the look in his eyes that fired into Emily.

"I don't want to be alone," she whispered, and the tears began to fall.

Henry Anonymous watched her through cautious eyes.

Then he opened the door wider.

Detective Ramone: Ms. DeBleu, I'd like to understand more about the rift between Ginger and

Emily. How is it relevant when all this happened
over a decade ago?

Whitney DeBleu: That's such a *man* thing to say,
no offense, Detective. There's a certain code of
conduct between women, between friends. See, when
all this happened, Ginger and Frank were still
recently broken up. Best friends aren't supposed
to date each other's ex. They just aren't.

Detective Ramone: Isn't Ginger married to Frank?

Whitney DeBleu: She is *now*. But back in college,
they took a break. Emily was also freshly out of
a relationship with this guy she really liked—
Daniel. Emily swore he was the one, so she was
heartbroken when he broke things off.

Detective Ramone: So, then, Emily dated Frank?

Whitney DeBleu: Not exactly. They got all hot and
heavy one night after a few bottles of wine. When
Ginger came home, she found them on the couch.
I wasn't there, but I hear Emily had her shirt
off and Frank could barely see straight… Suffice
it to say, it didn't look *good*. But I seriously
don't think it meant anything. After all, Frank
had come over to win Ginger back.

Detective Ramone: It doesn't seem like his plan
worked.

Whitney DeBleu: It's no wonder you made detective.

Detective Ramone: What happened after that night?

Whitney DeBleu: Ginger and Emily's friendship fizzled after that evening, but I don't think it was long before Ginger went back to Frank. I think it shocked her to see him with someone else and spurred her to get back together with him. Ironically, I think Emily ended up back with Daniel too. In a way, maybe it was a good thing this all happened. But what do I know?

Detective Ramone: You mentioned earlier that you don't keep in close contact with your college friends anymore. If that's true, why did you invite them to your wedding?

Whitney DeBleu: Because they were my best friends for several years! And when I floated the idea to Kate—we still text now and again—she agreed it would be fun to get together. After all, college was so long ago. Things all shook out how they were supposed to. Ginger is married to the love of her life with three great kids. Emily is a preschool teacher in Chicago—or at least she was when I last asked. Kate is Miss Megabucks out in New York. I thought it would be a fun reunion. I mean, I never thought it would *kill* anyone.

thirteen

Here we are." Sydney came to a stop in front of a small market that doubled as a gift shop and smiled up at Kate. "Will this work?"

"It will do the trick." Kate spotted a refrigerator in the back that likely housed overpriced bottles of water, soda, and other snacks. "Do you need anything while we're here?"

"No, I'm good."

However, when Sydney didn't make a move to head back inside the resort, Kate surveyed the young woman—hip bones jutting out beneath a pair of ill-fitting jeans—and was struck by their peculiar new friendship. It was odd how Sydney had eased into a group of much older women solely because she had a child. Without Lydia on her hip, Sydney would be just another young twentysomething enjoying the spoils of an unworried youth.

Kate didn't envy Sydney's youth; she cherished her lifestyle of luxury, along with the respect she'd garnered from a highly success-ful career. But a hint of jealousy was still there, hidden behind Kate's expensive foundation and overpriced antiaging creams—because this young woman had a child, and all the money in the world couldn't buy Kate that gift.

"Oh, I'll wait with you," Sydney said at Kate's expectant stare. "I'm not in any particular rush, and it's not like I've had a ton of adult interaction recently. I can't afford to *do* a whole lot without a salary, so…" She shrugged. "What are you gonna do?"

Sydney said the last phrase in a deep imitation of Tony Soprano that made Kate laugh. It felt good. Kate hadn't realized it before, but her relationship with Max had begun to morph over the last year and a half, ever since she'd realized they were going to have an uphill battle trying to conceive. There'd been less laughter, less silliness, less frivolity. Kate wasn't a frivolous person by nature, but she appreciated a witty joke here and there.

When she thought back now, there hadn't been much in the way of humor between her and Max for the past several months—there'd been the exchange of schedules (weekly and on Sunday evenings), polite niceties when they'd been in good moods and biting snips when cross, and the dreaded ovulation updates. They'd become business partners with sex on the side. How dreadfully unromantic.

"Kate?" Sydney asked. "Are you feeling okay?"

"Yeah, sorry. Can I at least hold something for you?"

"Oh, I don't need help—"

"Give me that," Kate said, beckoning toward the baby bag. Even a bit drunk, she knew how to take charge. "Your arms are full. Don't be silly."

"You must think I'm such a mess." Sydney shook her head after foisting the diaper bag over to Kate. (A horrific hand-me-down from Goodwill, Kate noted.) "I can't afford anything, I keep my baby out until all hours of the night, and I let strangers help me do everything."

"Of course not," Kate said, pushing away the guilty, fleeting thoughts that'd flashed through her brain. (I can afford nice things! I can manage a schedule and bedtimes and bath times. I can stick to a routine and afford professional help!) "I think you're a wonderful mother. It's clear you love your daughter more than I can probably understand."

"I do love her. You know, you'd make a great mother," Sydney said almost wistfully. "You'd have your baby dressed in the trendi-est clothes, and you probably wouldn't have spit-up in your hair, and you'd be back at the gym miraculously quickly." She gave a hoarse laugh. "The opposite of me. I'm sorry."

"Why are you apologizing?" Kate hoisted the bag onto her shoulder. She often wondered why mothers as a general group tended to offer apologies for things out of their control. "You didn't do anything wrong."

"I know, it's…" Sydney heaved a huge sigh. "It feels like I'm not doing right by Lydia. I'm not organized, nor am I particularly prepared. It feels like I don't deserve her. I don't have this high-flying job, or even a husband. Er—" Her face turned red. "Not that a woman needs a husband to be complete."

Kate let the comment slide past and feigned interest in the kitschy, manufactured little market. It'd been lit with twinkling lights, noxious candles, and loud sweatshirts in desert shades of neon pink and painful yellow, with a backdrop of soothing music piped through the surround-sound speakers. Kate felt crowded with the fake, overpriced tacky bundles of junk.

"Oh, this is too cute." Sydney joined Kate in the shop, pulling a bright-pink onesie toward her with the words *Serenity Spa & Resort* printed on it. "A souvenir."

"Get it," Kate said. "Lydia will look great in that outfit."

"No, I shouldn't." Sydney's face crumpled in a ball of frustration as she shoved the onesie back, almost angrily. "Forget it. Did you say you wanted coconut water?"

"Now that I think about it, I could use some aspirin too. My travel pack is in Max's bag, and I most certainly won't be using that. Here, hand me the onesie."

"But—"

"Please, it's all going on Max's credit card. He'll be buying a lot worse than baby clothes on this trip. It's not a big deal."

"It is a big deal to me," Sydney insisted. "I don't need it, and neither does Lydia. And I'm sorry, but I can't accept favors from you, especially when we've just met."

A twinge of annoyance had Kate watching Sydney more carefully as she shoved the onesie still farther back onto the table and turned away. It wasn't often that people argued with Kate, and it wasn't often that Kate backed down. But this felt somehow different.

"I didn't mean to imply I was doing you a favor," Kate said. "It's a gift. It's nothing, really. What's a few extra dollars on Max's tab?"

Sydney gave a wan smile. "I don't think you understand, Kate. To me, it is a lot. And I don't like having debts. I can't pay you back. End of story."

Kate sidled over to the refrigerator at the back of the store. It was rare for her not to argue when she knew she had a valid point, but to be quite honest, she didn't know what to say. Kate selected several Fiji waters and coconut drinks and put them into a basket, noting Sydney's wince as she glanced at the price list.

"I'm sorry. I really didn't mean to be rude," Sydney said. "Things aren't that bad, not always. But for now, I do have a finite amount in my bank account. I've been a little stressed with the separation and having to make do without my own source of income. Everything has to be budgeted—and I mean *everything*. And souvenirs like this aren't in the budget."

Kate felt an uncomfortable bubble building in her chest. Over the years, she'd donated to one charity cause after the next because *it's a tax write-off!* and *my, won't this look great for the business!* when there were real people who needed help and weren't getting it. Kate had always assumed there were programs to assist people like Sydney, people in need of financial help. Especially young mothers.

Was Kate really so naive to think she'd been doing a world of good, tossing her money at one cause after the next, when there were so many struggling every day to make ends meet?

"Really, ignore me," Sydney gushed. She tugged her flannel shirt tighter around her shoulders. "I didn't mean to make things awkward. I know you were only trying to help. I hope you can understand where I'm coming from."

"Of course," Kate said. "And I hope you can understand where I was coming from, as well. It isn't a big deal to Max, and I thought it'd be nice for Lydia to have something from the resort."

Sydney hesitated, sighed. Her gaze flicked at Kate. "If it'd make you feel better, and you're sure it's not an imposition, I think Lydia would love a gift."

"I'm glad." Kate smiled. "I'll pay for this, then, and we can head back inside. It's getting late."

Sydney backed gratefully away as Kate went to pay at the counter.

"All of this, please," Kate instructed the shopkeeper, gesturing to the aspirin, the waters, and the onesie. Kate fished in her purse for her own credit card and handed it over, preferring to buy the gift for Lydia and not taint it by billing the cost to Max's room. "I'd like to pay for it by card."

"No problem," the clerk said, swiping the card and handing two bags over to Kate. They were both puke green with cacti printed on the front and smelled faintly of plastic. "Have a serene evening!"

Kate took her things and met Sydney outside. It was a lovely night, quieter and calmer than the bustle brought on by daylight. The resort had been built into the rolling desert hills with cement sidewalks carefully zigzagging back and forth, cutting through exactly the right amount of nature. No path strayed too far from the resort, and every inch was lit in a carefully construed way—a hint of romance, a relaxing dimness that blended easily into the night beyond. A few critters skittered across the sidewalks, and still, resort staff bustled under the never-ending pummeling of guests' wants, needs, and desires.

The two women made pleasant small talk as they returned inside, past the nearly deserted lobby bar, and to the first-floor elevators. Sydney hesitated before several decorative vases topped with succulents, eyeing the bag on Kate's arm.

"I'm this way," Sydney said, nodding down the hall. "I can take things from here. Would you mind slinging the bag over my arm so I don't wake Lydia?"

"Don't be silly—I can drop it at your door for you," Kate said. "Nobody's waiting for me in bed tonight."

"If you don't mind, I'm right…here…" Sydney stopped outside a room, shuffled Lydia to her hip, and inserted the card into the reader. "Oh, shit. I forgot to order extra pillows. I've been meaning to do that all night."

"I can stop by the front desk on my way back, or I'm sure you could give a call."

"No, no. I'll get them tomorrow. I hate to be a nuisance. Speaking of, thank you so much for your help. You've done too much."

Kate waited outside in the hall until Sydney gave a nod for her to step through the door. Carefully, Kate laid the diaper bag on the stand near the entryway and surveyed the somewhat basic room. "It's no problem. Here's the onesie from the gift shop, and I grabbed an extra water for you too. I can't stand tap water."

Sydney's pink cheeks showed her desire to accept the gift warring with her pride. "I don't actually mind tap water."

Kate waited patiently, the bag extended on her wrist.

"Right, *Max*," Sydney said. "Well, thank you. I really appreciate all you've done for us."

Kate didn't bother to correct her about the purchase; whose money was spent wasn't important to anyone except Kate. She waited as Sydney pulled a few pillows down to create a soft cradle on the bed. She laid the sleeping Lydia between, and once she'd secured her daughter, she turned back to Kate.

"I don't know how to thank you for all you've done for us." Her eyes watered. "We've only just met, and your kindness is—well, very much appreciated."

Kate's level of discomfort shot through the roof. She didn't like "feelings" all that much more than Max, and she didn't know how to deal with them—her own, or anyone else's. "It's nothing.

Really, it was me being selfish. I deal with grief through retail therapy, and I don't have an excuse to buy baby clothes on my own, so Lydia gave me the excuse I needed. If there's nothing else, I'll head out..."

Sydney launched herself across the room as Kate trailed off, almost childish in her joyous appreciation as she clasped her arms around Kate and squeezed. Kate stood stock still, concerned, wondering if this was normal behavior for a cheap, thirty-dollar flippant gift.

"Sydney, please, don't worry," Kate said. "I didn't mean to offend—"

"You didn't offend." Sydney took a huge sniff and embraced Kate tighter for one long, extended moment. "It's been so long since anyone's done something to take care of me, or Lydia, and it means so much. You'll never know how much."

"It's nothing," Kate said, disentangling herself from the young mother before she, too, got emotional. Kate felt the stirrings of something in her chest, an almost teary sort of tickle, and she banished it with a sharp turn of her heel. She headed straight for the door before anything else could set her off.

"Hey, Kate?" Sydney called after her. "I hope—I hope you don't leave for New York tomorrow. I think you should stay the week. Not for Max or Whitney, but for you. For us."

Kate gave a half smile. "If I stay, will you consider joining us for a massage tomorrow? I'm sure the resort has professional child care. Both will be fully paid for by me. Or Max."

"I couldn't—"

"Think about it."

"I'll think about it," Sydney acquiesced. "Good night, Kate."

"Good night." Kate's heels clicked like miniature pecks of relief as they carried her away from the emotional bomb of a person that was Sydney Banks.

Sydney seemed to be stirring up all sorts of friendships and emotions among the group of women, and no one quite seemed able to pinpoint why. She'd drawn two feuding ex-best friends together—albeit tenuously—with the help of Lulu, and reunited a group of women without much in common except a shared apartment floor in college and memories of better times. Maybe it was Sydney's rawness, the joy and desperation, the hope and pain all wrapped into one person. It was too much for one soul to carry.

Where is this foolish husband of hers? Kate wondered for the millionth time. *Why isn't he taking care of his wife and child?*

Kate couldn't help it. Her feet pulled her toward the lobby of the resort as she strolled away from Sydney's room. Unlike the young mother, Kate didn't mind being a nuisance. She'd seen Sydney use all the pillows to form a crib for her baby and assumed they'd be doing some sort of co-sleeping arrangement. If Sydney needed more pillows, she should have them. They were paying enough to stay in the damn spa, after all.

"Hello," Kate said, leaning against the heavily polished front desk. She waited impatiently for the young front desk clerk to look up, thanking heavens it wasn't the same woman who'd offered her champagne after Max had dumped her in this very spot hours before. "I'd like a few extra pillows ordered to the room of Sydney Banks."

"Certainly." The front desk clerk smiled, her fingers clicking against the keys as she typed. When she stopped, a furrow appeared between her eyebrows. "Um, I'm sorry. Are you Sydney Banks?"

"No, I'm Kate Cross. This is for my friend. I came from her room, and she asked me to send some pillows for her baby."

"I'm sorry, but there doesn't appear to be a Sydney Banks staying at Serenity Spa & Resort."

"You're wrong," Kate said. "I just came from her room. She's in 114."

The front desk clerk shook her head. "I'm sorry, that's not right.

There's no Sydney Banks staying in room 114—or anywhere in the resort for that matter."

"She's part of the Banks/DeBleu wedding," Kate said. "She's family, I mean."

"And you're sure that's her full name?"

"For Pete's sake, yes! Is there a manager here I can talk to?"

"I'm sorry, but he's dealing with another issue."

"Well, fine. Can you get some pillows sent for me to room 114?"

"Sorry, that room was paid for in cash."

"So?"

"We require a credit card for incidentals."

Kate rolled her eyes and pulled a fifty from her wallet. She slapped it on the counter. "See that the woman in 114 gets pillows, and double-check her name is documented correctly on the paperwork, will you? This is ridiculous."

"Yes, ma'am," the front desk clerk said. "I apologize for any inconvenience."

Kate didn't wait for further confirmation before she left and headed to her own room. She needed to start the aspirin and the Fiji water, and her nighttime ritual, or she'd be waking with horrible skin and depressing bags under her eyes in the morning.

It wasn't until she reached the elevator that she stopped short as several of Sydney's odd behaviors clicked into place. Sydney's ambiguous stories about her husband and the cause of their separation. A fake name given at a resort—which would surely require some sort of false identification. A room paid for in cash. Her lack of funds or any sort of job that would keep her in one place for too long.

If Sydney Banks was her real name, and she had, in fact, given false identification to the front desk clerk, it wasn't much of a leap to assume the young mother had something to hide. Most people didn't bother to cover their tracks, unless…

"Holy shit," Kate muttered, pressing manicured fingernails to her forehead. "She's on the run."

fourteen

Ginger felt buzzed as the elevator doors clinked open, and not because of the alcohol—she'd had one, maybe two glasses of wine and a sip of champagne. She'd found it much more entertaining to sit and listen to the fascinating women congregated at the bar than sip herself senseless on drinks. The—what had Kate called it?—the itty-bitty pity committee. *How cute*, Ginger thought fondly.

Even Emily's presence hadn't completely derailed Ginger's mood. In fact, there'd been something a little off about her, like a puzzle piece that looked like it should fit but didn't quite match with how Ginger remembered her old friend. On the outside, Emily looked to be as Ginger would have expected—well-dressed, attractive enough, an average almost-forty-year-old meeting old friends at a bar for drinks.

But something underneath the exterior had seemed a little forced, a little over the top. And when the topic of Ginger and Emily's feud had been broached, Emily had practically been too distracted to notice.

Looking back, Ginger would have thought her somewhat snippy (and wine-infused) comments might have sparked something in Emily. An argument at the very least, or maybe an apology, but Emily hadn't taken the bait. It wasn't quite right, and the replay of the evening's conversations haunted Ginger as she slipped back up to her room. Had something happened to Emily that caused a vital shift in her personality? And if so, what?

Ginger battled with her thoughts as she weaved her way down a hallway filling slowly with flowers that dripped across doorways and signs boasting the wedding of Whitney DeBleu and Arthur Banks for anyone who hadn't noticed the first nine hundred indications of their weeklong extravaganza. The amount of love was stifling in this resort. Photos of the couple were set everywhere, in neat, crystalline frames surrounded by bouquets of fresh flowers. The family had spared no expense for this hurrah.

Humming with the pleasantry of adult, girlish conversation, Ginger stopped to inhale the scent of fat white roses blooming in a vase on the table in the hallway before her room. With a quick glance in either direction, Ginger plucked one of the roses out of the vase and continued toward her door, reminiscing about her reunion with Kate and Emily, and the meeting of Sydney and Lulu.

How exotic, Ginger thought with a wave of pleasure. (Lulu was from South Carolina!) These women with their big problems and fast-and-furious lifestyles. Kate, now the glamorous millionaire. Sydney, the struggling young single mother. Emily, the… Ginger hesitated, sighed. Emily, a shadow of her former self.

Try as she might, Ginger couldn't seem to remember college life without Emily. The two had been inseparable since they'd met at one of those stupid first-year orientation seminars. They'd sat next to each other in a class where every student was forced to make a candle with their school colors and talk about the major they'd chosen and what great things they were going to do with their lives.

While everyone else had taken the exercise seriously, Ginger had been unable to resist a snarky comment about this being the most expensive art class she'd ever taken in her life, thanks to the amount she was paying in tuition to build candles. Only one person in the room had laughed. Ginger had turned around and given a grateful smile to Emily, and after splitting a pizza for lunch, they'd become fast friends.

They had also managed to finagle their way out of the default roommates they'd been assigned to move in together in a tiny dorm room. Ginger then convinced Emily to flip around her class schedule so they'd be able to share homework duties. Emily had wanted to be a teacher from day one; Ginger was going the management route. While Emily had gone for a degree in English, Ginger had opted for the communications path. Ginger wondered if Emily had ever gotten her master's, if she'd ever gone on to teach.

With a huff, Ginger pictured the Emily from college and compared that girl to the version she'd seen this evening at the bar. Something told Ginger life hadn't gone exactly as Emily had planned—the master's degree, the husband, the children, maybe a dog. Then again, it wasn't as if Ginger had taken the time to actually engage Emily in conversation, so maybe Ginger had it all wrong. It'd been a long time since she'd considered Emily a friend, and it was really none of her business whether Emily was a thriving thirtysomething or not.

Maybe it's time, Ginger thought. Time to truly let that stubborn grudge go. Kate had made a good point: all had worked out as it was meant to be. And if Emily hadn't kissed Frank that one awful night, maybe Ginger would have taken Marcus Strait up on his offer of a second date. Maybe she would have staunchly continued to ignore Frank's phone calls in an effort to prove a point with her indifference until she'd pushed him away for good. Maybe she never would have gotten the courage to drop her stubborn facade and reunite with Frank, a union that had given her nearly two decades of love and three beautiful children.

Ginger reached her door and let those frightening thoughts slip away. A sense of warmth and comfort wrapped around her as she inserted the handy little key card into the lock. Her life wasn't so bad, after all. So what if she had to work long hours and sometimes got irritated by her free-spirited husband? Frank loved her, Ginger loved him, and their kids were healthy. She didn't have things as bad as she liked to think—and the little issue with Elsie could be solved by her and Frank teaming up together, like they always did.

A familiar rush of gratefulness settled over Ginger's chest as she paused in the entrance to her room, half expecting to find two little monkeys jumping on the beds and one teenage monkey sullenly staring at the screen of her phone. Frank wasn't exactly strict when it came to bedtimes, especially when Ginger wasn't home. It was as if a whole new set of rules descended on the house the second Ginger stepped out the door, and most of the time, she pretended not to notice.

However, tonight, Ginger was wrong. She was surprised to feel a sense of disappointment at the quiet room, her monkeys dozing, perfectly at peace without her. One lamp glowed over the bed she'd share with Frank like a porch light left on for a teenager rushing home to make curfew.

Beneath the glow sat Frank, perched halfway up in bed, one of Poppy's picture books spread open on his lap, his head bowed in sleep. Tom, similarly hunched over in a deep slumber, had likely pretended to be "so bored" by a little kid book, while simultaneously inching his way suspiciously close to Frank's lap—just close enough to see the images. Ginger's heart felt heavy, sopping with the weight of her love for them.

The biggest surprise of all, however, was Elsie. The teenager had changed into her tight black tank top (completely uncomfortable for sleeping, but *try* to tell her that and she'd bite your head off) and a pair of neon-pink shorts. She sat on the bed next to her father with Poppy in her lap, both sisters conked out in a deep sleep. Their mouths had cracked open in the same, drooling sort of way that indicated they were siblings even in unconsciousness.

Ginger covered her own mouth and hid a smile, thinking maybe Frank had been right this whole time. Maybe all they'd needed was a little vacation. They'd needed to blow up at one another and then come back down to earth and discuss. All was well! Her family was happy and together. Ginger didn't have to work for a full week. They were on vacation, and it wasn't killing them, despite Ginger's predictions of doom and gloom.

With a sigh of relief, she turned to grab her own pajamas from the suitcase. She'd wake Frank and cover the babies with blankets after she got changed and brushed her teeth and shut out the light. If she was quiet enough, they wouldn't even stir.

As Ginger headed to the bathroom, the loud blare of a cell phone interrupted the peacefulness of the room, threatening to wake the sleeping crew. Ginger leapt for it like a wild woman, silencing the phone and checking the damage it had done. One little snore from Elsie and a twitch from Tom, and then they were back to sleep.

Ginger glanced down, realizing the phone was Elsie's. Who was calling her daughter at this hour? Ginger didn't like to think of herself as one of those helicopter mothers, but when the phone landed in her lap, it was hard not to peek.

Not to mention, so long as Ginger and Frank paid for Elsie's phone, they had full access to everything that happened on it. Social media, texts, emails—whatever. If Elsie didn't want Ginger to see it, Elsie shouldn't be doing it on her phone. Freedom at fifteen was merely an illusion, and Ginger had explained that to her daughter in no uncertain terms.

Ginger flicked the screen open and found the name Phoebe Brimhall—one of Elsie's schoolmates—under the missed call log. With a frown, Ginger glanced up at her daughter. Elsie wasn't exactly chatty, but Ginger generally knew the sort of friends she kept, and she didn't run with Phoebe's crowd. Phoebe was a senior. She was the head cheerleader, the queen bee, the straight-A suck-up. What was she doing calling Elsie at this hour?

Ginger ducked out of the bedroom and slid into the bathroom, closing the door behind her and beginning to dig. Her snooping led to no immediate cause for alarm. There wasn't a history of calls from Phoebe, nor were there any text messages.

On a sudden impulse, Ginger pulled up the Facebook Messenger app and struck gold.

fifteen

Lulu had promised herself she wouldn't snoop. But it was dark, and Lulu hadn't turned on the light to search for the face cream she'd asked Pierce to pack in his bag. She'd been shuffling through his suitcase in the near-blackness while he slept deeply, and that was when she'd stumbled upon it. A second sheet of loose-leaf paper, this one with Lulu's name on it.

Her heart sank at the very sight of it. The letter obviously wasn't intended for her eyes—at least, not yet. Not like this. It had been tucked inside a little used pocket of his suitcase next to Pierce's work phone and shoved between the pages of his planner.

When her hand brushed against it, she'd recognized her name in familiar handwriting and figured it belonged as much to her as it did to her husband, so she'd pulled it out. Even though she was sure if they'd been at home, he'd have kept this little note in his office drawer. The locked drawer of secrets.

Lulu felt her heart begin to break as she unfolded it further. When she'd returned to the room after her evening at the bar, she'd been overwhelmed with feelings of love toward her husband. She'd found him sleeping in bed, one arm extended toward the empty space next to him as if waiting for Lulu's return. He was the one, the very last one, the only one for her. She'd been certain of it. And just when Lulu had finally succumbed to true love, it was slipping away through her fingers.

She knew that reading this private letter would do no good. It would be like tearing at a scab that had started to heal. The wound was already there, Lulu knew. It'd been hurting her for some time now, and her only regret was not broaching the subject with Pierce sooner. Maybe, if she'd caught it early, she could have nipped it in the bud. Now, it was much too late.

But she couldn't *not* look.

It was with a cautious hand that Lulu slipped the sheet against her body and strode toward the bathroom, feeling like a criminal. How depressing! Here she was like a teenager, crying over a diary in the restroom stall.

Retirement wasn't supposed to be like this. Life was supposed to get easier, empty of responsibility, of drama. Was it so hard for Lulu to grow old with her love and die? She didn't think that was asking for all that much.

Big, ugly tears welled in Lulu's eyes as she put the toilet seat down. She leaned over the letter addressed to her and, with a gulp, studied Pierce's careful, thoughtful handwriting.

Lulu,

I am trying to figure out what to say and how to say it. I'm up in our room desperate to explain things to you, but I know once I do…it will change everything. I know you sense something is wrong, and I owe you the truth, so that's what I'm going to give you. Here goes nothing.

I can promise you this: I never meant for things to happen this way, and all I can say is that I'm sorry. I wish there was a simpler way to tell you this, a way that wouldn't hurt so much, but I can't think of one. Maybe once I write it all down, I'll know the words I need to tell you when I look into your eyes.

I suppose I should start at the beginning. It all started back when

Lulu flipped the note over. She scoured the room. There was simply no more.

Pierce had run out of juice mid-confession, halfway through a letter that would have changed Lulu's life. And now, more than ever, she was desperate to know why.

Detective Ramone: Do you recognize this woman?

Ashley Pinkett: Oh, absolutely! Lulu Franc. My other friend Cindy was gushing about her when she and her husband walked into the resort. Ms. Franc had on that *fab* fur coat, so of course me and Cindy were admiring it all evening.

Detective Ramone: Did you see her any time after check-in?

Ashley Pinkett: Loads. She was hanging out at the bar with her friends all evening. And then once in the middle of the night.

Detective Ramone: How did Ms. Franc seem when she came down in the middle of the night?

Ashley Pinkett: It was interesting, actually. She seemed very calm, almost detached when I asked if she needed anything. She said she was getting some air. I felt like she was devastated about something but holding it together, and I only say that because it looked like she'd been crying.

Detective Ramone: Did she seem at all angry?

Ashley Pinkett: It was more like this cool determination. Like she knew exactly what she needed
to do and was prepared to do the damn thing.

Detective Ramone: Like murder?

Ashley Pinkett: I was thinking more like killing
a bottle of wine by herself. Speaking of wine,
Detective, I'm available for drinks tomorrow
evening, if you're interested…

sixteen

Emily's body thrummed on a high, on a magnificent cloud. She was weirdly wired, giddy almost, dangerously so, as she lay sprawled and naked on Henry's bed. She felt as if they were pushing each other, seeing how far they could go before bursting into flames.

"Thanks for letting me in," Emily said. "I'm glad I came by."

Henry gave a low, throaty cough. "I think we need to talk—"

"No." Emily pressed a finger to Henry's lips, then leaned over and drew his mouth to hers. "We don't. That wouldn't be good for either of us."

"But—"

"Look, Henry," Emily said, trying to sound breezy and unconcerned, as if she were truly just lounging on a luxurious bed, gloriously naked next to her lover. *Lover—what a fancy sort of word for a one-night stand*, Emily thought. This could still be called a one-night stand, right? It was within the twenty-four-hour window since they'd met, so technically, the term fit.

A sigh whooshed out of Emily as she rolled over, feeling something quite different from her normal pool of guilt and anger and loss. There'd been something about tonight—something about holding that baby, about feeling a man's touch again—that had her pulse pounding with optimism. A sort of optimism she hadn't felt in so long. In so, so long. Since she'd seen Julia's face, held her in her arms, knew the all-consuming, gut-bursting sensations of motherhood.

She glanced over to Henry, who was waiting with the quiet, reserved sort of patience she'd grown to expect from their brief, albeit intense, encounters. He rested there with his shirt off, tanned and gorgeous, those abs on display in stark contrast to the blindingly white sheets. He was the sort of stud who could have almost any woman he wanted with one flash of a smile.

Henry had mastered the rugged, mysterious sort of aura that told Emily he might be a con man, or a rancher, or a nerdy billionaire. There was a bit of a thrill for Emily in pretending he might be any (or all—a con man/rancher/billionaire?) of those things. If she found out he was an investment banker looking for a weekend fling and nothing exotic at all, she'd be gravely disappointed.

"You never finished your thought," Henry said, extending a hand toward Emily's face. He brushed back her hair with slightly rough fingers. Definitely not an investment banker. Rancher—maybe. "What were you saying?"

"I was thinking, you and I are probably somewhat alike," she said. "And I think we both know this isn't going anywhere; it's a little vacation romp to blow off steam. Let's not complicate it."

"We're alike?" Henry asked. "How do you figure?"

"You have secrets; I have secrets," Emily said. "I'm guessing yours aren't all sunshine and rainbows."

"You've been hurt," he said. "You flinch when I touch you."

"No, I don't. And this is exactly what I didn't want to do." Emily shifted away and turned her back to Henry. "Talking about reality doesn't make this romantic."

"What's the 4:00 a.m. hour for if not sharing secrets?" Henry leaned over, his breath a spicy spearmint. Emily figured she could live off the scent of him alone—a sort of woodsy crispness. "You don't know my last name. You don't ever have to see me again."

"You know my last name."

"I promise I won't chase after you."

Emily snorted. "You're a charmer."

"That's what you want me to say, isn't it?" Henry asked. "You're not married, are you?"

"No."

"In a bad relationship?"

Emily swallowed, her eyes stinging. "I'm alone. I plan on being that way for a long, long time. Forever."

"I understand secrets," he said, gruffly rolling away from her. "We don't have to discuss them."

Emily reached for him, pulled him close. She begged for his lips to touch hers just once more, to steal a kiss that had her heart thumping. Henry's arms suddenly felt like a small haven, where she could shout her secrets and they'd never echo back to hurt her. If anything, maybe it'd relieve the ache in Emily's chest that held her apart from the person she used to be.

"I can't—" Emily broke the kiss, gasping for breath. "I can't. He was awful, Henry. Horrible."

"Did you report him to the police?"

"No," Emily said, her chest constricting. "He would have killed me. He—There was a child involved." She hugged her stomach and crunched over herself, still feeling the ache that had destroyed her in a visceral way.

Henry shifted onto his elbows, but he didn't interrupt.

The sobs came freely as Emily rocked back and forth. "We had a child. A little girl, *Julia*. The doctors told me her death couldn't have been helped, couldn't have been stopped, that SIDS can happen to any baby, at any time, for no reason at all." Emily struggled to find her breath. "But I don't believe them. If only I'd left sooner, maybe things would have been different."

"It's not your fault. The doctors said so."

"I was..." Emily stopped crying suddenly. She sat up, picturing Daniel. Picturing the man she'd needed so desperately during college. The man she'd thought would give her everything, when all he'd given her was pain.

If it weren't for Ginger, maybe none of this would have happened. If Ginger hadn't broken their friendship because of one stupid mistake—Emily hadn't been thinking the night she'd kissed Frank! She had apologized a thousand times over, but no. Ginger had been able to forgive Frank, but she hadn't ever forgiven Emily. Her one transgression had sat on their record of friendship like a stubborn pencil mark, and the more she tried to erase it, the more permanent it became.

In her loneliness, Emily had fled to Daniel's bed, begging for him to take her back. They'd fallen into a whirlwind romance soon after. She'd been weak and tired, lonely and angry at the loss of her best friend. Daniel had seen something in her then, she realized. Something broken, and he'd capitalized on it with the prowess of a hunter finding its prey.

When Emily closed her eyes, she could still feel the slap of his hand against her cheek. She could see the blood spurt from her nose when he came home drunk and angry and sometimes armed. But if she hadn't gone back to Daniel, she wouldn't have had Julia. Emily remembered the times she'd stood over her baby's crib with the grinning stuffed animals nearby, singing softly, praying his mood would blow past. That he'd leave their daughter alone. That he'd focus on Emily instead.

"I was unconscious," Emily said evenly. She heard herself speaking, but it sounded hollow, as if someone else were retelling the story from the police report. "I don't remember exactly what happened. It was a blur, a nightmare. I woke to find my nose broken. I was lying in the bathtub. When I came to, the first thing I did was go to Julia's room to check on her, but…"

"I'm sorry," Henry said. His hand came to caress her cheek tenderly.

She struggled to find a breath, and when words weren't enough, she fell toward Henry with a ferocity that had them clawing at one another's clothes, a bit drunk, wildly angry, painfully aware of their dysfunctional partnership as they tore at each other until they both were gasping and spent.

"I'm going to shower," Emily said, shame creeping up the back of her neck. She crawled from the bed. "Don't follow me. I–I need to be alone."

Before Henry could respond, Emily crossed the room, forgetting to be self-conscious about her naked figure as moonlight pierced through the windows. He'd already seen her anyway—all of her—and he wouldn't be seeing her again.

Emily slammed the bathroom door behind her a little too hard, then cursed when she stepped on a duffel bag Henry must have left in the corner of the bathroom. Emily had surprised him when he'd opened the door earlier, so he must have been unpacking and forgotten it there.

"Fuck!" she snarled, holding her injured toe.

But when she leaned down to catch a glimpse of the offending object, her heart stopped.

A gun.

Henry Anonymous carried a gun in a duffel bag on a weekend retreat to a spa and resort.

Emily's tears stopped at once, and her survival mode kicked into high gear.

Maybe he was a cop, but she sincerely doubted that. He didn't have any other identification in his bag. Emily checked desperately for some sort of badge, but there wasn't so much as a gym card with Henry's name on it. Even if he was some sort of police officer, would he travel to a family event with a gun thrown carelessly in a duffel? It was possible, but...

Henry didn't feel like a cop.

So, why the hell did he have a gun?

Detective Ramone: You said you stole a gun from Henry's room.

Emily Brown: That *is* what I said. Good on you for listening.

Detective Ramone: Why did Henry have a gun in the first place?

Emily Brown: I wondered the same damn thing when I found it. But I have to say, I'm certainly glad it was there.

Detective Ramone: Did you steal it with the intent to shoot the victim?

Emily Brown: As a matter of fact, I didn't.

Detective Ramone: Then why did this man end up with a bullet in his chest?

seventeen

"Oh, hello, Lulu!" Kate straightened in surprise as the elevator doors opened to reveal a familiar face. "Is everything all right? It's late—I thought you'd gone to bed."

Kate was still reeling from the shock of her newly developed theory about Sydney and was slower to process Lulu's presence than normal. She'd been headed back to her room to begin her hangover prevention routine after her stop at the front desk to get Sydney pillows. Kate learned during the early days in her "big girl" job that even elegant happy hours led to very un-elegant mornings after if she didn't take control of the situation in advance.

Even in her dreariest of drunken nights, Kate took pride in her careful ritual: aspirin, face cream, half a gallon of water, herbal tea, and a hair mask. Call her obsessive, but while everyone at the office was showing up to work with bleary eyes and headaches after the Christmas party, Kate flounced in looking fresh as a daisy. It was particularly helpful to have such a firm routine on nights like this, when her mind was occupied by thoughts of second identities and resort rooms paid for in cash.

Lulu exhaled slowly. "I'm out to clear my head for a bit."

Kate flicked an impatient look at her watch. If she didn't get started soon, she'd be a mess tomorrow, and Kate did not want to be a mess the first time she ran into Max after their breakup. Not to try and win him back, but to flaunt what he was missing.

"Oh, Lulu," Kate said, instead of the terse excuse she'd prepared to use before slipping off to her own room. She made an effort to add sympathy into her words this time despite (*ticktock*) her routine being pushed back again. "Are you sure you're feeling okay?"

The woman looked older than before, almost elderly. Lulu dressed with elegant flashiness—brilliant rings, dazzling earrings, a stunning necklace—but now, she just looked tired. The makeup on her face had worn thin, and her shoulders drooped forward. She didn't seem to care.

"We can grab a glass of wine, perhaps?" Kate suggested, fighting the urge to look at her watch again. They'd already spent hours at the bar. What more could be said at this hour? "It might help to talk things over."

Kate's offer had come courtesy of the relationship books she'd read in hopes of better understanding the rest of the population. She wanted to associate with others on a normal, sympathetic level, but it just didn't come naturally to her. (Did people truly feel that many emotions *all the time?*) Sometimes, Kate had to manufacture sympathy for others. A sort of fake-it-till-you-make-it mentality.

The older woman looked up hopefully, but after a moment, she shook her head. A surge of guilt flooded through Kate. Surely her aspirin and beauty scrubs could wait half an hour to provide support to a…friend? Kate wasn't sure what constituted friendship, but it had sure felt like all five women had developed or redeveloped some sort of bond in the bar earlier in the evening.

"No, I don't want to take up your time," Lulu said. "It's late, and this isn't your problem. I'm going to read in the lobby for a bit and then head up to bed."

"Fine, but if you change your mind, I'm on the ninth floor, room 913. Knock if you want to have a drink on my balcony and talk—I'll be up for another hour at least."

"I appreciate that," Lulu said. "But I'll be fine. Have a good night, Kate."

"You too." And with that, Kate stepped into the elevator and punched the button twice before Lulu had time to wave goodbye.

As the elevator shot upward, Kate pondered her recent run-in with Lulu. In a way, Kate could see similarities between herself and the older woman, and she was startled to realize the very notion frightened her. Lulu was wonderful—it really was nothing to do with her personality. She was classy and wealthy, exquisite, a woman to be admired, without a doubt.

But what woman honestly wanted to turn seventy alone? Lulu hadn't said it outright, but she was obviously troubled by something this evening, and based on their earlier conversation, Kate could only imagine it had to do with her husband. If Pierce left her, Lulu would have no husband, no children, probably few family members to speak of. And while grace and charm and hefty inheritances had likely carried Lulu far in life, what did it matter now?

Kate reflected on her own life, on what had actually changed over the fifteen years since she'd last seen her college friends. Not Kate, that was for sure. Aside from an expanding taste for the luxurious and upgraded living quarters, wasn't Kate exactly where she'd been at twenty-five? Single, childless...alone.

The next decade promised to be drearier, if anything. At twenty-five, she'd been searching for success. Now, Kate had it—and more. She'd made partner already, and while she could collect more money, more clients, more fame (or infamy—was there really such a thing as a famous lawyer?), it was all incremental. For the first time, the thought felt exhausting to Kate. She'd been chasing money for ages. She'd caught it, bottled it, had it.

While Sydney (or whoever she was) longed for money to make her problems go away, Kate longed for problems money could fix. More money, more problems—so the saying went. *In a way, Sydney's issues are so simple*, Kate thought as the elevator dinged on the ninth floor. She stepped out and strode to her room, let herself in, and collapsed on the bed.

Sydney's problems were real, concrete. Not enough money? Find a job. Not enough food? Buy more. Yes, of course Kate realized things weren't *that simple*, but in a way, they were. They were primal needs that needed to be fulfilled with a clear path leading toward improvement.

But spreadsheets and answers had no place in Kate's inability to get pregnant. Doctors had no answers. They had all the tests and no answers. All the shots, all the medicines, and no solutions. They could transfer embryos into her body and force her to ovulate until she turned blue in the face, and yet, no amount of money could fix the broken pieces of Kate. Though she dreamed about it. Boy, did she dream. What she'd give for an easy, simple solution. She could see the advertisement now: *Is your uterus giving you problems? Fix it with three easy payments of $999.99!*

"Dammit, uterus!" Kate said to her stomach. "Why are you so *fucking* inhospitable?"

The outburst brought Kate back to reality. She dug in her bag for the recently purchased aspirin and Fiji water and sat on the bed. She popped a pill and guzzled water, barely feeling the weight of the medicine on her tongue.

The light of her computer blinked blue from the desk, and she figured she might as well give a quick scan of her emails—she'd told a few coworkers she'd log in and check things, but she'd gotten carried away at the bar and had ignored everything else.

She snapped her laptop open, but instead of clicking into the Outlook folder that would bring up standard drudgery from her colleagues, she found herself typing a newly familiar name. The letters spelling out Sydney Banks shone back from the Google bar on Kate's computer as her finger hovered over the Enter key.

Finally, she pressed it and sat back, waiting for the results to load. Or maybe nothing would show, Kate admitted to herself. If Sydney had given them all a fake name, there wouldn't be anything to find.

It took mere milliseconds for Google to return results, and it turned out, there were multiple women named Sydney Banks, along with one (very handsome) man down in Australia. It was quick work to sort through the first few listings that were decidedly not the woman Kate had met claiming to have the same name. However, when Kate clicked on the *Images* tab, the results were more surprising.

Indeed, there she was—Sydney Banks—smiling back from the blue-tinted screen. Admittedly, there weren't many photos of her, but there were enough. While Kate had her image splashed across newspaper articles and her law firm's website, she knew others preferred their privacy, and Sydney appeared to be one of them.

Kate clicked on the top link associated with Sydney's profile and was brought to a Facebook page. The settings were set to friends only, so while Kate couldn't see much, it was clearly Sydney's profile. A few more minutes of digging turned up an article about Sydney's high school cheerleading days and a short essay about her afternoon volunteering at a homeless shelter, and Kate was convinced Sydney Banks was exactly who she said she was.

So why had she paid in cash and used a fake name to register at the resort? The only solution was the one Kate had already come to, that Sydney was on the run—from somewhere, or someone. Kate suspected it had something to do with Lydia's father. Sydney had been vague about the details of her separation, and the rest of the women had been too polite to press. But could it extend further into dangerous territory than any of them had suspected?

Still mulling over the recent developments, Kate closed the Google browser and scanned through a few emails from her assistants and partners, letting the dull monotony of work take over. Kate went through the motions of responding to urgent emails and scanning the ones that weren't before thoughts of the evening returned, and Kate's click finger became itchy all over again.

Opening a new tab, Kate's fingers again hovered over the keys. She wasn't exactly sure what she was looking for yet. All Kate knew was she didn't want the next twenty years to look the same as the last ones. She couldn't bear if she ended up alone and childless. *Like Lulu, in a way*, Kate thought sadly. *Poor Lulu.*

Kate had never let herself Google the word *adoption* before. It had always felt like failure. Kate wasn't pleased to admit it, but she'd always thought of adoption much like she'd thought of donating money to charity: It was an excellent, wonderful thing. A truly magical way to connect parents wanting a child and a baby in need of a stable home. Kate loved it! Supported it. She went to an adoption event at least once a year in a jaw-dropping gown with an open checkbook.

But she'd never considered it for herself. Kate was used to getting her way, to having things work as they were supposed to. She'd never considered that she herself might be a lemon, and there was no manual to repair her.

Kate found her fingers pounding furiously at the keyboard as she dared to start thinking realistically about her future.

Adoption.

Surrogate.

Exhaling a deep breath, Kate felt an almost giddy sense of adventure. Maybe this was how things were meant to go. Maybe she was meant to take the road alone. A single mother, much like Sydney—except with money. And not on the run. And child care, and organic food, and… Okay, she wasn't like Sydney at all, except for the fact that they would both be going the road alone.

It wasn't as if Kate was greedy either. She knew the risks; she was thirty-eight and not getting any younger. She wasn't asking for triplets or a family of five like Ginger, just one tiny human for herself. Someone to hold and clothe and feed and love.

With a surge of adrenaline, Kate filled out a form on one of the websites requesting more information and a consultation. The little pop-up box informed her she'd receive a call during the next business day.

Kate wiped her hands (which had somehow begun to sweat) on the bedspread before standing. She was already picturing the meeting with the adoption agency: "Yes, I'll take one handsome man for the father, please! Intelligent—definitely intelligent. Maybe a professor? An astronaut? And the mother, how about a doctor?"

Yes, Kate thought with a smile. She didn't need Max at all.

Kate knew she was getting a little ahead of herself. She trembled with anticipation, which was ridiculous. She'd done no more than Google a website. But it was as if a path had opened before her, and if there was one thing Kate appreciated, it was a specific route and straightforward steps to solve her problems.

She was still buzzing with adrenaline as she moved to the bathroom and began her hangover routine. Letting the warmth of the rain shower wash over her, Kate's thoughts seesawed between surrogates and adoption and her ever-growing list of to-dos that'd begin once she returned to the city.

It was halfway through her routine that Kate noticed the beginnings of a queasy stomach, which she promptly ignored. A bad idea, seeing as she barely managed to step out of the shower before she reached the toilet, stuck her head over it, and relieved her stomach of its contents.

If only she'd started her hangover routine sooner.

eighteen

Lulu woke slowly.

Sunlight sprayed across the spacious, almost-penthouse resort room. Blue skies spanned for miles in the distance, stretching across the tops of palm trees and cacti and other desert-dwelling species. Lulu fluffed her pillow, sighing with the bliss of luxury comforts, of resort rooms created specifically to relax their guests and help them unwind from the bustle and stress of the real world.

Reaching a hand out beside her, she felt for Pierce's arm to signal she was awake; he'd be up already, reading the paper and waiting patiently for his wife to join the waking world.

Her arm touched nothing except bedsheets. Crisp, starched sheets and an additional fluffy, hypoallergenic pillow. And her husband's head wasn't on it. Flying into a sitting position, Lulu sucked in a deep breath as reality slowly descended on her like a heavy blanket around her shoulders.

Lulu glanced around the room she shared with Pierce, fighting a hint of disorientation. Usually, her husband waited beside her until she woke. Had he left the room? Gone on to breakfast without her?

Her eyes pricked with tears as the shower clicked on in the bathroom. She was ashamed at the relief that flooded her body to realize Pierce was still here. Even if he wouldn't be for long.

Shifting out of bed, Lulu wrapped herself in a fluffy, white robe, one with the resort's emblem embroidered onto it. She found an elegant little coffee arrangement waiting for her on a room service tray. One of the two cups had already been used, the last dregs of deep brown staining Pierce's cup.

Lulu helped herself to the other, selected one of those brown sugar cubes—the fancy kind in misshapen blobs with raw sugar imported from some Caribbean island—and dropped it into the delicate cup of black coffee. Steam spiraled upward as Lulu topped off her beverage with a dash of cream from an exquisite little milk jug, then picked up the minuscule rose-gold spoon to stir in the fixings.

Carefully raising her dainty cup, so thin it might crack from the breeze, Lulu made her way to the patio and let herself outside, easing onto one of the comfortable loungers adorned with a fresh towel.

As she leaned back, she felt the sun play hide-and-seek with the clouds on her face, and for once, she didn't worry about SPF or wrinkles or cancer. She closed her eyes and soaked it in and tried not to think at all.

But Lulu had never been very good at meditation, and as her eyes flicked open, she caught a glimpse of herself in the window's reflection. This morning, she was without makeup, without jewelry, without creams and lotions to help mask her age. Leaning closer to the glass pane, Lulu raised a hand to touch her cheek.

It was odd how the wrinkles outside didn't match the youth she felt inside. Some days, Lulu felt as giddy as a young girl. Then she'd catch a glimpse in the mirror and remember that actually, she was of the age to be a grandmother. It was a mismatch, and to Lulu, it seemed her inner self had never caught up with her aging body.

Lulu had never been particularly concerned by the number dictating her age. Her whole life, she'd had youth and beauty and charm on her side. Plus, she'd always chosen to marry older men. Not only did they tend to be more well off financially, but she enjoyed being the youngest in a pair.

However, Lulu was at the point in her life where men older than her were starting to die. But that wasn't the point. Lulu didn't *want* to look for someone else. She didn't want to search for love again, to go through the whole rigmarole of swapping life stories, meeting families, dreaming about future togetherness. She'd lost the will and the drive for it, quite possibly because she'd thought that portion of her life was over for good.

Love had never been so exhausting.

The ring of a phone startled Lulu from her reverie. She shuffled inside from the balcony and returned her coffee cup to the tray with a clink. She reached for the room phone and came to a halt when she realized the sound wasn't coming from the landline.

The ringtone was unfamiliar. Lulu glanced at her phone, but the screen hadn't lit with the sign of an incoming call. It wasn't the familiar chime of Pierce's ring, though Lulu glanced at his charger in the wall, which was empty. A prickle crept up the back of Lulu's neck as she spun around, listening for the direction of the sound.

Her feet pulled her toward Pierce's suitcase. She bent, unzipped it, and thumbed cautiously through his clothes. The sound was near, so near she was sure it was coming from his bag. Lulu cursed as she shuffled through her husband's familiar slacks and shirts, flipped through his pajamas and activewear, and poked through his socks. She pulled out his work phone, which she'd seen late last night, but the screen on it was empty and there were no missed calls.

The mysterious jingle continued to ring. It wasn't until Lulu discovered a tiny little zipper along the interior of his suitcase, hidden behind the bulk of Pierce's things, that she felt the vibration. With shaking fingers, Lulu tugged the pocket open and stuck her hand in, securing the slim mobile device and pulling it toward her, hesitant to look at the name.

In place of a full contact name was simply the letter *S*. Lulu's blood ran cold as everything clicked into place. Late night meetings, little black books with appointments designated by a single letter, notes referencing meetings Lulu hadn't been aware of... It was *her*.

Sensing the call was hovering on the verge of voicemail, Lulu reacted on impulse. Clicking the answer button, she held the phone to her ear and waited.

"Is that you, Pierce?" a female voice asked. "You were supposed to call me last night. I thought you said you'd be reachable, even though you'd be gone this week. Hello? Pierce?"

"Who is this?" Lulu asked, a strange gargle sounding in her throat. "And what do you want with my husband?"

Detective Ramone: Ms. Franc, I understand you spent time with Kate Cross last night at the resort bar.

Lulu Franc: You say that as if we had a wild affair. We had several drinks with a few friends.

Detective Ramone: Did you get a sense of whether Kate was harboring anger over her breakup with Maximillian Banks? Enough to kill a man?

Lulu Franc: What does that matter? I already told you, *I'm* responsible. I bonked that man over the head with a wine bottle and knocked him right out. This must be the third time I'm telling you the same thing.

Detective Ramone: That's funny, Ms. Franc. Because I have three other women with the exact same story. Four confessions, all women claiming to have acted alone, and one dead body—the math doesn't add up.

nineteen

After her discovery on Elsie's phone the previous evening, Ginger was relieved when breakfast with her family turned out to be a successful affair. She sat in the brightly lit seating area before a gargantuan buffet—the resort promised an impressive food selection, and according to Ginger's children, the resort had exceeded all their dreams.

It wasn't the relaxing, room-service fancy coffee she had envisioned for herself—lying on a glam lounge chair, wrapped in a fluffy resort robe, listening to nothing but the *whoosh* of the breeze and feeling drenched with sunlight—but at least her children were happy. And she couldn't afford to tip the busboys anyway, so that canceled room service.

Speaking of which, Ginger absolutely must remember to get to the petit fours before they were delivered for the evening. Otherwise, there would be all sorts of questions from her (suddenly perceptive) children about where the ones had gone from last night. Ginger couldn't help but think there was something to be said for the way her hotel back home did things—no room service, no petit fours, no problems.

Despite her daydreams, Ginger was thrown unceremoniously back into the breakfast chaos as a splatter of milk landed in her eye. She sighed and tuned in to her family's conversation.

Tom: "Dude, did you see the pasta for breakfast? And pizza—score!"

Poppy: "Mom, can I mix and match cereals? All of them? There's one, two, three… Did I say three? Four, five—I think thirty cereals!"

Frank: "Honey, did you see they have a coffee bar? Free lattes. This would cost six bucks at Starbucks. It's criminal!"

Even Elsie had managed to fill her plate with bits of this and that, primarily doughnuts with a touch of yogurt on the side for looks, and a banana she'd stick in her bag and never eat. A different day, Ginger would have demanded Tom eat fruit before pizza, and she would have insisted Poppy pick no more than two or three cereals. Then, she'd casually mention to Elsie that eating doughnuts for every meal was not acceptable. But this morning, Ginger didn't have the energy for it.

Ginger looked down at her double espresso and doughnut (she was stressed and it was vacation) and figured she couldn't exactly be preaching from a soapbox. She was still distracted from the messages she'd found on her daughter's phone. Even worse, she hated how her conversation with Elsie had ended.

"You okay, honey?" Frank asked, easing an arm around his wife. He looked pleased with himself as he shot a conspiratorial glance around the table. "You look tired. Little too much fun at ladies' night?"

"Something like that," Ginger said. She hadn't gotten him alone to discuss the messages, so she played along for the kids' sake. "Mommy's a little under the weather."

"Well, it's about time you had some fun." Frank hopped to his feet. "Come on, kids. Quick game of beach volleyball. Who is ready to get smoked by Dad?"

"You're not gonna smoke us." Tom leapt up, then scurried back to his plate and grabbed the last of his pizza with a skinny arm. "I'm so good, you won't even know what hit you."

"I want to play!" Poppy tried to hop up, but she elbowed the cereal and sloshed a mixture of Lucky Charms, Fruit Loops, Cheerios, and some chocolatey things onto the table in a sea of milk. "Oops."

"It's fine," Ginger said quietly, with eerie calmness. "I'll take care of this. You guys go with your dad, and I'll meet you out there soon."

"Right-o, kids! Poppy, what do you say to your mother?" Frank demanded with a stern expression. "You have to be more careful, sweetheart."

"Sorr-*ee*," Poppy wheedled. "Okay, Dad, can we go?"

"Elsie, can you wait here for a moment?" Ginger murmured. "I'd like to talk to you for a second. It's—not about what you think."

Elsie stood and glared at her mother. "No."

Ginger debated trying to stop her by pulling the mom card, but she'd already threatened her children enough this trip. She was tired. Exhausted. Someone needed to come up with a road map that navigated teenage years and sell it. She'd pay good money for that program.

Ginger had heard that teenagers came back around to being humans sooner or later, but Elsie was only fifteen. She had a lot of years to go, and Ginger suspected things would get worse before they got better. Not to mention the fact that Ginger had two more children who hadn't even started on the teenage journey yet. God help her.

As Ginger watched her eldest daughter trot along behind her father, she saw Elsie give the smallest flicker of a smile at something Frank said. Ginger's gut clenched with jealousy.

She worked damn hard to keep this family clothed and sheltered and fed. So did Frank, but somehow the kids were drawn to him like sunflowers to light. They tilted toward him, brightened whenever he was in the room. When Ginger walked into a room, her kids seemed to cower or clam up. Ginger wasn't scary, was she? She loved her children dearly. She'd die for them. Wasn't that clear? Where had that gotten lost in translation?

Fuming with the injustice of it all, Ginger mopped up the spilled cereal and cleared the trays from the table as a member of the resort staff came over and waved for her to stop.

"We'll take care of all that," the young man said with an exuberant smile. "Relax. You shouldn't be working on your vacation."

Ginger's hands shook, and she nearly burst into tears. "Thank you," she said, her voice catching in her throat. "Thank you so much."

As she made her way to the lobby, she found a woman in a tennis outfit was serving coconut water out of champagne glasses. Ginger accepted one gratefully before taking an unused corner of the lobby and sitting down with a sigh. She rolled her neck in slow circles and closed her eyes. She tried to count to ten and lost track at eight. She didn't know what to do with Elsie.

"How about that massage?" A crisp, efficient voice spoke from behind her, and Ginger recognized it as belonging to Kate. "You look very stressed out. I haven't seen you like this since finals week."

"I am." Ginger opened her eyes to find her impeccably dressed old roommate standing over her. Kate had no kids, no problems, Ginger couldn't help but think with a bit of bitterness. Instead, she had money to burn, an ex-boyfriend's credit card to tear through, and a week of relaxation at her fingertips. "You know how I mentioned I caught my daughter carrying condoms?"

"Yes," Kate said. She held a glass of coconut water in her hand and looked like she was heading to the French seaside in her huge, floppy hat and one-piece swimsuit. A sheer cover-up barely masked her beautiful figure. "I remember."

Ginger realized she'd been staring. "Sorry. You look so put together, and I feel like a frump. I can't believe we're the same age. You don't even wrinkle."

"Your daughter?"

"Oh, right," Ginger said. "Well, I came down hard on Elsie for it—or I tried to, but she won't listen to anything I say. I can't even get her alone in the same room as me. Then last night, I made things worse. I snooped on her phone, and I... Well, I won't bore you with the details."

Kate glanced at her fingernails and nodded, as if that was perfectly fine by her.

"But now I have a dilemma." Ginger shook her head. "If I tell Elsie I snooped on her phone, there's going to be a whole big blowout and the moral of this will be lost. I need her to know I love her and just want to keep her safe."

"Why don't I have a chat with her?"

"What?" Ginger gave a shake of her head, thinking she'd heard Kate wrong. "I'm sorry, but how would that help with anything?"

"I didn't lose my virginity until I was twenty-three," Kate said, her eyes landing crisply on Ginger. "I think I have you beat by... oh, eight years?"

Ginger's face heated. "It was with my husband!"

"I don't care when you gave it up; I just thought she might want to talk to someone who chose to wait," Kate said. "If you think she'd like to hear from me, that is. I might not have turned out perfect, but I did all right for myself in most categories."

"Oh, Elsie would adore you," Ginger said. "Are you kidding? But you don't owe me anything, Kate, and...I wouldn't even know how to bring it up."

"Let me handle it," Kate said. "I'll work it into the conversation without bringing you up. I can't promise it'll help, but it sure as hell can't hurt."

Ginger inclined her head toward Kate. "I suppose. I don't know. I have to talk to my husband first. He's busy with the kids, and he doesn't even know I checked Elsie's phone last night. I've really made a mess of the situation."

"We'll get it all sorted out," Kate said. "Go touch base with your husband and see if you can sneak away for a massage this afternoon. Trade him for...oh, I don't know. Sexual favors. You need a massage, Ginger. You look like the Incredible Hulk all hunched over like that."

"I know." Ginger expelled a breath. "Are you heading to the massage now?"

"No." Kate spoke sharply—too sharply—and quickly corrected herself. "I mean, I have something to take care of first. I'm going to find Sydney."

If Ginger wasn't mistaken, Kate left the slightest of pauses before Sydney's name. Ginger frowned. "Is everything okay?"

"I don't know," Kate said uneasily. "I'll find out soon enough. See you in a bit?"

Ginger rose, watching as Kate walked away without waiting for an answer. The woman was distracted, that much was for certain. Ginger found herself wondering what on earth had happened last night between Kate and Sydney. Because Kate was on a mission, and Ginger knew from experience—one didn't mess with Kate unless they were ready to pay the price.

———

Detective Ramone: Did you notice anything odd about a young woman called Sydney Banks during your stay?

Ginger Adler: I don't think so. We spent all evening together on the night of our arrival, and she sort of reminded me of myself a bit. You know, a young, struggling mother. How I was with Elsie back in the day. What would you have done about the condoms, Detective?

Detective Ramone: So you didn't notice anything off about Sydney?

Ginger Adler: No, not really. There was something weird between Kate and Sydney the morning of the seventeenth. But they must have worked out their issues, because Sydney was at the massage, and Kate didn't seem to be acting weird anymore.

Detective Ramone: What if I told you there's nobody at the resort by the name of Sydney Banks?

Ginger Adler: That's ridiculous. I met her.

Detective Ramone: Either the woman known as Sydney Banks gave a false name to resort registration, or she gave everyone else a fake name so that she could fit in with the wedding party.

Ginger Adler: Well, which was it?

Detective Ramone: You're telling me you don't know?

Ginger Adler: I met a woman named Sydney Banks with a daughter named Lydia. Why would I lie to you?

Detective Ramone: That's what I'm trying to find out, Mrs. Adler. Because from where I'm sitting, you're all lying.

twenty

A knock on the door startled Emily awake.

    She sat up in bed, cautiously letting her mind place her at Serenity Spa & Resort as she glanced around and took in the resort surroundings. At the second knock, she got a sinking feeling in her gut. She really, really wanted that to be maid service. She knew it wasn't.

Slipping into a plush robe, Emily gave a resigned sigh before padding over to the peephole and taking a look through. With an even bigger sigh, she pulled the door open. "What are you doing here?"

"Good morning," Henry said, leaning against the door. "You left rather quickly last night."

Emily crossed her arms. "We're having a fling, Henry. You're not very good at flinging."

"I thought I'd check on you." Henry gave a crooked smile, looking uneasy as he spoke, as if this were the limit to his sentimentality. "Like I said, you left in a rush."

After Emily had found the gun last night, she'd calmed her racing heart and talked herself out of a full-on panic attack. This was America. Plenty of people had guns, and enjoyed guns for sport, and kept guns for God only knew what purpose—safety? Henry might be an enthusiast who wanted to be armed in case of an intruder. Or he could have someone after him. Or he could be after someone himself. It was impossible to know.

"I didn't mean anything by it," she said. "I took a shower, and when I got out, you were sleeping. I figured I'd just slip on back to my room."

"Uh-huh."

"What?"

"I wasn't sleeping." Henry took a step closer to her, the motion intimidating, bordering on dangerous. "I watched you tiptoe out of the room like your ass was on fire. Did I do something? Say something? You didn't even give a backward glance."

"You're not supposed to ask these questions. You're supposed to be anonymous!"

Henry watched her. "It wasn't hard to Google you, you know. The obituary. The father. His name was Daniel, wasn't it?"

Emily froze. She hadn't allowed herself to say his name since their relationship ended rather abruptly. And violently. Clearing her throat, she gave a stiff shake of her head. "You don't know anything about what happened. I want you to leave."

"Fine." Henry raised his hands. "I'll leave."

"Now." Emily's entire body felt as if it'd been submerged in ice water. She was stiff all over, aching, and exhausted.

She'd need to get Sharleen on the phone again. Her head was spinning, and the drinking had only made things worse. She was sinking into a dirty, insipid pool of quicksand that had the potential to turn toxic...fast.

"It's true you don't know my name, and it's true I met you yesterday," Henry said, keeping his distance and his hands raised in a nonthreatening gesture. "But I figure you told me your darkest secrets last night. Maybe I know you better than your closest friends."

Emily's jaw set in a firm line, horror building in her gut, racing through her body. It was unfair, cruel even, how Daniel had destroyed her ability to have even a thoughtless fling without it turning twisted. "I found your gun last night. That's why I left. Who the hell are you, Henry?"

Henry's face went blank. "I think you're right. This is where we part ways."

"Good." Emily glared at him. "We can consider this fling, flung."

Emily watched as Henry turned and stalked away, stiff, tall, broad. Even if a part of Emily was upset to see him go, it was for the best. Who did he think he was anyway? Robin Hood? He shouldn't be digging up the past when it wasn't his to dig. Emily didn't want to know what Daniel was up to now—or ever. He was someone else's problem. She'd escaped, and she'd paid a bitingly steep price for her freedom.

She slammed the door behind her and picked up the phone.

"Sharleen," she said when the woman on the other end answered. "I need help."

twenty-one

Kate left Ginger in the lobby to ponder high-school problems while she went to tackle adult ones. Kate made an effort to keep her head held extra high this morning… because something was most definitely off. Despite her (belated) full beauty ritual the night before, she'd experienced a hangover this morning. Full-on queasy stomach and bleary eyes and shaky limbs.

Kate didn't normally get hangovers, so this was quite troubling. She wore huge sunglasses and a swimsuit with a cover-up to hide her frustration. Had she really had that much to drink? She remembered feeling bubbly and energized last night, not horribly drunk. There were no massive blank spots in her memory, just a touch of fuzziness around the edges. All things considered, she remembered having a wonderful time.

So why the hell was she so shaky? Was this what heartbreak felt like? Maybe it was finally hitting her that Max had left. Except Kate hadn't even thought about Max beyond using his credit card. He almost felt like a slightly unpleasant dream she'd had a while back.

She didn't buy a gallon of ice cream. She didn't feel like crying. She didn't feel like doing any of the traditional heartbreak rituals. Mostly, she wanted to get a massage, lay out in the sun, and find out who the hell Sydney Banks really was. Mourning Max fell so far down her to-do list that it didn't even make the first page. And if she really wanted, she could always book a first-class ticket home on Max's card whenever she was ready to leave if a week's stay felt too long. Sydney was right in one regard: having money made some things a lot easier.

Speaking of money, Whitney's wedding really was shaping up to be a ghastly, opulent event, as Kate was forced to halt mid-lobby to allow for a wreath of white roses to be wheeled past her. She took two more steps, then paused as Miranda Rosales—voted best wedding coordinator for *Bridal Digest* four years running—scurried past, shouting for someone to wash their hands before touching the veil.

Kate wondered if all this hoopla would be worth it. If all the money—hundreds of thousands, easily—would be well spent. Would it honestly cement Whitney's union with Arthur Banks for life?

Having never been married, Kate probably couldn't judge, but even to her—this seemed a bit obsessive. Kate had texted Whitney upon landing to schedule time for a drink, just the two of them for old times' sake, and Whitney had texted her back an image of her schedule. She hadn't even had time to personalize the text. It'd been an image that listed back-to-back activities in the salon and spa.

Not that Kate was particularly offended. She even wondered if this was karma's sneaky little way of getting back at her for the way she'd treated Whitney throughout college. They'd been friends, sure, and had plenty of great memories together, but Kate had always enjoyed being the rich one. The bossy one. The admired one. Kate had always been one step ahead of Whitney, and they'd both known it on some level.

Pulling up the day-old text on her phone, Kate bit her lip as she glanced over it. She had to wonder if this was Whitney's passive-aggressive way of telling her that the tides had officially shifted. It seemed Whitney was out to prove once and for all that she had obtained everything Kate had, and more. While Kate might have a leg up on the career path, Whitney would have a husband by the time the weekend was over. And soon after, Kate imagined, Whitney and Arthur would be adding children to the mix.

Kate sighed, flipped the message off her screen. Maybe she was reading too much into things. Whitney was probably just busy, not diabolical. What did it say about Kate that she was interpreting everything through such a twisted lens?

With a jolt, she remembered her first year exchanging Christmas presents with Whitney at school. Whitney had somehow scrounged up the money from her depressing little barista job to splurge on a two-for-one pack of tanning sessions at the local salon. To go along with it, she'd added matching sets of press-on, French-tipped fake nails from the pharmacy down the block.

The look on Whitney's face when she'd produced the gift for Kate—explaining it was the ultimate girls' pampering package—had been so thoroughly joyous that Kate had felt a moment's hesitation about the present she'd gotten for Whitney. Kate reluctantly pulled out the envelope and handed it to her roommate; it wasn't as if she could junk the two round-trip tickets she'd purchased that would fly the girls to her parents' Hawaiian timeshare.

Kate remembered Whitney's thrilled squeal and astounded expression. With a hint of remorse, she wondered if today's Whitney had outgrown such unfiltered outbursts of excitement. Kate highly doubted Whitney would *squeal* in front of Miranda Rosales, and a part of her felt slightly depressed at the thought.

Maybe Kate had liked showing Whitney the ropes, the finer things in life. And in turn, Whitney had made their outings gleefully fun. Once, Kate had swiped a pair of tickets to a black-tie charity dinner without her parents' knowledge, and the girls had snuck into the grand event wearing swishy dresses and sparkling tiaras until, giggling quite profusely on pilfered champagne, they were shown the door by a less than amused security guard.

To her surprise, Kate's face split into a grin from her brief trip down memory lane. It was the first time during the trip that she could truly say she'd been smiling for no particular reason. The thought made her somewhat itchy, uncomfortable.

She shifted her weight from one foot to the next as she was

offered yet another glass of coconut water and declined it with a distracted wave of her hand. She was too busy dealing with a pulsing question that'd hit her hard: What if she had it all wrong?

What if, this whole time, Kate had thought Whitney had been the one needing her—her guidance, her money, her connections—when really, it was the other way around? What if Kate had needed Whitney—her innocence, her devoted friendship, her willingness to accept Kate exactly as she was, flaws and all? What if Kate had needed Whitney more than Whitney had ever needed Kate?

Her hand trembled at the thought. She looked around for an open lobby chair where she could sit and think, and shoo away the attentive busboys giving her concerned looks.

Kate's parents had always been too busy for frivolities and silliness and spending time with their daughter. The most attention Kate had gotten from them during college was when she'd purchased those first-class tickets to Hawaii without their permission. She'd gotten a mere slap on the wrist before her credit limit was lowered so she didn't overspend again.

Whitney, however, with her shoestring budget and wealth of creativity, had given Kate some of the best presents she'd ever received. Customized photo books of their friendships. Tickets to a free and utterly ridiculous school play that was the worst they'd ever seen but somehow had stuck in Kate's memories as one of her favorites. The fake nails, which had prompted an evening's worth of wine drinking and movie watching by the light of their sorry little Christmas tree.

Thinking back, Kate realized it had always been Whitney who'd made up silly games in the library to get the four of them through late-night studying. It was Whitney, too, who'd smuggled in rolls of raw cookie dough to nibble on during finals week. It was even Whitney who had introduced Kate to Max, and while it'd taken them years to actually get together in a romantic way, it was only because of her friendship with Whitney that it had happened at all.

Kate was stunned to realize the impact Whitney had made on her life. It left her a bit shaky as she looked around and took in the stunning tabletop centerpieces currently being wheeled in amid shouts and a flurry of activity. Kate had to wonder if some of this was her doing. If she'd guided Whitney into thinking that excess, money, riches, was the best way. The only way to success. As Kate considered the text she'd received from Whitney in a new light, she found herself wondering if it was Whitney who had changed... or if it was Kate.

There was no room in the bride's "Wedding Week Countdown by Miranda Rosales" for such trivial things as a friendly chat— Whitney's time would be taken up getting plucked and pampered, waxed and dyed, suctioned and stapled, and God only knew what else. Kate thought back to Ginger and Frank's ceremony—they'd gotten married in a freaking barn, and they were still going strong some fifteen years later. Kate had never really pictured Whitney having a wedding where she was too busy to talk to old friends, and she hoped, for Whitney's sake, this was truly the right choice for her.

Disoriented enough for one morning, Kate released her thoughts of Whitney—content to imagine her friend exactly the way she'd been in college—and eased up from her chair. She made her way to the glossy front door and pressed it open, feeling the heat surround her like a familiar blanket as she stepped outside. Only a few steps later, and Kate was doused in a light layer of perspiration, tugging the cover-up away from her body where it stuck to her skin.

Kate hated sweating. While the desert heat was certainly scorching, Kate had good pores. She didn't sweat like an animal after two seconds outside. What the hell had she had to drink last night? She felt like she was dying, and death was *not* a good look on Kate.

Even the sight of the carefully numbered umbrellas lined in blue didn't ease Kate's discomfort. She normally loved this kind of exclusive lounge area with the blue-capped, white-shoe-wearing handsome young men rushing around to supply her with fluffy towels, sunscreen, coconut oils, aloe, and iced lemon water. She adored the fact that loud children were reprimanded while she sprawled out to sunbathe, and families who hadn't forked over the money at exclusive resorts were neatly ushered past the white, sandy path for "Members Only." Kate was a fan of "Members Only."

Instead of stretching her legs on a lounger as she longed to do, Kate turned her Tory Burch sandals toward the juice bar she'd meant to visit the previous evening. She found it easily and put in an order for a Detox Delight. Kate wasn't sure exactly what was in such a beverage, but she knew she could use both *detox* and *delight* in large doses.

Once the barista handed over a huge, frosted glass with an extra-long, curly straw, Kate headed for the resort doors again, only to find herself coming to a stop outside the market she'd found with Sydney the night before. Eyeing the little onesie she'd purchased for Lydia, Kate hesitated a moment before stepping inside. It didn't take long for her to get sucked over to an entire table of baby supplies: cute sweaters, diapers, miniature swimsuits, and dolls.

"Isn't that adorable?" The middle-aged shopkeeper came over, a different woman from the previous night, and smiled. "Do you have a little one?"

Kate cleared her throat. "No, but I'm—looking for a friend."

"I adore those little swimsuits. Look at these ruffles." The woman held a one-piece against her chest. "I have three boys. What I'd give for one girl. I wouldn't trade the boys for anything, of course. But the ruffles!"

"I'll take it," Kate said quickly. "And some of the diapers, and whatever else you think might be helpful to a new mother."

"Oh, well, this store is mostly trinkets and souvenirs and basic food and beverage items, but—"

"Diapers, the suit, a few onesies," Kate instructed briskly. "The baby is about four months old."

"Of course." The clerk bustled around, adding things to a large bag. "How much—"

"Money isn't an issue," Kate said with a prim smile. "Go wild."

The woman smiled back, a bit of confusion scrawled across her face, but she obliged. "Here we are," she said finally. "I've included a variety of things that should tide her over for quite a bit. Plenty of wet wipes—can never get enough of those!—diapers, onesies—also can never get enough—and I varied the sizes so she can wear some now and some later."

"Perfect."

"Your total will be"—the woman's voice dropped almost in embarrassment—"with tax…"

"Doesn't matter. You can put it on the room of Maximillian Banks."

"Oh, you're here for the wedding." The woman looked quite relieved. "The Banks family. It's a big to-do around here!"

"So I hear," Kate said with a forced smile. "Have a nice day."

Kate had only meant to buy one tiny gift as an excuse to swing by and talk to Sydney, but she'd gone a little wild. *Not a huge deal*, Kate thought as she turned her sandals toward the lobby. If Sydney didn't like the items, she could return them for cash and use the money. Max would be claiming it as an expense on his taxes anyway, so at least some good would come out of it.

She brought herself before room 114 and raised a hand to knock. It took a few rounds of rapping her knuckles against the wood before Sydney's hurried voice called back, "One second, please!"

Kate stepped back and waited patiently. When Sydney pulled the door open, she had the rushed, breathless look of someone who'd been running around seconds before and was trying for composure. She adjusted the strap of her plain tank top, and Kate wondered if she'd been feeding Lydia.

"Good morning." Sydney greeted Kate with a bright, slightly confused grin. "You look all ready for the pool. Maybe we'll join you. Did you want to come inside? Lydia is just fussing on the blanket."

"I grabbed a few things for you this morning," Kate said, holding the bag out in a proffered gesture. "Please don't turn it down. I saw the most perfect little bathing suit, and then the woman at the shop and I went a little overboard gathering some things for Lydia. It's not anything but a gift for her, so please don't give me trouble for it."

"Oh, um…" Sydney watched the bag as if it were infected. "Is everything all right? You seem anxious."

"Who the hell are you?" Kate watched Sydney carefully, so she saw the exact moment the young mother's face dropped. It sort of slid downward, like chocolate sitting too long in the sun, drooping and sad.

"I think you should come in," Sydney said, scanning the hallway, appearing anxious herself.

Kate glanced behind her, saw the hallway was empty, and took a step inside the room. "Who are you and what, or who, are you running from?"

"My name is Sydney Banks," she said, easing the door shut behind Kate. "I didn't lie to you."

"I figured. Google told me that much, though I suppose a good hacker could have faked your history," Kate said. "But you paid for your room in cash under a different name."

"I promise you, I am who I say I am." Sydney turned without hesitation and reached for her purse. "I have something to show you that might count as proof. Here—does this help?"

Kate leaned forward as Sydney held out a license from the state of Minnesota. The name and picture matched the Sydney Banks standing before her. "It could be a fake."

"I thought you might say that," she said. "But it's fine. I have additional proof."

Kate nodded, trying not to give anything away from her expression. She set the bag of gifts on the bed and spared a moment to glance at the gurgling baby snuggled between the extra pillows Kate imagined had arrived sometime the previous night.

"Thank you," Sydney said in a hushed voice. "You didn't need to do that—the pillows, the gifts—but we appreciate it. I do, for Lydia."

"If you don't like whatever's in there, return it for cash to the market," Kate said. "I don't care."

"Am I that obvious?" Sydney turned a chastised smile up at Kate. "It wouldn't hurt for us to have some extra gas money."

"Gas money?" Kate's eyebrows cinched together. She didn't even own a car in New York. She hadn't driven for many years. "Where are you going?"

"We drove here," Sydney said. "It was safer."

"Safer," Kate parroted.

She watched as Sydney crept across the dark space. After Kate's near penthouse of a room, this basic setup felt almost claustrophobic.

"I thought your aunt booked your resort room," Kate ventured while Sydney dug through a ragged, old knapsack. "Why wouldn't she book it under your name?"

"She transferred the money to my account," Sydney said, turning back with a photo book held to her chest. Her face was red, either from embarrassment or from the effort of digging it out. "I requested we do things that way. I told her I needed to check my schedule and be flexible with arrangements."

"But you didn't."

"I didn't want to be easily found," Sydney said. "Just in case."

"Your last name is Banks," Kate said. "Wouldn't that be your husband's last name? Is this his family gathering?"

"I kept my maiden name when I married."

"So Arthur Banks *is* your cousin, then. Are you close with your family?"

"My parents have been dead for some time. My aunt, Arthur's mother, helped out when they passed away, but I was almost an adult at that point, so I did most of it on my own," she said. "I don't really keep in touch with my extended family. I'm sure a few people are surprised to see me here with a baby at all, but that's their problem, not mine."

"Sydney," Kate said, shaking her head. "What happened to you?"

"I married a man thinking it was love," Sydney said. "It was love, actually. I still love him. He loves me; I know he does. He was older than me, much older, and sexy. He had money."

"You're running from your husband," Kate surmised. "What did he do? Why didn't you report him if things got so bad?"

"We got married and pregnant really fast," Sydney said. "I loved him. He's charming and gorgeous to look at. He had money and a stable job, and he made all sorts of promises. I'd never have to work! I could stay home with the children! He'd take care of me!"

"Until he hit you."

"Stop!" Sydney said, then glanced at the baby and lowered her voice. "Sorry. It's been a few weeks since I left him, and he's looking for us. We're running out of funds, and I'm running out of places to hide. Lydia and I have been camping out in motels. It probably wasn't smart of me to come here, to a family event, but I couldn't pass up a week of paid lodgings. It's what was best for Lydia. Even if my husband does think to check here, there's no one registered by my name at this resort—and he'll know I can't afford to put myself and the baby up here for long."

Kate felt a surge of outrage on Sydney's behalf. "Have you gone to the police?"

"He said he'd kill me and take Lydia," she said. "I know that's what he's planning to do anyway, but if I went to the police, it would only slow me down. I'm safer on my own."

"You can't keep living like this! This wedding was in the paper. It won't be hard for him to track you to the resort."

"He wouldn't dare come here. I'm surrounded by family."

"Family you don't talk to on a regular basis," Kate pointed out.

When Sydney didn't respond, she gestured toward the album in her arms. "What's in the book?"

"A record of my so-called accidents. I made specific notes below each of the photos, documenting how the injuries really occurred. In case you didn't believe me," Sydney said, "this is sort of my insurance policy. Evidence of abuse in case the police ever catch up to me. To him. To us. Look, I know you think I'm stupid, but I'm not. I know I was being abused. I know what he was doing is wrong, but I'm trying to do what's best for me and my baby."

"Let me see," Kate demanded, gesturing toward the book. "I'm a lawyer, you know. There are systems in place to help women in your position. I went to school and interned in Minnesota, and if you do actually live there, I can set you up with some great contacts to help you get an order of protection. The Minnesota Coalition for Battered—"

"I don't want help!" Sydney interrupted, panicked. "I'm just explaining myself so you don't get suspicious and rat me out to the resort. We can't afford it."

Sydney forfeited the book to Kate's outstretched hands, then turned to the bed, where Lydia squirmed in her little nook. Sydney fussed over her baby while Kate took the album and rested it on the resort's built-in desk.

Kate opened the first page while Sydney hummed lazily in the background to her restless daughter. It seemed wrong for Kate to leaf through evidence of Sydney's abuse while a lullaby floated over to her, a soundtrack to the pictures that showed bruises in the shape of fingermarks and cuts from what Sydney had claimed were accidents.

As Kate flipped from one page to the next, Sydney hummed louder, giving Kate a buzzing in her ears that made her uncomfortable and queasy. Image after image. Most of them close-ups of a woman's body. A burned shoulder, a cut lip, a bruised tummy. None of them showed Sydney's face. Probably, so if the book fell into the wrong hands, she couldn't be identified.

"You dated for six months," Kate said, making an effort not to vomit. Her damn queasy stomach. "Then you got married."

"Yes, and pregnant within the month," Sydney said. "It was a whirlwind."

"The first time he came after you…"

"I was probably pregnant but didn't know it yet. We were already married," she said. "It wasn't too bad that time. He'd… well, he'd had a bit to drink and was angry about something. I don't remember what. Probably a dish in the wrong place, or the lights. I used to leave the lights on when I left a room, and it drove him nuts."

Kate cleared her throat, biting back her vile comments. She flipped another page. "This went on," she said, hoarse, "through your pregnancy?"

"Not horribly," she said. "But yes, enough for me to be concerned. He promised me he'd stop. I thought maybe when the baby arrived, it would shock him into realizing there was something else to live for. Someone else to let me live for," she corrected. "He asked me to quit working. I thought it was sweet at first, but in retrospect, it made it harder for me to leave. He probably knew that all along."

"But you managed to tuck money away before you quit?"

Sydney nodded. "I would have left him sooner, but I needed the insurance for my pregnancy. He did have a good job, and he didn't let me go without. And whenever I had a trip to the hospital, he always bought me something nice after. He was very apologetic."

"He shouldn't have had to be," Kate said with poison on her lips. "'Here, honey, I sent you to the hospital. Have a silver watch.'"

Sydney's eyes flashed in frustration. "He did love me. He still loves me. He just doesn't know how to manage it."

"It doesn't seem like he's learning, and he will kill you before he does," Kate said. She stood. "I need to use your bathroom. I'm going to be sick."

Kate left the page open as she stood and strode across the resort room, falling to her knees before the toilet. As she relieved every last bit of the contents in her stomach, she swore to herself she was never drinking again.

But Kate knew that wasn't the real issue. The real issue wasn't the champagne, or Sydney's justification for her husband's horrendous actions, or even the fact that that sweet, innocent baby Lydia might have been affected if Sydney hadn't left when she did. It was the photograph on the page of the album that showed a woman from the neck down, thin-limbed and gawky, her belly swollen with pregnancy, with bruises up and down her thighs.

A carefully written line across the bottom read:

February 2, 2018. Eight months pregnant.

Went to the hospital for "injuries" because I incorrectly loaded the dishwasher.

Dropped all charges because he threatened to kill me and the baby if I didn't stay.

Kate pulled herself off the floor, feeling a dry sort of primal urge to find the man who'd done this to a young mother and strangle him herself. She felt a surge of rage that the law hadn't protected this woman or kept her and her child safe. With that ugly, festering feeling in her stomach, she wiped a sleeve across her mouth and splashed water on her face.

"You can't keep running from him forever," Kate said, stepping out into the room. She noticed Sydney had closed the book, and her face had turned ashen. "I'd like to help you if you'll let me."

"I'm sorry," Sydney said with a shaky tremble of her lip. "But it's far too late to help me."

Detective Ramone: Let me get this straight: Four women all book massages at the same time—all

paid for by you. Then, the same four women all
confess to killing one man, each of them acting
on their own authority. You expect me to believe
that's a coincidence?

Kate Cross: I met new friends, reconvened with
some old ones, and paid for their massages. So
what? I was racking up my ex-boyfriend's room
bill. If you don't have anything new, can we wrap
this up? It's after midnight, and we've been at
this for hours.

Detective Ramone: Not so fast, Ms. Cross. One of
you ladies doesn't have your story straight.

Kate Cross: Oh?

Detective Ramone: Three of you have told me that
you killed a man by swinging a wine bottle at his
head. One of you confessed to shooting him. Who
should I believe?

Kate Cross: Don't be ridiculous. Nobody was shot.

Detective Ramone: I can assure you, a man was
shot this evening.

twenty-two

Emily did a double take as she stepped onto the sandy path, huge sunglasses masking her bloodshot eyes, and caught a glimpse of a mini Ginger strolling down the path. Despite the haze of the previous evening, Emily recalled Ginger's daughter was named Elsie. *Elsie Adler*, she thought, watching the gangly teenager roll her eyes at her father as he tossed a football miles over her head.

Flinging a beach towel over her shoulder, Emily inhaled a slurp of some nasty kale smoothie that she'd had to infuse with vodka from the minibar. She tried to sort through the feelings in her stomach, but they were mixed with last night's hangover and this morning's alcohol, and she didn't like what she was finding. Not only were her emotions a mess, but so were her thoughts. She couldn't shake the mantra that'd begun to play on repeat.

Julia should be here too.

Her daughter should be gossiping about boys with Elsie, or tanning her awkward teenage limbs in the sunlight, or snarking to her mother about being overly watchful and annoying and uncool. Emily wouldn't complain about Julia like Ginger did about Elsie; she'd bask in the joy of being a mother.

"I'm not getting that," Elsie snapped across the sand. "I'm going to find Mom."

"Heya, Emily!" Frank Adler waved over his children's heads. "I haven't said hello to you yet."

Emily shoved her glasses higher on her nose and sucked down

the rest of the smoothie to fortify her confidence. It was hard to know how to feel about Frank. Emily wanted to hate him for his part in the destruction of her friendship with Ginger, but it wasn't entirely his fault. The blame went equally to them both. Plus, Frank was just too damn hard to hate with his huge heart and huger smile.

"Hi, Frank." Emily moved an inch closer. It was all the friendliness she could muster on only two shots of vodka. "You've got quite the clan out here."

"They're the best." Frank paused. "Tom, go get the football before it's lost at sea. Elsie, come meet your mom's old pal."

Before Emily could wave off the herd of Adlers, Frank swooped down to gather a giggling little girl in his arms. He tossed her over his shoulder before striding across the sand and offering Emily a handshake while his youngest daughter swung like a pendulum behind his back, laughing in a high-pitched wail that hurt Emily's hungover ears.

Emily returned the shake, watching a completely unfazed Frank carry on a conversation with a child hanging like a sack of potatoes behind him. Somehow, Emily wasn't surprised. Both she and Ginger had known Frank would slip into fatherhood like he would a used baseball glove. Frank was made to be a dad.

"You knew my mom when she was younger?" Elsie hovered a safe distance from her father and looked curiously at Emily. "My mom had friends?"

"Your mom was a firecracker," Frank said with a whistle. "She still is. Only we make her act like the responsible one. Ain't that right, Poppy?"

The littlest one let out another shriek as Frank tickled her stomach. In the next second, a football sailed across the sandy pitch and landed an inch from Emily's big toe. A few degrees north, and it would have knocked the empty glass right out of Emily's hand.

"Tom, come on, bud. We talked about that," Frank yelled. "Don't throw balls around the guests if you can't aim."

"It's fine," Emily lied. "Boys will be boys."

Frank gave a happy nod and completely missed all telling signs of Emily's dismay. He tossed Poppy in the air before setting her down, then challenged her in a race to catch up with Tom. Only Elsie lingered behind, pretending to watch her siblings and father, but really casting glances at Emily whenever she thought it was safe.

The interest was mutual. From the moment Elsie had sidled over, Emily had been hard-pressed to turn her gaze from Elsie's face. She truly did look like Ginger, minus the graying hair and stress lines on her forehead. Emily's heart lurched, picturing a younger version of herself standing there on the beach. She wondered if Julia and Elsie would have been fast friends like she and Ginger had been a long time ago.

"Do they always have that much energy?" Emily's voice cracked. She wasn't feeling well and knew she was staring too much at Elsie. Emily's phone call with Sharleen hadn't gone all that well, hence the vodka in her breakfast smoothie.

Elsie winced. "It's awful, isn't it?"

Emily offered a smile. "I didn't want to say anything."

"Did you actually like my mom back in college?"

"Yes, I did," Emily said. "We were good friends for quite some time."

"But you're not friends anymore."

Emily studied Elsie. It was strange how natural it seemed that Elsie existed. When Emily and Ginger had been in college, children for either of them—both of them—had seemed so impossible. Something so far off in the distance, it was barely a spec on the horizon, and certainly not something that might become real. Or rather, someone.

But looking at Elsie, seeing the hint of curiosity she'd inherited from Frank, along with the beauty she'd surely grow into from Ginger, Emily wondered how she'd ever doubted Frank and

Ginger would end up together. How she could have made such a stupid mistake that almost destroyed everything. Elsie was so real, so tangible and unique, it was as if her parents had been drawn together solely for her creation.

Emily studied her empty glass and desperately longed for a refill while she considered Elsie's question.

"No, we're not exactly friends anymore," Emily said. She was too tired to lie. "You could say we fell out of touch after college."

"I figured," Elsie said. "Since she calls you a bitch. But only when she thinks we can't hear her."

Emily snorted. "Yeah, well. At least you kids are honest."

"What happened to make you guys not friends?"

Emily thought back to Frank, and Daniel, and the mess she'd made, then glanced to Elsie. "Your mother can tell you the story when you're older."

"Why does everyone think I'm a child?" Elsie shot a dark look in the general direction of the spa. "My mom punishes me like I'm an adult and then treats me like I'm Poppy's age. It's not fair."

"What do you mean?"

"You wouldn't understand."

"Try me," Emily said, then raised her empty glass in cheers. "I'm ready to listen. And you know your mom doesn't approve of me, so there you go. Isn't that what teenagers love? Going against their parents' wishes?"

Emily felt mildly bad about toying with Elsie's mind, but she was too curious in studying Ginger's daughter to let her go so quickly. She wanted to understand what Julia might be like, what problems she might be dealing with had she lived to reach high school. When Elsie talked, Emily tried to picture her daughter and pretend this was real. Just a mother and daughter hanging out on the beach, hashing out high school drama.

Emily could see Elsie considering, and she could see the moment when the young girl decided to take a leap and trust Emily. Or at least get back at her mother by confiding in Ginger's well-known enemy. It had been a strategic ploy on Emily's part, and it had worked. She certainly didn't regret it.

"That's the problem." Elsie toed the sand in her flip-flops, then glanced over her shoulder to make sure nobody was in earshot. "She doesn't listen to me. Ever. She's punishing me now for… Well, it's stupid. And super embarrassing."

"I heard something about it," Emily said vaguely.

"I'm sure you did. Because my mom talks to everyone but me about my problems."

"Try me," Emily repeated. "I've heard it all. Nothing will alarm me."

"My mom thinks I'm carrying…condoms around." Elsie studied Emily's face for a reaction, and then looked disappointed when she didn't get one. She lowered her voice to a whisper. "You know… *to have sex*."

Emily shrugged. "And?"

"And I'm not! I mean, they were in my bag, but I'm not using them."

"So what if you were?"

"I'm not even sixteen. I don't even…" Elsie's fingers clenched into fists. "I haven't even held hands with a boy."

"Well, your mother's probably worried about you making the same mistakes she did."

"What sort of mistakes?"

Emily had to tread carefully, she realized a moment too late, or she could very well insinuate that Elsie herself had been somewhat of a *happy little surprise*, as Frank had lovingly called their bundle of screaming joy.

"What do I know?" Emily mumbled. "Like I said, I don't have children. I'm only spouting crap to you. Why are you carrying condoms if you don't want to have sex?"

"A senior at school gave them to me during lunch. I didn't

know what to do, so I stashed them into this little pouch I never open and my mom never sees. I was in the cafeteria when it happened. It's not like I could just throw them out in front of anyone. Afterward, I guess I forgot about them until my backpack ripped on the plane."

"Ah."

"Anyway, the girl who gave them to me, her name is Phoebe." Elsie shook her head and pasted a mightier-than-thou expression on her face, though Emily caught a shadow of vulnerability underneath it. "She's, like, the most popular girl in school. The head cheerleader. President of student council. Prom queen. Anyway, this year, I decided I'm going to try out for the cheerleading team."

"Did you tell your mom?"

"No." Elsie scowled. "She wouldn't understand. She thinks cheerleading is stupid. Plus, it's not like she has the money to buy me a uniform anyway."

"How would you explain practices to her?" Emily pressed. "You'd be spending a lot of time at school learning routines and going to games and whatnot."

"My mom works a lot. She usually doesn't get home until late these days, so it's not like she'd notice. My dad is nice and all, but he's totally oblivious to my schoolwork. If I told them I joined a study group, it'd solve that. I suppose if they did find out at some point, it'd be too late by then to make me quit."

"What about the expenses?"

"I've saved up. I have some birthday money," Elsie said. "It's not like I buy anything—I get all my books for free and the only thing my mom allows me to do for fun, practically, is read."

"It sounds like you have it all planned out." Emily shrugged. "Good luck. I'm sure you'll do great at tryouts. If you're anything like your mother, you'll be running that team before the season's over."

Elsie shot a surprised look at Emily before she burst into laughter. "You know, I don't think you're... Well, I don't know why my mom's not still friends with you. You're easy enough to talk to."

Emily struggled to find the proper response. Her head swam with the fresh hit of alcohol on an empty stomach, and the familiarity of conversing with a carbon copy of "young Ginger" was forcing Emily to revisit years that had long since expired. Years that should remain behind her.

"She has her reasons."

"Stupid ones, probably," Elsie said. "I'd rather talk to you than my mom."

Emily's stomach constricted, and a wave of guilt slid down her spine over her earlier jab at Ginger. Emily wondered what exactly had made Elsie open up to her. Had it really been Emily's strategic conversation, or was it something more? Was it so obvious that Emily was an awful adult that even a teenager didn't mind talking to her?

No matter how big Elsie's problems might be, she probably felt secure in knowing that Emily was more dysfunctional than her. Emily was willing to bet that Elsie could sense instability and felt more comfortable around a train wreck like Emily than someone like Ginger or Kate or Lulu—women who had their lives sorted and organized and shiny. Teenage life wasn't sorted and organized and shiny, and neither was Emily.

Emily wondered briefly if Julia would feel the same way, or if, had things been different, her own daughter might lash out to someone else—someone like Ginger—as a way to get back at her mother. *It doesn't matter*, Emily thought, *because it would never be*. She would never discuss the birds and the bees, boys and magazines, prom dresses or wedding gowns with her daughter. Because she had failed as a mother.

"I enjoy listening to you," Emily finally mustered, her voice weirdly throaty with pent-up emotion. "Although, I'm still not quite sure how the condoms come into play or why someone would have given them to you."

"Well, Phoebe heard that I'm the only one trying out for the team who's still…" Elsie's face looked instantly sunburned with embarrassment. "You know…"

"A virgin?"

"Yes," Elsie said. "Phoebe is the one who slipped the condoms in my bag. I think she was trying to help me out, but I'm not really…I'm not interested. I was planning on lying to Phoebe when we got back. If I tell her I did some stuff with one of the neighbor boys who doesn't go to our school, she won't be able to check out my story, and I don't have to worry about being the odd man—er, woman—out."

"Your mother was very concerned you were having relationships without her knowledge," Emily said. "She'd probably be relieved to hear the truth from you."

"I can handle this myself. Don't say anything to her, okay?" Elsie asked anxiously. "Please."

Emily waved a hand. "None of this is my story to tell. Though I do hope you know that you shouldn't feel pressured into having sex before you're ready."

"Of course I know that! I'm not an idiot. And I want to wait until…well, I'm in love." Elsie stared up at the sky as if it pained her to admit such a thing. "Phoebe was only trying to help. She wasn't doing it to be mean."

"If you say so," Emily said. "Though Phoebe sounds a little misguided herself. Not the sort of friend I'd want to be spending my time with."

"It's high school," Elsie said miserably. "Everyone is misguided."

Emily couldn't have agreed more, but she was running out of things to say. Their conversation was getting too real, too personal. "Well, I should really be finding the other ladies. I think another of our old friends—Kate, the one waving—is gathering people for massages, and I'll have a bullet in my brain if I don't cooperate."

"Another friend from Mom's college days? I'll go with you," Elsie said, surprisingly chipper. "I'm bored."

"Should you tell your father?"

"Bye, Dad!" Elsie yelled. "I'm going with Emily to find Mom and meet her other friends."

Emily found a convenient trash can and dumped her cup as she headed for the gathering of women near the pool. She'd caught Lulu looking at her the previous evening, and Emily knew—she just *knew*—that Lulu suspected there was more to Emily. Two shots of vodka first thing in the morning would surely tip her hand. If Emily had mastered one skill in recent years, it was faking sobriety. Unfortunately, that didn't do much for her résumé.

"Are you sure you don't want to explain to your mom about what really happened?" Emily mused aloud. "It seems like that could clear things up quickly."

Elsie considered, her face thoughtfully transforming into an adult-like expression. "If my mom doesn't want to trust me, then why should I do the same for her?"

Emily didn't have much time to respond, because at that moment, Ginger joined Kate, Lulu, and Sydney on the sandy path and caught sight of Elsie and Emily. Ginger's face darkened as her eyes shifted to Emily, but as she glanced at her daughter, she became cautious, like one might be when defusing a bomb.

"Elsie," Ginger said as her daughter approached. "Did you have fun with Emily?"

"Oh, this is your daughter?" Kate asked. "She's beautiful. My name's Kate."

"I'm Elsie," the teenager said, firmly ignoring her mother. "Pleasure to meet you."

"Pleasure to meet you," Kate said. "We're all going for a massage. Would you like to come? My treat."

"No, she wouldn't," Ginger said. "She's a minor. I think the spa is eighteen and older."

Emily saw Elsie's fists clench. She could understand both sides, the protective mother instincts and the daughter desperate for freedom. Was there a right answer? A compromise? Or were mothers and daughters destined to never quite see eye to eye during those awkward teenage years?

"Shame," Kate said. "I think you'd really love a nice massage. Well, ladies, we're going to be late. Elsie, maybe I can buy you a drink later?"

"A mocktail," Ginger said. "She's fifteen."

"Of course," Kate said. "I meant a coffee."

"She's not allowed coffee," Ginger said. "She's still growing, and it's bad for—"

"It's okay," Elsie said, interrupting. "Thanks, though. I'm stuck here with my sister and brother."

Sydney cleared her throat. "Speaking of, I'm going to swing by the child care drop-off with Lydia."

Emily struggled to keep her eyes off the baby, but it was difficult. It seemed daughters and mothers surrounded her, flinging their existence in Emily's face. She didn't fit in. Didn't belong here.

"That's fun," Elsie said. "They have this awesome playground for the kids. It looks pretty great. I'm sure she'll love it."

"Elsie is a wonderful babysitter too," Ginger said, whispering as if Elsie wasn't allowed to hear the compliment. "If you're interested, I'm sure she'd be up to watch Lydia."

Elsie nodded, brightening. "If you'd like, I can watch your daughter. I babysit once a month for my neighbors."

"I wouldn't want to put you out," Sydney said. "Child care is free for an hour. Might as well use it."

"I really wouldn't mind. I love babies," Elsie said. "And I'm bored."

"Keep her busy!" Ginger encouraged. "Busy is good."

"I might as well take advantage of resort services," Sydney insisted again. "But, ah, if you wanted to help out, I'm sure you could stay with her there."

"Sure, I could do that," Elsie said, and Emily could see the gears turning in her head. *It'd be better than sitting around with her parents.* "I'd like that."

"Don't leave the playground," Ginger instructed as if she were dropping Elsie herself off at the facility. "And let the nursery know if you go anywhere. And tell your father."

"Mom, I know," Elsie snarled. "Go get your massage, okay? It's not like I could even leave the resort if I tried—we don't have a car."

Sydney approached the woman in charge of child care behind the formal, lavishly outfitted check-in table. A sprawling outdoor playground built to entertain all ages was littered with employees dressed in Hawaiian-style shirts and ugly hats. Behind her was the indoor portion of the facility with big, arching windows through which play blocks, a kitchen, and bookshelves promised a stimulating environment.

Emily hung back as the woman in charge stepped forward and introduced herself. She had on a big, ugly hat and the signature flowery shirt standard for all resort employees. Her name badge declared her to be Barbara, and she wore bright-red lipstick and a painfully large smile.

"Hi there, and who do we have here?" Barbara asked, looking to Lydia as if the baby could talk. "We have one cutie, don't we?"

"This is Lydia," Sydney said, gently peeling the baby away from her shirt. "And I'm Sydney."

"Room number?" Barbara asked, again with the smile.

"913," Kate said, stepping forward as Emily struggled to follow. "I'm her sister. The name on the room is Kate Cross."

"Ah, okay." Barbara gave a quizzical glance between Kate and Sydney. "Great. Well, it's complimentary for the first hour, and then eighteen dollars an hour afterward."

"Great," Kate said. "Where do I sign?"

"I'll need you to sign here for the rooms, and the mother"— Barbara looked up at Sydney—"to sign the consent forms."

Emily understood Barbara's confusion at the sisterly relationship between Kate and Sydney. What she didn't understand was why Kate was lying about being related to Sydney. They looked the least alike of any of the women in their party.

Kate was all glossy black and oversized sunglasses while Sydney was a scrawny blond who looked like she should be studying for finals. They didn't even look like they came from the same generation.

"This here is Elsie," Ginger said, fluttering toward Barbara. "She's my daughter, and she's fifteen. She'd like to hang here and help with Lydia if that's okay."

"Sure," Barbara said, still confused. "Family?"

"Sort of," Sydney said. "We're all here for the Banks/DeBleu wedding."

"Oh, I see!" Barbara gave a tinkling laugh as if that made everything acceptable. "Getting pre-wedding spa treatments?"

"Massages," Kate said. "And we have to head that way now, or we'll be late. Are we good to go?"

"Yes, yes." Barbara lifted Lydia from Sydney's arms. "She'll be in great hands!"

Elsie reached for Sydney's proffered diaper bag and shouldered it. Emily felt suffocated as the four women around her made tittering sounds of goodbye and lots of waves. She pretended to be swept up in the festivities when really, her head ached and she wanted to be left alone.

Finally, Kate grabbed Emily's elbow and dragged her away. As they shuffled toward their massages, Emily overheard Elsie asking if she could hold Lydia for a little bit. And, Emily realized, she wanted to be left behind too. She wanted more time alone with Lydia too; she wanted to hold the baby and look into her innocent little eyes and wonder *what if*.

"Emily," Lulu said softly. "Honey, it's time to go."

Emily turned, feeling her gaze harden as she looked at Lulu. "I need a drink."

Detective Ramone: Ms. Clint, I understand you are in charge of child care here at Serenity Spa & Resort?

Barbara Clint: That's right, officer.

Detective Ramone: A baby by the name of Lydia Banks was dropped off today, correct?

Barbara Clint: Yes, and boy, was she adorable. What's more, I barely had any work to do with her. The girl, Elsie, watched her the whole time. She was such a doll with the baby.

Detective Ramone: As for the baby's mother, do you remember who dropped her off?

Barbara Clint: Absolutely. I have the sign-in logs. It was Kate Cross and Sydney Banks—here for the wedding, of course. And then there was the baby's father.

Detective Ramone: The baby's father? He was there when the women dropped him off?

Barbara Clint: No, no. He swung by while the women were getting their massages.

Detective Ramone: Did he give you a name?

Barbara Clint: Well, no—not exactly. But we didn't let him inside either. Like I tell all the

parents who check in children with us, nobody
signs their children out except the person who
dropped them off. It's a safety precaution.

Detective Ramone: What exactly did the baby's father
say to you? Did he tell you he was the father?

Barbara Clint: Well, no. Now that I think about it,
he didn't say much of anything at all. He sort of
swung by the entrance and stopped there. I thought
he was looking over at Lydia, who sat on Elsie's—
the teenager's—lap. It's really hard to say for
sure what happened now that I'm looking back.

Detective Ramone: Did he speak to you specifically, Ms. Clint?

Barbara Clint: Well, now that you mention it, he
didn't say anything at all. I asked if he was
checking on Lydia, and he nodded. I assumed… Are
you telling me the man I spoke to *wasn't* Lydia's
father?

"Here they are!" Barbara called as Kate approached the children's
play area with Sydney post-massage. "I have to tell you both, this
young lady is the best babysitter I've ever seen. I didn't even have
to look over here more than twice the entire time! And she even
got the little sweetheart to sleep."

Kate wasn't sure if it was the masseuse (who'd really done a
number on her neck) or Barbara's falsetto cheery voice that made
her reach for the aspirin she'd purchased the previous night. She

offered one to Sydney, who shook her head, her eyes glazed with motherly love as she held her arms out to retrieve Lydia. It was almost painful to see how much Sydney loved her daughter.

"Oh, my," Sydney cooed to Lydia, then looked genuinely amazed at Elsie. "I can't believe you got her down—that's a real task. Most days, she doesn't take any sort of nap without a fight. She's a screamer, this one."

"Really?" Elsie bounced Lydia a bit longer before offering her to Sydney. "She didn't cry once for me. She giggled a lot, though. Thanks for letting me hang out with her."

"No, thank you," Sydney said. "Will you be at the rehearsal dinner tonight? I'm sure Lydia would love to see her new friend there."

Elsie felt herself grinning. "I think my mom is forcing me to go. Maybe I can babysit for a little bit so you can have some time with your friends."

"I wouldn't ask you to do that," Sydney said, her hip jutted out as she bounced the baby. "But I'm so happy to hear we'll see you there. Maybe save a little dance for Lydia. I hear they'll have a live band after."

Elsie was about to agree, but Kate jumped impatiently into the conversation. She had a job to do and not a lot of time to do it.

"Your mother mentioned on the way back from the spa that she had to go check on the little ones," Kate said, her eyes landing on Elsie. "I told her that maybe the big girls—me and you, I mean—could have a coffee?"

"I can't—"

"We'll get you a decaf Frappuccino thing." Kate waved a hand impatiently. "Let me introduce you to the most magical drink of the rest of your life."

Sydney and Lydia were already headed off, presumably for more naps and eats. Elsie looked over to where her family was doing their own thing. Kate saw a glimpse of frustration in her eyes before Elsie responded.

"Sure," she said, turning back to Kate. "I suppose nobody would miss me."

"Great. How old are you?"

"Fifteen," Elsie answered sharply, as if on a job interview. "Almost sixteen, I guess."

"Ah, I remember that age. Quite a while ago for me. You know, I knew your mom in college."

Elsie's face was filled with skepticism. "So I heard. Honestly, I'm surprised my mom would hang out with someone like you."

"Like me?"

"You know," Elsie said, shrugging uncomfortably. "Cool. It's not like my mom is cool."

"We shared an apartment," Kate said, glancing down at her nails. "We don't keep in touch regularly anymore, but...well, I suppose we should."

Elsie shrugged. "Friends don't really last."

"No, I'd suspect not—especially at your age." Kate pushed her glasses up onto her head. "You're pretty, you know. I'm sure you have a ton of boys trailing behind you like dogs at school. They're ridiculous at that age."

"They are ridiculous." Elsie wrinkled her nose. "But I'm not interested in dating yet."

"Really?" Kate stopped walking, quite pleased with the way things were going already. She and Elsie were moving quickly through her agenda, and with any luck, she would be able to report back to Ginger after a single cappuccino. Kate really should have a daughter—she wasn't all that shabby at this mothering business. "I hated dealing with boys at your age, but I felt like I was about the only one who did."

"Yeah, no," Elsie said. "The ones at my school are all so immature."

"Huh," Kate said and resumed walking so as not to appear too eager. "Good for you. I didn't have a serious boyfriend until I was twenty-three. My friends thought—"

"Hold on a second." Elsie put up her hand and paused. "Did my mom put you up to this?"

"What?" Kate gave what she imagined was a convincing look of surprise. "What are you talking about?"

"I can't believe she did this!" Elsie's face darkened like a tornado cloud. "She's so...*ugh*!"

"What is it?" Kate asked, bending her eyebrows together in manufactured concern. "What did your mother do?"

"She set you up to talk to me about boys." Elsie barely managed to mutter it before shaking her head. "Dating, whatever."

"I know what you're thinking," Kate said, "but you have to give me a chance. Your mom didn't set this up. She was moping in the lobby, worried about you, and I suggested she let me talk to you."

"Why?"

"Because I waited until I was twenty-three to have sex," Kate said as Elsie's face bloomed bright pink at the mention of intercourse. The girl really was innocent. "And will you look at me? I made out okay. I thought—maybe I had something to say that could help with what you're going through. Talking to moms about this stuff is so...*ugh*. But I'm not your mother."

"Yeah, but I'm not interested in...that," Elsie said with a wave of her hand that indicated the magical, adult expression of love. "If my mom would have stopped for a second to ask me about my feelings on the subject, I would have told her the truth. An older girl at school put the stupid *things* in my bag. I didn't buy them."

Kate gave a bark of laughter. "Pranks have changed since I was a kid. We used to...I don't know, flush people's heads in the toilet."

"You actually did that?"

"Not me. But I heard the stories. I would never do anything so barbaric. However, I might have put laxative in a girl's lunchtime soda when she stole my prom date."

Elsie's mouth fell open. "You didn't. Did it work?"

Kate gave a tinkling laugh. "Don't try it. You're not like me,

Elsie. You're kind and sweet and beautiful and funny. So...leave the stupid girls alone to do their thing. The second they graduate from high school, it stops being cute."

"She wasn't trying to be mean. She was trying to help me out. It's just...high school is complicated. My mom doesn't understand."

"It feels like high school is your whole life," Kate said, "and it is right now. But by the time you get to be my age? I barely remember it. High school is this ugly little scar where a big fat pimple used to be. It was unpleasant and embarrassing, and I hated nearly everything about it, but I got through it. The experience passed, and I scarred over, and now I don't even remember the names of my high school friends."

"Wow."

"You remind me a little of myself when I was your age," Kate said. "So please don't be mad at your mom because I volunteered to talk to you—it was my idea. I was only trying to help. When I was your age, I wish someone had told me it was okay to wait and do my own thing. There's plenty of sex to be had post-college."

Elsie shuddered and averted her face. "Thanks, I guess."

"I think you should talk to your mom about what actually happened," Kate suggested. "It sounds like a big misunderstanding. She really does love you. I promise."

"Then why would she accuse me of things I didn't do without even asking? She waved that strip of"—Elsie shuddered—"you know, the..."

"Condoms," Kate filled in.

"Yeah," Elsie said. "She dangled them in plain sight on the plane. Everyone could see her. It was the worst! I would have been happy reading my book and letting the flight pass, but the whole time, she kept trying to talk without stopping to listen."

"Moms," Kate said. "I had one. I know."

Almost as if on cue, Elsie's phone dinged in her hand, and she looked down, blanching at the message on the screen. Her shoulders began to shake; her fingers trembled. Kate wondered what could possibly have been said that was ruining their perfect mother-daughter (but not really) bonding moment.

"What is it?" Kate asked. "What happened?"

"Nothing," Elsie said, bringing the phone toward her face to presumably study the message closer. "My mom ruins everything!"

"Elsie, what happened?"

Elsie flipped the phone around and showed Kate the message.

"Well," Kate said, trying and likely failing to mask her surprise. "Yes, that's certainly not ideal."

Detective Ramone: Who was present under the pergola when the victim was killed?

Emily Brown: Me. I was alone. And Sydney, I guess, but she wasn't very helpful.

Detective Ramone: I have three other reports—and I'm sure more to come—that state at least five people were there.

Emily Brown: Sure, maybe they were outside, but I wasn't looking around for them, and they certainly weren't with me.

Detective Ramone: Why are you all lying? What happened out there, Ms. Brown?

Emily Brown: I refuse to answer any more questions.

Detective Ramone: Ms. Brown—

Emily Brown: I don't know what more you want me to say.

Detective Ramone: Do you have any regret for what you did?

Emily Brown: No, Detective. With all due respect, it felt great.

twenty-three

Ginger kept her eye on Elsie and Kate from a distance as her daughter and old friend walked and talked. A surge of pride had hit her when she'd seen Elsie gently hand Lydia back to Sydney.

"Mom, pay attention!" A Nerf football hurtled at Ginger. "Duck!"

Ginger was too busy watching a smile light Elsie's face to react in time, so she took a smack to the back of the noggin. "*Ow*, Tom! Don't throw it if I'm not looking."

"Well, what are you looking at?" Tom called. "The game is over here."

"Tom, apologize to your mother," Frank said. "You've messed up her lovely hair."

"Mommy, can I get ice cream? Can you walk me there?" Poppy tugged on her mother's shirt. "The one that swirls. It's free, you know. There's no reason I can't have it."

Ginger suppressed an eye roll, thinking the scariest thought of all was that she had to go through this again. At Poppy's age, Elsie had been a sweet, completely innocent, unargumentative, happy little girl. Poppy was already a manipulative little trickster who had picked up some moves from her older sister and brother. She just might be the death of Ginger.

"Throw the ball with your brother for a few minutes," Ginger said as she watched Elsie from across the sand. Ginger sensed a shift in the conversation between Kate and Elsie. "I have to take care of something quickly. Don't wander away from your dad, and we can get some ice cream when I come back."

Poppy gave a stomp of her foot, mostly to prove she wasn't happy. Ginger made a sign to Frank that she was going over to Elsie. He saw her, nodded, and gave her the thumbs-up, as if that'd help arm her for battle. Ginger would need a lot more than a thumbs-up to get through this war.

Making her way across the sandy path, Ginger raised an arm and wiped the sweat from her brow thanks to the scorching afternoon heat. So much for the relaxing massage! Then again, it hadn't been all that relaxing in the first place. The masseuse had taken one look at Ginger's back, rested her hands on her shoulders, and made a sound of dismay.

"Tense?" she had asked.

"Yep," Ginger had said.

"It's not good to be so tense all the time."

"Yeah, thanks," Ginger had said. "That's helpful."

The woman had proceeded to take out all her frustration on Ginger's back, leaving Ginger sore and achy and popping an aspirin borrowed from the ever-prepared Kate.

Ginger closed in on her daughter and Kate, feeling a sense of trepidation in the air. Something had gone awfully, horribly wrong. What had Kate said to Elsie? How could Ginger have let this happen?

"Hey, you two," Ginger said carefully, purposefully stepping in front of her daughter. "How's it going? Looks like the baby really loved you. You were great with Lydia, and I'm sure Sydney really appreciated all the attention you gave her."

"It's a good thing someone loves me," Elsie retorted. "Because you certainly don't seem to even like me!"

Kate hovered in the background, pretending to order a drink from a nearby beverage cart, quite obviously watching the show through her huge dark glasses. Ginger gritted her teeth against her daughter's resentment and ignored Kate. If Kate had children, they probably wouldn't grow up to hate her. They'd have cute little shopping dates and manicure nights, and if Kate ever needed a break, she could hire a nanny and have a week full of massages.

"Don't talk to me like that. I am your mother, Elsie. Of course I love you. That should never be a question."

"Then why are you going behind my back?" Elsie held her phone up, and on it was a screenshot from Phoebe Brimhall. "Did you message Phoebe from my phone? On *Facebook*?"

Ginger felt a flush rising in her neck. "I shouldn't have done that. I'm sorry, but, Elsie, you are obviously keeping secrets from me. I'm your mother."

"That's not the point. You peeked at my stuff!"

"Hey, your phone is public property to me," Ginger said with a low growl in her tone. "I am your mother. Your father and I pay all your bills. We agreed when you got the phone that anything on it was subject to parental inspection without warning. I didn't overstep any boundaries."

"Clearly, you don't trust me!" Elsie shouted. "You don't even listen to me!"

"I do too listen to you," Ginger said, feeling her blood pressure rise. "But it's sure hard to listen when I ask you a question and you give me a one-word answer. I don't get all that much information from you."

"I'm stringing at least ten words together right now! How do you like them apples?"

"Don't quote movies at me, Elsie. I'm trying to have a serious conversation with you. This isn't a joke."

"No, of course not. You wouldn't actually want to have fun with me, God forbid."

"What has gotten into you?" Ginger positively shook with emotion. Frustration, despair, sadness. "You used to be my little girl—me and you. We'd talk and play all day long, and we'd go for walks to the park, and now, I can't even get you to look at me. Where did I go wrong?"

"You're still not listening to me," Elsie said. "I would have explained the situation if you'd freaking asked—and then shut up long enough to hear it."

Ginger started in surprise. "Explained what?"

"It's too late." Elsie waggled the phone with the confused message from Phoebe on it. "You've already done your damage."

Ginger glared at the screen. "I saw your phone last night when you were sleeping. You don't even talk to Phoebe Brimhall. Isn't she a senior? I only read it to see what she'd said. She was asking if you'd used the condoms yet! What was I supposed to think? I won't stand for other girls pressuring my daughter to have sex."

"She wasn't pressuring me to do anything! You don't even know half the story. And worst of all, you most certainly didn't have to respond with 'This is Elsie's mother'!" Elsie cringed. "I can't even bear to look at the rest of your note. That alone is plenty embarrassing. Now everyone on the cheerleading squad will know you monitor my phone. Scratch that, the whole school. Nobody will ever text me again."

Ginger's gut flooded with shame. "Maybe I shouldn't have done that. But I don't think you should be hanging out with girls who are talking about condoms like they're, I don't know, sticks of gum to be handed out willy-nilly."

"You don't know what's going on! Phoebe was trying to help me. She wasn't pressuring me to do anything."

"I'm only saying, it's not as if you have a committed, loving boyfriend to use them with," Ginger continued. "If you did, I might think differently about the situation, and we could talk about that too. Don't you know you can talk to me about anything?"

"You are not freaking listening!" Elsie cried again. "Just go away. I am going to the room to read. Can I have the room key? I—I can't be around you."

"Elsie!"

"Can I have the room key?" Elsie jutted her chin forward and stuck out her hand. "If you make me stay out here, I'll be miserable, and I will make the rest of the family miserable. I only want to read and be away from you."

Out of the corner of her eye, Ginger saw Kate approaching, but she didn't register it. "No. This is a family vacation, and—"

"What if you let Elsie have the key to my room for an hour or two?" Kate barged in, taking control as she always did. "I have a room on the ninth floor with a fabulous view. You can read out on the balcony in quiet, Elsie. Hell, order room service. My ex-boyfriend is footing the bill."

"I'd like that," Elsie said quietly. "Thank you, Kate."

Ginger felt weak as she looked at this woman, a stranger to Elsie, winning favor with her child while Elsie couldn't bear to have a conversation with her own mother. "Elsie, you can't run away from this. It's not going to disappear."

"I don't think she's running," Kate interrupted, driving up Ginger's blood pressure even more. "She needs a bit of time to cool down. What do you say, Elsie? Cool down, then have a chat with your mom before the rehearsal dinner tonight. Final offer."

"Fine," Elsie snarled.

"Fine," Ginger said, knowing if she denied Elsie this, she would be hard-pressed to speak to her daughter all trip. "What's the room number? I'll walk you there."

"I'll walk her there," Kate said, "since I have to shower anyway. Elsie, do you have some things you need to grab? Ginger, I will be with her all afternoon. Come up to 913 whenever you're ready for a chat. I won't let her out of my sight, I swear."

Elsie nodded. "My dad's hanging onto my bag. I have my book in there."

"Go get your things and meet me back here." Kate directed traffic like it was her job. "I want a word with your mother."

Elsie slouched away to pick up the small Nike backpack that likely contained a book and her signature bottle of Diet Coke.

"What the hell do you think you're doing?" Ginger rounded on Kate the second Elsie was out of earshot. "How dare you come between me and my daughter when we're trying to have a difficult conversation. It's not like you have any experience with your own children."

Kate's eyes widened, the biting remark hitting its spot in the sore, aching crevice that would surely have existed because Kate wanted children, and Ginger had them, and she'd rubbed it in.

Ginger massaged her forehead and immediately felt multitudes of guilt. "Oh, Kate. I'm so sorry. I didn't mean that. I'm—"

"It's fine," Kate said crisply, dismissively, as if she didn't have time for an apology. "It was probably wrong of me to interfere, but I thought you should know something. If you'll just listen for one second."

Ginger's legs and arms felt shaky, as if she'd binged on espresso all morning and was approaching the crash. "You have to let me apologize to you," Ginger said. "I'm so sorry. I'm jealous. You talked to her for longer than I have in the past year. At least, that's what it feels like."

"I don't need an apology," Kate said, her words still chilly. "I don't have children—it's true. But my experience with children aside, I'm not actually here to talk about Elsie this time."

"Who are you here to talk about?"

"You," Kate said, her eyes landing on Ginger. "You aren't listening to her."

"But—"

"You're doing it right now. If you want my honest opinion, shut the hell up, Ginger." Kate's eyes flashed with frustration. "You have a good kid, and Elsie told me some things I think you should hear. So, I'd suggest giving her some time to cool down and then ask her to explain the situation—and then give her time to talk.

You might be surprised. I'll take Elsie up to my room, and I'll be there with her—I need a shower and a nap. Here's an extra key to get in whenever you're ready."

Ginger stood stock-still, reeling from the shock of it all, as Kate brushed past her and met Elsie with a smile. Ginger watched as Kate began to talk, probably issuing orders, and by some miracle, Elsie listened. By the time they rounded the corner, Ginger caught a glimpse of Elsie smiling.

Watching the two walk away, smiling and laughing, Ginger was suddenly thrust into a vicious time loop that sent her back to college. She was struck by the way Elsie was maturing so quickly, as if before her very eyes. Some of the awkward gangliness of her limbs had seeped out and left her looking elegantly tall and thin, especially when she lifted her chin and straightened her shoulders like she did now, walking beside Kate.

Ginger could almost imagine herself and Kate twenty years younger, back when Ginger had probably done the same thing— straightened her shoulders, flipped her hair, pretended to be a new level of sophisticated while hanging with Kate.

Ginger remembered one particular morning in college shortly after her breakup with Frank. Kate had stormed into Ginger's bedroom and yanked the sheets off the upper bed, demanding she get ready for brunch. It didn't matter that it was a Wednesday, or that finals were the next week, or that Kate was skipping her internship to rescue Ginger.

It also didn't matter that Ginger had shoved an entire box of Oreos down her throat the night before and had a stress pimple the size of Pompeii across her forehead. All that mattered was that Kate had drawn Ginger out of a funk, and while sluffing it to brunch in pajamas hadn't solved all her problems, there was something cathartic about having a woman like Kate in one's life. Kate always knew best, and there was no possibility of ignoring her once she'd made up her mind.

That was the power of Kate Cross. And now, it seemed, her daughter had learned the very same lesson that she had, once upon a time.

Another pang of jealousy wormed its way through Ginger, hot and toxic. How had Kate managed to get Elsie to talk when Ginger had been prying at her daughter for months with zero success? And what did Kate mean when she told Ginger to listen? Of course Ginger listened! She tried to ask her daughter questions—

Ginger stopped.

Is Kate right? Now that she thought about it, Ginger couldn't remember if she had actually asked Elsie about the condoms or if she'd leapt to conclusions in a public place. Conclusions that were based on Ginger's own past behavior instead of the way she knew Elsie to be. As much as they were similar, Elsie wasn't Ginger.

Ginger knew that Elsie had turned down a boy named Brendan for a winter dance. (It wasn't really snooping to peek in Elsie's journal if it was for safety purposes, was it?) Brendan was a nice kid, popular too, and frankly, Ginger would have understood if Elsie wanted to spend some alone time with him, to explore the confusing hormones sending messages shooting in every direction through her body.

But instead, Elsie's journals had contained pages of musings on books, of beginner attempts at poetry and song lyrics (oh, the teenage angst), and some general grumblings about her brother, sister, and parents.

How could Ginger have been so stupid? What had she missed that Kate hadn't? Ginger took a step toward the disappearing duo, thinking maybe she should offer Elsie an apology, but she hesitated. Maybe Kate was right. Maybe Elsie needed some time to cool off—especially if she was anything like Ginger after a fight.

The rehearsal dinner was only a few hours away, and Elsie had promised to talk beforehand in exchange for some space. In the meantime, Ginger had a son who wanted to throw footballs at her head and a daughter who "needed" ice cream this very second.

And so it was with a combination of sadness and hope that Ginger approached her family minus one. When had Elsie grown up? When had she become her own person, an almost adult who was far more responsible than Ginger had been at that age? With a sigh, Ginger looked at her husband and finally returned his thumbs-up.

"All is well? Great! Elsie is hanging out with your old college gal pals?" Frank called over. "How neat. Catch, Mom!"

Ginger ducked, missed the ball, and was tackled by her son. Then Poppy came over and sat on her chest.

"Mom, can we get ice cream now?" she asked. "My sugar levels are low."

"Come on, sweetie," Ginger said. "Let's go. On the way, you can tell me what other sorts of things you want to do this vacation."

"Really?" Poppy frowned, looking skeptical. "I get to pick?"

"You get to pick within reason," Ginger amended. "And I promise I'll listen."

Detective Ramone: Thanks for meeting me here, Ms. Jones. Can you please state your name and job title for the record?

Jenny Jones: My name is Jenny Jones. I work in hospitality, sir. I do whatever's needed. Some nights I'm working the front desk and other times I'm restocking the minibars. I've called Ubers and escorts and 911 for our guests, Detective. No task is too big or too small for Serenity Spa & Resort.

Detective Ramone: Thank you. Were you able to

question the maids about the rooms on the list I sent over earlier this evening?

Jenny Jones: Absolutely. As requested, I contacted all employees who went into the rooms listed on the document and asked if they'd found anything unusual.

Detective Ramone: Let's start with Kate Cross. Anything unusual in her room?

Jenny Jones: Nothing, sir. The woman is neat as a pin.

Detective Ramone: What about the room of Pierce Banks and Lulu Franc?

Jenny Jones: Not much there either, sir. It's very neat and barely lived in. There were several books left out, most of them on the subject of war, but that's the extent of it.

Detective Ramone: And Emily Brown?

Jenny Jones: It appears she didn't stay in her own room, sir. She stayed with a gentleman friend, and I had the maids check there as well. They didn't find anything particularly unusual. There were a few…personal items as noted by the maid service in that room.

Detective Ramone: Such as?

Jenny Jones: Condom wrappers. Several of them scattered about. It appears he was intimate with someone last night, likely a woman.

Detective Ramone: And Ginger Adler's room?

Jenny Jones: Well, sir, there was one thing.

Detective Ramone: Yes?

Jenny Jones: There was a condom wrapper in the trash.

twenty-four

Lulu carefully inserted her diamond earrings and took pleasure in inspecting the resulting shimmer. She basked in the brilliance of them. They were a gift from Pierce, of course, along with the ruby ring on her finger and the diamond wedding band that was upwards of three carats. Lulu didn't apologize for liking expensive gifts, especially when the men she married could afford them.

She had dressed in a gorgeous, over-the-top, gold ball gown that was probably "too much" for a rehearsal dinner of any variety, especially at her age, but Lulu didn't care. It might be the last time Pierce laid eyes on her. She wanted—no, she needed—to feel confident for the conversation that loomed before them.

Lulu hadn't yet decided how to deal with the phone call from S. She was still in shock to discover her husband had a third phone in the first place. This was the sort of thing that happened in movies and books, the sort of underhanded shenanigans of criminals and adulterers and the like. Pierce wasn't criminal. He was… Lulu hesitated. What was he? Did she even know her husband at all?

After a dial tone met Lulu's ear earlier that morning, she had carefully wiped the phone on her shirt (God knows why she was worried about fingerprints on her husband's spare phone) before slipping it back into the suitcase pocket where she'd found it. She'd then eased out of the room and left her husband a note saying she'd gone on to breakfast for a bite to eat and not to wait around for her as she had a ladies' day planned at the spa.

Lulu had proceeded to spend the next few hours alternating between a state of speechless shock and the slow burn of a building rage. Just over an hour before returning to the room to get ready, Lulu had watched the lobby from a secluded corner—holding a trashy magazine over her face as camouflage—and waited until Pierce came downstairs to join his family for cocktail hour, as she knew he would.

She had felt like Harriet the Spy. She knew it was petty and childish of her to watch her husband without his knowledge, but she also wasn't yet ready to broach the subject of his secret phone. Frankly, she didn't know what to say.

So she had waited and watched as Pierce met up with two of his brothers at the bar. They clapped one another on the shoulder with the sort of enthusiasm that came from family ties that had existed long before Lulu had come around. And they would remain long after she'd gone.

The groom's father bought a round of drinks for the men, and Lulu watched as Pierce sipped his whiskey neat and clinked glasses with Arthur's father, celebrating a happy time in their safe little circle of wealth. Lulu felt rage bubbling in her chest as she watched her husband enjoying his family. It didn't look as if he'd had a second thought about Lulu's whereabouts.

In the past, Lulu had always appreciated the relationship Pierce had with his family—politely distant, in a few words. There was no nagging mother-in-law (she was long dead) and no demands from siblings that required Lulu and Pierce to uproot their lives to "help out" with family matters, aside from the occasional wedding or funeral. And when the Banks family did gather, it was often around delicious food and drink, easy topical conversation, and a thoughtful gift exchange at Christmas.

It had been a family Lulu was happy to join. And one she would miss.

While there was a tainted sort of thrill in watching her husband without his knowledge, Lulu realized she'd have to forfeit her post in order to get ready for dinner. Once she was certain Pierce was dressed for the evening and tucked into his whiskey, she'd pulled on her sunglasses and used the magazine as a fan to shield her face while stealthily returning to her room. She'd left herself half an hour to get ready before appetizers were served.

As Lulu painted red across her lips, she tried (and failed) to fight off the agonizing sense of loss in her gut. She knew she had to speak with Pierce after dinner. She'd managed to avoid her husband for one day, but he'd become suspicious if she pulled the same stunt the next. With a trembling hand, Lulu dabbed at a smear of red she'd accidentally placed on her front tooth.

As the hour rolled to a close and Lulu cemented waterproof mascara onto her lashes (Lulu had never cried during a divorce yet, but you could never be too careful), she slipped into a gorgeous pair of low pumps that lifted her glimmering gown a hint high enough off the floor so it wouldn't drag. She looked at herself in the mirror and raised her chin with pride.

Battling with the proud stance was a persistent pooling of moisture in her eyes that simply wouldn't do. With a sniff and a bit of focus, Lulu found it easy enough to chase away the tears if only she let the pool of rage simmer until it boiled over and engulfed her sorrow.

What is Pierce thinking? He was throwing away a perfectly good relationship. While Lulu had theorized there might be another woman in Pierce's life, she'd never believed it. Not until she'd heard the woman's voice. Then, it had all come crashing down, thrusting her into reality.

With a pinch of regret, Lulu wondered if her past husbands had felt the very same things she was feeling now before she'd ended their marriages. But Lulu had to believe that couldn't be the case. Since she'd married Pierce, she'd found herself coming around to the idea of soul mates, the spiritual notion of one true love. There was no way she would ache so badly if Pierce weren't meant for her, if they didn't belong together. It had never hurt like this before. Why couldn't he see that?

With one final dab at the corner of her eye, Lulu set off toward the elevator armed with an extra tissue in her clutch and a balloon of anger inflating her chest. She eyed the button for the penthouse suites as she stepped into the elevator. With a wry twist of her lips, Lulu thought that if she and Pierce were on better terms, she would have gently suggested he upgrade their room to the highest floor so they could spend their evenings wrapped around each other as they watched the lights twinkle in the distance. Instead, she pressed the button for the ground level.

Lulu stepped from the elevator and made her way down the hall, following several signs inlaid with a beautiful script that directed her toward an elegant ballroom. She passed underneath a dainty arch of roses and came to a stop before an exquisite table laden with white lace linens and glasses of a pinkish champagne bubbling merrily on a tray.

A woman in stilettos moved with the authority of the president of the United States, barking into an earpiece for *More appetizers, stat!* and scurrying about with her elbows out like daggers. She wore a sleek, black dress that form-fitted her clearly starved body and a black choker necklace that looked vaguely sexual in nature.

Miranda Rosales, Lulu mused. Then, she heard someone ask for her name and turned, unimpressed, as a man dressed in a suit smiled at her, introduced himself as Ralph, and repeated the question.

"Lulu Franc," she said, "though if you're looking at the guest list, it might be under my husband's name, Pierce Banks."

"Ah, yes," Ralph said with a delicate clip to his voice. "He arrived about five minutes ago with a large Banks party. He mentioned you'd be along shortly—told me to look out for the beautiful young woman named Lulu."

Lulu rolled her eyes but felt a rush of validation as Ralph gave her a playful wink and passed her a glass of champagne. Damn this *S*! Lulu still loved Pierce. She loved the way he lavished her with gifts and attention and love. The way his formal manners dictated he call her beautiful whenever possible and open car doors whenever Lulu didn't throw them wide with impatience first.

Maybe she'd ask him for the other woman's full name after confessing to Pierce that she'd found his secret phone and spoken with *S*. And then maybe Lulu would strangle her. (Probably not, as she'd heard strangling required a lot of strength, but the thought sounded somewhat appealing.)

Lulu stepped through the doorway into the formal area that had been elegantly decorated for the rehearsal dinner. With a glance around the space, Lulu calculated the evening was costing the Banks family upwards of fifteen grand on the low end. Garlands of pearls and twinkling fairy lights decorated the vaulted ceiling, while white lamps resembling marshmallows gave off a romantic, puffy sort of glow.

A live, seven-piece orchestra—the ladies and gents dressed in all white attire—played at the far end of the room before a vacant dance floor. Servers, also dressed in all white, bustled about with bite-sized nibbles of food that wouldn't keep a squirrel fed.

Lulu loved money. She loved weddings. She loved *love*, but this was spending for the sake of spending. If this were Lulu's wedding, she'd ax the overbearing wedding planner and go with someone a bit more relaxed. For Christ's sake, it was just a wedding. It was one day.

She'd bring in a jazz quartet and get the dance floor occupied with guests. She'd flit about with her husband on her arm, greeting her guests, nibbling the nibbles, drinking the drinks. A wedding was a verb, something to be cherished and enjoyed. In her case, a number of times.

Instead, the bride and groom sat demurely behind their chosen table, listening to the wedding planner in one ear and guests in the other. It appeared they weren't allowed to eat, judging by their empty plates and the sheer tightness of the corset around Whitney's torso. One bite of cheese, and Lulu had the feeling the poor bride's buttons would pop right off.

Before today, Lulu hadn't spent more than a few minutes in the same room as Whitney DeBleu, though she'd run into her a time or two at large family gatherings. Lulu had interacted with her enough to feel qualified to say the bride seemed like a nice enough young lady—and that was the extent of it. Lulu did briefly wonder if it was Arthur's idea or Whitney's to have a budget the size of the national debt for their weeklong celebration.

Beyond the heavily decorated (candles, chandeliers, confections, *oh my!*) dining area sat a sprawling patio closed off to the public. Lulu headed straight for it to get a breath of fresh air. Her timing was impeccable; as she turned, she caught one of Pierce's brother's beelining toward her and managed to deftly avoid running into him. She wasn't in the mood for small talk.

Lulu was here for one purpose: to put on a brave face until dessert was served, and then gently pry the truth from her husband's lips. After that, well…she'd have to play things by ear.

The air outside still held remnants from the harsh desert temps during the day, but with the setting of the sun, a chill had begun whipping up from beyond the edges of the patio. The neatly printed cement was surrounded by a hedge of *Sansevieria trifasciata*—a plant more commonly known as mother-in-law's tongue, Lulu knew. A fitting name for the occasion. Lulu knew all about mothers-in-law. She'd had plenty of them.

On the far end of the patio, just beyond a gleaming koi fish pond, sat a pretty, antique-looking white gate between a gap in the greenery. Beyond it stretched a walking path that led into a deeper darkness. Lulu strolled toward it, noting the wooden platform just on the other side of the hedge, which had been set up like a stage.

Resort staff had been preparing all day for the looming nuptials, and evidence of their hard work was everywhere.

Chairs tied with gauzy white ribbons sat beside tables covered in fresh linens, the fabrics blowing lightly in the breeze. The centerpieces hadn't yet been placed, but Lulu spotted a rack of wine bottles needing to be unloaded near a tall pergola—the same custom bottles that had been provided to each of the attending guests in their welcome baskets.

Lulu shivered against the painfully chill wind as she looked out at the abandoned courtyard that, at first light, would be transformed into a fantasyland most women could only dream of having on their wedding day. For now, however, there wasn't another soul outside.

"You look beautiful."

The voice made Lulu jump and rest her ruby-ringed hand to her chest. "Pierce! You startled me."

"You've been avoiding me all day." His eyes were serious, melancholy against his otherwise handsome, tanned face. "Why?"

"Please, let's not discuss this now." Lulu felt a sudden chill as she glanced at her husband's stony features. She'd never noticed the hardness of his jaw, or the way his eyes glinted under the moonlight. "It's almost time for dinner."

Pierce didn't respond. Instead, he looked down at his hands and toyed with the wedding band around his fourth finger. Lulu felt her shoulders go tight, and suddenly, she wondered how she could have been so stupid. *He knows.*

Of course Pierce knew. If he had been expecting a call from *S,* he would have eventually checked his phone. It would have taken two seconds to draw up the call log and see an incoming call had been answered. He'd know the phone had been found, and the only logical person who could have uncovered it was his wife.

Lulu mentally berated herself—she'd thought to wipe her damn fingerprints from the phone, but she hadn't erased the call log? And even if she had, it would only have been a matter of time before *S* called again, or before Pierce noticed the silence and called her first. It wouldn't take the conniving pair more than a breath to put two and two together. The only question that remained was…what was Pierce planning to do about it?

"Pierce," Lulu said, urging herself to remain calm despite her racing heartbeat. "Please, can we discuss everything later? I don't want to be all in a tizzy in front of your family. Let's focus on getting through dinner, and then we can have a chat afterward in private."

"As you wish." Pierce's response was even, calculated. He stepped closer to Lulu, forcing her to edge back against the gate. He raised a hand, trailed a finger lightly down Lulu's cheek.

She wondered if he could feel her tremble.

His voice came out in a whisper. "You really do look magnificent. I love your earrings."

Lulu touched a diamond, forcing her fingers to steady against the gems. "You chose them."

"I remember." Pierce's eyes flashed as he met her gaze. "They bring out your eyes."

As if on cue, bells began ringing from inside the dinner area. Lulu was surprised to find herself exhaling a sigh of relief as Pierce turned his intense gaze away from hers and directed it over his shoulder. Someone else had popped out on the patio for a smoke. Lulu had never been so relieved to have company.

Pierce grasped Lulu's hand firmly and led the way inside, stopping to greet a plethora of family members with painstaking caution, introducing Lulu with flattery and grace. He pulled out her chair. He whispered in her ear and rested a thoughtful hand on her thigh. He was the picture of a perfect husband.

Lulu made it through the first round of appetizers before the panic set in. Those marshmallow, puffy lights seemed to be closing in, going dark around the corners. The room had grown packed and full, and the murmur of voices seemed deafening. A server asked if she wanted a refill, and Lulu winced, shook her head, and stepped back.

"I need some air," Lulu said suddenly to her husband. "I'm sorry. Don't follow me. I'll only be a minute."

"Where are you going?"

"Outside," she said. "Wait here."

Pierce met her gaze. "I don't think that's a good idea."

Detective Ramone: Walk me through the rehearsal dinner.

Lulu Franc: The decorations and food were quite extraordinary. I'm sure the family spent a fortune on it all. If I'd done the same for my weddings, I'd still be in debt, and I've married well, Detective.

Detective Ramone: What happened after dinner? When did you return to the patio?

Lulu Franc: I didn't finish dinner. Halfway through, I went outside for a breath of fresh air, and that's when everything went south.

Detective Ramone: Who else was there?

Lulu Franc: It was me and, well, Sydney. She was already unconscious.

Detective Ramone: Sydney was unconscious when you arrived?

Lulu Franc: Yes, and there was a man standing over her. I was convinced he hit her hard enough to knock her out because he had blood on his knuckles, and Sydney's head was bleeding. Head wounds bleed a lot.

Detective Ramone: Was her baby with her?

Lulu Franc: No.

Detective Ramone: Where was the baby?

Lulu Franc: I don't know.

Detective Ramone: There's one other tiny detail with your story that doesn't make sense to me, Ms. Franc. When security arrived on the scene, there was no woman lying unconscious on the ground. If Sydney was injured so badly, then where did she go? And how did she get away?

twenty-five

Sharleen told Emily to take things easy until she got back home.

Of course, she'd said so in more professional terms.

Emily grabbed her fourth champagne from the bar, thinking Sharleen didn't really understand. It was easier to forget. What better way to help her forget than an open bar? Appetizers had barely begun to make the rounds by the time Emily made fast friends with the bartender, the exchange of a healthy cash tip ensuring a full glass all evening.

Screw Sharleen, Emily thought. *Screw Henry, screw Daniel, screw them all*. Emily had escaped from a horrible, toxic relationship and was working to put it all behind her. She'd only recently come to terms with the word *abuse*. She hadn't wanted to think of herself as a victim, yet that was what she was. A poor, helpless victim.

Weak people were supposed to be victims. Kate Cross in her fancy getup would never be a victim. Sydney with her baby wasn't a victim; she was a warrior taking care of that baby all on her own. Ginger wasn't a victim—she would set her husband straight the second he stepped out of line, Emily was sure of it. She'd seen it happen. Emily had never wanted to be weak.

But the truth was that she had been weak. All those years ago in college, from that very first time Daniel had laid eyes on her, she'd crumbled. She'd made her choices. She'd gone back to him over and over again, even when she had seen cracks in his exterior that leaked glimpses of the cruelness he hid beneath. Even when she should have known better.

Emily's mouth tasted bitter. She ordered a shot of whiskey, downed it. Ordered another. Ordered a tequila and watched as the bartender's fuzzy-looking face frowned as he slid it over, a little less full than the previous ones.

"Another tequila, please," Emily said to the bartender. "No training wheels this time."

"Um, ma'am—"

"Give me the drink," she said. "And I'll leave you the hell alone."

Emily flashed back to the present, thinking of Henry's words that morning. He'd meant to help, but he hadn't. The truth was, he'd hurt her. In looking up the obituary for her daughter, pulling up an image of the man who'd ruined Emily's life, confronting her with the dirty details of her past when the two of them were supposed to be nothing more than a fling in the present, he'd hurt her badly.

Henry had gone where he shouldn't have gone; he'd dug deep, torn at old scratches and wounds inside her, opening the scars to bleed. Then he'd gone, leaving her to die a lonely death because she'd asked him to go.

Emily sipped her champagne and looked around the room decked out in love and hearts and shitty buffet food. (The food was actually quite good, but Emily's mood tainted it to the equivalent of steamed spinach without butter.) She wondered if Daniel had a new wife by now. A new woman to batter, a new child to destroy. Emily really should do something about him...but what? What could a weak woman like herself do against a force like Daniel?

Emily closed her eyes, sinking into the memory of the night she'd left. She'd done this before, multiple times, usually when she was drinking. If she let go enough, she could almost visualize the scene as if she were right there in the moment all over again.

The night had been murky, black, and that was how her visions always began. She only remembered bits and pieces of it. She'd been sober back then, even before she'd gotten pregnant with Julia. Emily hadn't even enjoyed alcohol all that much before Daniel. She'd never had more than a glass of wine with dinner. Alcoholics had seemed so undisciplined to her. *Why not just stop drinking?* she'd thought to herself. *It can't be that hard!*

Now, her memories were often patchy, thanks to the liquor, but that night, it was due to sheer terror and pain that certain parts had been blocked out. Her recall of the specifics was broken. She knew he'd had a knife. There was a struggle. She remembered trying to leave through the sliding patio deck doors when he'd come home raging drunk and began whaling on her. She'd tried to protect herself, her baby. There'd been stairs, falling, blood.

He'd panicked, thrown her in the bathtub.

Emily had always suspected he'd wanted to try and make it look like a suicide.

When he'd realized there would be no explaining the bruises on her head, he must have changed his mind, because he tried to take her to the hospital. By the time Emily had come around, however, she'd fought him off and run to get Julia. *This is it*, she'd said. *I'm taking the baby.*

He was going to let her go too. She could see it. See the horror in his eyes at what he'd done. The fear of Emily reporting him, ruining his successful career, destroying his life.

"If you ever come near me or the baby ever again, I'll kill you," she'd said as she reached for Julia, and she'd meant it.

A tear slipped down Emily's face, over her cheek. She was sinking, spiraling into the black hole, a flushed toilet dragging her into the sewage of the world, the muck and filth that had become her subconscious. There was no escaping it. It was too late. She'd already lost Julia, her heart, her very soul.

She opened her eyes, her knuckles white as they gripped the stem of a champagne glass. (When had she gotten champagne?)

And she knew exactly what she had to do. There was only one way out of this mess.

Emily spiraled from the bar, pausing, taking a second to note the room before her. It all seemed like too much. Like a Barbie wedding complete with the blushing bride. Whitney really did look beautiful in a sweeping, long white gown that skimmed over her impossibly trim hips.

The coordinator, Miranda something-or-other, bustled about with a pen stuck behind her ear that she'd likely forgotten there, barking orders as if her life depended on this very dinner going off without a hitch. The flowers—white roses—filled the centerpieces of every table and spilled over onto a floor strewn with fresh petals.

Several chefs worked quickly to keep the smell of expensive foods pungent and permeating the room—stuffed zucchini flowers, mouthwateringly thin strips of prosciutto, a cheese platter lovingly arranged so it was impossible to eat. The flowers, the scents, mixed with the gauzy, draping fabrics and the dim twinkle of fairy lights made the patio look otherworldly, exquisite...perfect. And this was only the rehearsal dinner.

I don't belong here, Emily thought with a smile.

She didn't belong anywhere.

"Sharleen," Emily muttered as she pulled her phone out and began to dial. "Sharleen, pick up the phone."

Sharleen's answering machine clicked on as Emily fought her way through heart-shaped photo arrangements of the bride and groom. There were no goodbyes she needed to say, except to her therapist. To let Sharleen know there was nothing she could have done.

"I'm sorry," Emily said into the phone. "But this is for the best."

Detective Ramone: Thanks for joining me on the phone, Dr. Love.

Sharleen Love: What's this about? Is Emily all right?

Detective Ramone: She's…fine. But the situation is a little complicated. We found your number had been dialed a few times on her phone over the last forty-eight hours. Did you speak with Ms. Brown during any of these calls?

Sharleen Love: What's this about? I'm not answering questions without speaking to my lawyer. We have doctor-patient confidentiality.

Detective Ramone: I'm not asking you to breach confidentiality, I only need to know what she said to you the last time she called. A few minutes later, a man was murdered.

Sharleen Love: Emily didn't kill anyone, I can tell you that. She wasn't… She was calling about something else entirely.

Detective Ramone: Doctor, has Emily ever discussed suicide with you?

Sharleen Love: I think I'd like to confer with a lawyer before we continue.

"Oh, God." Emily stopped walking abruptly as she reached Henry's floor and stepped out of the elevator. "Ginger, I didn't expect to see you here."

Ginger looked harried, an ice bucket in her hand and a frenzied look on her face as she stopped short at Emily's voice. Ginger spun around, and Emily realized she must have caught her in the middle of getting dressed. She had on beach sandals with a half-unzipped dress and hair pinned to only one side of her head.

"Emily," Ginger said evenly. "I'm in a rush and can't talk. Poppy threw up everywhere, and the whole room is a mess."

"This… I'm sorry, but it can't wait." Emily found herself being pulled toward Ginger, her arms outstretched. The alcohol was clouding her vision and making words difficult to find, but she desired closure with her old friend. Craved it. "I need to talk to you."

"You've had fifteen years to talk to me, Emily," Ginger said. "I'm not interested in talking to you right this very second. I need to sort out my daughter."

"It's about Daniel."

"I don't care about the past," Ginger said. "I got Frank, you got Daniel—it all worked out. We all got what we deserved. Is that what you wanted to hear?"

Emily stopped cold. Was Ginger right? Had she deserved Daniel? Had she deserved all that happened to her? The thought was sickly and black and wormed its way through the alcohol to the hole in Emily's heart. Maybe she'd known the truth all along, and it had just taken an outsider to bring Emily's worst fears to life.

"You don't know what I've been through," Emily said in a whisper. "It's been awful. I've paid for my mistakes a hundred times over."

"Look, I'm not happy to hear you're hurt, Emily, but what can I say? Karma has a way of catching up to people. Now, if you'll excuse me, I really do need to get this mess cleaned up and my daughter in the bath. I haven't finished dressing myself, and I'm already late to dinner."

"I don't have a family," Emily whispered. "I don't have anyone, Ginger."

"Jesus, what do you want me to say? Seriously, I don't have time for this right now." Ginger cradled the ice bucket to her chest and sidestepped Emily, stomping past her before whirling back around and coming to a stop. "You're so selfish, Emily. What don't you understand? You're quite clearly drunk, probably on some ridiculously expensive champagne, and I'm here clearing up fucking vomit."

Emily felt weak as she looked at Ginger, too preoccupied to even give her the time of day. It was with startling clarity despite her hazy mind that she knew it was time.

Without thinking, Emily stepped forward and reached an arm toward Ginger. As Emily's fingers connected with the fabric of Ginger's dress, Ginger flinched and looked down. Emily stepped closer and brushed a quick kiss against Ginger's cheek. When Emily pulled away, she could barely speak.

"I'm so sorry, Ginger," Emily murmured. "I hope someday you'll understand."

Emily could feel Ginger's eyes on her as she turned and left, but she didn't look back. If she did, if Ginger offered even the slightest words of friendship and forgiveness, Emily's resolve might crumble—and she couldn't let that happen. Her mind had been made.

Emily arrived outside Henry's room, dressed in the red gown she'd saved for months to buy—if for no other reason than to put on a good show for Kate, Whitney, and Ginger at their reunion—and knocked. Her mind was fuzzy, dark.

She closed her eyes, swaying against the door, as the doctor's voice played in her head. *I'm sorry, there's nothing more we can do. There's nothing you could have done.*

"Emily, are you all right?" Henry opened the door and helped her to stand. "You collapsed on me there."

She glanced up, closing one eye to focus on Henry. "You're—ah, you're off to dinner."

Henry was dressed in a suit, sliding a button on his wrist through the hole. "You're drunk."

Instead of sounding sympathetic, he sounded annoyed. "Get in here. You need to lie down."

"I will, but, ah—I can't."

"Why not?"

Henry was definitely upset, Emily realized. Even through her fogged mind, she could tell he was not happy to see her. "I'm—you're angry with me."

"Fuck," Henry said. "I didn't come here to babysit a grown woman, Emily. No, I'm not happy to see you, and especially not in this state. You can barely open your eyes."

Well, that, Emily thought, *isn't very nice.*

But it was the proof Emily needed. Sharleen hadn't answered, Ginger hadn't forgiven, Henry had flung their fling, and there was nobody on earth who wanted her. Nobody who needed her. Pathetic, weak old Emily, taking up oxygen that someone else deserved more.

"Why don't you go on," Emily said. "Let me sleep on your bed. Go to the party and forget about me."

Henry cursed again, helped Emily to the bed. When she lolled onto it, he gave her a look—one filled with such disgust, it caused tears to burst from Emily's eyes.

"I'm sorry" was all she could whisper as Henry stormed out and the door slammed shut behind him.

Detective Ramone: Tell me exactly what happened on the patio.

Emily Brown: I stole a gun from Henry Anonymous. I already told you I slept with him, so it was

easy enough to lie my way back into his room. You
men are all the same.

Detective Ramone: So you had the gun when you
reached the courtyard?

Emily Brown: Yes. I got a little lost when I left
his room—I'd been drinking, see—but eventually,
I made my way downstairs. I was headed outside. I
thought it'd be awful for Henry, or a poor maid,
to find me dead in the resort room. But when
I got to the patio, Sydney was already unconscious. And that bastard was standing over her.

Detective Ramone: What did you do when you found
him there?

Emily Brown: I raised my gun and shot him.

Detective Ramone: Where was Lydia during this
time?

Emily Brown: The baby?

Detective Ramone: Yes. The baby.

Emily Brown: I don't know.

Detective Ramone: Ms. Brown, I have a huge problem
with your confession, as you call it.

Emily Brown: Why? I had the means and the motive.

Detective Ramone: Imagine my confusion, then, when three other women all testified that there was no bullet in the victim's body at the time of his death. An autopsy will be able to corroborate that detail easily enough. Which would lead me to believe, Ms. Brown, that the victim was shot postmortem. [Pause] Why don't we review your story one more time?

twenty-six

P oppy ate too much ice cream," Elsie said, hanging up her cell phone. "My mom doesn't have time to talk before the rehearsal dinner because Poppy is puking."

"I'm sorry," Kate said, cautiously watching the teenager. "Are you upset your mom isn't able to swing by for a chat? It must be hard having siblings. I was an only child."

"Upset?" Elsie barked laughter. "Don't be silly. I'm only upset because she's still making me go to the dinner thing, even though Poppy and Tom get to stay back with Dad."

Kate watched as Elsie turned to her floppy paperback, a book worn into so many grooves, Kate wondered about its history. Who else had read that dirty, little copy? Who else had held it and complained about their parents while dog-earing pages or licking their finger to flip to the next? The way Elsie sunk into the book within seconds of turning her eyes to the page had Kate thinking she should get back into reading for pleasure. The joy on Elsie's face, the unerring focus with which her eyes flitted from one line to the next, spurred something in Kate.

Unfortunately, the very thing spurred in Kate sent her running to the restroom to bend over the toilet and expel the contents of her lunch. "What the hell?" she murmured, flushing to get rid of the smell, the sight of vomit making her even more sick.

Once she'd cleaned up and brushed her teeth, Kate returned to the living area. "Don't drink too much champagne, kids," she said in a cheesy voice to Elsie. "I have one hell of a hangover."

"Maybe you're pregnant," Elsie said without flipping her gaze from the page. "My mom threw up all the time with Poppy. I used to tease Poppy about making Mom sick even when she was in her stomach."

"No," Kate said automatically. "That's not possible."

Now, Elsie looked up. "Why are you so sure?"

"Because my ex and I tried everything money could buy to help us conceive a child," Kate said. "Before we broke up, obviously. In fact, we tried for so long, and so hard, that it ruined our relationship. A few months ago, we decided to take a break from it all in hopes to get ourselves back on track. In fact, that's why—" Kate stopped, squinted at Elsie. "Are you old enough to hear this?"

Elsie rolled her eyes. "I go to public school."

"But you've never had sex."

"Of course not!" Elsie recoiled. "I haven't even... I mean, the only time I've even *seen* a condom was when..." Elsie's face turned red. "Oh, never mind."

"What is it?" Kate urged. "God knows I don't judge."

"I mean, I've seen one." Elsie's cheeks grew pinker and pinker. "But the first time I ever touched one was last night."

Kate tried not to let her surprise show. "Oh?"

Elsie rolled her eyes. "It's not what you think. After my mom went down to the bar, I went into the bathroom and opened up one of those stupid packages to see what the thing looked like. I mean, it's been causing this whole big issue on our trip; I figured I should investigate and know what it was."

Kate raised a hand, held it over her mouth to prevent her reaction from showing. "And?"

"You know..." Elsie shrugged. "It looked like a balloon. It smelled gross. I filled it with a little water and then threw it at Tom when my dad went to get ice."

Tears leaked from Kate's eyes, and she couldn't tell if it was due to the hilarity of Elsie's innocence or the fact that this was something Ginger might have done back in their dorm days—sneak into Kate and Whitney's room with Emily as her sidekick to pelt one another with water balloon condoms.

"Right, well," Kate said. "I guess you've never had to worry about taking a pregnancy test. I have, and I'll tell you—I never am."

"Oh-*kay*," Elsie said, adding extra vowels to show she really didn't care either way, but could Kate please keep her worrying to herself, so Elsie could stop talking about such mortifying subjects and read in peace?

However, while Elsie sunk back into her novel, something clicked in the back of Kate's brain. Something that made her angry.

With horror, she realized that Max had been manipulating her for months. It'd been *his* decision to take a break, his ultimatum that had forced Kate to choose between a boyfriend and a baby. He'd convinced her to feel guilty for wanting to continue trying for a child, for wanting to jump straight into that sixth round of IVF because they could. Because they could afford it, because they were two people (supposedly) in love, because they had the means and the drive and the slim shred of hope that was the only thing that truly mattered.

Kate now saw Max's plea for a break more clearly, for what it truly had been from the start. It had been a way of distancing himself from the relationship. Even if it had been subconscious on his part, it had been a sign, and she should have recognized it. Max had been over their relationship for some time. Only he hadn't seen fit to end it until months later, wasting precious minutes of Kate's life as they barreled toward a dead end together.

However, even during their so-called break, Kate hadn't truly been able to shut her mind off. Even when she'd been trying her best to cooperate for Max's sake. She'd tried not to pay attention to her erratic periods. She'd tried not to reach for the pregnancy tests she kept stashed in every drawer of the house. She'd tried not to reach for the thermometer, but she knew. And she knew that her last period had been extraordinarily light. She'd chalked it up to stress, but maybe…just maybe…she'd been wrong.

Kate shuffled into the bathroom, leaving an oblivious Elsie to read in peace, and removed a test from her bag. She stared down at it. She must have taken hundreds of these in the last year. Sometimes twice a day, just to be sure. Could this time be different?

As Kate finished her business and washed up, turning the test facedown on the counter so she couldn't see the results, she closed her eyes and breathed deeply. Could she be pregnant with Max's child?

Kate considered carefully. She had been queasy and sick all day. She'd chalked it up to a hangover, but in retrospect, it could have been early signs of morning sickness.

A breath crashed out of her as she leaned forward and gripped the counter with shaky knuckles.

The answer was yes. Technically, she could be pregnant. The window of ovulation, along with the timing of their sexual encounters over the past few weeks, made that entirely feasible. But did she want to be pregnant? Would it be worth tethering herself to Max until the end of time for the sake of a child?

Reaching for the test, pulse racing, Kate knew the answer.

Yes.

With a shaky hand, Kate flipped over the slim stick and rested it against the counter. She stared at it, and stared at it, and stared longer. She felt her heart drop toward her knees. Then she picked up the plastic, snapped on the cover, and threw it all into the garbage. It clanked off the side and landed facedown in the bin.

"Everything okay in there?" Elsie called.

"Fine," Kate replied.

But as she looked in the mirror, bleary-eyed and exhausted, she knew everything wasn't fine. The test was negative. And despite the complications a pregnancy would have caused under the circumstances, the result had broken her heart.

It had all been in her head. She'd wanted to be pregnant so badly that she'd turned a hangover into morning sickness, when the reality was that Kate was simply getting older. She couldn't drink like the college student she used to be, nor, it seemed, could she make the naive dreams of her past come true.

Kate composed herself with a few deep inhalations. She had a wedding to attend, an upset teenager in her bedroom, and an ex-boyfriend to face before the week was over. She could push her sorrow off for another few days. She'd done it before.

"Are you sure you're okay?" Elsie asked, looking up from her book as Kate appeared in the doorway. "You look a little, I don't know, tired."

"I'm fine. But you should be getting to dinner, missy." Kate brushed a wayward strand of hair from her face. "Are you going back to your room to change?"

Elsie looked down at her athletic shorts and tank top. "Do I have to?"

"Let me find something for you."

"Your clothes won't fit me," Elsie said, but there was a distinct gleam in her eye as she finally peeled that magnetic book from her hands and set it on the bed. "Your clothes are, like, for supermodels."

"You're very pretty, Elsie. A bit shorter and skinnier than me, but nothing a few pins can't help. I have a sort of flowing gown that will make you look like a queen. What do you say? I'm already bored thinking about my breakup and want a distraction."

"I thought you loved him."

"Yes," Kate said, not wanting to discuss him any longer. While Kate had loved Max, she'd loved the idea of a child more. If she hadn't been so desperate for a family, she would have seen Max for the asshole he was a long time ago. "I think it was a blessing in disguise that he ended things when he did. I can move on now."

"Well, I have no doubt you'll find someone else. Or you can

adopt a baby, if you wanted to be alone. Sometimes I think that would be easier."

"Me too," Kate whispered before she realized she'd said anything at all.

"You should think about it," Elsie said in the confident way that only teenagers can. "I know you'd be a great mom."

"You're only saying that to be nice."

"No, I mean it." Elsie rested a hand on one of the gowns, testing the luxurious fabrics beneath her fingers. She looked surprised to be touching something that wasn't from Target. "I've only known you for, like, a day, and already you're sort of like a cool big sister that I'm not really related to. I wish you were my mom, even though you're probably not old enough to be."

"Don't be ridiculous." Kate cleared her throat. "I'm the same age as your mother. And she'd be hurt if she heard you talking like that. She does love you, Elsie."

"Er, okay." Elsie shifted uncomfortably. "I mean, I know my mom loves me, and my dad does too. But my dad's a goof, and my mom's all intense about everything, and you're a nice mix of both. And you listen to me, and you talk to me like I'm a normal human being, not an idiot."

Kate cleared her throat again, annoyed by the sudden tickle tormenting her esophagus. She ran a hand over her forehead and took a few deep breaths in an attempt to pull herself together. This rush of emotions was unprecedented for her, and she didn't particularly like it.

"Let's get you dressed." Kate focused her sights on Elsie as a distraction. "You will be the star of the show."

"Isn't the bride supposed to be the star of the show?"

"Not when I'm on the job," Kate said. "I have the perfect shade of lipstick to bring out your eyes."

Once Kate finished with Elsie's hair and makeup, she helped her slip into the pretty French dress Max had insisted Kate wear. Kate realized, suddenly, that it had been made for Elsie.

The dress hit right at Elsie's feet and had demure straps that hung off her shoulders. There was no cleavage. (Kate was only a tiny bit concerned about Ginger's reaction to her using Elsie as a human dress-up doll.) But Ginger could hardly object to the beauty that was Elsie Adler. She looked like an elegant prom queen. But older, more mature somehow.

And when Kate saw Elsie look in the mirror and smile, it was the only confirmation Kate needed to know she'd done a good deed. It almost made her forget about the pregnancy test tainting her trash can. Almost.

"I love your hair out of your face like that," Kate said. "You have such pretty features. You should show them off more often!"

"I'm not interested in dating yet, really." Elsie scrunched up her nose. "Do you think I'm weird?"

"No, I think you're brilliant! Don't let yourself get distracted by boys now. You have plenty of time in and after college." Kate crossed the room to where Elsie stood in front of the mirror and adjusted a bobby pin before leaning down to whisper in her ear. "And let me tell you a secret. Women don't dress for men. At least, not the sort of woman I want to be. We dress for ourselves."

Elsie gave an open-mouthed nod of realization, as if Kate had turned into Yoda with her sage advice. "I suppose you're right."

"Dress in a way that makes you feel good, and confident, and powerful," Kate said. "And it'll be your most attractive self. I guarantee it. Whether that's in a business suit, a ball gown, or a sports bra."

"What if I don't know who I am yet?"

Kate squeezed Elsie's shoulder. "I'd say that's perfectly normal, and it's more than okay."

"How'd you figure out what you want?"

Kate considered, thinking back to her late-night Googling, and her misguided relationship with Max. "I'm still not sure I know what I want." She forced a smile in the mirror, toyed listlessly with Elsie's hair. "But I'm working on it."

"Will you let me know when you figure it out?"

"Of course." Kate looked at the clock, her fingers still intertwined in Elsie's new curls. "*Shit!* Here we are chatting away, and we're already late for dinner. Come on. We need to go, or your mom will be pissed at me."

"You swear a lot for someone who wants to be a mom," Elsie said. "My mom only swears when she thinks we can't hear or when she's driving."

For someone who wants to be a mom. Kate stilled in the doorway, shaken by Elsie's flippant phrase. She was beginning to wonder why the hell everything the teenager said seemed to be affecting her so strangely this afternoon when her phone beeped with a text message and graciously offered her another easy distraction from trying to decipher what it all meant.

"Perfect. That was your mom saying she's running late and will meet us there. If we hurry, we can still beat her downstairs. Do you think she'll be upset at your dress?"

"Who cares?" Elsie said. "I look fabulous."

Kate gave a nod of approval at her confidence, then rested a hand on Elsie's back as they scurried from the room and closed the door behind them. The pair hopped in the elevator and made it to the lobby area where a beefy rent-a-cop named Ralph sat with his arms across his chest, frowning at an arch of white roses.

"Name?" he grunted, obviously tired of the old song and dance.

"Elsie Adler," the teenager said, shooting Kate a conspiratorial look. "And, ah, Ginger Adler."

Ralph merely gestured toward the party. "Have fun," he said with all the enthusiasm of a dead fish.

"What was that all about?" Kate asked, giving Elsie the side-eye as they shuffled toward the entrance. "I'm on the invite list—Whitney was my friend. Although, truth be told, I was planning to skip tonight's dinner. I haven't dressed for it."

"You're always dressed for a fancy dinner. Plus, I thought you might want to come inside for a minute, and I wasn't sure if Max would have tried to take your name off the invite list when he broke things off," Elsie said. "I know you're friends with the bride, but even I know men can be assholes."

"Your poor mother," Kate murmured, but she didn't feel all that bad. Ginger would get in one way or another. Ralph was no match for Ginger Adler, and Kate was certain Miranda Rosales wouldn't have approved of last-minute guest changes. Max might have fooled Ralph into taking Kate's name off the list, but once Kate got inside, it would be an easy task to clear up the matter with Whitney.

"Whew," Elsie said. "We beat my mom here. Hey, I see Sydney and Lydia out on the deck. I'm going to go say hello to them if you don't mind."

"Okay, well, I'll stick close until your mom gets here."

"I think you should find Max," Elsie said. "Maybe it would give you some closure."

Kate paused midstride and looked down at the girl. Except, she realized, *girl* was the wrong word. Elsie stood quietly still. She watched the bride and groom from the entrance, looking not like an awkward child but like an elegant young lady. Her chin tipped high and her shoulders were straightened. What was more, Elsie Adler had made a surprisingly good point about confronting Max.

As Kate stepped past another majestic floral arrangement, she considered the teenager's advice. Maybe she did need closure. After all, it was ridiculous what Max had put her through. Just yesterday, Kate had been desperate to conceive a child with this man. A man who had proceeded to dump her at a family wedding without having the courtesy to discuss their future—or lack thereof—in private. Worse, Max hadn't bothered to check in with Kate one measly time in the ensuing twenty-four hours to make sure she was all right.

Yes, Kate thought. One last conversation with Max should do the trick.

Appetizers had already begun to circulate the perfectly decorated room. Servers dressed in snappy suits carried trays of custom cocktails between the guests, each sparkling beverage garnished with a spear of exotic fresh fruit or a sprig of greenery. Tiny sweets adorned with edible flowers and sparkling sugars sat on a dessert table, and the marvelous three-tiered cake next to it was surely only a precursor to the real thing.

Kate might have been uncomfortable surrounded by so much *love, love, love* if she weren't so distracted with her own thoughts. She hated the bitter disappointment another little white-and-pink stick had brought upon her, and the fact that it still had the power to drain her soul so completely, even after all this time. At the same time, she felt energized by brand-new dreams of adoption and surrogacy. The latter had sparked the first hopes of something real that Kate had felt in a long, long time.

Kate clung to those hopes as she spotted Max over by the bar, his hand around a gorgeous blond with a huge bottom. The woman wore a lacy white dress that Kate thought was a little tacky considering the bride had on a flowing, white lace dress as well. Somehow, Kate suspected, this woman suited Max better than she ever had.

But that didn't mitigate her annoyance at being dropped like Max's discarded socks. Kate walked across the room and gave a twitch of a smile as she leaned up against the bar next to him. The bartender scooted toward her looking interested, but Kate took cheery pleasure in brushing him away with a flippant, "Oh, I don't plan on sticking around."

Kate cleared her throat, but Max didn't budge. He was too busy inviting his new girlfriend to Cancun for a long weekend. He'd always said he would take Kate to Cancun. They'd never gone.

She listened idly for a few minutes, and when Kate tired of the conversation, she gave her fingers an impatient tap against the counter.

Max heard and turned, a look of angry frustration on his face until he saw who'd made the noise. "K-Kate?" he stuttered. "What are you doing here?"

"I came to see you."

"But…" Max's gaze flicked nervously to the front door. "There's…er, a guest list, and…"

"If you thought tricking poor old Ralph into removing my name was going to stop me from attending the festivities, then I suppose you don't know me very well," Kate said, silently thanking Elsie's intuition. "You wouldn't want me to get Whitney and Miranda involved to clear up matters, would you?"

Max's face paled.

"Don't worry, this won't take long. Surely your girlfriend can wait a few minutes."

"She's not… Kate, you don't understand. We've just met," Max said. "We were only talking."

"I think you and I should talk for a few minutes."

"Honey," Max said, and both Kate and Blondie looked toward him, as if he might have directed the endearment to either one of them. It was a very awkward moment for Max.

"Er, Angela," Max said more clearly. "Can I have a second?"

Angela blew out a breath, gave a succinct nod, then sashayed off to find a table, drink in hand. Kate gave her plenty of time to leave, watching leisurely as Angela found a new man, an older gentleman sitting alone, and eased into the seat next to him with a flirtatious pose.

"You've been doing a number on my credit card," Max said. "What else do you want from me?"

"I truly hate to interrupt your date, but I wanted to say thank you."

Max raised his eyebrows. "For?"

"Breaking up with me."

"But—" Max frowned, squinted. He rubbed tension out of his forehead. "Are you sure you're feeling okay?"

"I'm feeling great," Kate said, realizing that, as a matter of fact, she was. She was battered and crushed, sure, but she would get over it. She would hope again. Elsie had helped her see that much. "After I check out of here, I'll leave your credit card alone."

"So…" Max blinked, his eyes slightly bleary. Kate suspected he had a hangover too. Probably from being up all night with Blondie. "Why'd you come here tonight?"

"I want the answer to one question," Kate said. "Or rather, two. Did you ever love me? Did you ever truly desire to have a child with me?"

"Kate…" Max sighed. "It didn't matter how much I wanted it, because you can't have children. It's not going to happen for you. I'm sorry."

Kate felt as if he'd pressed a dagger through her rib cage, dangerously close to her heart. Her breath came in sharp gasps and she released a noise that sounded like a deadly hiss. Kate shook her head. "To think I wanted this so badly, and you didn't want it at all."

Max gave a patronizing shake of his head. "You wanted it enough for both of us. I was just…there. A sperm count, if you will."

It was with unbridled fury that Kate raised her hand and brought it in a clean slap across Max's cheek. "You should have dumped me a hell of a lot sooner if that's how you felt. I loved you!"

Max put a hand on his cheek, worked his jaw as if she'd hit him hard enough to do any damage. (She hadn't; it'd been mostly for show, and for the satisfying sound her palm on his cheek made.) He shook his head as if to straighten everything out.

"I told you before—you're broken, Kate. Even the doctors can't find out what's wrong with you. All the money in the world can't solve your problems, and we both know it. It's time to move on."

Kate wanted to smash his head against the bar, but she was too shocked to do much of anything. She'd come into the rehearsal dinner to find out how a man she'd loved so desperately days before could move on from her so easily. And in doing so, she'd managed to completely forget the power Max had over her.

No, Kate thought with fury. *No longer.*

It was a teary mixture of rage against Max and aching pain at her inability to have children that gave her the willpower to storm through the love-festooned hall toward the exit. She punched a heart-shaped balloon for good measure, though it retaliated by bouncing back and making her duck as she reached the doors.

At the same moment, Ginger burst into the entryway, barreling toward the outdoor patio in a hurry. When Kate glanced outside, she saw Lulu—with a look of surprise on her face—holding the door open for Ginger's rampage.

That's it, Kate thought. She needed air. Fresh air. And a distraction.

Kate followed a few paces behind Ginger. Lulu let the thick glass doors shut behind Kate, opening her mouth with a greeting when she was cut off by a scream.

An earsplitting, pulse-pounding scream.

Detective Ramone: Ms. Cross, I've got a bill here that says an hour of child care was charged to your room today. Do you have children?

Kate Cross: No, I do not. Thank you for pointing that out, seeing as my inability to have children was the very reason my boyfriend dumped me this weekend. You should know that, since I'm sure you've asked everyone about it already.

Detective Ramone: I apologize. So are you saying this charge was a mistake?

Kate Cross: No, I am not.

Detective Ramone: How close are you to Sydney Banks? And why did you pay for the care of her child this afternoon when she was a guest of the very same resort? She could have easily charged it to her own room. I've cross-checked the sign-in logs, and Barbara verified Sydney was with you at drop-off.

Kate Cross: It was a gift.

Detective Ramone: A gift?

Kate Cross: Is there a problem with that?

Detective Ramone: Not exactly, Ms. Cross. But I am wondering if you've been telling me the truth about your relationship with Sydney Banks. Did you see her daughter, Lydia, anytime during the rehearsal dinner?

Kate Cross: Detective, I've cooperated enough. I've confessed. Please leave the child out of this.

twenty-seven

"Oh, Poppy," Ginger said, rubbing her daughter's back. "I told you not to eat too much ice cream."

"But…" Poppy's lip trembled. "It was free."

"You don't have to eat everything because it's free."

"Y-yes, I do. It saves us money. We never have enough money," she said. "That's what you always tell Dad."

"Honey, it's a figure of speech," Ginger said. "We have plenty of money to live on. Don't worry. I need you to rest here with Daddy and Tom while I pop down to dinner. I'm going to say hi to the bride and groom, and then I'll be back to put you to bed."

"Okay," Poppy said, exhaling a huge sigh of air and popping her thumb in her mouth. She hadn't done that regularly in years, but she reverted to the old habit when she was under the weather. "Is Elsie coming back?"

"Do you actually miss your sister?"

Poppy shrugged.

"Elsie's coming with me, and then she'll be back," Ginger said. "Okay, climb under the covers now. Tom, behave, okay?"

Tom nodded, curled up on the corner chair in a most awkward position. He had one leg crossed over his knee and was slouched halfway down, eyes glued to the screen of his tablet.

"Great, love you both," Ginger said, popping kisses onto their heads. "Love you too," she said, saving a forehead kiss for Frank. "Are you sure you don't mind that I'm heading down there alone?"

"*Die*, Tom!" Frank shouted toward his own tablet. "Dang, son. How'd you get out of there? I taught you too well. You're kicking my rear end."

Ginger straightened, appalled. "I'm taking those tablets away from you both if you can't watch your language. I don't want to hear any of that talk about death—got it?"

"Sorry, honey," Frank said, flicking guilty, puppy-dog eyes up at her. "Have fun. Er—did you say something?"

"Forget it," she said. "I'll be back in an hour. Love you. Watch so Poppy doesn't get worse, and call me the second anything changes."

"Sure, honey," Frank said, his eyes back on the game as Tom let out a banshee-level wail.

"Come on, Dad," Tom said. "You pushed me off that cliff. You did it on purpose!"

Poppy ignored both boys (the small one and the big one) to watch Olaf sing on the set of *Frozen* across the big television. Ginger bit back an affectionate sort of smile for the chaos that was her family. Now, to get Elsie back into the mix, and all would be well in the Adler nest.

Ginger had been calling and texting Elsie all afternoon, and her daughter had replied with enough terse responses to let her know that she was alive and having a great time…without her mother. When Ginger had called to say Poppy was sick and she wouldn't have time to visit Kate's room before dinner, she imagined Elsie had squealed with glee.

"Hi there," Ginger said, slightly breathless as she swatted an errant rose from her face before ducking under a flowery arch. She checked in with the security guard—a red-faced man named Ralph. "Sorry I'm running late. My name is Ginger Adler. I'm a friend of the bride."

Ralph surveyed her up and down. "Sorry, but I can't let you in."

Ginger looked down, offended. She'd worn a pretty navy dress that she thought made her look a bit like a classy sailor. (*Frank had particularly enjoyed that very fantasy the last time I wore this*, Ginger thought with heated cheeks.) It was a far cry better than her normal yoga pants and sweatshirt.

"Excuse me?" Ginger shook her head, not understanding. "I'm on the list. I didn't fly across the country not to see Whitney DeBleu."

"Lady, a *Ginger Adler* already checked in," Ralph said. "There aren't two Ginger Adlers on the list."

"It must be a mistake," Ginger said. "Here's my license."

Ginger pulled out her license and handed it over, watching as Ralph's ears grew increasingly pink.

"If there's another Ginger Adler here, she's the fake one," Ginger said. "Do you remember what she looked like?"

"Hot," Ralph blurted, almost as if he had no control over his words. "I mean, she was an attractive woman, a bit younger than you. She came here with someone I thought was her daughter— even though she didn't look old enough to have a teenage kid."

"Dammit, Kate," Ginger snarled. "That's a friend of mine. I'll send her out. I think she wanted to walk my daughter into the party because they spent the afternoon together."

"I'll get her," Ralph said, a gleam in his eye. "It's no problem."

"You can't leave your post," Ginger pointed out. "And for the record, she's older than me. Got it? We're both thirty-eight. I'm a few months behind her."

Ralph looked surprised by the numbers, but not overly surprised. As if raising his eyebrow would require too much effort. "If she's not out here in a few minutes, I'm calling backup security."

As Ginger brushed through the doors, she spotted Whitney and Arthur along the far wall, situated behind the head table, deep in conversation with their bridal party. Ginger continued her scan, looking for Elsie. After she located her daughter, she'd deal with

Kate. Once they were both squared away, Ginger could show her face around the room, say her hellos, and be upstairs by bedtime.

Why had Kate lied to get in here, anyway? Ginger pondered this as she came around the corner. Was her ex-boyfriend really so awful he'd try to get her uninvited to the rehearsal dinner? That seemed a bit ridiculous, seeing as Kate was on the invite list in her own right as a friend of the bride. It wouldn't have taken more than a word with Whitney to set the record straight, but maybe Ginger was missing the point. Maybe Maximillian Banks was just that unpleasant.

Ginger spotted Lulu first, standing at a table next to her husband, and wondered if she'd gotten answers from him yet. It was hard to say. The look on Lulu's face wasn't happy, and neither was the way she stormed through the crowded tables in a beeline toward the rear exit. She shoved a large glass door open and a wash of fresh air filtered into the dining area.

Ginger barreled after Lulu as someone began clinking a champagne glass. The bride-to-be and groom-to-be stood and gave each other a swooping, romantic sort of kiss that would have had Ginger swooning and nudging Frank on any other occasion. Then Frank would have good-naturedly given Ginger her own swoon-worthy kiss, and they would have convulsed in fits of laughter after.

God, she loved Frank. And her kids. *Where is Elsie?* Something didn't feel quite right. It was nothing Ginger could put her finger on—nothing concrete. It was like a tremor in the air, a promise that because of all this love and happiness in one room, somewhere else, a darkness balanced it out.

Ginger picked up her pace. Lulu caught sight of her and paused in the doorway, holding the glass panel open. But Lulu's eyes were focused on something behind Ginger.

Glancing back, Ginger caught a glimpse of Kate—also hurtling toward the outdoor patio—and noted that she didn't look good at all. Her eyes were bleary as if she'd been crying, but that couldn't be right. Kate wasn't a crier. But her makeup was gone, wiped clean, and there was a raw sort of determination in the set of her jawline.

"Kate?" Ginger called, but it was too noisy in the room, and Kate didn't hear her.

"Hey, Ginger," Lulu said as Ginger passed through the open door. "Looking for Elsie?"

"Yeah," Ginger said. "Have you seen her? And is Kate okay? It looks like she's upset."

"I think Elsie's outside," Lulu said and then lowered her voice as Kate approached. "I haven't talked to Kate yet tonight. Seems like everyone's having a rough go of it."

"What about you?"

Lulu's gaze darkened. "I'm not entirely sure."

"Kate, where—" As Ginger turned toward Kate, her words were drowned out by a scream.

twenty-eight

It came from deeper outside, past the glittering koi fish pond and the charming white gate, past the arms of foreign-looking, stiff green plants reaching sharp little fingers toward the sky. The scream didn't seem to have penetrated through the thick glass walls to the indoor dining area. There was too much clinking and kissing going on at dinner for anyone to be bothered by the call of distress.

"What was that?" Lulu asked. "It sounded like it came from over there!"

"Elsie," Ginger breathed and then took off.

She barely noticed a door at the side of the building as it opened, one staircase or another leading from the belly of the resort to the wild outdoors. Emily emerged out from the black hole, something deep black, metallic, glinting with moonlight in her hand.

"Elsie!" Ginger cried again. "Elsie, where are you?"

Ginger passed through the sectioned-off lounge area flanked by a waterfall and rock fixture—closed to the public—and out through a little white gate and onto the walking path beyond. A few cautious steps down the path brought her to a private court-yard. Ginger recognized it as the location where Whitney and Arthur were to be married the next day. Already, the decorations were out in full swing.

But Ginger didn't take the time to study her surroundings, nor did she care that the courtyard looked like a fairy tale. She didn't see the palm trees standing guard before the tall brick walls, or the various succulents that watched her movements quietly, draping the desert backdrop in shades of green and pink and purple and orange.

A platform stood at the far end of the courtyard, and just before it, an elaborate pergola peeked out from beneath beautiful white cloths that twitched charmingly in the night breeze. A large crate sat forgotten near it, stacked high with replicas of the same customized, lovely bottle of wine in Ginger's room upstairs, ready to be placed on tables for the next day's wedding. The scream had come from behind it.

Ginger raced through it all, coming to a halt when a body seemed to materialize at her feet. Ginger's first thought was *Dead! She's dead!* Familiar blond hair sprawled out in a matted, bloody mess, and there was no movement from the young mother.

"Sydney," Ginger said, collapsing to her knees to feel quickly for a pulse. "Someone help! Sydney's hurt!"

Shit, is she dead? But Ginger couldn't linger. Her heart, her very essence pulled her elsewhere, to her daughter. To Sydney's daughter, Ginger suspected. Elsie and Lydia would likely be together.

Elsie might have come out here to play with the baby, but who had attacked Sydney?

"Mom!" Elsie's voice came with a sob. "Over here!"

The call came from a distance, and Ginger's heart lurched. She stood and barreled forward, slowing her pace only as she neared the pergola and spotted Elsie crouched before the stacked bottles of wine, partially obscured from view.

Ginger would have continued running, but the sight of a man standing before her daughter stopped her cold. Elsie clutched Lydia to her chest, appearing terrified but unharmed.

"I want my daughter," the man said. "I'm unarmed. I only came to get my little girl back."

"But you—" Ginger halted. "Your daughter?"

"Lydia is mine."

"You're Lydia's father?" Ginger asked hoarsely. In horror, she glanced over her shoulder at Sydney. "How could you hurt your wife? Have you killed her?"

The man blinked, shook his head. "For Christ's sake, I didn't kill my wife."

"But Sydney—"

"She's a lunatic," he said. "She stole my daughter."

Elsie gasped. "I don't believe you."

"*Henry.*" Emily appeared from behind the towel rack, holding the gun extended. "Get away from her, you bastard."

"I don't want to hurt anyone." Henry raised his hands under the moonlight. "I only came here to find Lydia."

"Well, you've already hurt Sydney, and now you've sure as hell hurt me too!" Emily said. "I don't understand."

"Don't be pathetic, Emily." Henry faced her. "I haven't hurt you. We both knew what we were getting into the second you joined me in the airplane bathroom. You're not innocent."

"No, I'm not," Emily said, her voice a low, throaty growl. "But I'm not the one who deserves to die." Emily raised the gun higher, her eyes narrowed. "And I wasn't back then either."

"Stop!" Ginger shrieked. "Emily, wait. Henry, back away and leave my daughter alone. We can figure this out without hurting anyone else."

"I don't mean your daughter harm." Henry glanced toward Ginger. "I'm here because Sydney stole my daughter. She's mentally unstable."

"Bullshit." The tremble of words came from Kate. "You're all the same, aren't you? All of you *fucking* men—nothing is ever your fault! God."

Kate's voice was hoarse and raw with anger. Tears streamed from her face. Ginger ached for her; she'd had no idea. Kate's perfect life…wasn't so perfect.

"I saw the whole damn book," Kate said. "Every last, ugly

picture. What sort of monster abuses his pregnant wife? Yes, Henry, is it? I saw every last fucking bruise. It's documented. You're finished, no matter what happens tonight. It's over. You'll not so much as look at your daughter ever again."

"You don't understand," Henry said, his hands raised higher. "Sydney doesn't deserve—"

"How dare you." Emily spoke softly, her voice ice cold and deadly sharp. "She's Lydia's mother. And you are a disgusting, manipulative, *abusive* man."

Ginger watched as Emily's finger tightened on the trigger. Her heart thumped, blood speeding through her veins. Henry was still too close to Elsie for Ginger to make a break for her daughter, and the only thing she could do was stand and watch as the situation fell apart.

Henry was Lydia's father. Sydney was on the run from him because, from the sounds of it, he'd horribly mistreated her. Emily looked miserably sick, her face pasty, hair stringy, while Kate stood next to her, cheeks damp with tears of silent rage.

"I should have had the guts to do this ten years ago," Emily said in the earth-shattering silence.

"Emily, *no*—" Ginger shouted, but it was too late.

The shot rang loud, an ear-shattering *boom*.

twenty-nine

Everything happened at once.

The pergola lurched as Henry stumbled back against it. The frame wobbled, shook. Gauze whipped in a dance with the wind, tangling around the compromised structure. The flowers woven over the weathered wood trembled; petals spiraled to the ground. And then, in its entirety, the pergola began a steady descent as the supports crumbled beneath it.

Elsie screamed, curling Lydia closer to her body as she hunched forward into a protective crouch, too close to the free-falling structure. If she didn't move, Ginger knew, her daughter would be crushed.

The bullet had wildly missed Henry. It'd lodged itself into the pole behind him, but the shock had startled Henry into taking the fixture down with the sheer brunt of his weight. Unfortunately, as he peeled himself off the trembling beams, he was prepared to act.

While the floral-laden beams swayed and waned, bone-white against the moonlight, he hurtled through the chaos toward Elsie and the child. At the same time, Ginger flew toward her daughter. But she was a step behind, a little too late, a little too slow, a little too…

Ginger could only watch as her daughter, her beautiful daughter, harnessed the baby against her chest. Elsie was prepared for Henry's attack. She reached behind her for a bottle of wine and, as Henry neared her, she closed her eyes and swung at his approach.

Elsie clipped him on the side of the head with a sickening crack, just as the pergola gave its dying breath. With one final gasp, the white fabrics billowed and wheezed, along with the entirety of the structure. Hundreds of pounds of splintered wood, boughs of greenery, and festive fairy lights shivered with anticipation. Finally, the support beams bowed their knees in surrender.

Ginger could only watch as it happened. With a sharp inhalation, she realized it would land on Henry, trap him, if she did nothing. He was lying on the ground, dazed from the head injury. He struggled to roll over and Ginger leapt for him. But he was just too heavy, and his eyes were just too glazed, and she was forced to retreat. A piercing scream accompanied the swaying cracks of dying wood.

The world paused, stilled, stalled.

Then Lydia let out a cry, and time resumed.

And with it, gravity.

The pergola gave up, finished. Henry's hands were an ugly red, coated by blood from the rapidly growing pool around his head. Ginger returned to his side, tried again to haul him out from underneath it all, but her attempts were futile. As she looked into his eyes, she knew it had come to an end.

Ginger crouched to shield her daughter's eyes as Henry took one last, guttural breath.

"Are you okay, sweetie?" Ginger stroked her daughter's face. "Did he touch you? Lydia—she's fine. What happened?"

"Mom, I'm fine—I'm fine," Elsie said, shaking, pulling herself to a sitting position with Lydia pressed to her.

From behind them came a cry from Lulu. "Sydney needs help! I've found a pulse! Someone needs to call her an ambulance."

"I'm calling now," Kate said, pulling out her phone, a slight warble in her voice the only sign of a break in her efficiency. "Breathe, Elsie. It's going to be okay."

"Oh my God." Elsie's face paled as realization sank in. "Was that really... Did I kill Lydia's father? I hit him with the wine bottle, and he couldn't get up in time... I... *Mom...*"

Elsie let out a heartrending wail. The truth of what had happened was beginning to sink in, and fast. Ginger ached for her daughter, but there wasn't time for emotions. She needed to figure out a way to keep Elsie out of this—for good.

"Stop," Kate said decisively. "He was a monster."

"It was self-defense," Lulu called over. "I saw the whole thing. There's no doubt about it."

"He wasn't armed," Elsie said. "Am I going to prison—"

"We're not going to let anything happen to you. Not ever, do you understand me?" Ginger clutched her daughter to her chest. "Elsie, this wasn't your fault. It was my fault. I lunged for him. I'm going to confess to the police. This wasn't your fault, sweetie."

"It was self-defense," Lulu insisted. "There was a struggle!"

"I am not taking the risk," Ginger said firmly. "I'm not letting my daughter near this mess. What don't you understand?"

"I understand," Emily said quietly. "But you're not taking the blame, Ginger. I might as well have killed him. I shot the gun. I was just doing what I should have done a decade ago."

"Emily..." Ginger shook her head. "No. You were trying to save my daughter's life—"

"I was going to end my life tonight," Emily said, "and nothing more. I would be dead now if not for Elsie."

"But I—" Elsie gasped. "If I didn't knock him down, he would be alive, and—"

Ginger shook her head, gaining momentum. "I could have saved him at the end, but I didn't. Elsie is my daughter," Ginger said fiercely, looking around, demanding the others understand. "I'm going to confess, and I need you ladies to back up my story. Just in case. I swung the bottle of wine at his head, *do you hear me?*"

"Elsie, I need you to listen to me. You're to take a shower," Kate said briskly. "Get the blood off you. We'll take care of this, honey. I promise. It's what I'd want anyone to do for my daughter."

Either Elsie was in shock, or she was incredibly calm. Ginger could barely formulate a thought other than her need to keep Elsie out of this at all costs. Fragments of shattered information filtered through her brain, but nothing stuck. She wanted to listen to Kate and follow orders.

"Where's Sydney?" Lulu asked. "Wasn't she lying there unconscious? And where did Emily go?"

"Shit," Kate said, resting a hand across her head as she glanced around at the newly vacated patio. "Elsie, did you hear me? You need to get out of here. Go find your father."

"But I'm the one who killed him!" Elsie cried.

"Honey, you didn't kill him. He was alive when I got to him," Ginger said, her voice hoarse.

"If anyone's turning themselves in over that monster, let it be me," Lulu called, returning from the courtyard where she'd been looking for Sydney. "Elsie is only a girl, and she's going to need her mother by her side now more than ever."

"Elsie is my daughter," Ginger said, her mouth feeling parched. "If anyone gets to take her place, it's me. I have to protect her."

"I think I have an idea," Kate said.

thirty

Emily waited until the others had left. Shuffled inside to take care of Elsie, to carry out their little plan to save the girl. Not that it mattered; they wouldn't need it. Emily should be the one to shoulder the weight of Henry's death—alone.

He lay beneath the pergola, the exquisite symbol of lasting love and commitment that had brought about a painful end to his miserable life. *Fitting*, she thought, feeling for a pulse while averting her face so she didn't have to stare at his broken one. She didn't feel remorse, nor did she feel sadness. Just complete and utter exhaustion.

The emotions that swirled through her this weekend had swelled and built until she'd found herself drunkenly holding a gun to her head, and they now came hurtling back, stinging her eyes. Tears of tiredness, of sadness, leaked down her face, dripped from her chin until they mixed with the spatters of blood on the ground.

The regret pounded against Emily's skull in full force as she debated the what-ifs. What if she had stood up to Daniel when it was her own daughter in danger? What if that one action would have saved Julia's life? What if it had been her daughter shielding Lydia, facing off with a fucking monster?

Regret simmered, boiled, struggled to morph itself into rage. She'd slept with this man, allowed herself to be screwed by another woman's husband. A woman as lovely as Sydney with a darling daughter, with so much to live for, with the potential for a family mere inches from his now-cold, dead fingers. Another man had used Emily, abused Sydney, and still had a daughter to show for it.

Why should this monster get the opportunity to raise his daughter when there was no second chance for Emily? No matter how much she prayed, or how hard it hurt, or how desperate she felt, it would never bring Julia back.

A sob racked Emily's shoulders as her eyes clouded. She didn't belong here, drifting amid platters of exquisite champagne and expensive flowers and luxurious pools… She belonged at home with her daughter, with the sweet scent of newborn shampoo mixed with the warmth of a sleeping baby against her chest, but no. Thanks to men like Henry, like Daniel, Emily's life had been destroyed.

And so had Sydney's. The poor, young mother lying unconscious on the rocky ground, nearly murdered by her husband. If things had gone differently, that would have been Emily.

That *had* been Emily. And as Emily raised her gun, she felt a sudden influx of déjà vu, of waking in the bathtub with a splitting headache and a lump the size of a golf ball. Of padding silently across the floor, dripping blood on the white carpets. Of reaching for her daughter and not hearing a breath…

"He's already dead." Sydney's voice startled Emily. "What are you doing?"

Emily turned and found Sydney curled over herself, her hair matted with blood and eyes wide with frenzy. Emily couldn't respond for the tightness in her chest as the image of Julia swam before her eyes. "I'm doing what I should have done for my own daughter. Her name was Julia."

Sydney met her gaze, and the two women shared a chilled look. Then Sydney nodded and closed her eyes.

With a chest-crushing sob, Emily aimed the gun at Henry's chest. And pulled the trigger.

Detective Ramone: Hi, Ms. Adler. Thank you for agreeing to join me here again. Please state your name for the record.

Elsie Adler: I'm Elsie Adler.

Detective Ramone: How old are you, Elsie?

Elsie Adler: I'm fifteen. Almost sixteen.

Detective Ramone: What brought you to Serenity Spa & Resort this week?

Elsie Adler: My mom's college friend is getting married.

Detective Ramone: Thank you. Now, I understand you asked to see me.

Elsie Adler: Yes, my mom doesn't know I'm here. I'm supposed to be with my dad, but I snuck out when he went to the bathroom. He's going to be super mad at me.

Detective Ramone: Why did you sneak out?

Elsie Adler: Because you should know the truth.

Detective Ramone: What truth?

Elsie Adler: I know you're looking for a murderer, Detective, and the truth is—I killed that man.

I'm the one who hit Henry on the head with the wine bottle, and I can't stand that everyone is lying to protect me. I'm almost an adult.

Detective Ramone: That's very brave of you to come forward, Elsie. Please walk me through exactly what happened.

Elsie Adler: Well, I went to the ballroom for the dinner party with Kate. She's another college friend of my mom's. Once we arrived, I went outside to see Sydney and Lydia.

Detective Ramone: Do you know Sydney and Lydia well?

Elsie Adler: Not really, but I helped babysit Lydia this afternoon, and I wanted to say hi and play with her on the patio. She's very cute, and I liked them a lot.

Detective Ramone: Okay, so you found them. Was it just the three of you outside?

Elsie Adler: Yes, dinner had already started, so we were alone out back. We were just peeking at the pergola and all the pretty floral arrangements when he arrived. We probably weren't supposed to be out there, but we weren't doing anything wrong. We just wanted to look. Lydia liked the bright colors.

Detective Ramone: Elsie, what happened once Henry arrived?

Elsie Adler: Well, I was already holding Lydia. I heard a commotion and turned around, but by then, Sydney was already on the ground. She didn't even make a noise. He was standing over her.

Detective Ramone: Henry, you mean?

Elsie Adler: Yes. Then the baby let out a cry, and he heard it. I tried to keep Lydia quiet and hide by the huge rack of wine bottles, but I couldn't.

Detective Ramone: I understand. What happened then?

Elsie Adler: Sydney was bleeding a lot, and she didn't move. I thought she was dead.

Detective Ramone: That had to be very scary for you.

Elsie Adler: Yeah, but I wasn't even thinking about being scared. I was… I heard Lydia cry when her mom fell. It was like she knew. And I hid to protect her. I… Maybe I should have gone to help Sydney, but I think she would have wanted me to keep Lydia safe.

Detective Ramone: I'm sure she would have wanted exactly that. What did you do after you got to the rack of wine bottles?

Elsie Adler: I screamed. I thought someone from

the party might have heard me, but I don't think they did. Then, um… I think that's when he…

Detective Ramone: It's okay, Elsie. What did he do?

Elsie Adler: He pulled out a gun. I'm—I'm pretty sure that's when it happened. Everything is a little blurry.

Detective Ramone: That's understandable. Did he shoot?

Elsie Adler: No, he wanted Lydia. I figured he'd kill me either way after I saw what he did to Sydney, so I just reacted and held Lydia tighter. It was like I couldn't let her go, even if I wanted to.

Detective Ramone: Like I said, you were very brave. When you refused to give him the baby, what did he say?

Elsie Adler: Um, I don't really remember. Other things happened then. My mom was there, and her friends. I don't know how they all got there, but then they started talking to Henry.

Detective Ramone: Do you remember what they said?

Elsie Adler: Bits and pieces, but like I said, it's fuzzy. My mom tried to get Henry to go after her instead of me, but he didn't. I think he already knew Emily somehow. There was a shot—but

it didn't hit him. It hit the pergola and startled
Henry. Everything sort of sped up really fast
and then went into slow motion.

Detective Ramone: How do you mean?

Elsie Adler: Well, the shot was so loud, and
then Henry crashed into the wooden beams and
the whole structure started to collapse. People
started running and shouting, but all I could
see was him coming after me. So I grabbed the
only thing I could think of and swung at him.

Detective Ramone: Toward Henry? And are you
referencing the wine bottle?

Elsie Adler: Yes. He had his gun out. I think he
had it pointed at me. I don't exactly remember,
but I know I was terrified. I put Lydia against my
chest and closed my eyes. And, yeah, I just swung.
I felt it connect, and…crack. I was only thinking
of Lydia. How is she? Will she remember this?

Detective Ramone: Lydia is fine, and I'm sure
she won't remember any of it.

Elsie Adler: How's Sydney?

Detective Ramone: Elsie, please concentrate.
After you hit Henry on the head with the bottle,
what happened?

Elsie Adler: He went down, sort of limp, like

he couldn't really move. My mom went to help him, but the pergola was already going down, and then…he, um…

Detective Ramone: Are you okay, Elsie?

Elsie Adler: I feel a little sick. It landed on him. He was already bleeding everywhere, and then it was like the whole world stopped, and then when it restarted, he wasn't moving anymore. I think I killed him.

Detective Ramone: Nobody else had any contact with Henry? Please don't cry, Elsie. You were very brave for Lydia.

Elsie Adler: My mom tried to help him, but there was too much chaos. He was just too big and too heavy to move before the beams crashed on top of him. That's when they all decided to cover for me. Lulu because she is the oldest and has no children or anyone else to worry about. Emily because…well, I think she was very angry with him. Then my mom because, well, she's my mom, and Kate because she's my friend.

Detective Ramone: Elsie, I have one big question left for you.

Elsie Adler: Um, okay?

Detective Ramone: You said that Henry pulled a gun on you.

Elsie Adler: Er, yeah.

Detective Ramone: That would make the case pretty cut and dry—self-defense, obviously. But there's one piece of the puzzle I'm missing. Did Emily get the gun away from Henry at any point?

Elsie Adler: Um, no. I don't think so. I mean, I think she had her own. I-I'm pretty sure she didn't take Henry's.

Detective Ramone: You're sure?

Elsie Adler: I think so. I'm pretty positive. They each had a gun. There were two. Two guns, I remember now.

Detective Ramone: Unfortunately, Ms. Adler, I'm having a difficult time believing there was a second gun. Where would it have gone? You see, it wasn't anywhere on the premises—at least not that we've found, and we've looked everywhere. So while I appreciate you telling me the truth, you'll understand that I need to be sure you're telling the full truth.

Elsie Adler: I—Everything happened so fast. I'm not sure where it went.

Detective Ramone: That's the curious thing, isn't it? I first thought maybe one of you women took it, but that doesn't make sense. Without the gun, the case is a lot harder to prove self-defense. It's in your best interest that we find the second gun. If there is one.

Elsie Adler: He was…er, um…he was going after the baby.

Detective Ramone: Yes, but what if I told you… the baby belonged to him?

Elsie Adler: The baby belonged to Sydney too.

Detective Ramone: I'm going to ask you one more time, Elsie. Who killed Henry? Where's the second gun—or was there one?

Elsie Adler: It was me, sir. I killed Henry. A baby belongs with her mother.

Detective Ramone: That's not for you to decide.

Elsie Adler: It was self-defense.

Detective Ramone: Last question, Elsie. Where did Sydney Banks go?

Elsie Adler: Sydney? I've no clue. I imagine she's outside recovering with Lydia.

Detective Ramone: She was. An hour ago. But somehow, she got away from the medical examination team. She's gone.

thirty-one

Lulu dragged her old, weary bones up to the resort room. Her whole body, mind, and soul were weary. Maybe it was leftover adrenaline from the commotion on the patio seeping from her muscles, or maybe it was the thought of facing her husband for what could easily be the most difficult conversation of their marriage. Or maybe she was just getting old, dammit, and needed to get used to feeling tired.

With a hefty sigh, she placed her key card in the door. The detective was still downstairs sorting through testimonies, but once Elsie had come forward, the jig was more or less over. Except for the tiny detail of Sydney's escape…along with the baby. That, Lulu knew nothing about.

Poor Elsie, Lulu thought. She was one of the real victims in all this. Nobody, no child, should have had to see what she'd seen. Or have made the decisions she'd made.

Lulu pushed the door open, tears sprouting in her eyes the second she saw her husband pacing before the window. All thoughts of the case downstairs slipped from her mind at once.

Pierce looked worried, harried. Instead of his usual dress slacks and a fine shirt, he had on jeans and a long-sleeved, pale-gray sweater that looked like butter. The effect was jarring to Lulu. He really was out of sorts—either in worry over Lulu's whereabouts, or something else. Even his neatly trimmed hair stood at odd angles, and he had the beginnings of a five o'clock shadow. It made him look older, rougher.

Lulu didn't feel nervous around him any longer. She wasn't frightened by the glint in his eye or the story he'd likely try to spin when she asked about his secret phone. After a night of lies, all Lulu wanted was the truth.

"Finally," he said, turning around, an expression of relief on his face. "Lulu, I was so concerned for you! They said you might be involved in the death of a man, and I couldn't get to you. I tried to find you. What happened?"

"I'm sorry," she said, her lip trembling. "I—"

"Sit down," her husband said, gentle but firm.

He rarely took on a controlling tone, but when he did, there was no arguing with him. Lulu sat.

"Tell me one thing," she whispered. Lulu shifted onto the bed, her shoulders hunched over as her hands fiddled on her lap. "Are we over, Pierce?"

Her husband didn't look surprised enough by Lulu's question to make her feel any better. "I don't want us to be over."

"But we are." The tiredness came on stronger. Lulu closed her eyes. "Give me the truth. Who is she?"

"Who?"

"S," Lulu said. "You've got to have figured out by now that I found your secret phone. And I might be naive, Pierce, but I know about the locked drawer in the study. The calendar appointments. The late-night meetings. The money funneled out of our account. It all links back to S. So tell me, who is she?"

"Oh, Lulu." Pierce shook his head, ran a hand down his face. "It's not what you think. There's no one else. It's always been you."

"Don't lie to me!" Lulu wiped angry tears from her eyes. "All I'm asking for is the truth. I heard her fucking voice."

Pierce's body went perfectly still. That unfamiliar, stony expression returned. Lulu wasn't used to seeing her husband's face harden, nor did she like it. He seemed foreign to her, unfamiliar. As if she hadn't really known him the entire duration of their marriage.

"There's no easy way to tell you this," Pierce said. "But maybe if I show you…"

"Goddamn it, Pierce. I want a name," Lulu said, her voice raising. "If you're leaving me, I want to know—"

"There's a chance I'll be indicted, Lulu." Pierce's voice rang crystal clear throughout the room, like the sound of a flute echoing across a cold, winter morning. Soulful, piercing. Chilling. "My company has been under investigation for some time now."

"But—" Lulu looked up at her husband. "I don't understand. Your secret phone…"

"I use it to talk to my head lawyer—*Sheila*," Pierce said. "She's in my appointment book as *S*. I've not mentioned her to you on purpose. She was instructed to leave you entirely out of things, which is why she hung up when you answered this morning. I have been doing everything I can to keep this mess out of our personal lives, hence the phone, the meetings at the office, the appointments I couldn't tell you about."

"But the note I found… It said you met with *S* at a hotel."

"We often meet at the lobby bar or the restaurant at the Ritz," Pierce explained. "You can check my credit card—there are no room charges or anything of the sort. I wouldn't do that to you, Lulu. You have to understand, it's not good for company morale to take such frequent meetings with Sheila at my office during business hours."

"No, as a matter of fact, I wouldn't understand, because you haven't told me anything. Why wouldn't you trust me with this?" When Lulu spoke, her voice sounded flimsier than she would have liked. "If you're in trouble, I would have supported you. You're my husband, Pierce. What made you think you'd have to suffer through this alone?"

Pierce sat, the stony facade cracking as he took his wife's hands and grasped them in his own. "Lulu, what you have to understand is that I love you more than anything. The mistakes I've made—well, they happened long before I met you. If I'd known what I know now…if I'd known I could be as happy as I am with you, maybe things would have been different. But they're not, and I don't want your name and reputation sullied because of my choices."

"But I love you."

"And I love you. But I don't know how long this whole process will take. The investigation is ongoing and will likely end in an indictment."

"What does that mean?"

"There'll be an arrest, a grand jury, media attention…" He stared intently at the wall. "You're such a wonderful woman, and I hate what I'm doing to you, to us. If I'd known…"

Pierce had slipped into a pattern of not finishing his thoughts, leaving Lulu to pick up the pieces and place them together. "Are you telling me you'll be taken to jail? But that's impossible! You're a good man."

"I'm a flawed man. That's the beautiful thing about you—you see the good in everyone. Even me."

Lulu raised her hand, pressed it to her husband's cheek. "So there's nobody else? Sheila is…your lawyer? And the late-night meetings?"

"All related to the investigation. I may have told half-truths—or worse—in my professional career, but I swear I've never lied to you. It's always been you. Only you, Lulu."

Lulu's tears streamed down her face. "What did you have to show me?"

"Inside my locked drawer at home, along with a few papers related to the case files, I keep a notebook," Pierce said, brushing a kiss across Lulu's forehead before he stood and crossed the room. He retrieved a tiny black book from the same pocket in the suitcase where he'd stashed his secret phone and paused, holding it lovingly in his hands. "In it, I write down all the things I can't seem to voice now, and all the things I know I'd like to tell you later." He hesitated again. "That way, even if I'm not beside you physically in the future, you'll have a little piece of me left behind—if you want it, of course."

"Oh, Pierce," Lulu said, her throat clogged with emotion. "I confessed to cracking a man's skull tonight, rather than face the thought of life without you!"

"Lulu, honey." Pierce pulled her close. "What's all this nonsense about cracking a man's skull open? Who would ever believe you could do that to someone?"

"That's the least of our problems for now. Why didn't you tell me?" she whispered again.

"I—" He cleared his throat. "I've been alone a long time, Lulu. Almost seventy years I've been on my own, taking care of myself, making decisions that affected nobody but myself. If only I could have foreseen the fallout."

She pulled back with stark realization. "You thought I would leave you if I knew the truth."

"I am *encouraging* you to do so. See, I don't want to hold you back," Pierce said. "I wanted to make it to our five-year anniversary—for both our sakes—and then I was going to sit you down and explain everything. I would've told you next week. I wanted to give you the option to divorce me quietly before things got too difficult. I don't want to be a burden on you, Lulu. I love you too much for that."

"Sweetheart…" Lulu choked on her tears. "I'm not going anywhere."

Pierce gave a sad smile at his wife before he handed the booklet over and watched as she thumbed through pages of love notes, of words he couldn't say, of dreams he'd never live out next to Lulu. When she looked up, her eyes moist and full of love, she shook her head.

"I hope you'll tell me more when you're ready," Lulu said in a thin murmur. "And until then, will you come here, Pierce? If you will be taken away from me, please—at least let us enjoy the time we have left together."

thirty-two

Emily raised a hand and knocked on the room door. Her breath hitched. It'd been a long night of tying up loose ends, and by the time it was all over, it must have been 4:00 a.m. before she tumbled into bed.

Emily hadn't been able to sleep, nor had she been able to eat. She'd merely sat on her deck with a cup of cold coffee in her hand, frozen in thought, through the early morning hours. She'd considered all that had come to pass—and all that hadn't. How close she'd come to ending her life. How close she'd come to ending another's. How close she'd come to falling for Henry fucking Anonymous, only to find out he'd been no better than Daniel.

Eventually, she'd pulled herself from the gloom. The walls had begun to close in, to suffocate. The sour stench of milk from her creamer jug—left on the balcony to warm in the sun—spiraled into her nostrils and caused her stomach to churn. She vomited into the toilet for half an hour, then forced herself to shower, brush her teeth, and dab on some makeup that made her look less like the complete and utter mess she was.

Ginger pulled the door open, stopping abruptly the second she saw Emily on the other side. She gave a furtive glance behind her, as if concerned Emily might somehow rub off on her children.

A good fear, Emily thought. Because the darkness around her was all consuming, a growing, living thing that fed off her soul—all the good and bright and colorful. And left behind nothing but a brittle shell.

"What are you doing here?" Ginger asked. "I thought—is the wedding still on?"

The wedding had been pushed back a day, much to Miranda Rosales's dismay (and very loud shrieking). The entire resort had heard shouts about how the flowers were wilting, the ice sculptures melting, the food spoiling. Not to mention the new pergola that had needed to be ordered. They'd have to pay *tens of thousands of dollars*, she'd screamed at the concierge, but the resort had planted its foot in light of the circumstances—and declared the wedding venue closed.

"No," Emily said. "I came to say…I'm…"

"Just a minute, all right?" Ginger called over her shoulder to her kids. "You guys get ready for the pool. Have Daddy take you down when he's out of the bathroom. I have something to take care of."

"But, Mom," Poppy shouted. "I can't find my underwear!"

"I'll help," Emily heard Elsie mutter quietly. "Go on, Mom."

Late the previous night, after Elsie had slipped out of her father's clutches and come forward with a mostly true story, the gig had been up. The detective had called all four women back into the makeshift interview room to go over their stories one more time. Bit by bit, the real truth had slipped into place.

In light of the situation, and the circumstances, Detective Ramone had agreed not to hold Elsie in juvenile detention but to leave her under the care of her family. With four eye witnesses all claiming that Henry had lunged at Elsie and she had reacted the only way she'd seen how, self-defense had been reinstated as a viable explanation, even without the second gun Elsie had fabricated in her nervous confession.

Sydney's injuries and testimony had also backed up the women's stories. Before she'd escaped, she'd gone on record explaining that Henry had hit her over the head with something—she wasn't sure what—and knocked her unconscious. It was the last thing she remembered before waking up with a splitting headache in the courtyard.

The attack had been unprovoked, according to Sydney, which made Henry's aggression toward Elsie all the more believable. And, as Detective Ramone pointed out, it wouldn't be long before the autopsy confirmed or rejected the women's confessions. It would be easy enough to prove whether it was the bonk on the head, the pergola, or the bullet in Henry's chest that had delivered the killing blow.

Ginger slipped out of her room, closing the door against the noise of her children as they prepared for the day ahead. "What is it?"

There was a look in Ginger's eyes, a look of remorse, of trepidation, that somehow weaved its way into Emily's heart. A concern, almost motherly, as Ginger asked if she was feeling okay, told her she didn't look good, and would she like to sit down?

Emily felt the tears come. She hadn't cried in so long, in oh so long. After losing a child, what else was there to cry over? But somehow, she'd never allowed herself to feel the pain of it. To truly mourn Julia. She'd felt guilt—horrible, crippling guilt—over the fact that she hadn't left Daniel earlier. She hadn't been there to hear her baby—if there was anything to hear. Maybe there was nothing she could have done, but Emily had never let the thought cross her mind. It had always been her fault.

"Why couldn't you forgive me?" Emily gasped, then burst into tears all over again. The horrible, gut-wrenching, awful sort of cry that had her rocking against the wall like a maniac, curling against her knees as she slid to the floor. Howling, wailing. Doors popped open in the hallway, voices murmured over the hysterical woman.

"Come inside," Ginger said, opening the door and shooing Emily inside. "Kids, get out of here. Frank, *now*."

Ginger's family leapt to attention and vacated the room. Poppy was only half-dressed, but Elsie threw a towel around her, and Frank picked his littlest daughter up and slung her over his shoulder while Tommy scrounged for the rest of Poppy's suit. They worked in unison and vanished before Emily could breathe.

"I'm sorry," Emily said, her shoulders shaking as she exhaled her words. "I'm sorry I ruined our friendship. You have no idea how sorry I am."

"Really, it's okay," Ginger said. "I should have let it go so much sooner. It was stupid of me to hold onto a grudge for this long. I was hurt, but I got over it. Frank got over it. And I'm sorry, Emily—oh, honey, why are you still crying? Look, I was meant to be with Frank. It all worked out. You got back with Daniel, and there was no harm done. Maybe I should be thanking you for the kick in the pants that I needed to realize I belonged with Frank."

"I stayed with Daniel," Emily said. "We had a child together. Her name was Julia."

Ginger's shoulders stiffened. "I didn't know that."

"Of course you didn't," Emily said. "You were off having your beautiful children with nice, thoughtful Frank. And Daniel..."

Ginger looked mostly confused as Emily trailed off, and though she tried to offer comfort, she clearly didn't know what to say. "I'm—um, happy for you! Where is your daughter now? Is she with him?"

Emily raised her bleary eyes, looked at her ex-best friend, and shook her head. "She's gone."

The story flushed out of Emily, poured forth like it never had before. Every aching detail, every poisoned memory, every sweet, tiny detail she could remember from Julia's short time on earth. Every awful detail of her life with Daniel. Every wave of guilt she'd felt in the following years. She continued through to the previous night and explained that the reason she'd had the gun was so she could end her own life.

"Emily," Ginger said, and true sympathy gushed from her as she pulled her old friend into her arms. "None of this is your fault. You were a victim, sweetie. What Daniel did is inexcusable. It's *not—your—fault.*"

"If I'd only left—"

"I've had friends—wonderful mothers, wonderful fathers, wonderful families—lose children for reasons beyond their control. They never deserve it. There's always guilt. I can't imagine—if it had been me, or Elsie…"

The women both lapsed into silence.

"I see why you are so angry at me," Ginger said quietly. "I'm sorry I never knew, and I'm sorry I handled the situation so poorly and made things worse. While I had my children, and Frank, you had…"

"It's not your fault," Emily said quickly. "But, Ginger, I can't go on like this. I need…I need *help*."

Ginger ran her hand through Emily's hair, motherly, softly. "It's going to be okay, Emily. You'll get through this. You were ready to save my daughter's life yesterday. Whatever you need, whatever I can do for you—it'll be done."

"I don't know that there's a thing you can do for me. I am already lost."

"No, you're not," Ginger said firmly. "You're my best friend, Emily. And I need you back. Elsie needs you. And Julia…she'd want you back too."

Mindy King: Good evening, everyone. This is Mindy King with Channel 11, bringing you the most up-to-date breaking news as it's happening. Today, we have Detective Ramone here with us to answer a few questions about the case that has stumped the nation. Baby Lydia, barely five months old, has seemingly disappeared from the face of the earth after her father was tragically killed last week. The story came to light after a man's death disrupted a wedding at the highly esteemed Serenity Spa & Resort. Detective, can you help us to understand what truly happened behind the wedding veil?

Detective Ramone: Thank you for having me, Mindy. We are currently asking anyone with information on Sydney Banks, thought to be traveling with the young infant named Lydia, to call the police. We suspect she has kidnapped the child.

Mindy King: The man who was found dead—Henry—was a widower and the father to the baby our country has come to know and love as Lydia, correct?

Detective Ramone: Yes, that's correct.

Mindy King: If the rumors are to be believed, Lydia's mother, Carolyn, passed away just a few weeks before Henry in a surprising accident at home. She sadly left behind a husband and child.

Detective Ramone: That's correct.

Mindy King: Did Henry murder his wife, Detective?

Detective Ramone: Carolyn's case has been reopened due to the discovery of new information. We are exploring the possibility that Carolyn's death was not accidental, and we will continue to do everything in our power to leave no stone unturned. We *will* uncover the trail of events leading to Lydia's disappearance.

Mindy King: You mentioned that Lydia has likely been kidnapped by her nanny, Sydney Banks. Is it true that Sydney killed the baby's father in order to steal his child?

Detective Ramone: We suspect the child is with Sydney Banks, as I said, and we encourage anyone who thinks they've seen Sydney or Lydia to phone their local police. It's possible Sydney could be armed, so we urge everyone to take caution in the instance of a sighting.

Mindy King: Let me get this straight, Detective. We have a husband who kills his wife, only to find his daughter kidnapped by the nanny. When Henry tracks down his daughter, he's killed by… *who*, Detective? Who killed Henry Stone?

Detective Ramone: We're not releasing that information to the public at this point. The investigation is still under way. That's all for today.

Mindy King: So we've got a dead mother, a dead father, a kidnapping nanny, and zero leads from the police. Detective, what are the chances of finding Lydia Stone alive?

Detective Ramone: I've no further comment.

thirty-three

One Year Later

A re you ready to see them?" Kate bounced Emma up and down on her lap, chatting to the giggling little girl. "Because I know they're dying to see you, sweet cheeks! Are you going to show them how big you are?"

Emma laughed, but Kate didn't have time to coo a response before a knock on the door had her springing from her seat. "Here they are!"

Kate bounced across the condo that would be home base for a girls' weekend in New York City. After the incident a year ago, the women had all gone their separate ways, keeping in touch mostly thanks to Kate's bossy texts asking how everyone was doing once a month.

Kate hadn't broken the news to them about her adoption plans until the papers had been finalized. Within weeks of returning from the spa, Kate had submitted all the necessary documentation to all the finest agencies. She spared no expense and, after some thought, decided that she could do without an astronaut as a father or a doctor as a mother. All Kate wanted was a child.

While Kate had expected conflicting emotions to hit her as the adoption process went underway, they never came. It'd been a shock for her to realize there simply were none. Instead, she wondered if maybe she wasn't broken at all. Maybe she just hadn't met her son or daughter yet. In fact, Kate had never been more sure of anything.

The call had come nearly eight months later. Kate knew that was exceptionally fast—miraculously fast, even—but for the first time in her life, she found herself believing in miracles. The moment she laid eyes on Emma's face, she knew. They would be a family.

While Kate suffered an occasional ache that Emma would grow up without a father, nothing could diminish her joy at finally having a child. Not the sleepless nights, the hectic work schedule, the exhaustion, the destroyed social schedule, or even the fact that she hadn't made it to the gym in five whole days. Kate was head over heels in love, and she wouldn't have it any other way.

Plus, Kate thought as she pulled open the door, she wasn't really alone. She had plenty of strong women on her flanks who would be wonderful role models for Emma. Like the two standing on her doorstep now.

"Ladies!" Kate did an awkward one-armed hug to encompass both women. "I'm so glad you could make it. I hope you're ready for some massages—joking. But seriously, I have some fun things planned for us, so long as we can work around nap time."

"Can I hold her?" Elsie was barely through the door. "Emma is gorgeous, Kate."

"I know. Takes after her namesake." Kate winked. "Emma Elsie Cross."

Elsie blinked. "What?"

"After one very brave woman," Kate said with a broad smile. "Come on in already."

Kate knew, from her texts with Elsie, that the teenager and her mother had grown close over the last year, in no small part due to the horrors Elsie had witnessed at the resort. However, real life had caught up to them all, and Kate had been pleased to hear that Elsie had made the cheerleading team. (And that Ginger was very proud of her daughter's accomplishment.) The condoms had long been tossed in the trash, but the dialogue about such things remained open. And Elsie had made friends her age who had similar interests reading ragged little books and writing angsty songs and going to the movies. Kate knew Ginger was relieved.

"Where's Lulu?" Elsie asked, smiling at Emma as she reached for her. "And Emily?"

Like always, Kate felt a twinge of worry handing her daughter over to anyone, but she needn't have worried at all. Elsie was a pro. "Lulu's flying in shortly. She didn't want to crowd us, so she'll be staying at the same hotel as Emily. They'll meet us for dinner."

"And Pierce?" Ginger asked with a certain, unspoken curiosity.

"He's not able to make it," Kate said easily. "He can't get away at the moment, as he's needed in court. They're expecting a decision sometime in the next few months."

Ginger eyed her daughter who, despite her interest in the baby, was clearly listening attentively. "Is Emily in yet?"

"She's flying back from France, actually," Kate said with a sophisticated eyebrow wiggle. "With a man. A good one, from the sounds of it."

"I can't believe it's been a year since we've seen each other," Ginger said. "It almost feels like no time has passed."

Kate agreed. "It's been a year too long."

"Have you heard from..." Ginger hesitated, waiting until Elsie had taken Emma deeper into the living room. She bit her lip and dropped her voice. "Have you heard anything at all from Sydney?"

"Ginger, it's been a year since she took off." Kate reached for Ginger, squeezed her shoulder. "She's gone. You have to let this go. It's not our fault. We did the best we could with the information we had. How were we to know Lydia wasn't Sydney's child?"

"D'you still think..." Ginger hesitated. "Is Lydia better off with Sydney?"

"My opinion hasn't changed since the news story broke," Kate said. "I think Lydia would have been best off with her mother."

"I still can't believe it." Ginger's eyes widened. "That whole time, we were getting to know Sydney in person, and she was living someone else's life. All those stories she told us... They must have belonged to Carolyn. But I can't shake the feeling that we had it all wrong from the start. I have nightmares that maybe this was Sydney's plan all along, and we aided her in murdering an innocent man."

"Henry wasn't innocent," Kate said. "But like I've told you before, we are going to have to live with some unanswered questions. I saw the photographs. But we have to accept we might never know the truth."

Ginger gave a shrug. "I suppose someone killed Carolyn, and it probably wasn't Sydney. Right?"

Kate could barely meet Ginger's eyes.

"I think we should worry about ourselves," Kate said finally. "A year later and the police are still stumped as to the poor baby's whereabouts. What on earth could we possibly find out that they couldn't?"

"I suppose."

"Now, shall we get your things inside?" Kate said briskly. "Or would you like to sleep in the hall?"

epilogue

Kate pushed oversized sunglasses higher onto her face as she made her way carefully up the weathered front steps of a modest brick building in Southern California. Her black-and-white-striped dress had cost a mere two hundred dollars, and her shoes were six months old and had scuff marks on the sides. She didn't even care.

Ever since Emma had arrived on the scene, Kate found herself morphing slowly into the type of mom she'd always been terrified of becoming. She wore hoodies when there was a chill in the air instead of fur coats for playdates to the park. Her skin-care routine was much less important than making sure Emma was lathered in sunscreen during summer strolls in Central Park. She'd even eaten a box of sushi from a grocery store.

Right about now, Emma would be tucked away at the hotel with her nanny, a lovely young college grad with far more energy than Kate. Rebecca was her name, and Emma loved her. But not as much as she loved Kate, and that, Kate suspected, was what motherhood was all about.

Kate had agreed to fly to the West Coast on business—one of the few trips she'd taken since Emma's birth. Then again, this wasn't any old trip. Kate had tacked on a few personal days at the end that would, with any hope, answer the questions that burned and lingered in her mind.

Kate climbed to the second floor of an apartment building that looked dingy and worn, but well loved. Little cacti bloomed on balcony number nine, and a sheet of paper with a baby's handprint on it sat drying outside, tamped down by a misshapen rock.

Raising her hand, Kate expelled a breath, hoping the hours and hours of work, not to mention the thousands of dollars she'd spent, had paid off. She knocked twice.

When the door opened, Kate smiled. "Well, hello there, *Hannah.*"

Sydney Banks's face went pale—the sort of pale that meant the floor was dropping out from under her and the ceiling was caving in above her. The sort of pale that froze her blood. Kate knew she'd look the exact same way if Emma's birth parents ever tried to claim custody of her daughter.

"I trust you got the money I sent?" Kate asked lightly. "I didn't bother to sign the card, what with the police investigation and all. I have a daughter of my own now, you know, so I couldn't risk associating myself with you. But I believe you owe me some answers."

"Kate," Sydney stuttered, her eyes flashing with concern, then horror, then anger. "What do you think you're doing here?"

"If I'd come to turn you in, don't you think I would've spared myself the trip out here and simply contacted Detective Ramone?" Kate smoothed her dress. "I think the least you can do is invite me inside."

Without waiting for a response, Kate slid easily into the apartment, removing her sunglasses as she glanced around at the bright, colorful room decorated with pictures of a smiling mother-and-daughter combination.

Sydney stood stock-still in the doorway, her fingers twisting into knots before her body. She still looked thin, but less sickly than she had at the resort. She'd put on a few pounds, and her hip bones had disappeared, covered by a thin sundress patterned with pink flowers. Despite the breezy choice of clothing, the year that had passed since Kate last laid eyes on Sydney had aged her tremendously.

Instead of those bright, innocent eyes, Sydney now watched Kate carefully, cautiously.

Kate cleared her throat. "Where's Lydia?"

"*Carolyn* is sleeping," Sydney said, her chin tilted upward.

"Interesting choice in name." Kate gave Sydney a thin smile. "I've heard it a few times since you escaped."

"I didn't escape from anywhere," Sydney said. "I did what I had to do. The police wouldn't have understood."

"No? What about me?"

"There wasn't time to explain!" Sydney glanced over her shoulder as her voice raised. She shut the door, then pressed her back to it. "After that night, when Henry died and they were questioning you all, I wanted to say something. I really did."

"But you didn't," Kate said. "In fact, you lied to me. We all confessed to killing Henry. Then days later, the news breaks that you don't have any legal claim to Lydia, and in fact, both of her parents are dead. Henry was telling the truth on that patio."

"I didn't..." Sydney sucked in a fortifying breath and gained confidence as she went along. "You can't think I'd hurt anyone, or else you wouldn't have sent me money."

"Did you know who it was from?"

"To be honest, I wasn't sure." Sydney glanced toward her feet, which were bare against the carpet. "But I wasn't exactly in a position to ask questions, nor could I afford to give it back. So I accepted it. I'm not sure why you helped, but the money was a godsend. I'm sorry I couldn't thank you sooner."

"I did it for Lydia, not for you."

"How did you find me?" Sydney whispered.

"I'm a cutthroat lawyer with big-time resources and people who owed me some major favors." Kate glanced down at her nails, waited a beat. "But more importantly, I'm a stubborn bitch. I get what I want, Sydney. And when the police let up on the investigation, I figured I'd step in to see what I could do."

"The police let the case slide because they know my daughter belongs with me."

"No, they let up because it seems Henry killed his wife, and with nobody fighting for Lydia, more 'pressing' cases pushed hers to the back. Now, I'd like some answers."

Sydney's hands shook as she smoothed her dress. "Can I get you some lemonade? Congratulations on your daughter, by the way. Is she Max's?"

"No, she's mine. I adopted her on my own."

Sydney stilled, her eyes softening. "I see. Well, the same congratulations are still in order."

"Thank you," Kate said stiffly. "And yes, I'll take some of that lemonade."

Kate didn't care about the lemonade, but she did want more time in Sydney's apartment. She was genuinely curious about everything. About the past and the present, about Sydney's life and Lydia's too. As Sydney bustled about in the cramped kitchen with the cupboards that didn't quite close, and the sink that didn't quite drain, Kate found herself feeling like she didn't belong in the homey little apartment. Everything felt staged, just a little off.

"It's not much," Sydney said, handing over the glass of fresh lemonade and then gesturing for Kate to take the nicest spot on the couch. Sydney took the battered armchair that looked like it had been confiscated from a street corner and doctored back to life. "But we're happy here."

"I can see that," Kate said and found she meant it. "So you've set up a life for yourself. You're working, taking care of Lydia. Have you run into anyone else you know?"

Sydney's hands shook as she raised a glass of ice water to her lips. "No. I wished—I wanted to, but I couldn't. I wish I'd been able to speak with Elsie, but..."

"I recently saw Elsie," Kate said easily. "She's doing well."

"I wrote her a letter, ages ago," Sydney said. "Would you give it to her for me?"

"I think Elsie's been through enough without having to carry this burden too."

Sydney hung her head. "I was afraid to contact any of you. I didn't know if they were still watching."

"The police have been mystified," Kate said. "It was quite the news story for some time, though I suspect you know that. Don't you, Sydney?"

"I know what the media said—how they tried to make me out to be this evil woman." Sydney shifted uncomfortably at the mention of her old name. "But I swear I'm not the bad guy here."

"Then who is?"

"I was best friends with Lydia's mother," Sydney said finally. "I mean, I didn't know Carolyn all that well at the start, but I started as her housekeeper when she got pregnant and had to be on bed rest. We spent hours talking and talking and talking. Things started to come out."

"Things about Henry?"

Sydney nodded. "Carolyn wasn't well during the pregnancy, but that didn't stop him. You saw the book—it wasn't a lie. It wasn't *my* life, but it was Carolyn's. He did that to her."

Kate remained silent.

"He killed Carolyn," Sydney insisted. "I watched Henry push Carolyn down a flight of steps when he was stone-cold sober. I watched as she didn't get up. I watched as he tried to play it off like it was a mistake…and the police bought it. They ate up his lies. They did nothing."

"So you kidnapped Lydia."

"I'd been raising her since she was born, and even before—I loved her," Sydney said emphatically. "You must understand. You have a little girl who isn't biologically yours either—"

"Shut up," Kate growled. "Emma is my daughter. Plain and simple."

"Exactly." Sydney looked oddly appeased. "You and I understand each other. We're more alike than you know, Kate. Which is why you sent us the money. You knew I couldn't let him raise her, just as much as I did. Henry was a murderer."

"Why didn't you go to the police?"

"I did," she said. "But what right did I have to the baby? I was just the nanny, and there was no one else coming for Lydia. The police hadn't found Henry guilty of killing his wife at the time, so why would they take his child away?"

"We all wondered if this was your end goal from the very beginning."

"I swear to you, Kate," Sydney said. "I wish Carolyn were still alive. I didn't kill her, and if you think I did, then you're as bad as the police."

"I sent you money."

"Take your damn money back!" Sydney flew to her feet and stared at Kate. "Is this some sort of blackmail? I'm telling you the truth. I can't afford to pay it all back, but I will. And I'll go on the run again if I have to—Carolyn and I have survived worse."

"Going on the run last time didn't work out very well," Kate said. "Henry found you quite easily."

"I didn't think he'd paid me all that much attention," Sydney murmured. "I was the lowly help, the nanny, his *staff*. They paid me in cash; I wasn't even sure he knew my last name."

"How does a member of the Banks family end up working as 'lowly help,' as you put it?"

Sydney's lips drew into a thin line. "I'm a Banks only by name. My parents were estranged from the family. They were cut off financially and socially. I was shocked when Arthur's mother reached out after their death—she's the only one I'd spoken to in years."

"Well, Henry found you anyway. Discovered your real name, I'm guessing, and then a quick Google search would've turned up the DeBleu/Banks wedding. He probably didn't realize you were estranged from your family when he followed you there."

"It's possible," Sydney said. "Or he could have followed my trail. I didn't exactly get the opportunity to ask him. After Lydia and I left, we drove down to Chicago and stayed there for a while. It was one of the closest metropolitan areas large enough for us to disappear into the crowds."

"I see."

"As we know from Emily, she and Henry shared a flight out to California," Sydney said. "Which means he must have followed us to the motel where we'd camped out in Chicago and talked to people there. I'd told one woman we were headed out west to see family. From there, it would've been easy to find the resort details online, as you so kindly pointed out."

Kate gritted her teeth. "How do I know you're not lying this time too?"

"Trust me," Sydney whispered. "You're a woman, a mother now. You have to understand. The night I took Lydia, he almost killed me. I didn't hear him come home. I was supposed to hear him—the fifth step squeaks, the seventh step sighs. I never heard the *sigh*."

"What do you mean, he tried to kill you?"

"I was upstairs in the nursery, singing to Lydia, when he saw me. He had a gun, and I just kept singing, trying to keep him even tempered. I remember the very lyrics. 'Hush, little baby, don't say a word,'" she sung softly, "'Mama's gonna buy you a mockingbird…'"

An eerie chill settled on Kate's shoulders. "Why that song? You weren't her mother then."

"No, it was just a song then, but I am her only hope now." Sydney's feet seemed planted a little firmer, and a steely resolve developed in her eyes. "Carolyn belongs to me. She's mine. I love her, just as you love your baby girl."

"How'd you get away?" Kate asked. "You expect me to believe that you escaped from a confrontation with a man double your weight and armed with a gun? And still managed to kidnap his child?"

"Of course not," Sydney said. "I put the baby back in the crib and managed to talk Henry down from the ledge. He's cocky and mean, but he's not stupid. Two mysterious deaths in his house within a month? It wouldn't look good for him. Even if he managed to kill me and hide my body, someone would have reported me missing. The police might have been inspired to reopen Carolyn's file, and I assured Henry that he didn't want any such thing to happen because of what they'd find."

"And he believed you?"

"It's the truth," she said bitterly. "We both knew it. But it wasn't as if I could report the incident to the police. They would've seen what you see now—a nanny trying to kidnap a child she has no legal claim over. They wouldn't have understood."

"I'm not yet convinced that he was wrong. You told me you had a husband. You stole someone else's life story and used it for yourself." Kate stood, towered over Sydney. She hadn't taken her scuffed shoes off when she entered the apartment, and as she stepped forward, her heels depressed into the tattered carpet. "You showed me a book of photos, of your battered body. You had this whole sorry story, this whole life that was a lie. How you met your husband and why you separated. That is…quite bizarre, and you'll have to excuse me if I'm somewhat skeptical of your claims to be entirely sane."

"The photos were of Carolyn. I already told you that!" Sydney took another step backward, her hand clutching for the countertop. "I was helping her gather evidence to go to the police all through her pregnancy. We thought she'd be safe when the baby was born, but that didn't stop Henry. So, yes, when she died, and Lydia and I went on the run, I used Carolyn's story as my own. It's her truth. In a strange way, I think Carolyn would have wanted me to have that safety net."

"How do I know you didn't kill her?" Kate stood taller, trembling. "How do I know we didn't murder an innocent man, the father of Lydia, because you're a psychopath trying to live someone else's life in your own twisted fantasy?"

Sydney went very, very quiet. Absolutely still.

Eventually, without saying a word, she stood and strode toward the closet.

Kate watched her warily, her hand reaching for the pepper spray in her clutch. She didn't need it, however, for the only thing Sydney retrieved from the neat, overstuffed storage space was a photo album.

Sydney set it on the couch, flipped to the very back where there was a photo of her and another woman. The other woman sat upward in a hospital bed, her arms wrapped around a teensy little girl, freshly swaddled in hospital blankets.

Kate found her throat clogging with emotion at the sight of the young mother next to Sydney, that look of wondrous love—of utter, complete amazement—as she stared down at her brand-new daughter.

Kate knew, as only mothers can know, the unquantifiable amount of joy she was experiencing in that moment. The way her heart strained and burst with it all, expanded greater than ever before. Impossible to shrink back.

It's no wonder Emily had been in such pain, Kate thought. Her heart had stretched three sizes too big, and then been ripped apart, her love left to droop in the knowledge of what might have been. What could have been. *What if…*

"That's Carolyn?" Kate asked before the lump in her throat grew larger. "And Lydia?"

Sydney nodded. "I found this photo the day after Carolyn died. It was in an envelope with my name written on it—in the cleaning cupboard—where Henry would never have gone."

Kate watched as Sydney flipped the card over and found a note on the back.

Sydney, it said. *If you're reading this, then I'm probably dead. I'd like you to take Lydia. To someplace with palm trees or igloos, it doesn't matter. Keep her away from him.*

"I made her a promise," Sydney said. "She was preparing to leave him, as soon as Lydia was old enough. So, after I left his house that night—promising to move far, far away—I waited. It didn't take long. After all, Henry needed to return to work. He needed child care. He tried to be cautious, to warn the day care center, but what were they supposed to do? I am Lydia's mother. I simply picked her up from day care—"

"You weren't her mother! You kidnapped her," Kate corrected. "They wouldn't have let you take her freely. Especially not if they'd been warned."

Sydney didn't argue. "What would you have done in my shoes, Kate? What if it were your daughter?"

Kate gave a shake of her head, bit her lip. She thoughtfully tapped the photograph against her open palm. "How do I know you didn't make this up? Write a little note on the back to explain your whole sordid story?"

A wail sounded in the next room. Sydney flicked a glance over her shoulder, attuned to the child in a natural, instinctive way. "If you don't trust me by now, then you probably never will," she said, standing, leading Kate to the front door. "There's nothing else I can say to convince you. So, Kate, I guess the next step is up to you."

Kate waited in the doorway while Sydney moved to grab the child—her child—from the other room. The pair returned, Lydia looking ruffled and sweet after a nap, her cheeks flushed a pretty pink and her hair a staticky blond mess. As the toddler rested her head on Sydney's shoulder and nuzzled in closer, a pacifier tucked between pouted lips, Kate's heart pounded with the weight of her decision.

She studied Lydia.

She studied Sydney.

Abruptly, Kate turned on her scuffed heels and strode away from the apartment. This time, she didn't look back. And she knew, in her heart, she never would.

reading group guide

1. Lulu, Ginger, Kate, and Emily all have their different situations and secrets. Which woman did you enjoy reading the most? Who do you think you're the most like? Why?

2. What do the four women—Lulu, Ginger, Kate, and Emily—all have in common? What are some of their core differences?

3. Do you think Ginger handles the situation with Elsie and the condoms well? If you were in her shoes, what would you have done differently? Why do you think Elsie reacts the way she does?

4. Lulu begins to wonder if her marriage to Pierce is about to fall apart, so she calls on her ex-husband Anderson to ask why her relationships fail. Imagine being in Lulu's situation. Would you ever call an ex for this? Have you remained close to an ex before? What was that relationship like?

5. Describe the events that led to Ginger and Emily's feud. Do you think Ginger's reaction to seeing Emily after all these years was warranted? If you were Emily, how would you have responded in that situation?

6. What are some of the triggers Emily faces at the resort? Why does she begin to break down?

7. Why does Kate feel the need to help Sydney? What are some of the parallels between the two? What about between Emily and Sydney?

8. Describe the relationship each woman has with children and parenthood. How is that theme woven throughout the story?

9. Why do you think Elsie is able to open up to Kate? Did you ever have an adult or older confidant when you were that age?

10. How do all the women end up on the patio the night of the rehearsal dinner? Why do you think they all claim to be guilty? Who is actually guilty?

11. What happens to the women after the wedding ends? Why do you think Kate tracks down Sydney one last time? If you were Kate, would you believe Sydney's story?

a conversation
with the author

What inspired you to write *Pretty Guilty Women*?

Pretty Guilty Women started with one big question: Why would four very different women all confess to the same crime? The idea simmered in the back of my mind for months as I wondered what sort of women might be involved in such a bizarre scenario. How did they meet? What brought them together? Who was truly guilty? Eventually, I put pen to paper and wrote *Pretty Guilty Women* in search of the answers.

Which of the four—Lulu, Ginger, Kate, and Emily—did you enjoy writing the most? Which was most challenging?

For me, each character was both a joy and a challenge to write. I'm positive there are tiny parts of myself in each of the women—some more than others. Lulu was fun to write because she has such charisma. I love that she knows exactly who she is, and I admire the way she has aged with grace and confidence and a good bit of humor!

At times, Emily was challenging to write because her story is so raw. She grapples with huge, dark issues, and while I haven't experienced everything she's gone through personally, I truly tried to put myself in her shoes and imagine what she was experiencing. She believes she is weak and vulnerable, but despite her flaws, there is a strength inside of her that she is struggling to recover. I hated that she'd been through such hardships, but I was hopeful she would find the light at the end of the tunnel.

How did you map out all the twists and turns that happen throughout the story?

Lots and lots of editing!

While the bit about editing is true, I also focused on the four women as individuals first. I spent a lot of time thinking about who they were—their secrets, desires, and dirty little truths. Then I wove each story together until all four narratives overlapped as one.

Finally, I worked with my brilliant team of editors and agents to truly dig deep into the women's relationships, teasing out their individual motivations and exploring their strengths and weaknesses.

What does your writing process look like?

There's rarely a "regular" day for me when it comes to writing. My process morphs and changes all the time—some days I stay up late, working until four o'clock in the morning. Other times, I'm at my computer by 6:00 a.m. As for my actual writing process, I prefer to plot and brainstorm by hand, so when I'm starting a book, I will go to a coffee shop, put on some headphones, and write in a notebook for hours. When I get stuck on a scene, I take a long walk outside to clear my head. I don't write every day, but once I begin a project, I try to work on it until I reach *The End*!

If you had one piece of advice for prospective suspense writers, what would it be?

Write! Sitting down and writing is the absolute best way to practice the craft (in addition to reading a wide variety of books). I have always wanted to write suspense, and it took me more than thirty books before I felt confident enough to pen *Pretty Guilty Women*. My college degree is in mathematics and actuarial science, and I have no formal training in writing; however, I have always had a deep love of reading and a passion for telling stories. In my early twenties, I figured out that writing novels was my dream career. It took many years to make that dream a reality, but it has all been worth it a million times over.

The bond between mother and child is a central theme throughout the story. Are you a mother yourself?

I am! Or, I will be by the time *Pretty Guilty Women* hits bookshelves. At the moment, Baby LaManna is due any day, and my husband and I are thrilled to be welcoming a new member into our family. While I don't have as much experience (yet) in motherhood as Ginger, I'm looking forward to the journey!

At the same time, I'm very close with my own parents, which made the mother/daughter dynamic between Elsie and Ginger especially fun to explore. Teenage years can be a roller coaster, but if you can make it out the other side, that bond can be something very special.

Why did you decide to set a fast-paced suspense story at a beautiful wedding resort?

In a way, I think the beautiful wedding resort fits the theme of *Pretty Guilty Women* perfectly. The idea that things aren't always what they seem is prevalent throughout the story. Kate in particular spends a significant amount of time wondering if this glitzy, glamorous wedding is really going to make Whitney and Arthur's marriage last. Are looks everything they're cracked up to be? Sometimes, it seems, the most beautiful people and the most beautiful places house the darkest secrets.

If you had to be best friends with one of the women in the novel, which would you choose, and why?

Lulu! She's got wisdom to spare (along with ex-husbands), and I'd love to spend a day at her place in South Carolina sipping sweet tea and hearing her stories. She's lived a most unique life, and I would love to be able to pick up the phone and call her for advice.

When you're not writing, what can you often be found doing?

If it's summer, you will definitely find me outside! My family lives in Minnesota, so we try to take advantage of every day that's above freezing. I love to garden and go for long walks in the sun, head to my parents' house for a barbecue, or hit the lakes on a windsurfer or a kayak. I'm also a coffee fanatic and adore sampling local diners and coffee shops with my husband. This summer, we've got a baby arriving, so I'll be adding a stroller to my walks outside!

Are you working on anything new?

I'm always working on something new! I have another suspense book in progress. More news to come on this soon. It is in the same vein as *Pretty Guilty Women* and tackles complicated themes, along with a hefty dose of suspense. Taking place within the darker realms of Hollywood, this project explores the concept of reaching for the stars—and how sometimes our greatest dreams can be our greatest downfall.

To see more of my books, please visit ginalamanna.com, where you can find a complete reading guide. Register for my newsletter to stay up-to-date on new releases, special sales, and other big announcements. You can also connect with me on Facebook or Instagram, where I post frequently and love to chat with readers!

acknowledgments

Thank you to all my publishers and editors around the world for bringing this story to life. In particular, I am so grateful to the talented people at Sourcebooks and Little, Brown and Company, with special thanks to the incredible Shana Drehs and Lucy Dauman. Your excitement for this project has been contagious from the start!

To my agent, Sarah Hornsley, thank you for taking a chance and believing in this manuscript. Without your expert eye and insightful advice, it may never have seen the light of day. Thanks also to Jenny Bent and the Bent Agency for the support, encouragement, and guidance along the way.

Thank you to the most wonderful person in my life—my husband, Alex, for everything. But most of all, for believing in me, making me laugh, and feeding me when I'm on a deadline so I don't starve. To the newest addition of our family, thank you for providing a very pressing due date to get my work done. And more importantly, for making me a mom. I love you both!

Thank you to Mom, Dad, Kristi, and Megan for reading my books (or at least displaying them on your shelves). The love and fun and inspiration you've provided over the years have undoubtedly helped make my dreams of becoming an author come true.

A huge thanks to Rissa Pierce, Michelle Foss, Nicole Boelter, and Katie Hamachek for your friendship over the years. Your parenting advice, travel companionship, and long conversations and late nights have taught me what it means to have great girlfriends.

Thank you to Stacia Williams for making my life better in so many ways. I don't know what I'd do without you.

about the author

Gina LaManna is the *USA Today* bestselling author of more than thirty novels, including *Sprinkled*, *Hex on the Beach*, *Wicked Never Sleeps*, and *Shades of Pink*, among many others. She lives in St. Paul, Minnesota, with her family. Visit the author online at ginalamanna.com.